Befana

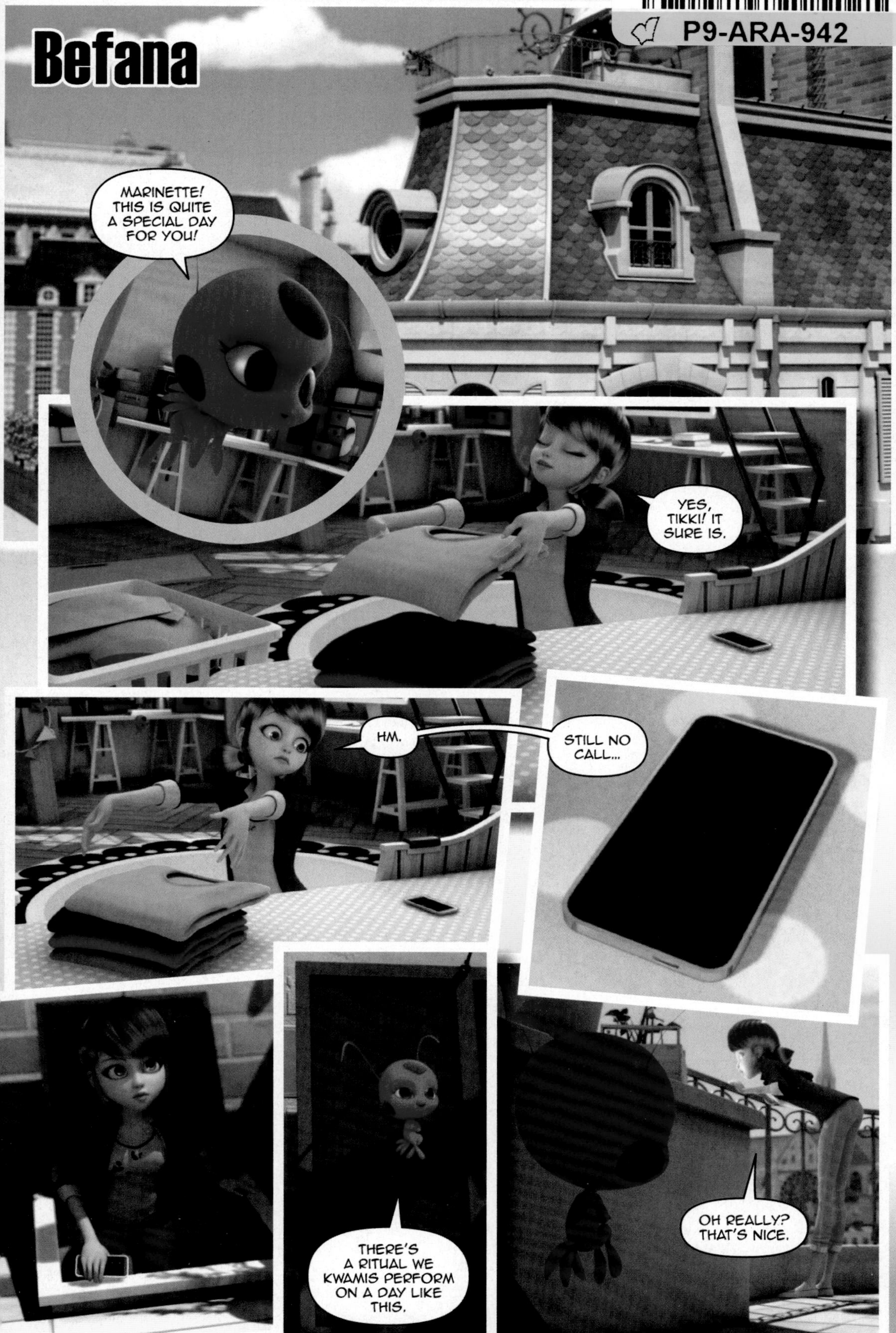
MARINETTE! THIS IS QUITE A SPECIAL DAY FOR YOU!
YES, TIKKI! IT SURE IS.
HM.
STILL NO CALL...
THERE'S A RITUAL WE KWAMIS PERFORM ON A DAY LIKE THIS.
OH REALLY? THAT'S NICE.

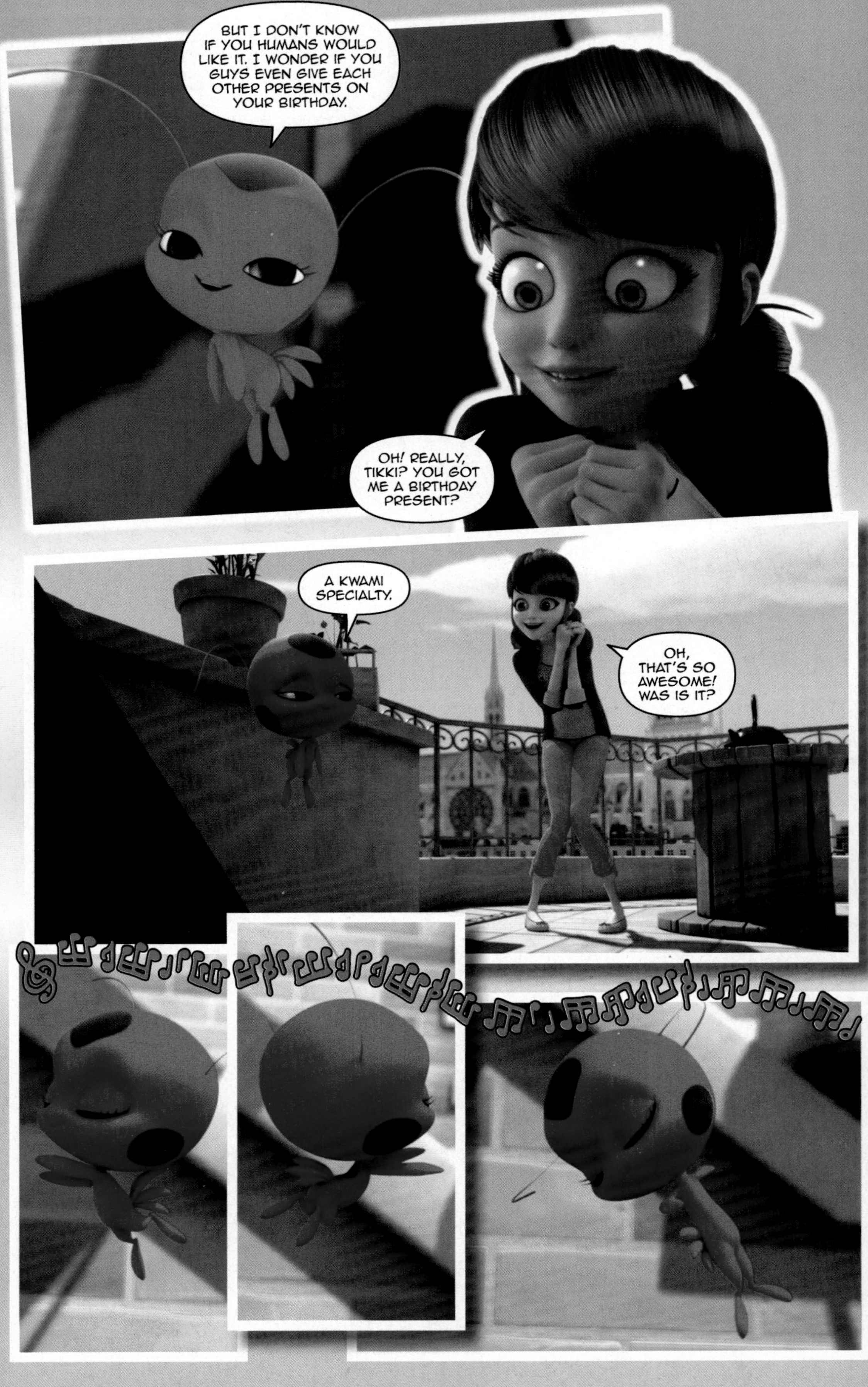
BUT I DON'T KNOW IF YOU HUMANS WOULD LIKE IT. I WONDER IF YOU GUYS EVEN GIVE EACH OTHER PRESENTS ON YOUR BIRTHDAY.
OH! REALLY, TIKKI? YOU GOT ME A BIRTHDAY PRESENT?
A KWAMI SPECIALTY.
OH, THAT'S SO AWESOME! WAS IS IT?

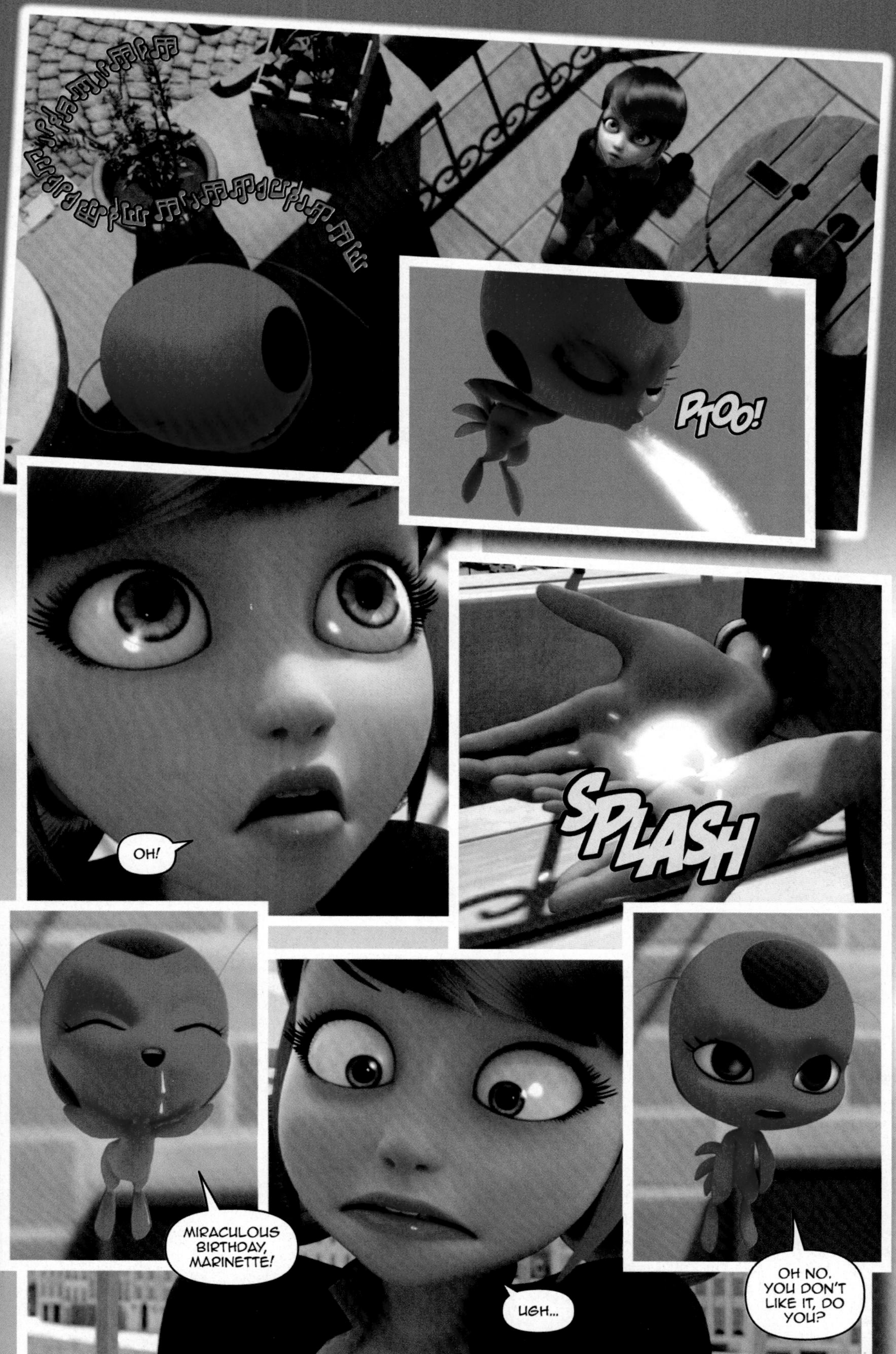
PTOO!
OH!
SPLASH
MIRACULOUS BIRTHDAY, MARINETTE!
UGH...
OH NO. YOU DON'T LIKE IT, DO YOU?

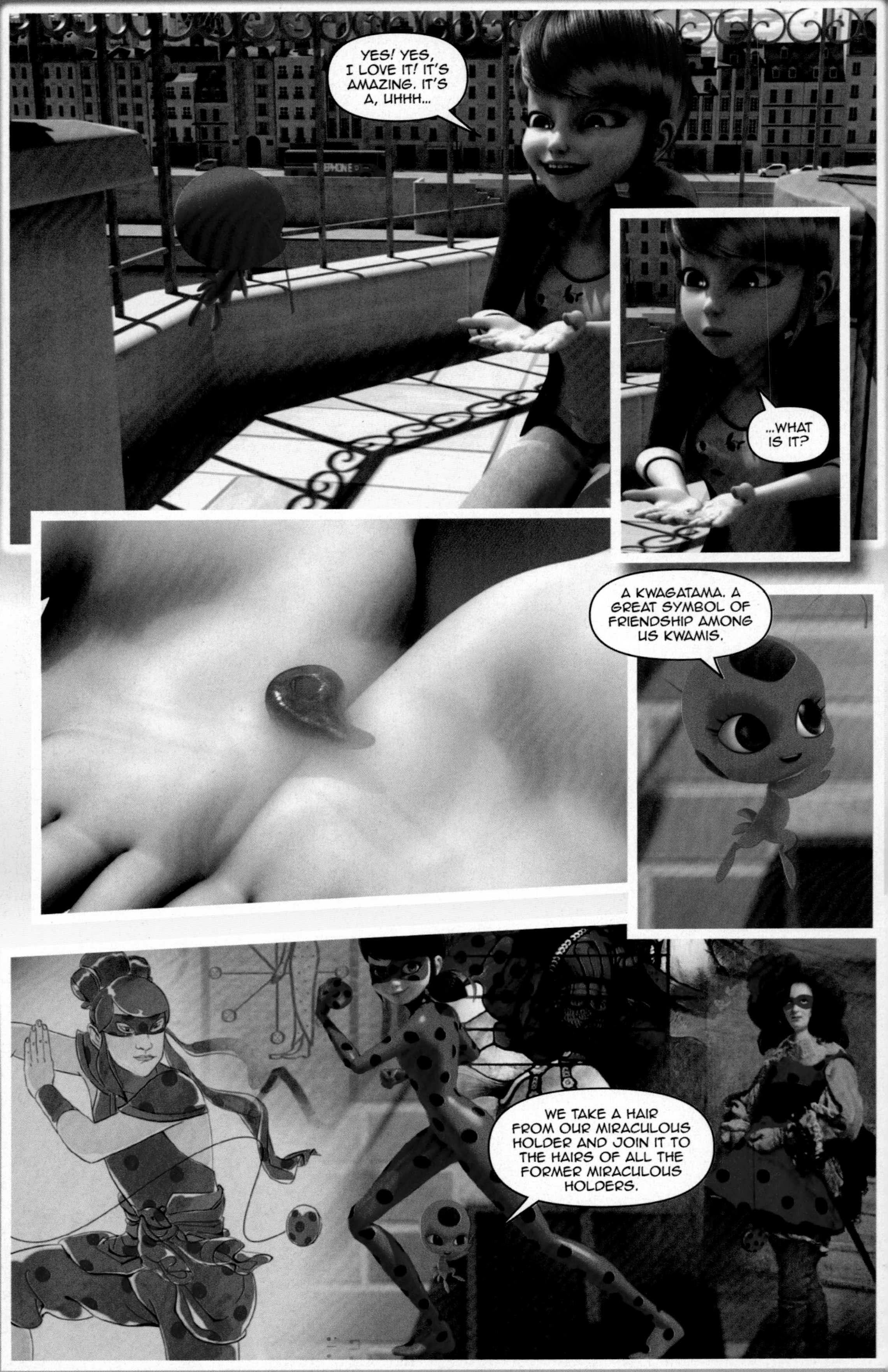
YES! YES, I LOVE IT! IT'S AMAZING. IT'S A, UHHH...
...WHAT IS IT?
A KWAGATAMA. A GREAT SYMBOL OF FRIENDSHIP AMONG US KWAMIS.
WE TAKE A HAIR FROM OUR MIRACULOUS HOLDER AND JOIN IT TO THE HAIRS OF ALL THE FORMER MIRACULOUS HOLDERS.

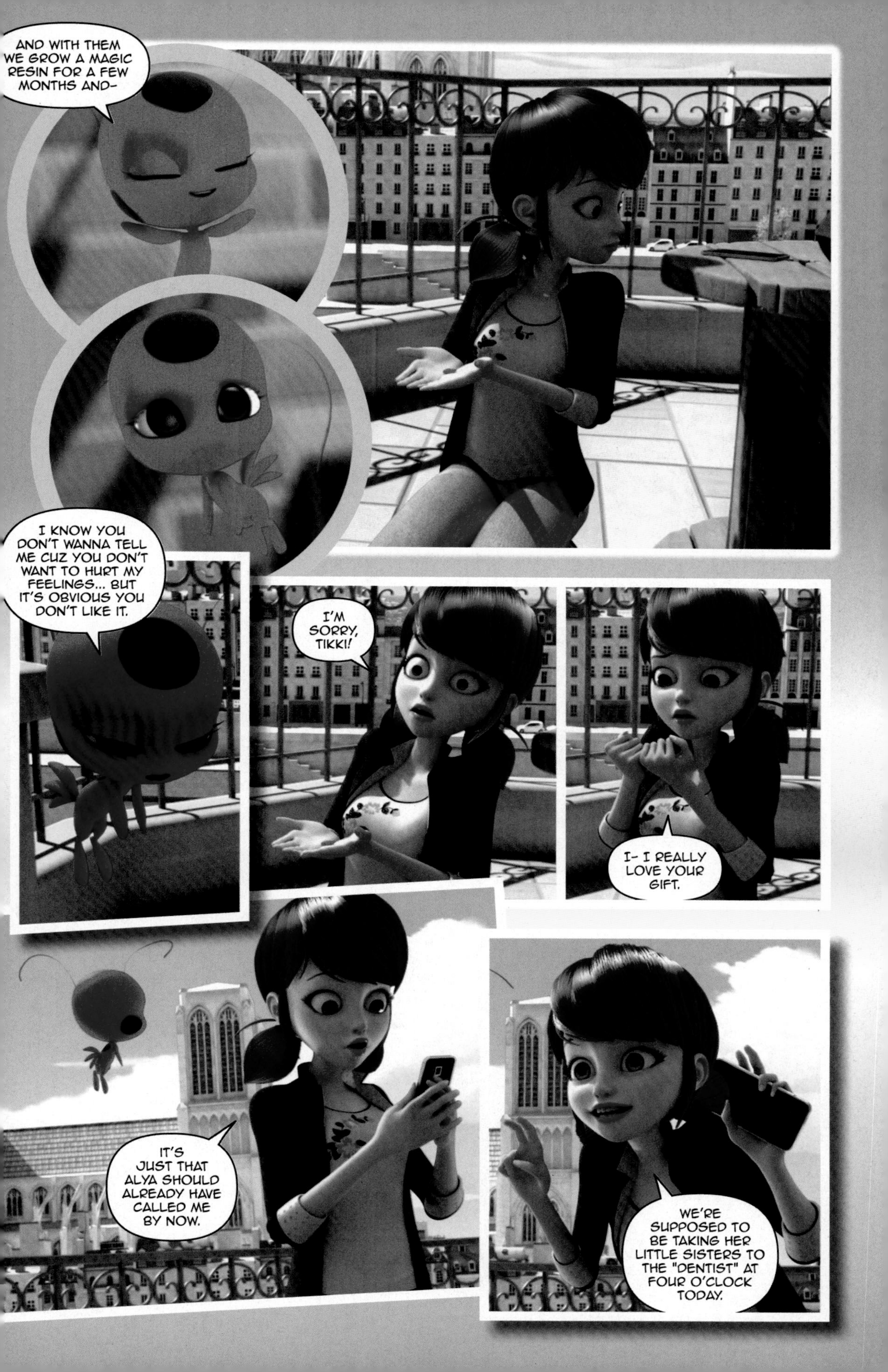
AND WITH THEM WE GROW A MAGIC RESIN FOR A FEW MONTHS AND-
I KNOW YOU DON'T WANNA TELL ME CUZ YOU DON'T WANT TO HURT MY FEELINGS... BUT IT'S OBVIOUS YOU DON'T LIKE IT.
I'M SORRY, TIKKI!
I- I REALLY LOVE YOUR GIFT.
IT'S JUST THAT ALYA SHOULD ALREADY HAVE CALLED ME BY NOW.
WE'RE SUPPOSED TO BE TAKING HER LITTLE SISTERS TO THE "DENTIST" AT FOUR O'CLOCK TODAY.

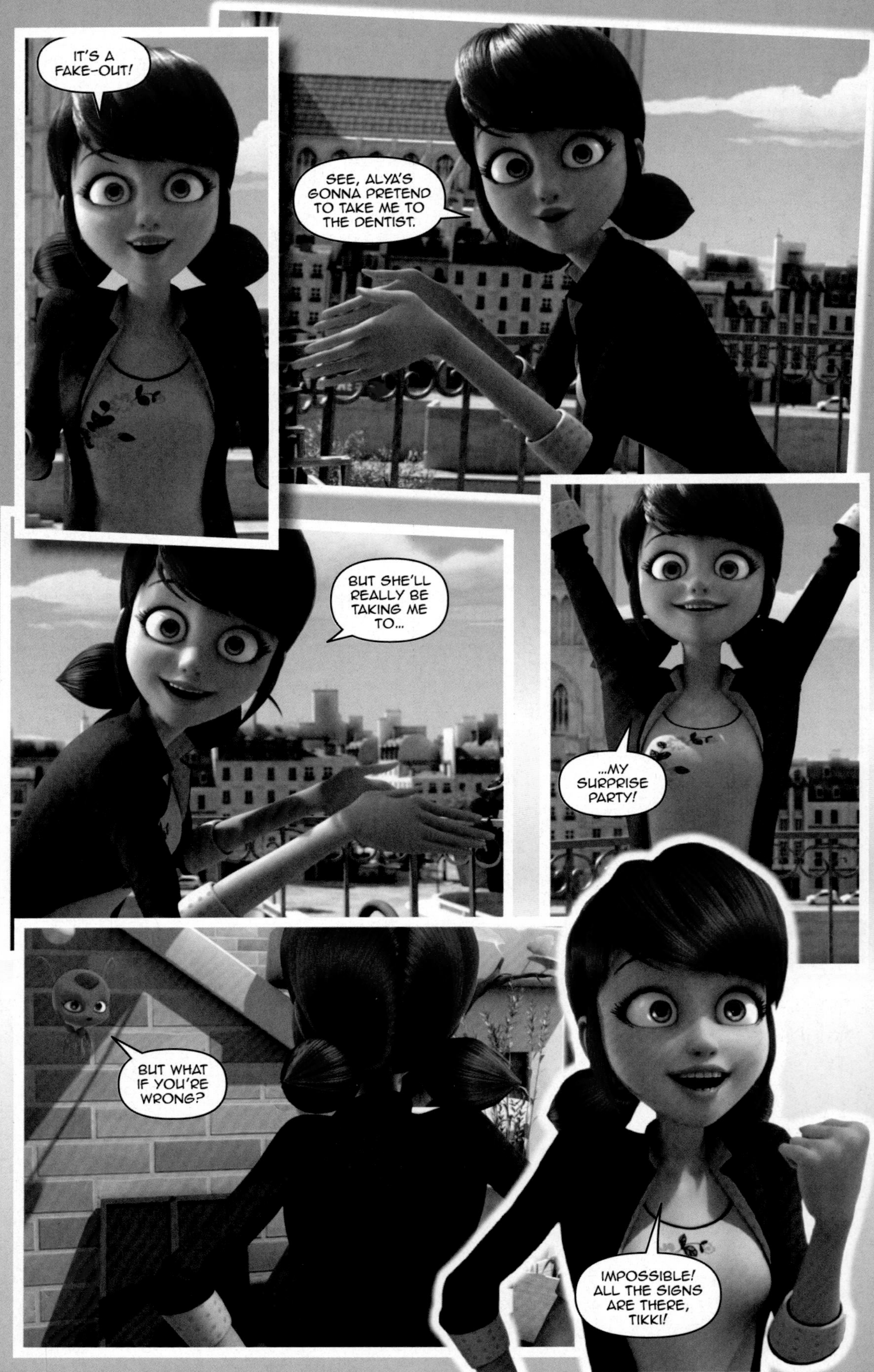
IT'S A FAKE-OUT!
SEE, ALYA'S GONNA PRETEND TO TAKE ME TO THE DENTIST.
BUT SHE'LL REALLY BE TAKING ME TO...
...MY SURPRISE PARTY!
BUT WHAT IF YOU'RE WRONG?
IMPOSSIBLE! ALL THE SIGNS ARE THERE, TIKKI!

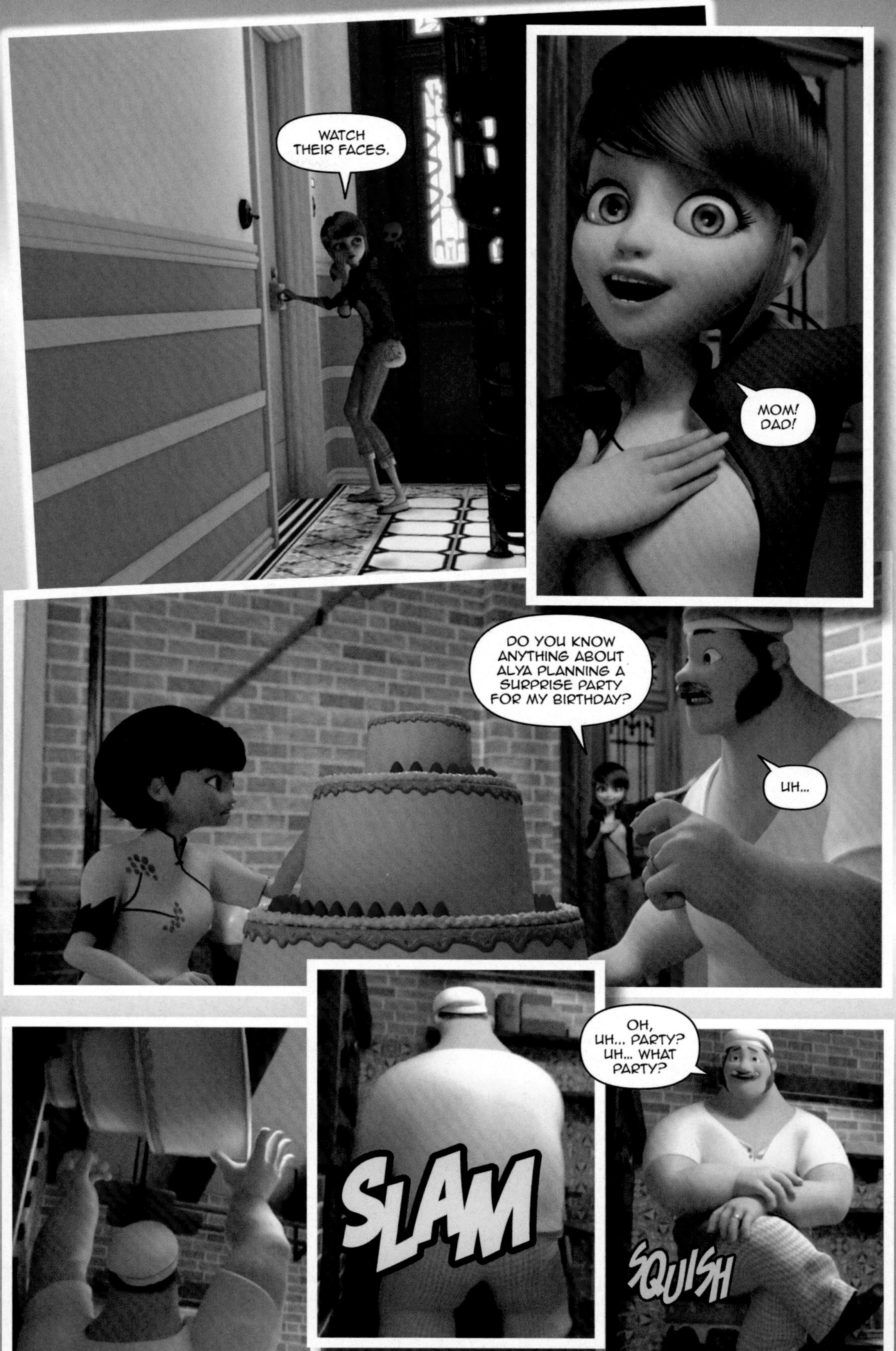
WATCH THEIR FACES.
MOM! DAD!
DO YOU KNOW ANYTHING ABOUT ALYA PLANNING A SURPRISE PARTY FOR MY BIRTHDAY?
UH...
SLAM
OH, UH... PARTY? UH... WHAT PARTY?
SQUISH

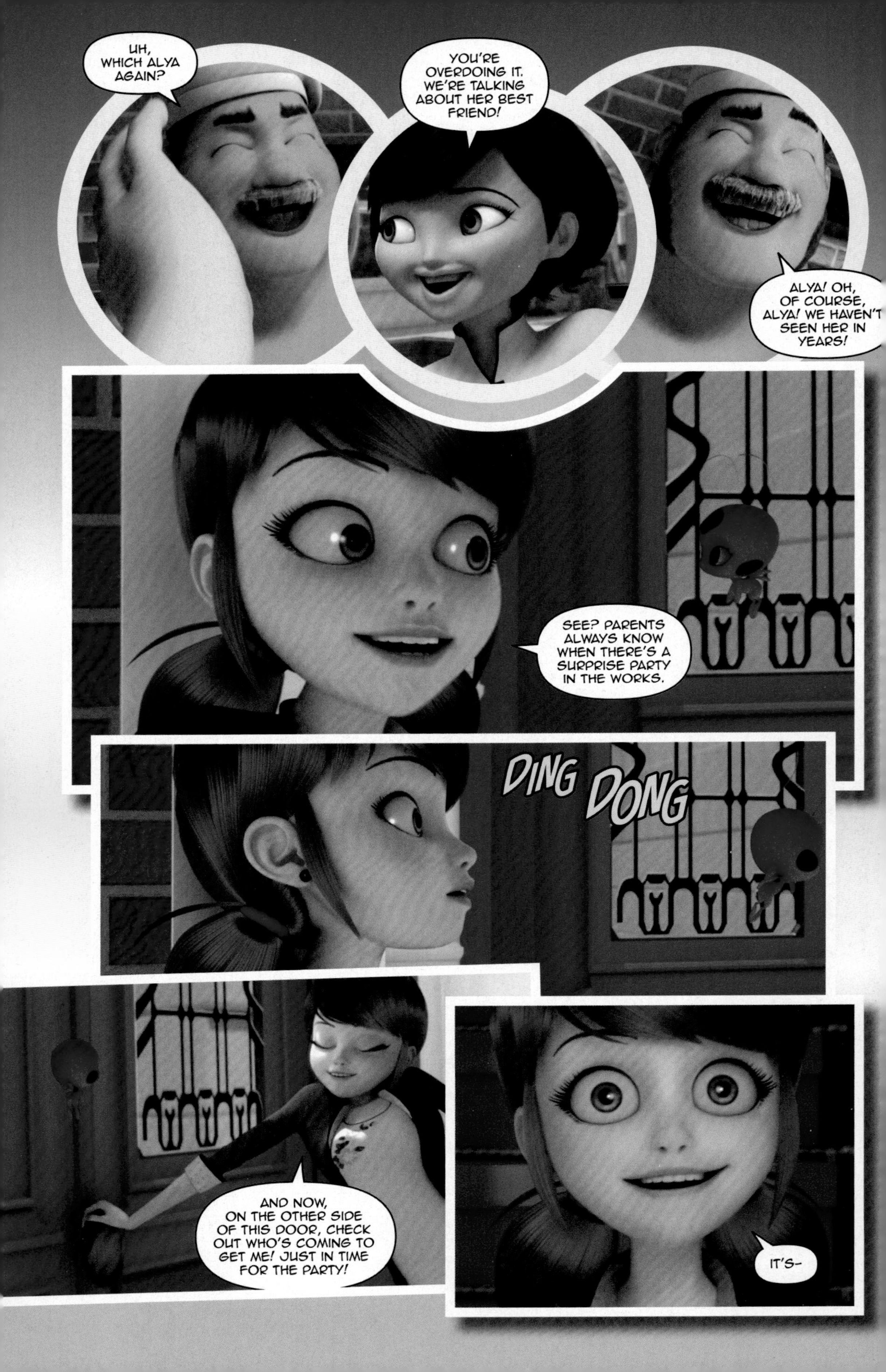
UH, WHICH ALYA AGAIN?
YOU'RE OVERDOING IT. WE'RE TALKING ABOUT HER BEST FRIEND!
ALYA! OH, OF COURSE, ALYA! WE HAVEN'T SEEN HER IN YEARS!
SEE? PARENTS ALWAYS KNOW WHEN THERE'S A SURPRISE PARTY IN THE WORKS.
DING DONG
AND NOW, ON THE OTHER SIDE OF THIS DOOR, CHECK OUT WHO'S COMING TO GET ME! JUST IN TIME FOR THE PARTY!
IT'S-

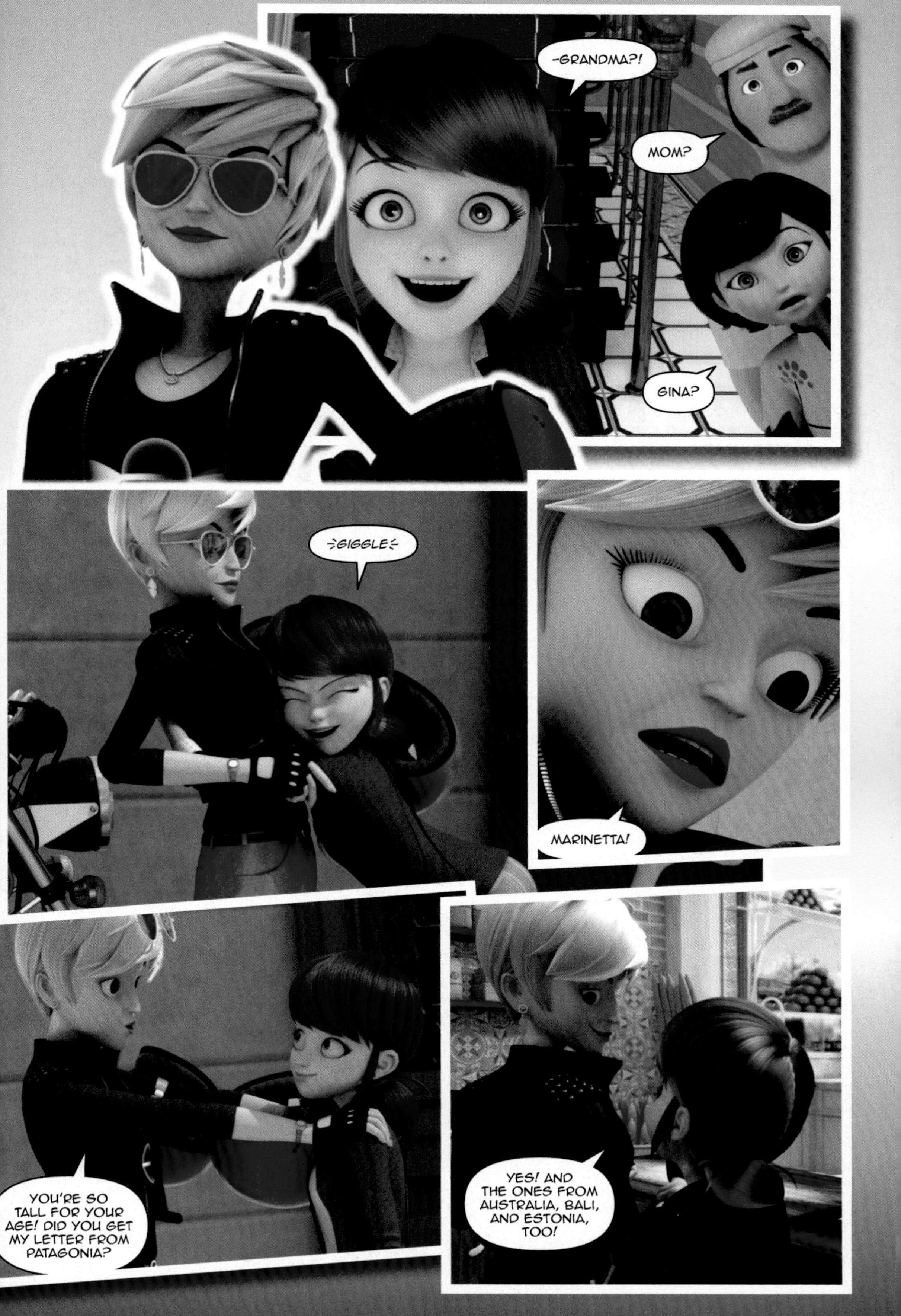

-GRANDMA?!
MOM?
GINA?
⋟GIGGLE⋞
MARINETTA!
YOU'RE SO TALL FOR YOUR AGE! DID YOU GET MY LETTER FROM PATAGONIA?
YES! AND THE ONES FROM AUSTRALIA, BALI, AND ESTONIA, TOO!

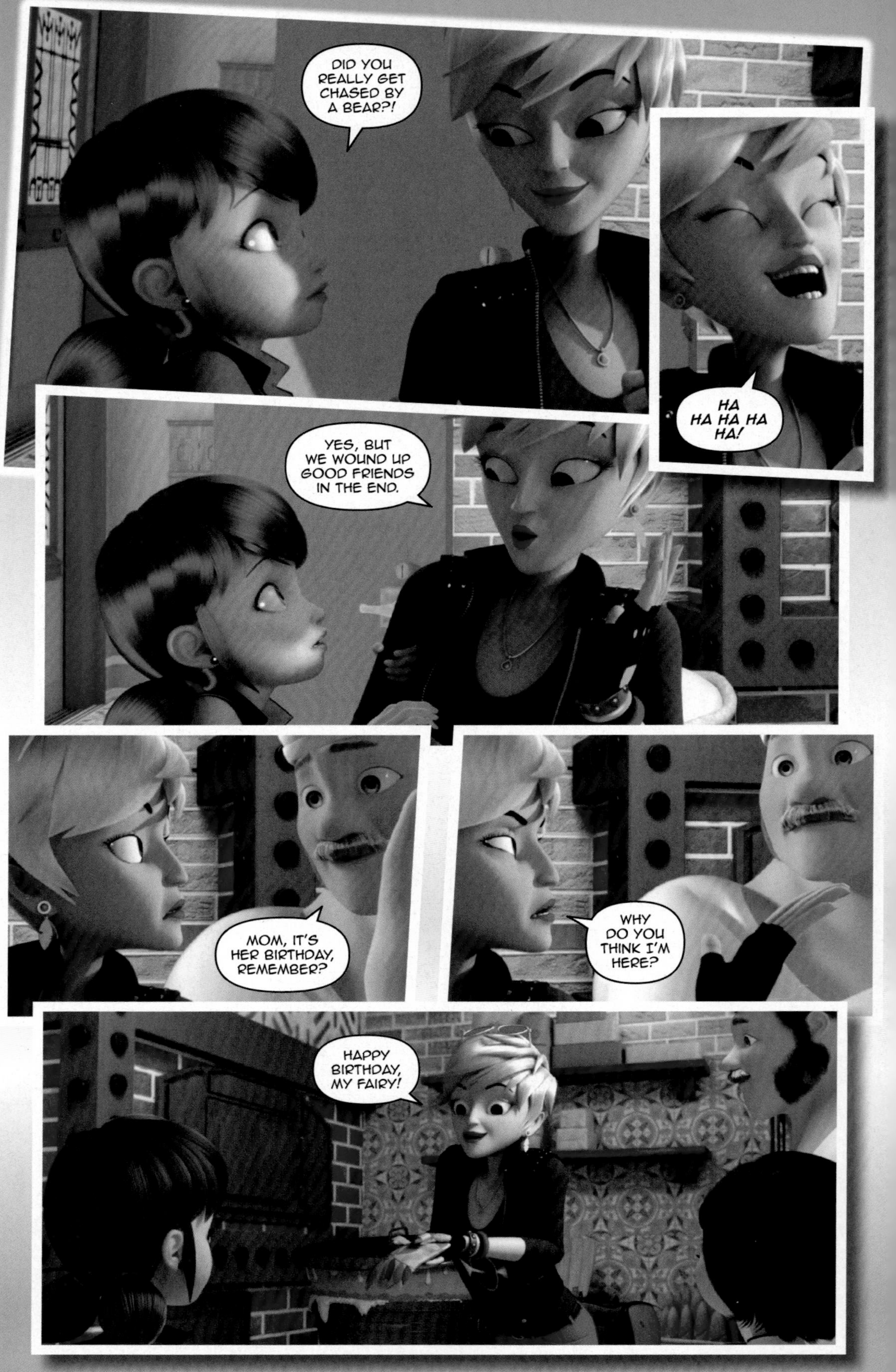
DID YOU REALLY GET CHASED BY A BEAR?!
HA HA HA HA HA!
YES, BUT WE WOUND UP GOOD FRIENDS IN THE END.
MOM, IT'S HER BIRTHDAY, REMEMBER?
WHY DO YOU THINK I'M HERE?
HAPPY BIRTHDAY, MY FAIRY!

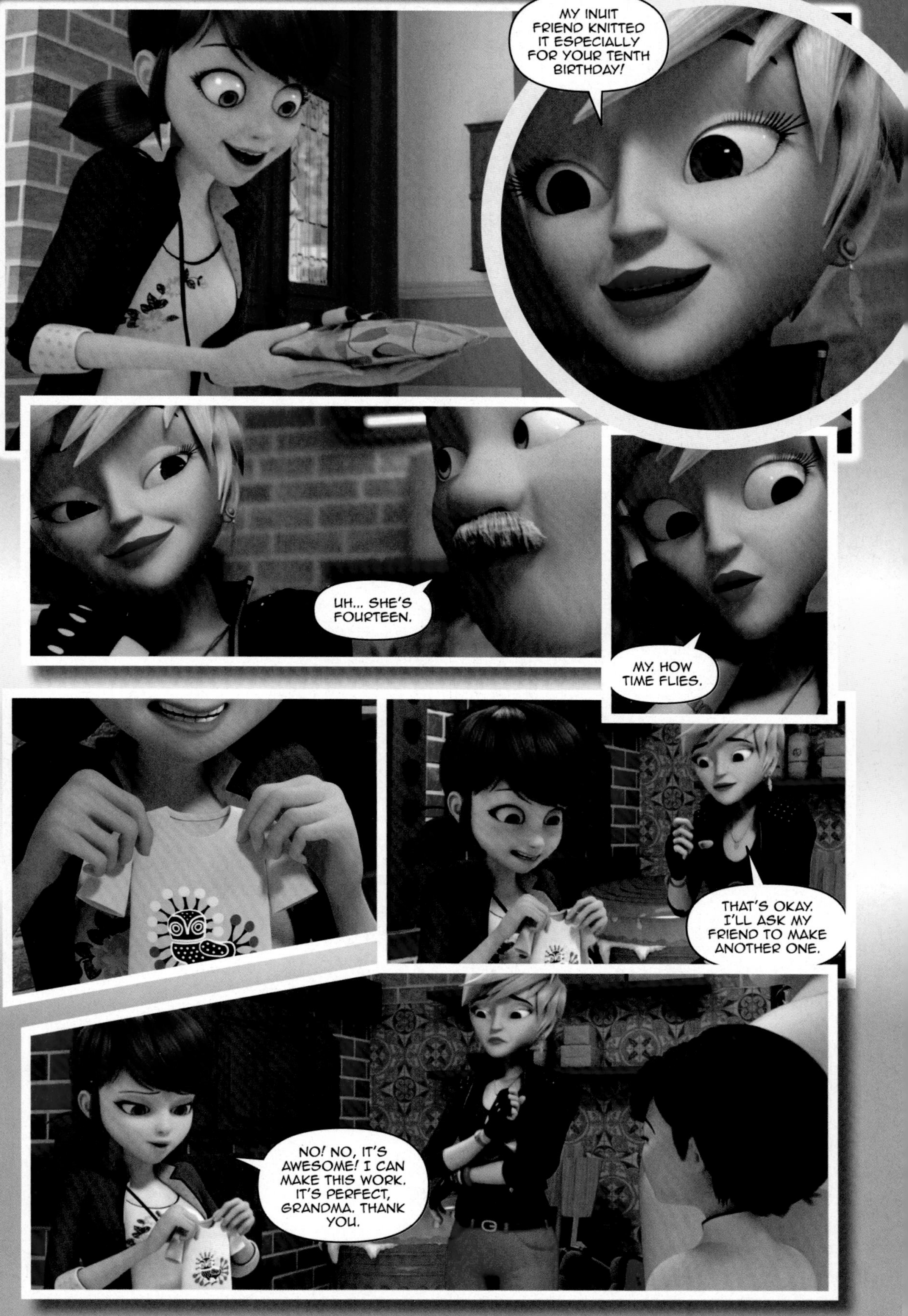
MY INUIT FRIEND KNITTED IT ESPECIALLY FOR YOUR TENTH BIRTHDAY!
UH... SHE'S FOURTEEN.
MY. HOW TIME FLIES.
THAT'S OKAY. I'LL ASK MY FRIEND TO MAKE ANOTHER ONE.
NO! NO, IT'S AWESOME! I CAN MAKE THIS WORK. IT'S PERFECT, GRANDMA. THANK YOU.

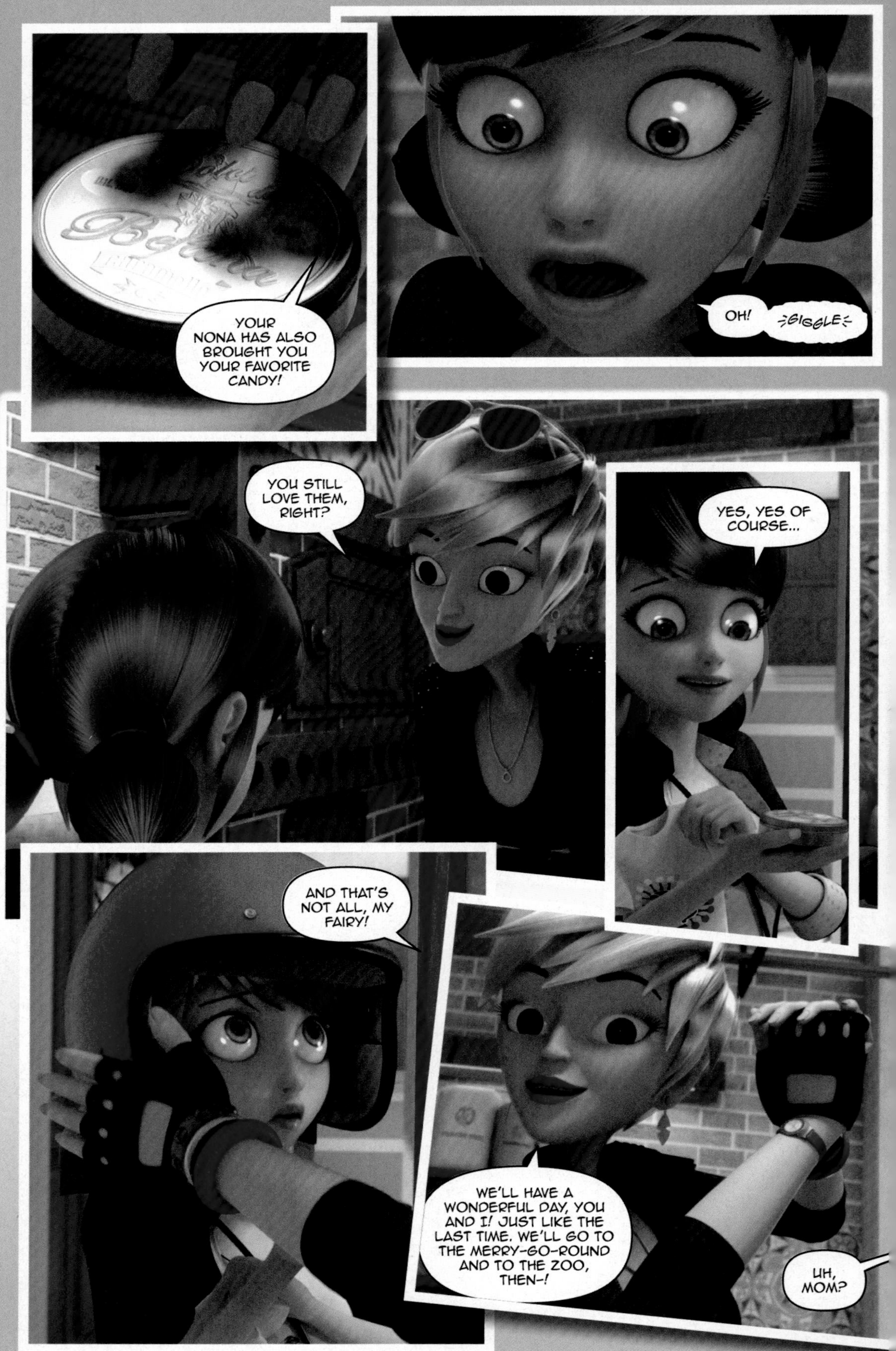
YOUR NONA HAS ALSO BROUGHT YOU YOUR FAVORITE CANDY!
OH!
GIGGLE
YOU STILL LOVE THEM, RIGHT?
YES, YES OF COURSE...
AND THAT'S NOT ALL, MY FAIRY!
WE'LL HAVE A WONDERFUL DAY, YOU AND I! JUST LIKE THE LAST TIME. WE'LL GO TO THE MERRY-GO-ROUND AND TO THE ZOO, THEN-!
UH, MOM?

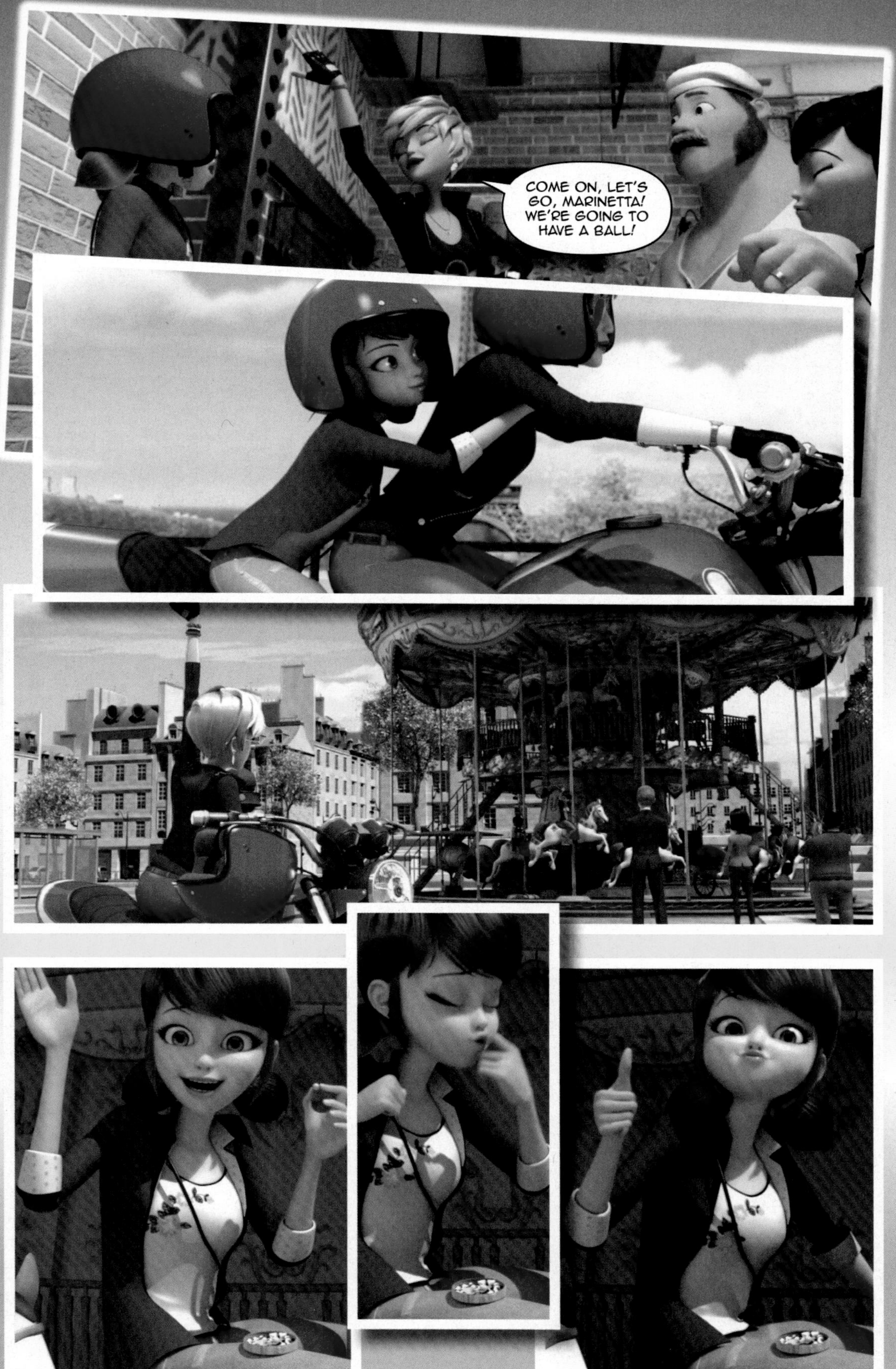
COME ON, LET'S GO, MARINETTA! WE'RE GOING TO HAVE A BALL!

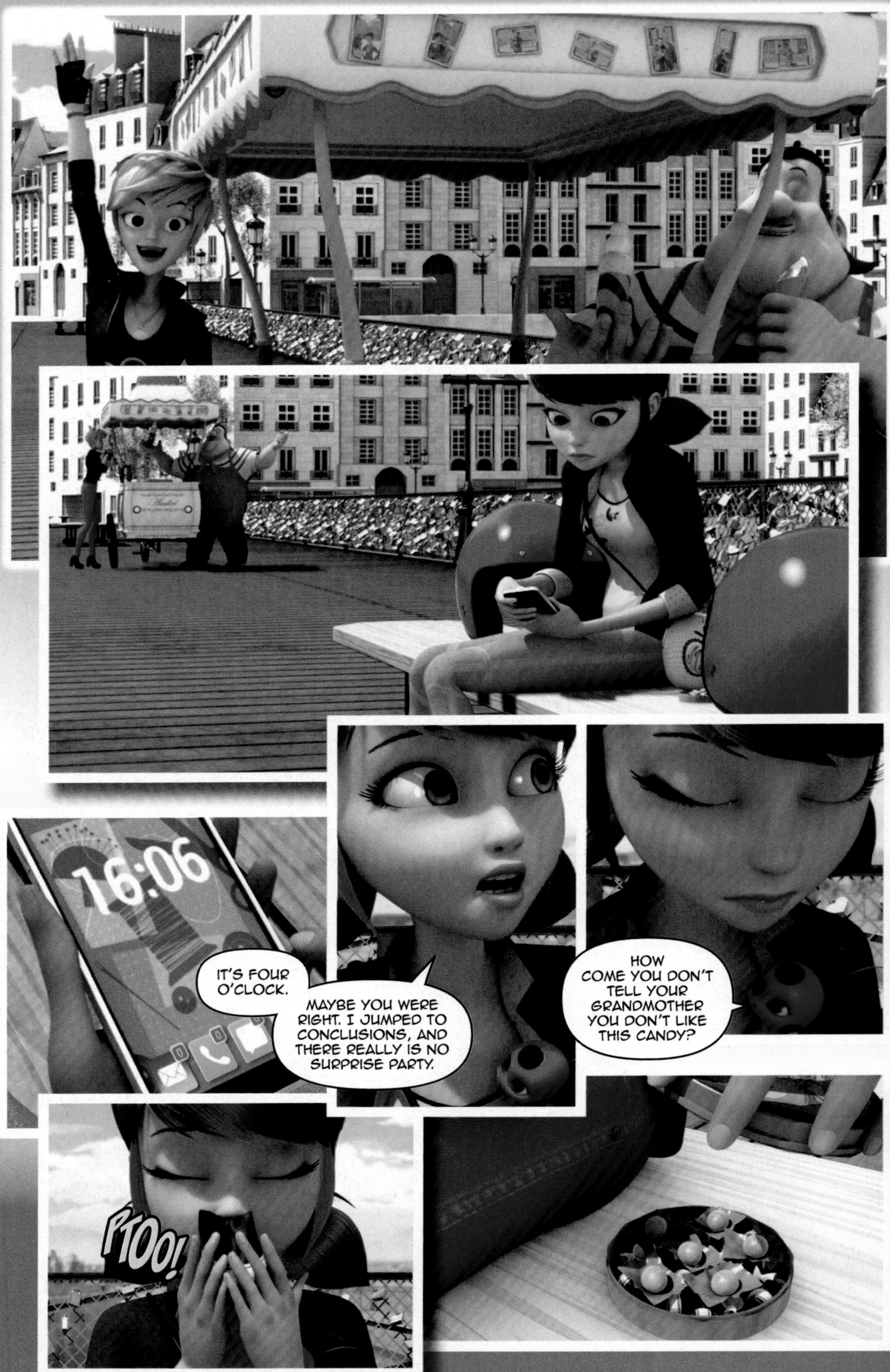
IT'S FOUR O'CLOCK.
MAYBE YOU WERE RIGHT. I JUMPED TO CONCLUSIONS, AND THERE REALLY IS NO SURPRISE PARTY.
HOW COME YOU DON'T TELL YOUR GRANDMOTHER YOU DON'T LIKE THIS CANDY?
PTOO!

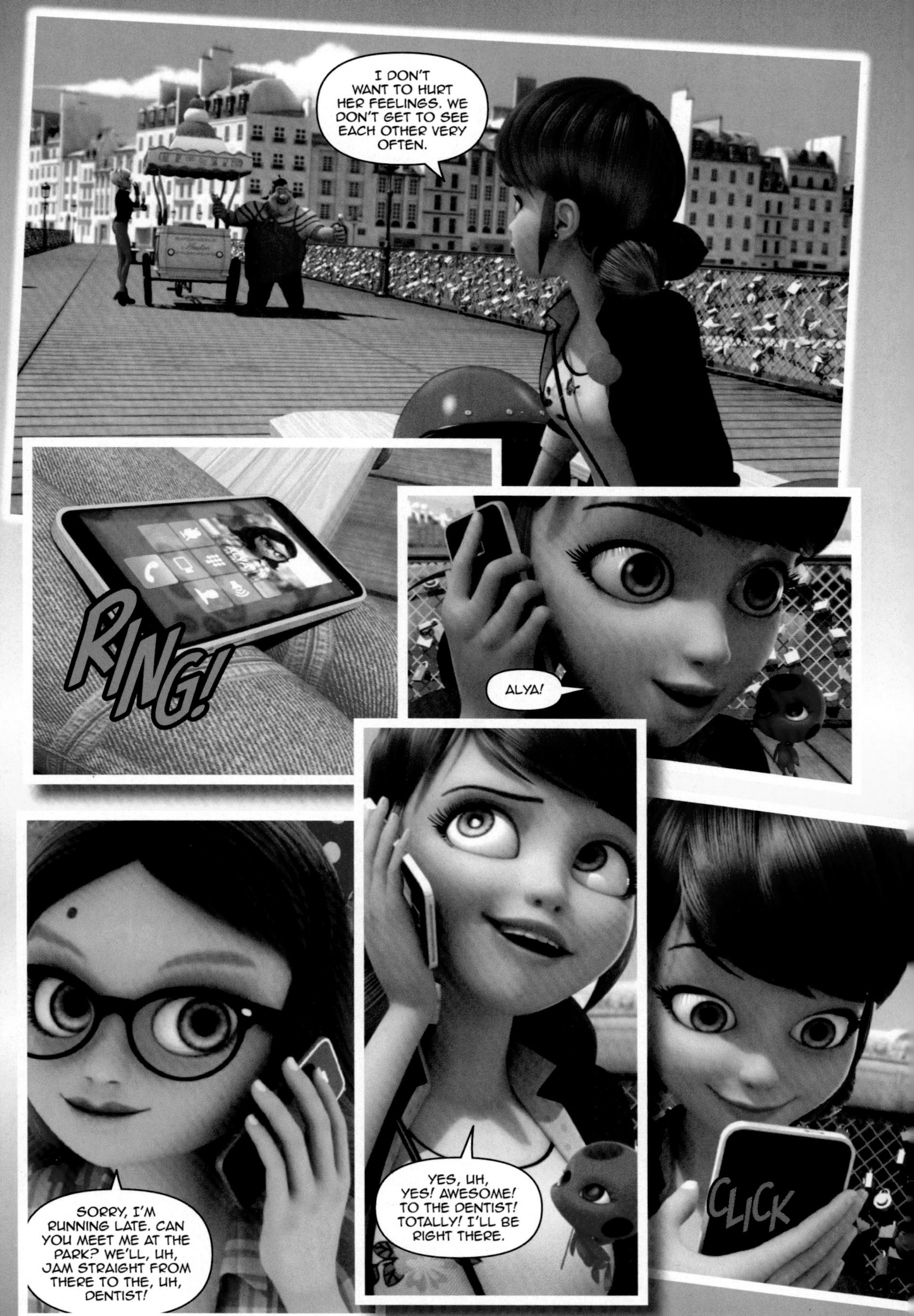
I DON'T WANT TO HURT HER FEELINGS. WE DON'T GET TO SEE EACH OTHER VERY OFTEN.
RING!
ALYA!
SORRY, I'M RUNNING LATE. CAN YOU MEET ME AT THE PARK? WE'LL, UH, JAM STRAIGHT FROM THERE TO THE, UH, DENTIST!
YES, UH, YES! AWESOME! TO THE DENTIST! TOTALLY! I'LL BE RIGHT THERE.
CLICK

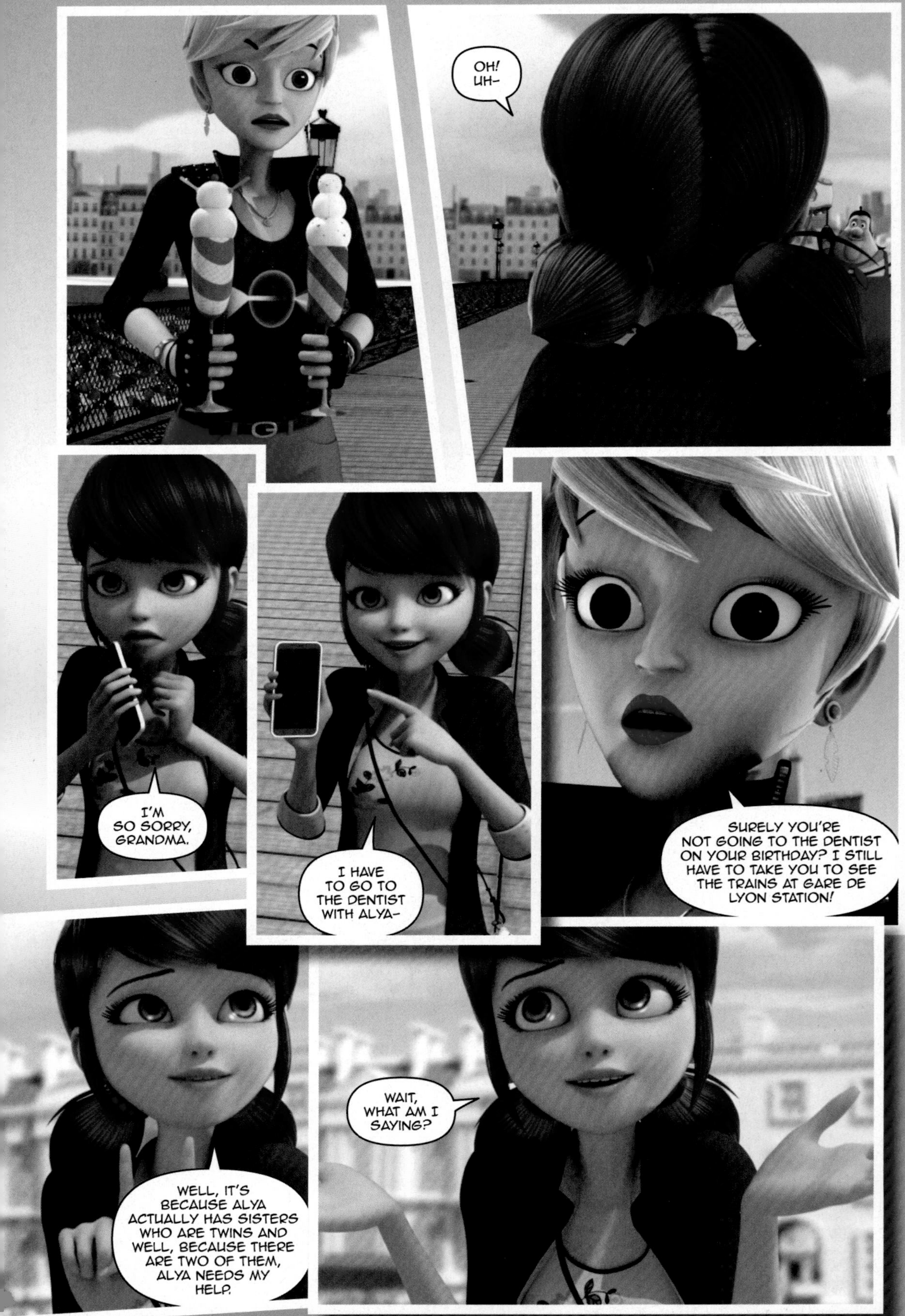
OH! UH-
I'M SO SORRY, GRANDMA.
I HAVE TO GO TO THE DENTIST WITH ALYA-
SURELY YOU'RE NOT GOING TO THE DENTIST ON YOUR BIRTHDAY? I STILL HAVE TO TAKE YOU TO SEE THE TRAINS AT GARE DE LYON STATION!
WELL, IT'S BECAUSE ALYA ACTUALLY HAS SISTERS WHO ARE TWINS AND WELL, BECAUSE THERE ARE TWO OF THEM, ALYA NEEDS MY HELP.
WAIT, WHAT AM I SAYING?

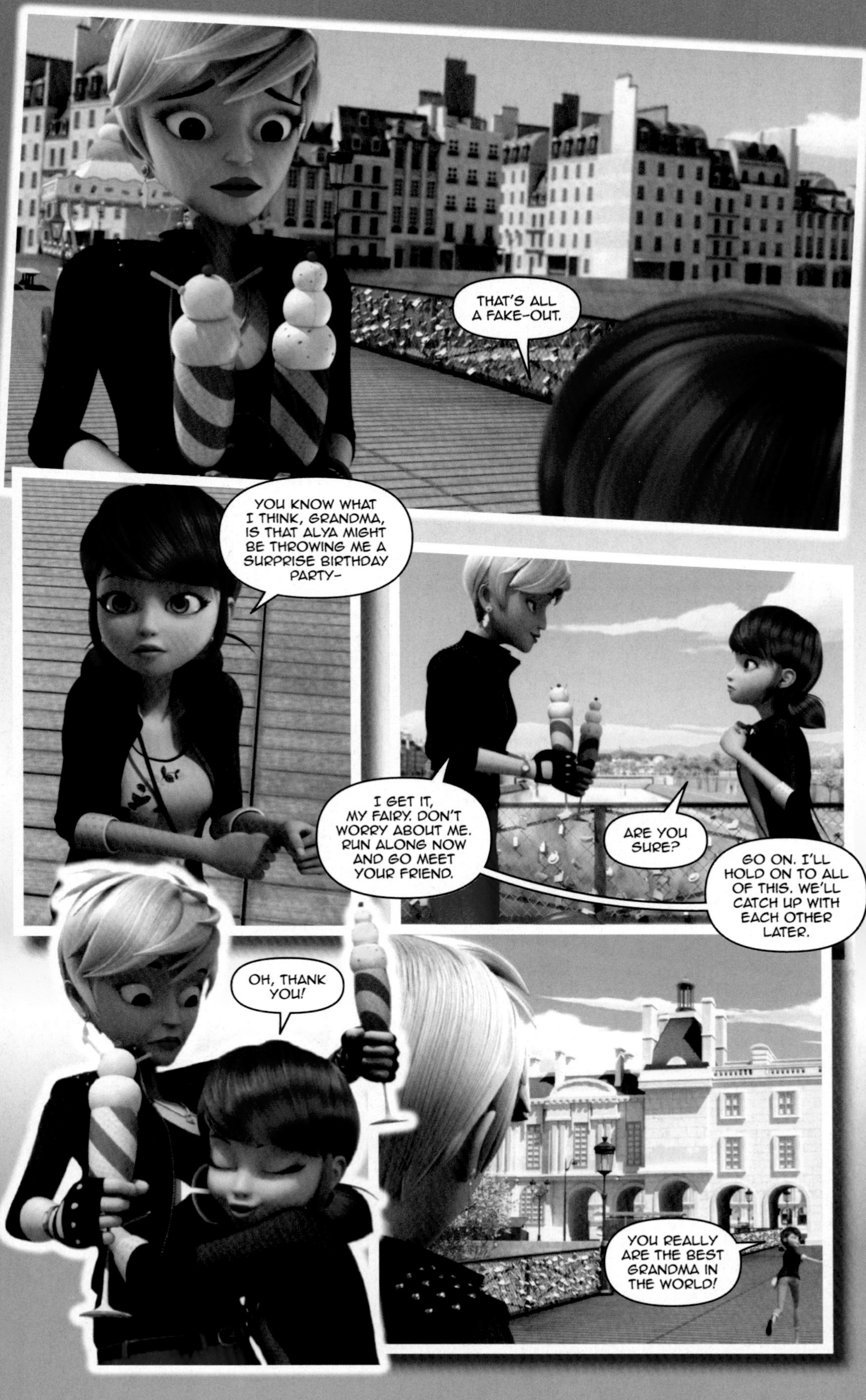
THAT'S ALL A FAKE-OUT.
YOU KNOW WHAT I THINK, GRANDMA, IS THAT ALYA MIGHT BE THROWING ME A SURPRISE BIRTHDAY PARTY-
I GET IT, MY FAIRY. DON'T WORRY ABOUT ME. RUN ALONG NOW AND GO MEET YOUR FRIEND.
ARE YOU SURE?
GO ON. I'LL HOLD ON TO ALL OF THIS. WE'LL CATCH UP WITH EACH OTHER LATER.
OH, THANK YOU!
YOU REALLY ARE THE BEST GRANDMA IN THE WORLD!

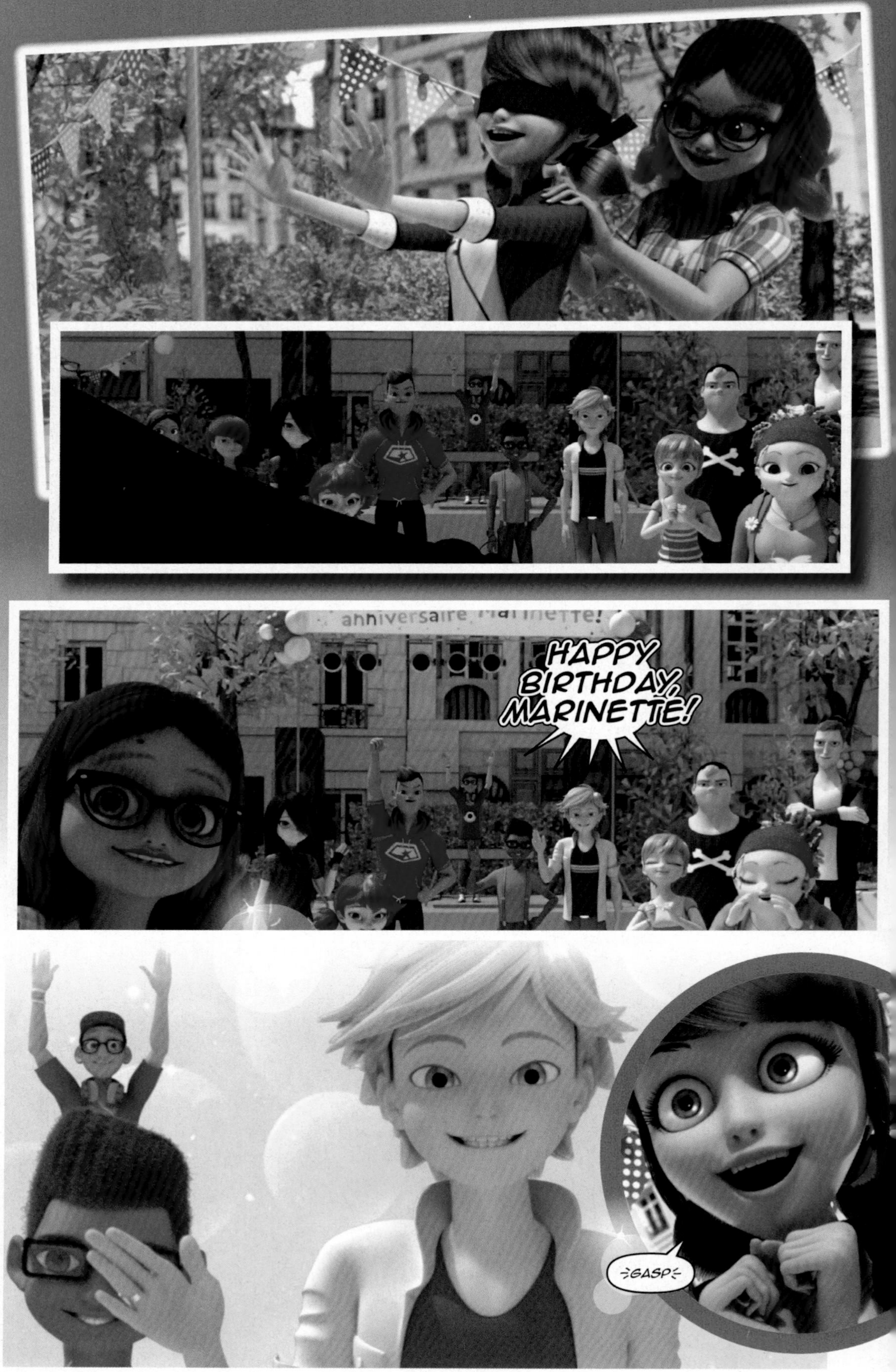
anniversaire Marinette!
HAPPY BIRTHDAY, MARINETTE!
GASP

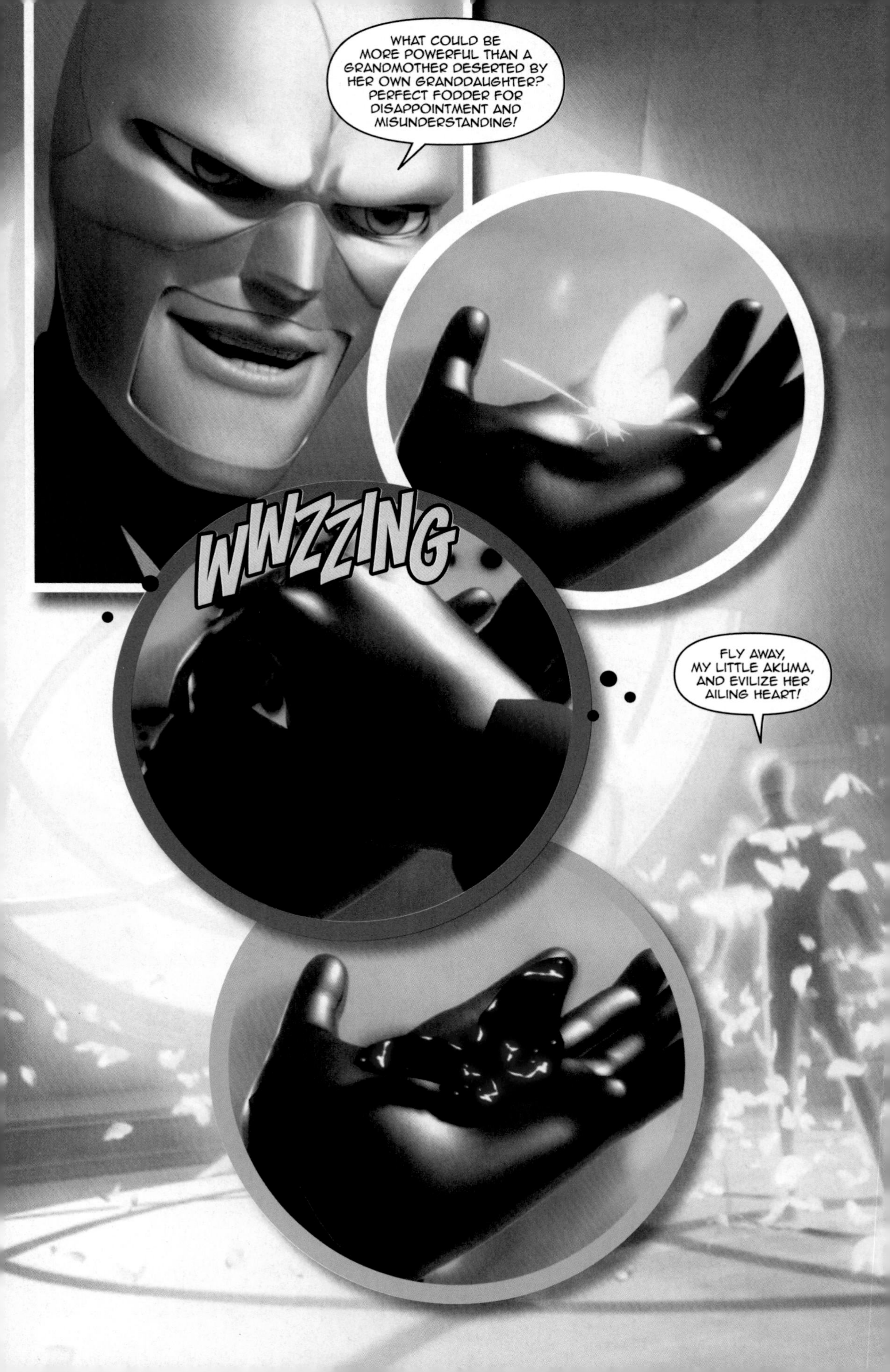
WHAT COULD BE MORE POWERFUL THAN A GRANDMOTHER DESERTED BY HER OWN GRANDDAUGHTER? PERFECT FODDER FOR DISAPPOINTMENT AND MISUNDERSTANDING!
WWZZING
FLY AWAY, MY LITTLE AKUMA, AND EVILIZE HER AILING HEART!

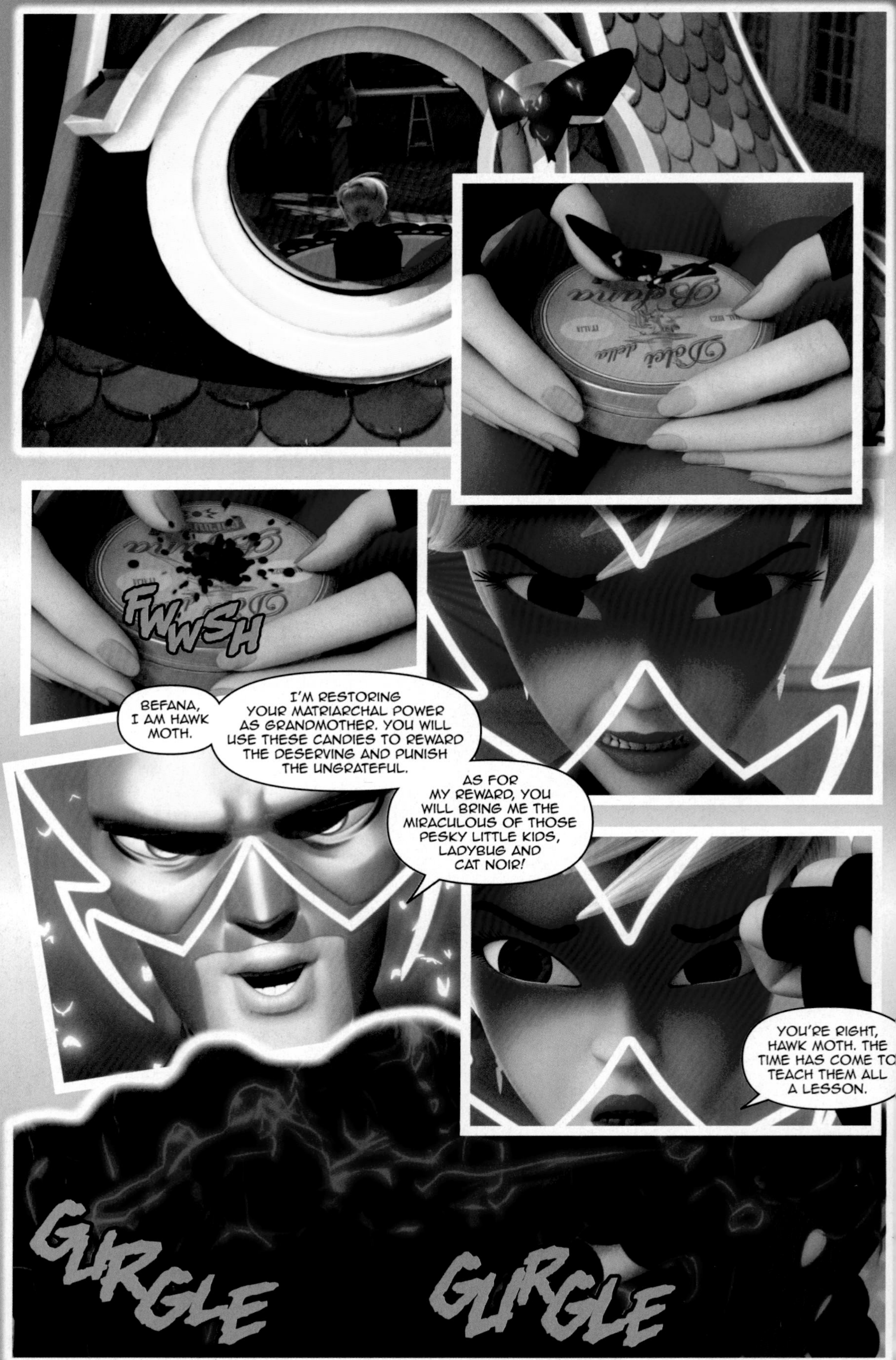
FWWSH
BEFANA, I AM HAWK MOTH.
I'M RESTORING YOUR MATRIARCHAL POWER AS GRANDMOTHER. YOU WILL USE THESE CANDIES TO REWARD THE DESERVING AND PUNISH THE UNGRATEFUL.
AS FOR MY REWARD, YOU WILL BRING ME THE MIRACULOUS OF THOSE PESKY LITTLE KIDS, LADYBUG AND CAT NOIR!
YOU'RE RIGHT, HAWK MOTH. THE TIME HAS COME TO TEACH THEM ALL A LESSON.
GURGLE
GURGLE

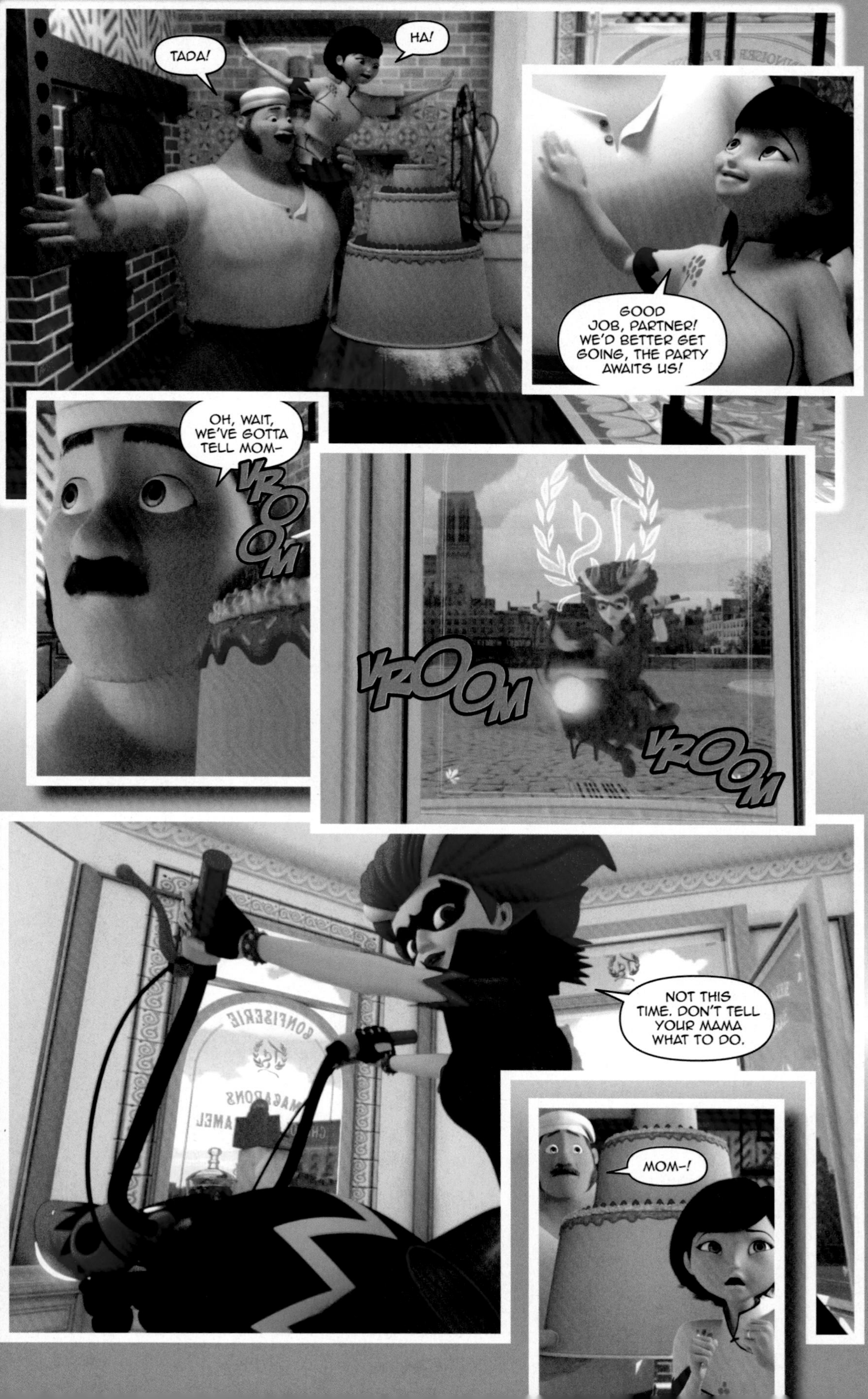
TADA!
HA!
GOOD JOB, PARTNER! WE'D BETTER GET GOING, THE PARTY AWAITS US!
OH, WAIT, WE'VE GOTTA TELL MOM-
VROOOM
VROOOM
VROOOM
NOT THIS TIME. DON'T TELL YOUR MAMA WHAT TO DO.
CONFISERIE
MACARONS
MOM-!

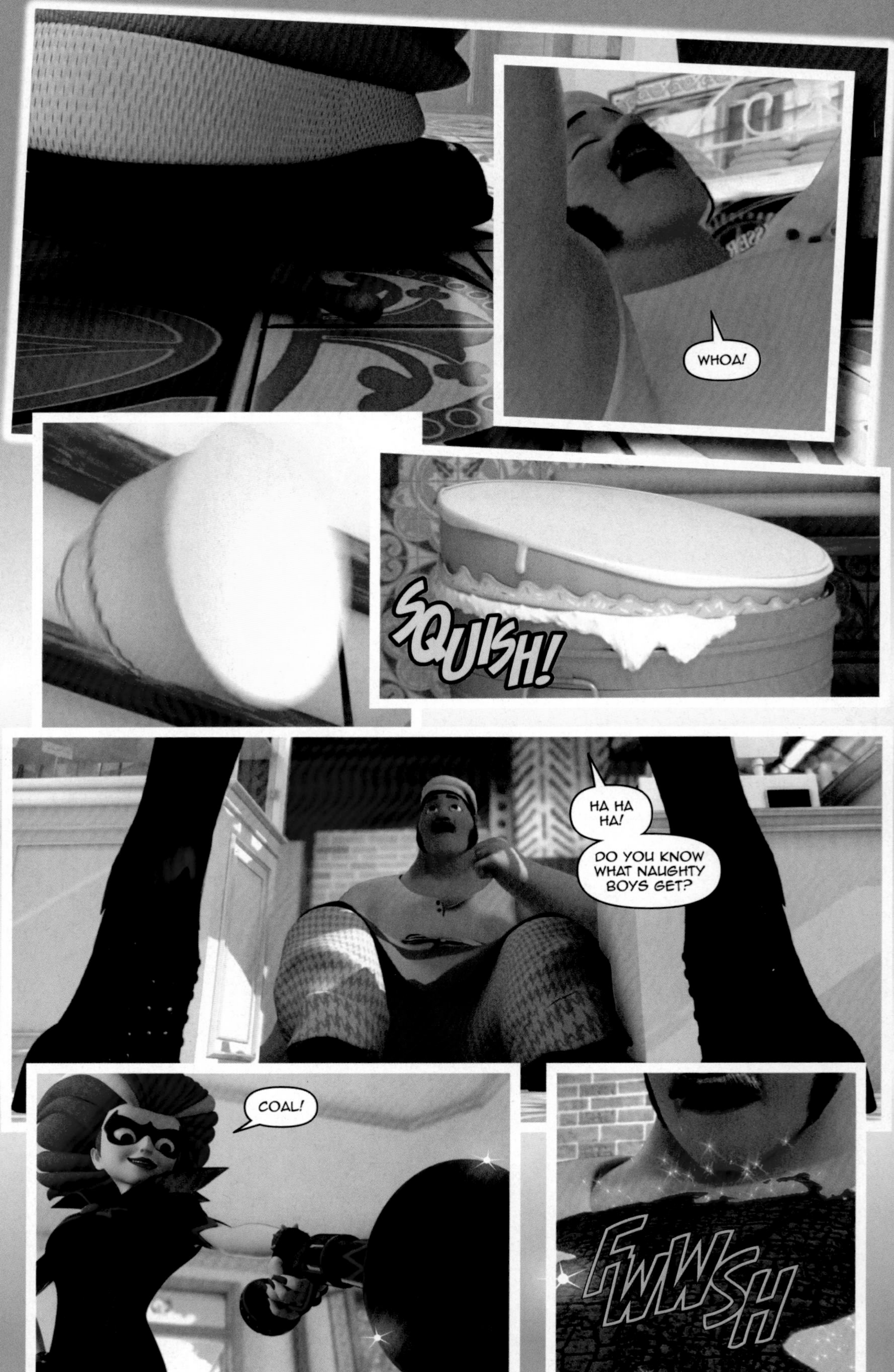
WHOA!
SQUISH!
HA HA HA!
DO YOU KNOW WHAT NAUGHTY BOYS GET?
COAL!
FWWSH

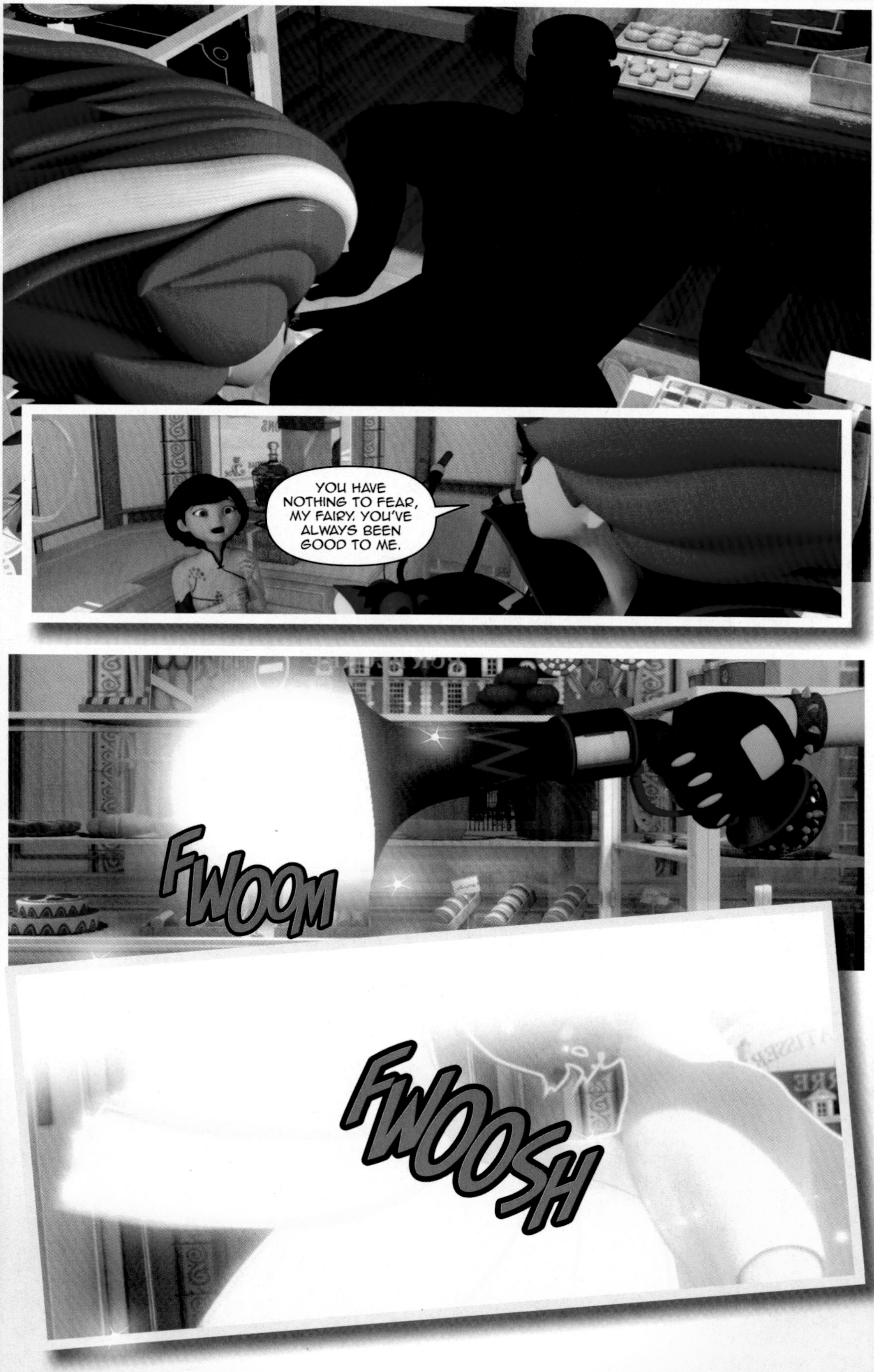
YOU HAVE NOTHING TO FEAR, MY FAIRY. YOU'VE ALWAYS BEEN GOOD TO ME.
FWOOM
FWOOSH

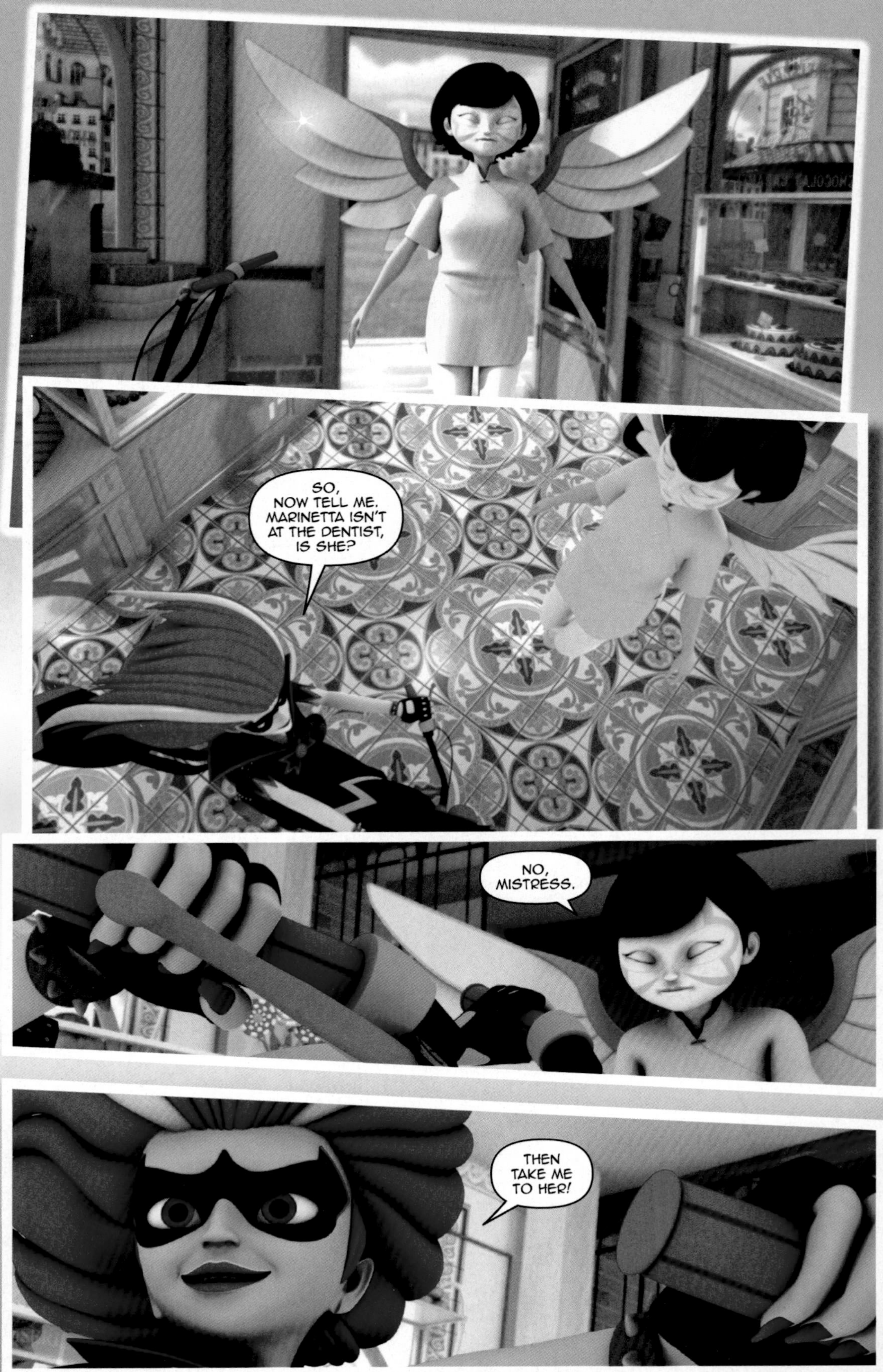
SO, NOW TELL ME. MARINETTA ISN'T AT THE DENTIST, IS SHE?
NO, MISTRESS.
THEN TAKE ME TO HER!

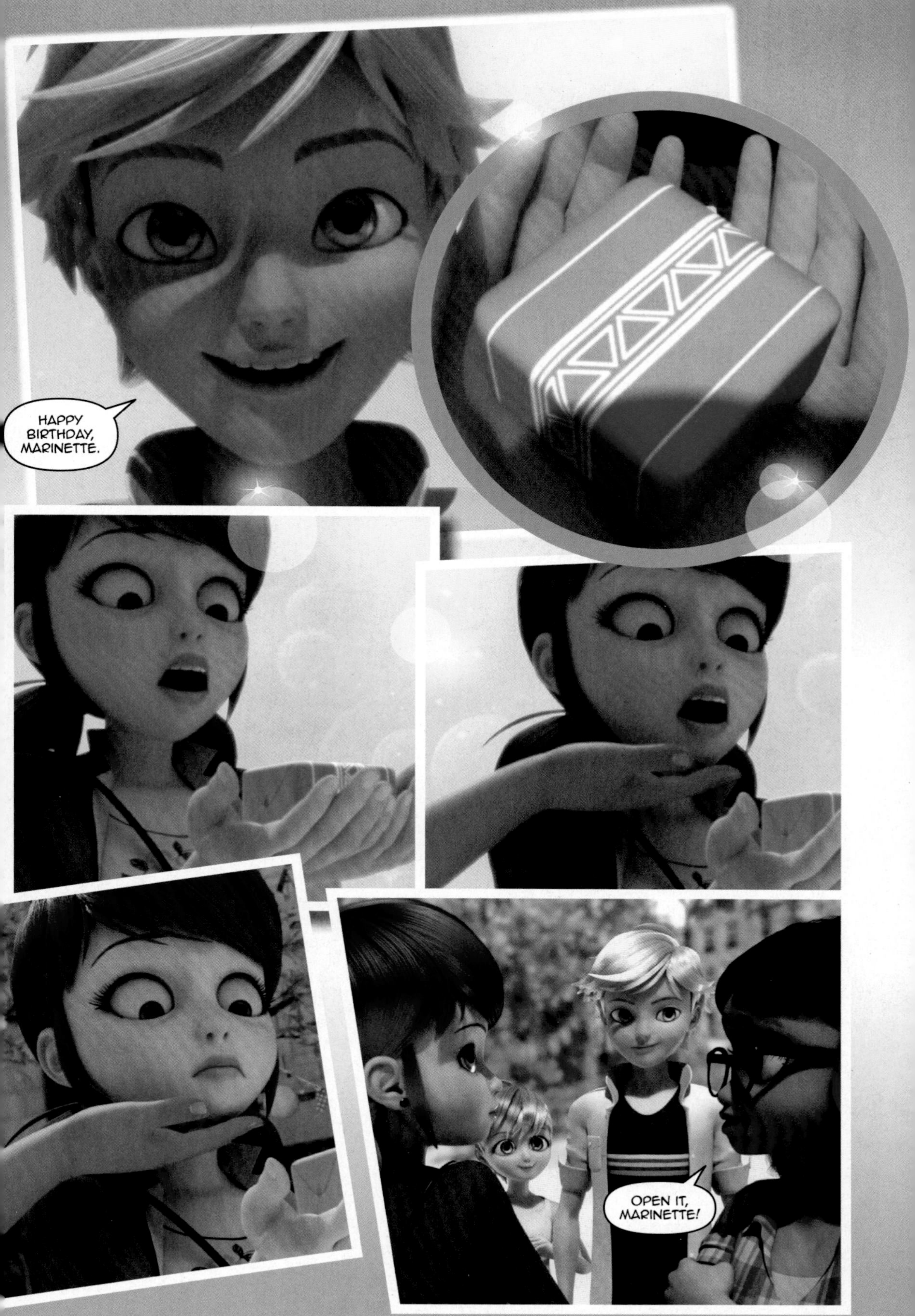
HAPPY BIRTHDAY, MARINETTE.
OPEN IT, MARINETTE!

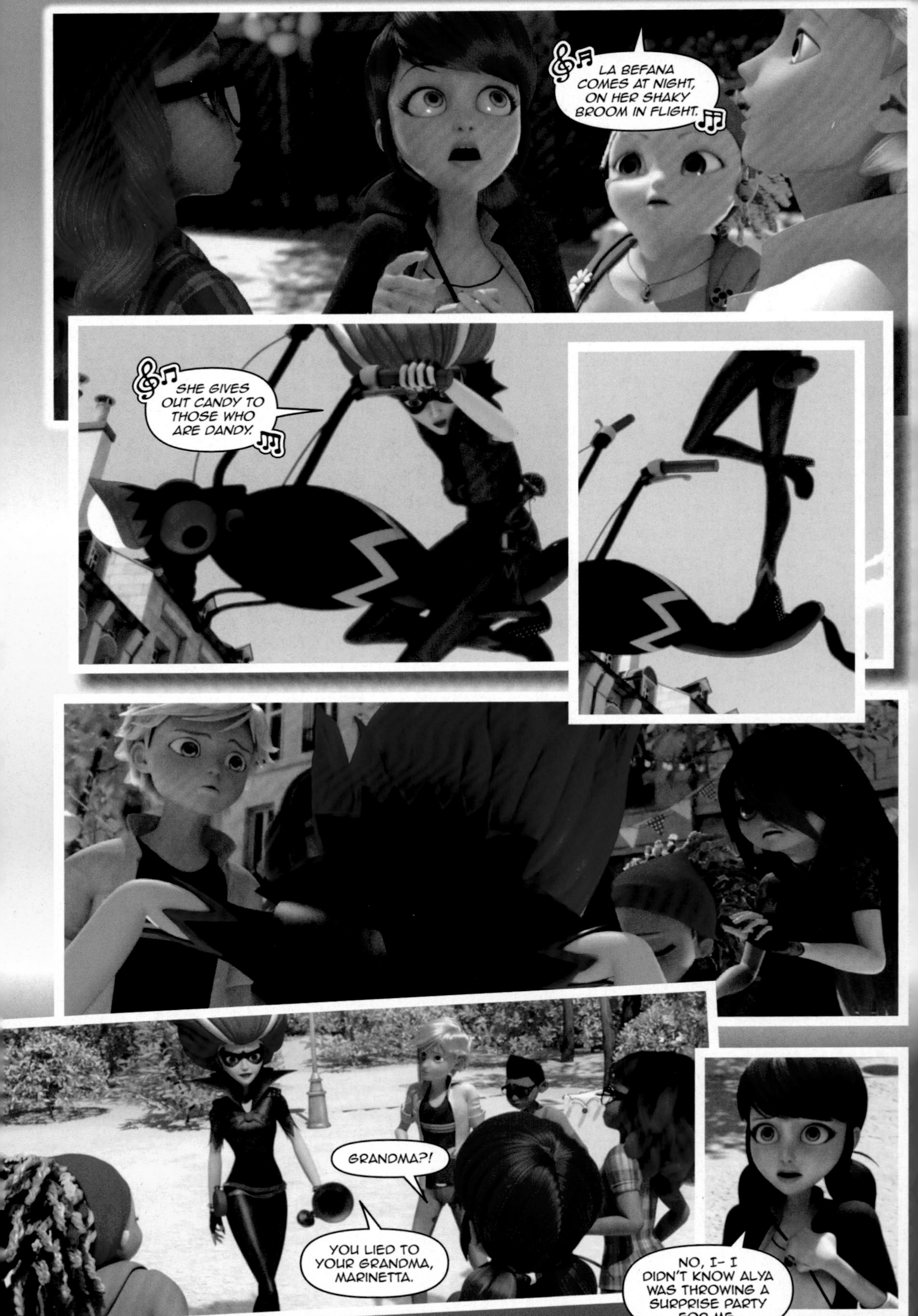
LA BEFANA COMES AT NIGHT, ON HER SHAKY BROOM IN FLIGHT.
SHE GIVES OUT CANDY TO THOSE WHO ARE DANDY.
GRANDMA?!
YOU LIED TO YOUR GRANDMA, MARINETTA.
NO, I- I DIDN'T KNOW ALYA WAS THROWING A SURPRISE PARTY FOR ME.

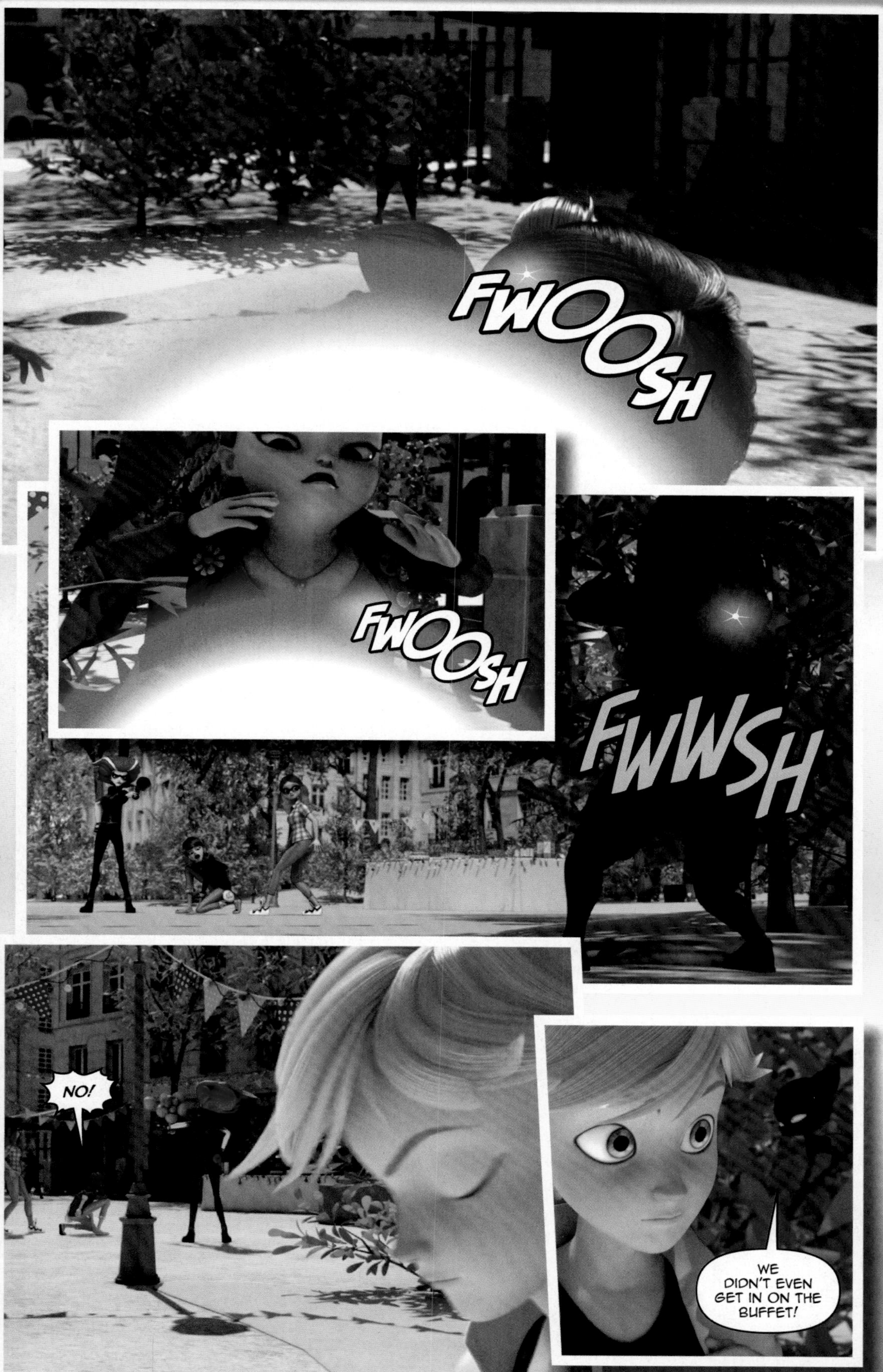
FWOOSH
FWOOSH
FWWSH
NO!
WE DIDN'T EVEN GET IN ON THE BUFFET!

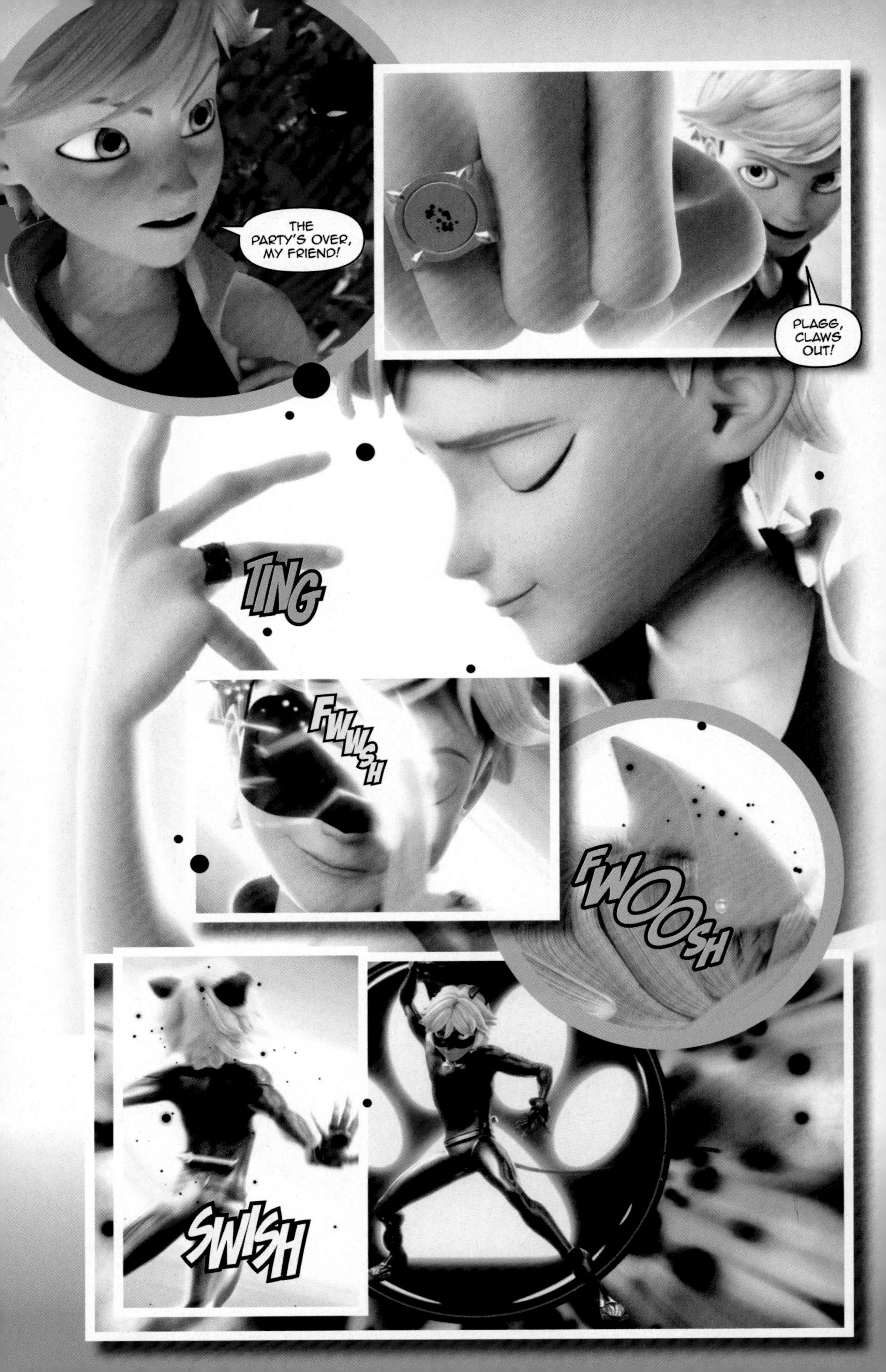

THE PARTY'S OVER, MY FRIEND!
PLAGG, CLAWS OUT!
TING
FWWSH
FWOOSH
SWISH

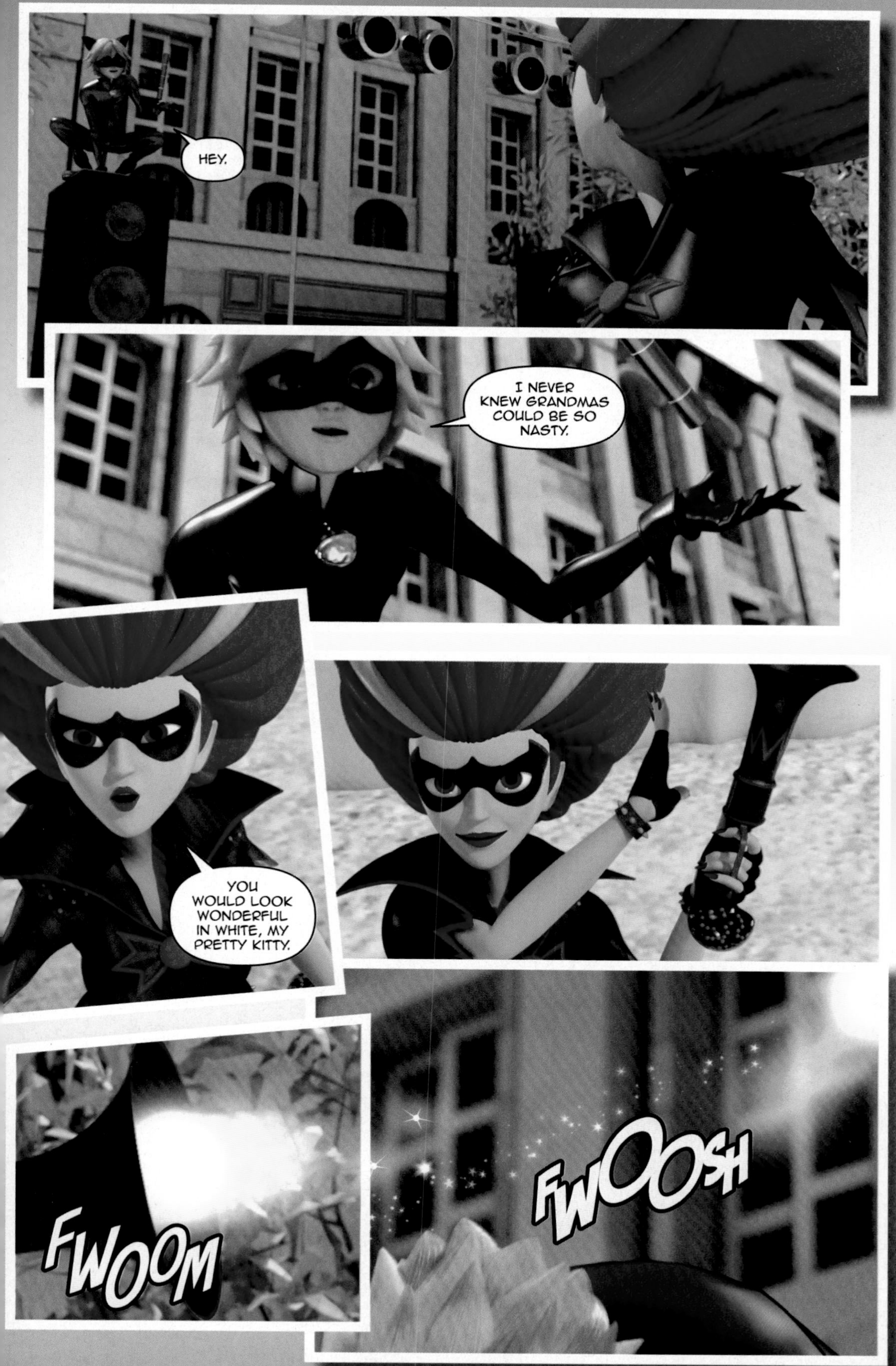
HEY.
I NEVER KNEW GRANDMAS COULD BE SO NASTY.
YOU WOULD LOOK WONDERFUL IN WHITE, MY PRETTY KITTY.
FWOOM
FWOOSH

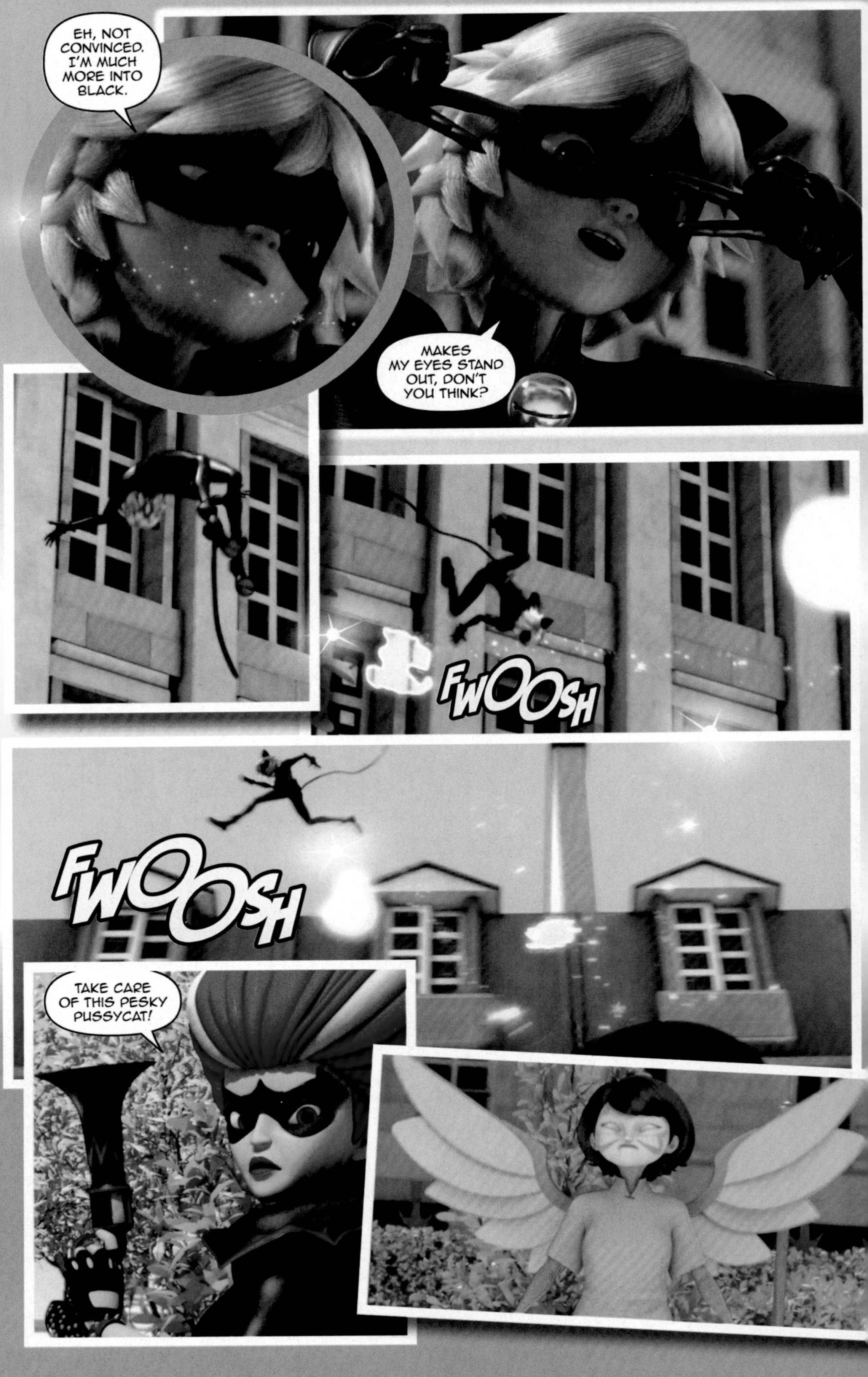
EH, NOT CONVINCED. I'M MUCH MORE INTO BLACK.
MAKES MY EYES STAND OUT, DON'T YOU THINK?
FWOOSH
FWOOSH
TAKE CARE OF THIS PESKY PUSSYCAT!

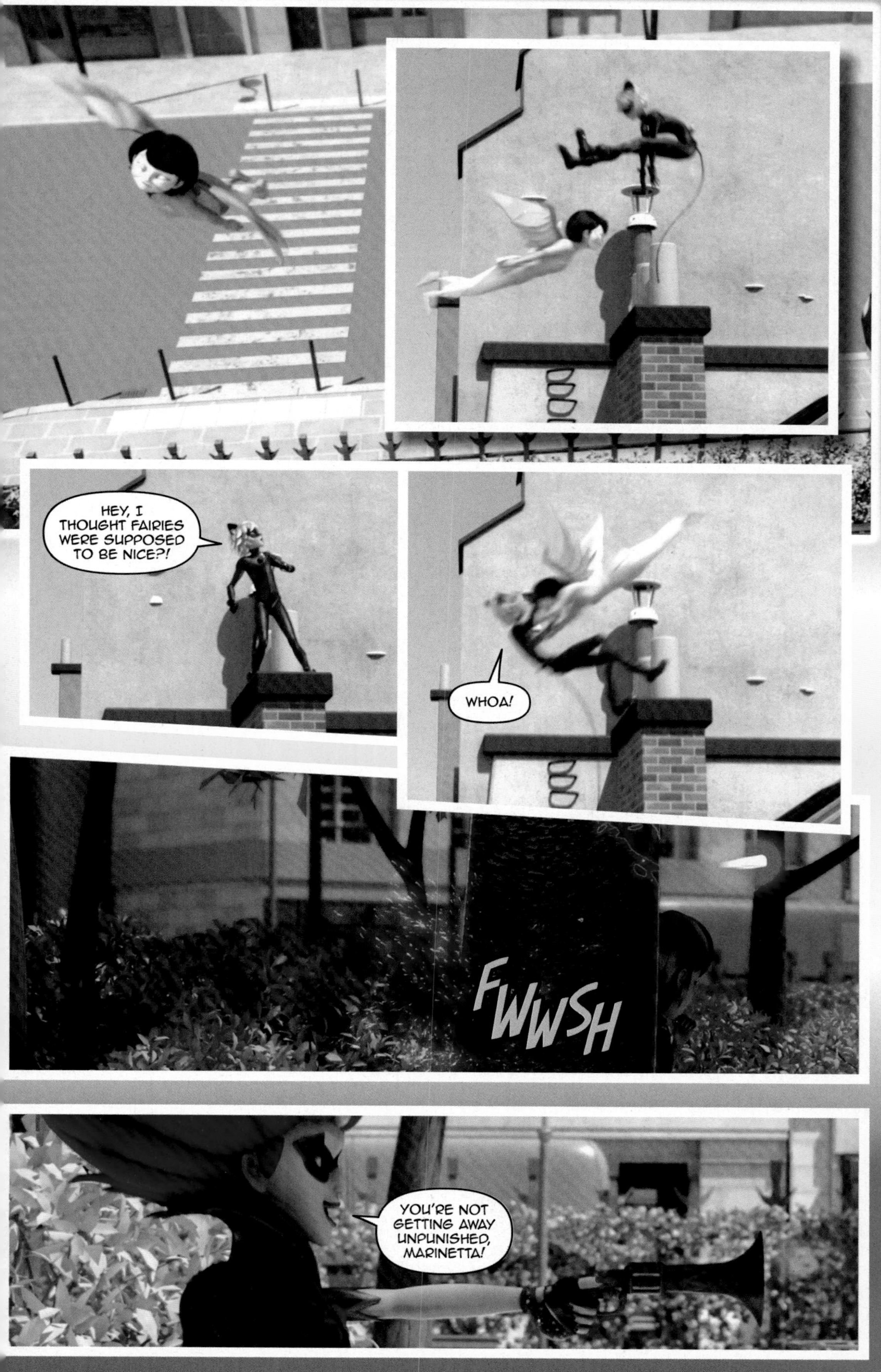
HEY, I THOUGHT FAIRIES WERE SUPPOSED TO BE NICE?!
WHOA!
FWWSH
YOU'RE NOT GETTING AWAY UNPUNISHED, MARINETTA!

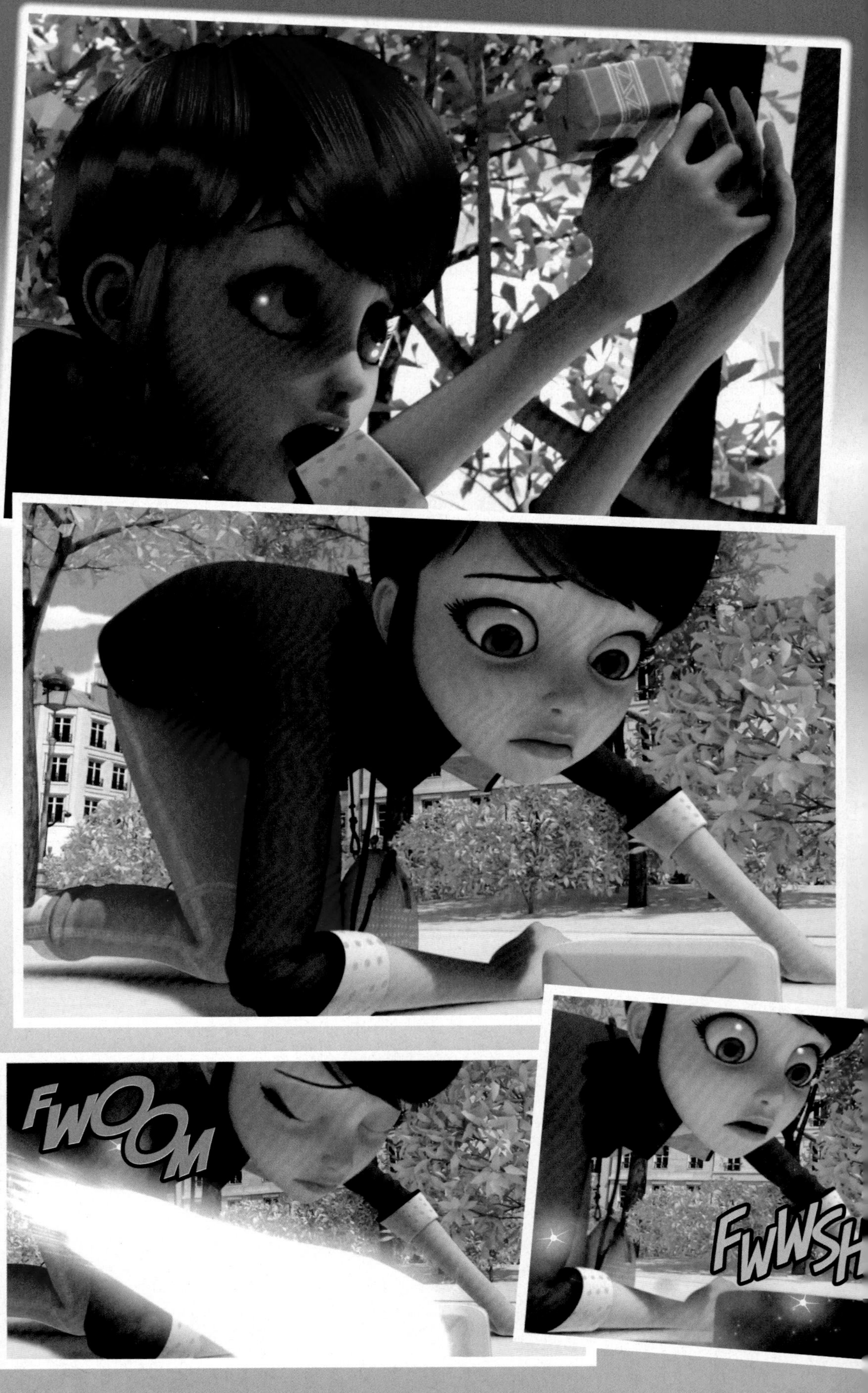
FWOOM
FWWSH

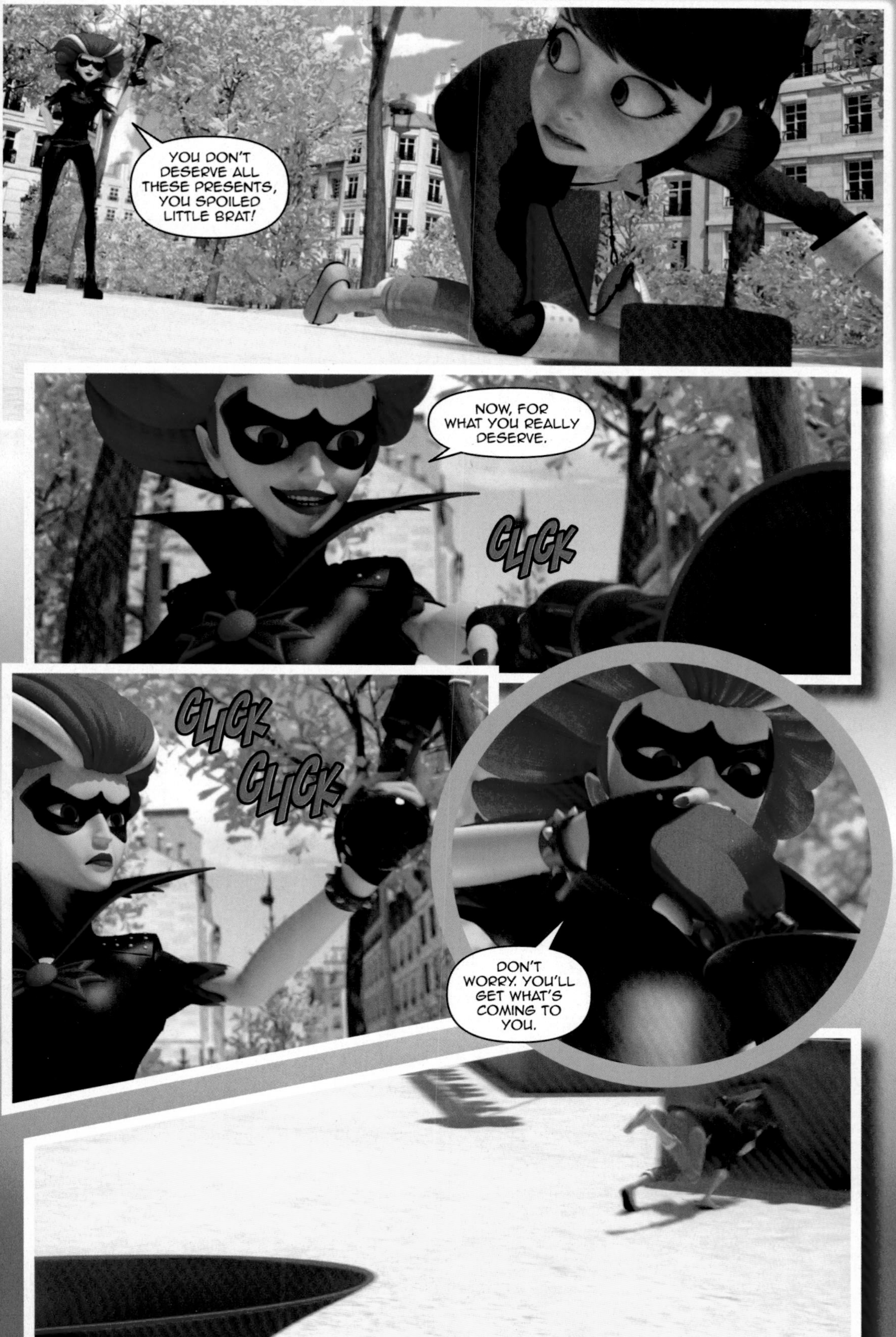
YOU DON'T DESERVE ALL THESE PRESENTS, YOU SPOILED LITTLE BRAT!
NOW, FOR WHAT YOU REALLY DESERVE.
CLICK
CLICK
CLICK
DON'T WORRY. YOU'LL GET WHAT'S COMING TO YOU.

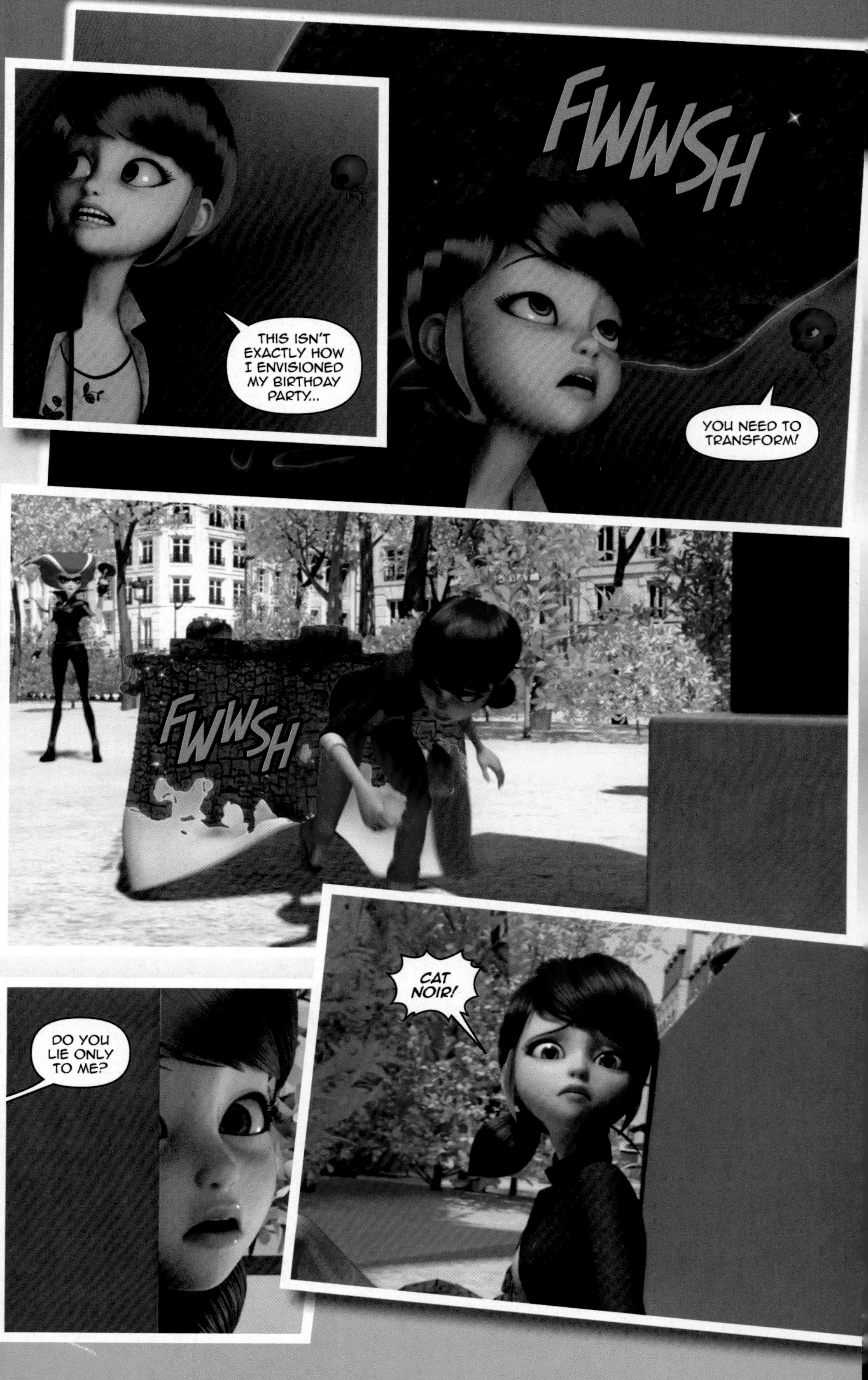
THIS ISN'T EXACTLY HOW I ENVISIONED MY BIRTHDAY PARTY...
FWWSH
YOU NEED TO TRANSFORM!
FWWSH
CAT NOIR!
DO YOU LIE ONLY TO ME?

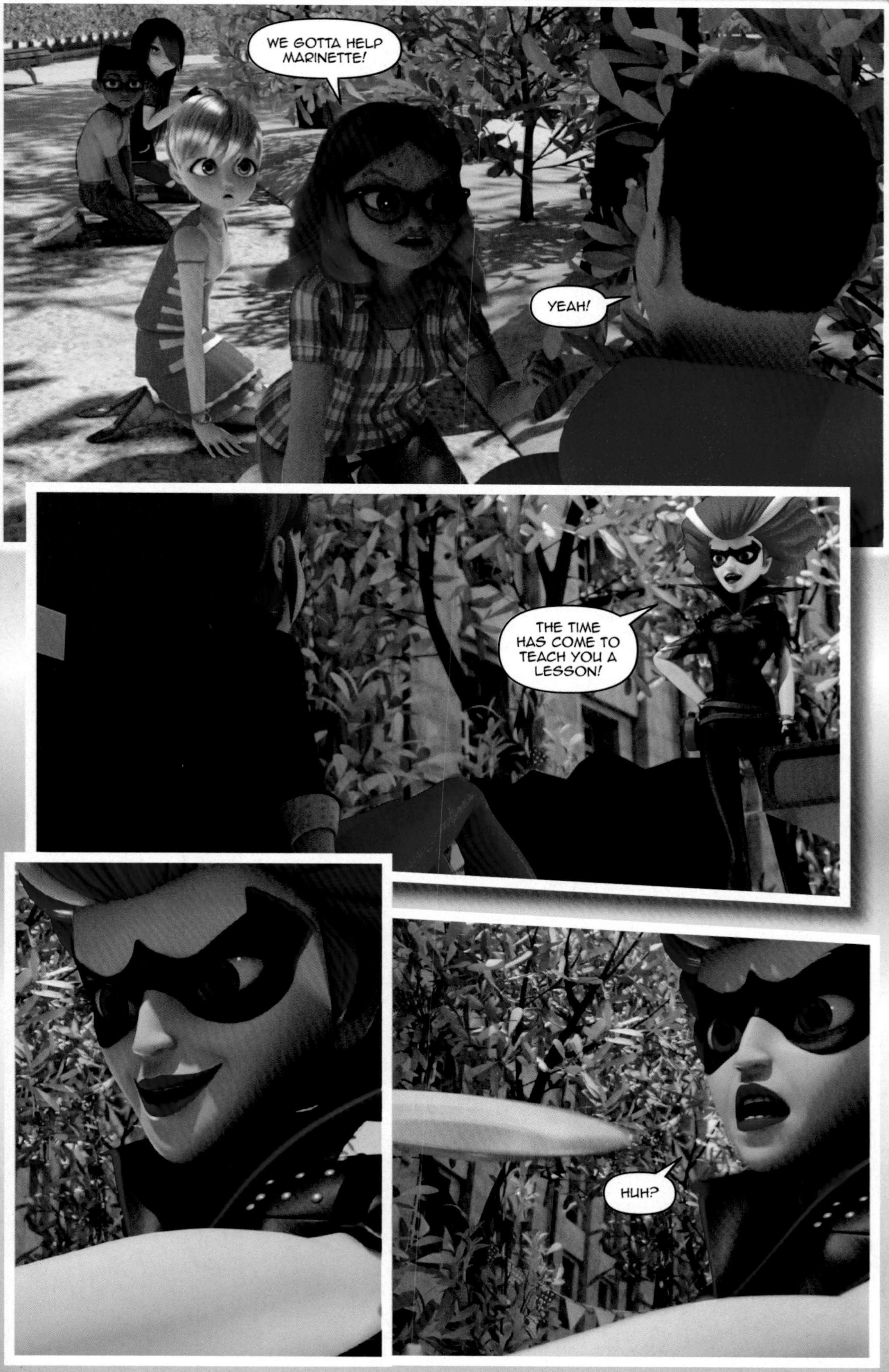
WE GOTTA HELP MARINETTE!
YEAH!
THE TIME HAS COME TO TEACH YOU A LESSON!
HUH?

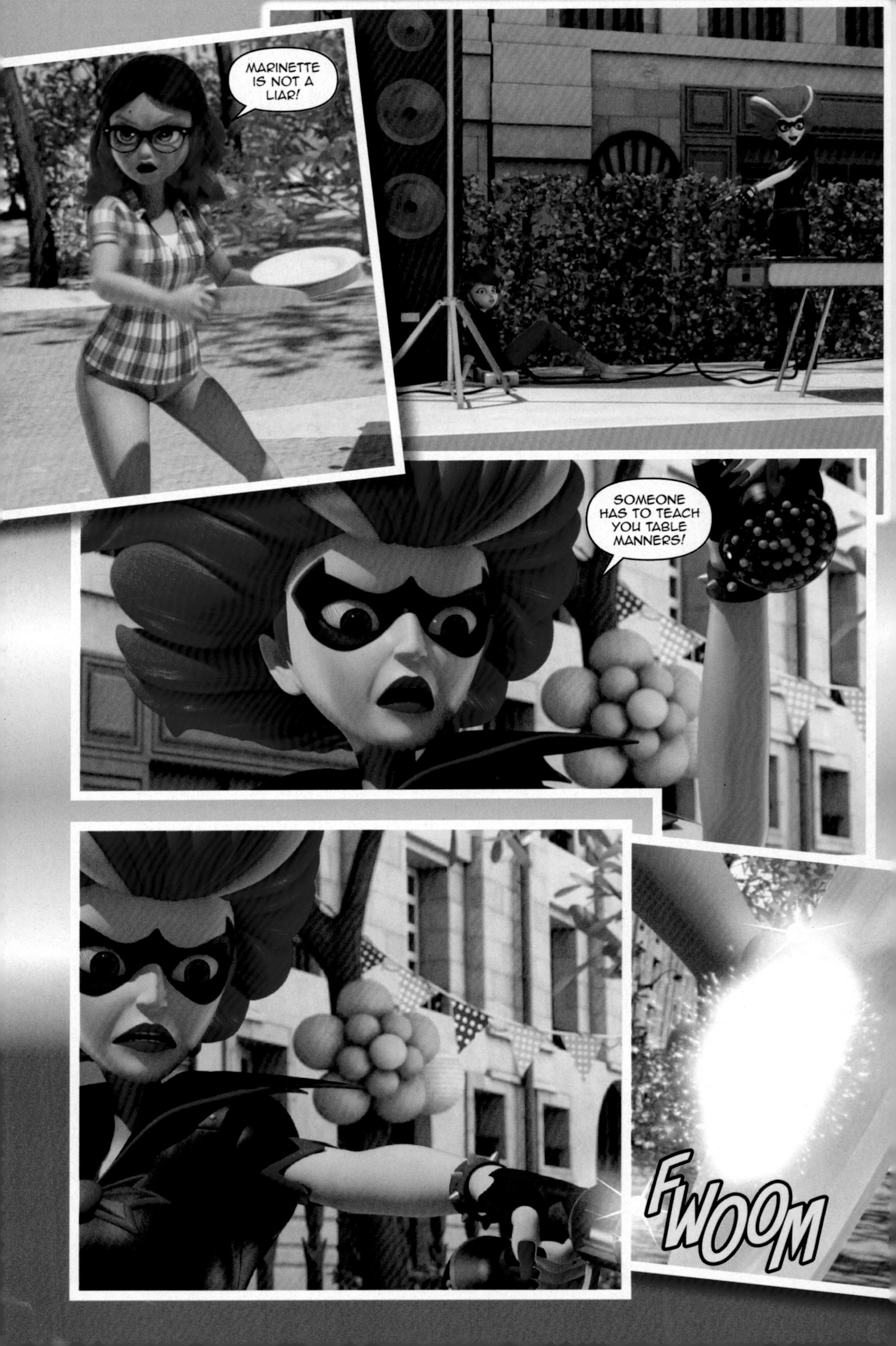
MARINETTE IS NOT A LIAR!
SOMEONE HAS TO TEACH YOU TABLE MANNERS!
FWOOM

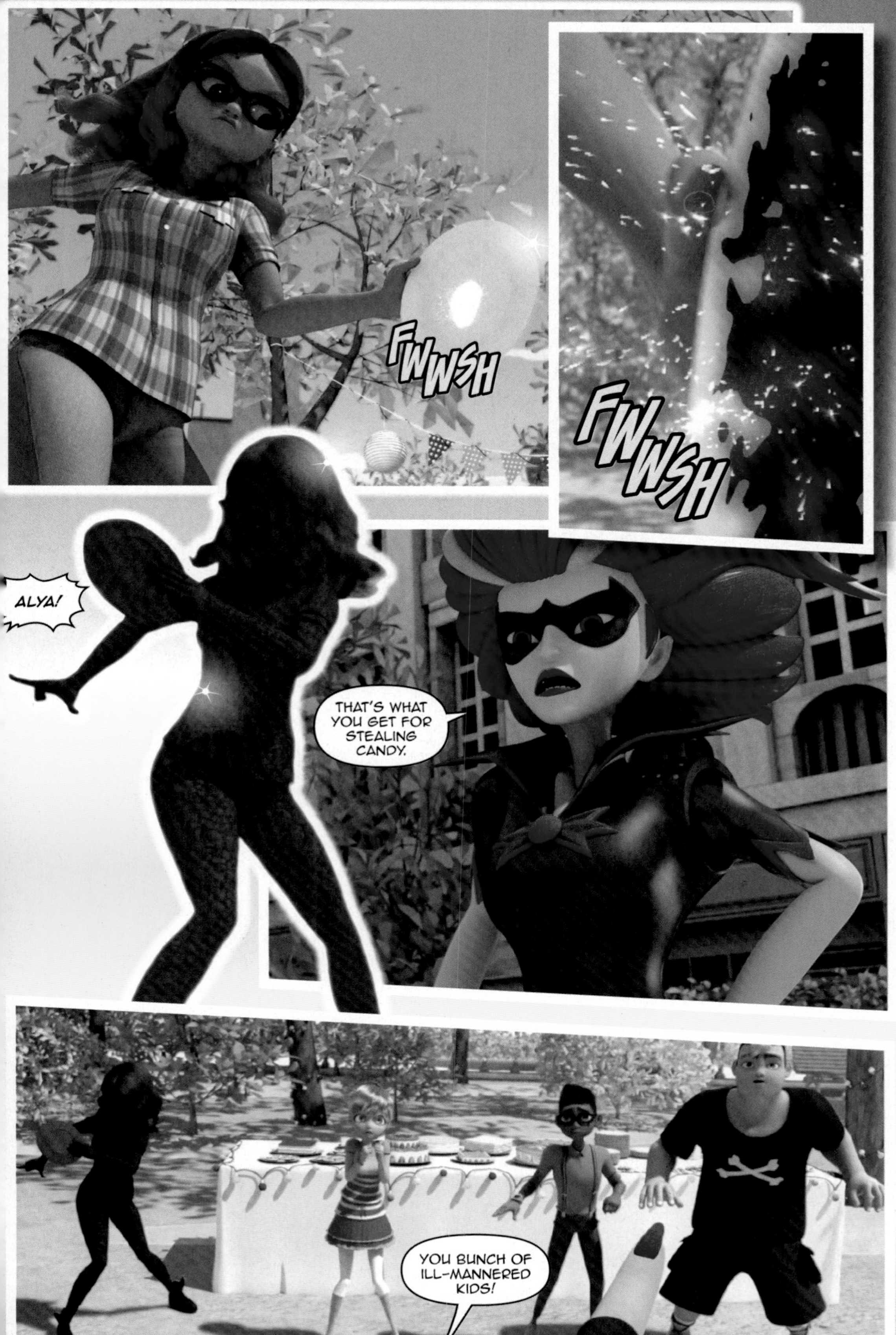
FWWSH
FWWSH
ALYA!
THAT'S WHAT YOU GET FOR STEALING CANDY.
YOU BUNCH OF ILL-MANNERED KIDS!

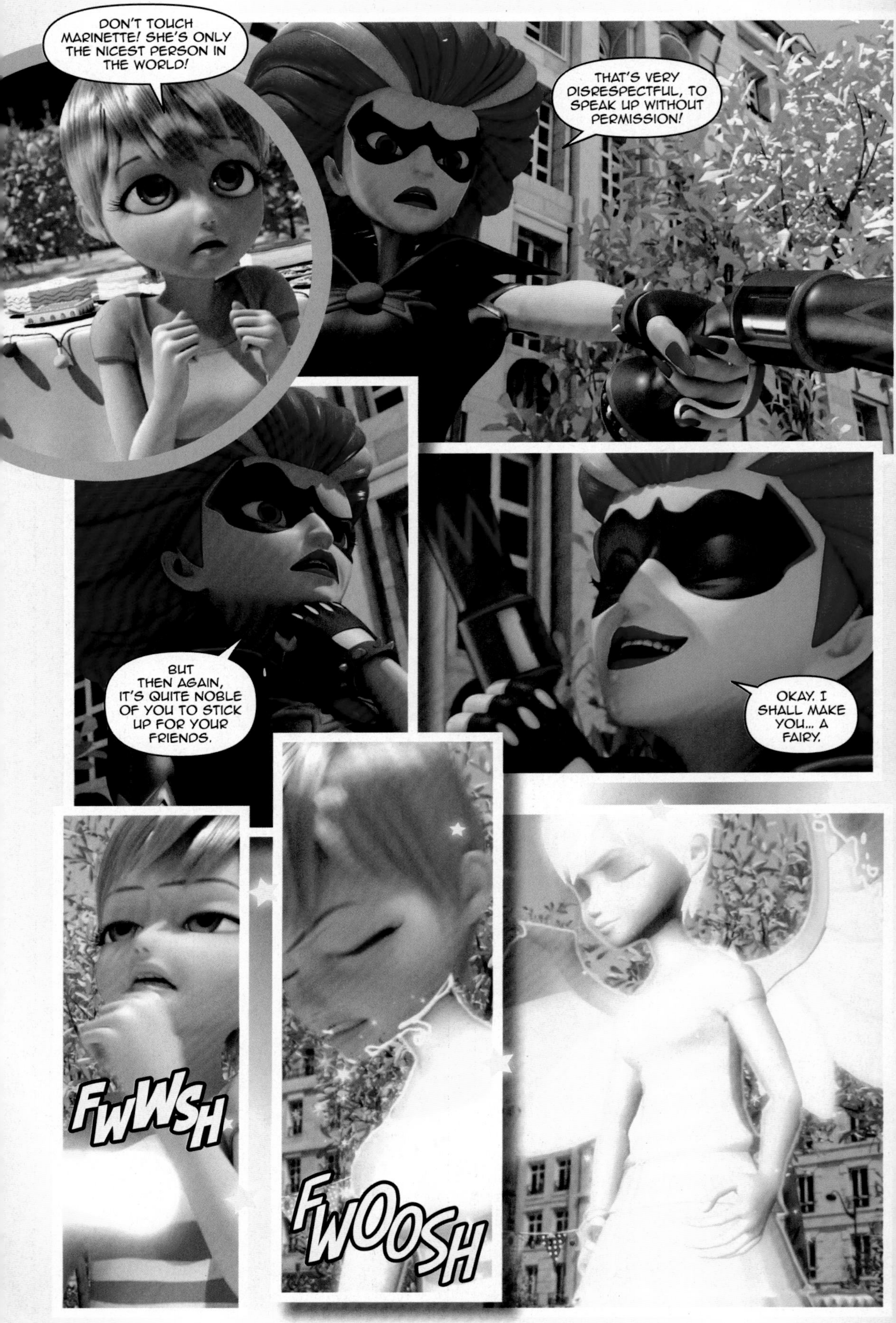
DON'T TOUCH MARINETTE! SHE'S ONLY THE NICEST PERSON IN THE WORLD!
THAT'S VERY DISRESPECTFUL, TO SPEAK UP WITHOUT PERMISSION!
BUT THEN AGAIN, IT'S QUITE NOBLE OF YOU TO STICK UP FOR YOUR FRIENDS.
OKAY. I SHALL MAKE YOU... A FAIRY.
FWWSH
FWOOSH

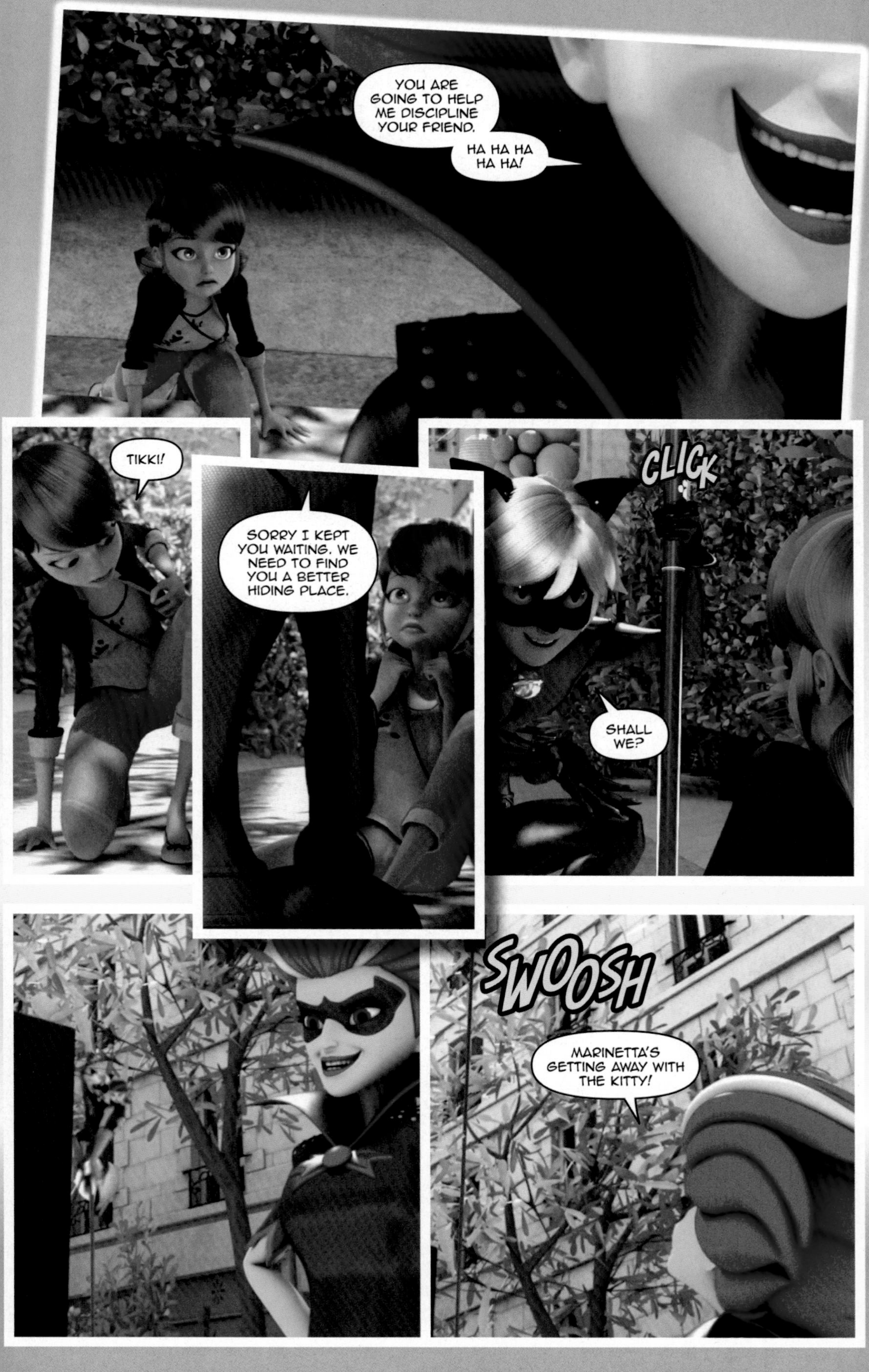
YOU ARE GOING TO HELP ME DISCIPLINE YOUR FRIEND.
HA HA HA HA HA!
TIKKI!
SORRY I KEPT YOU WAITING. WE NEED TO FIND YOU A BETTER HIDING PLACE.
CLICK
SHALL WE?
SWOOSH
MARINETTA'S GETTING AWAY WITH THE KITTY!

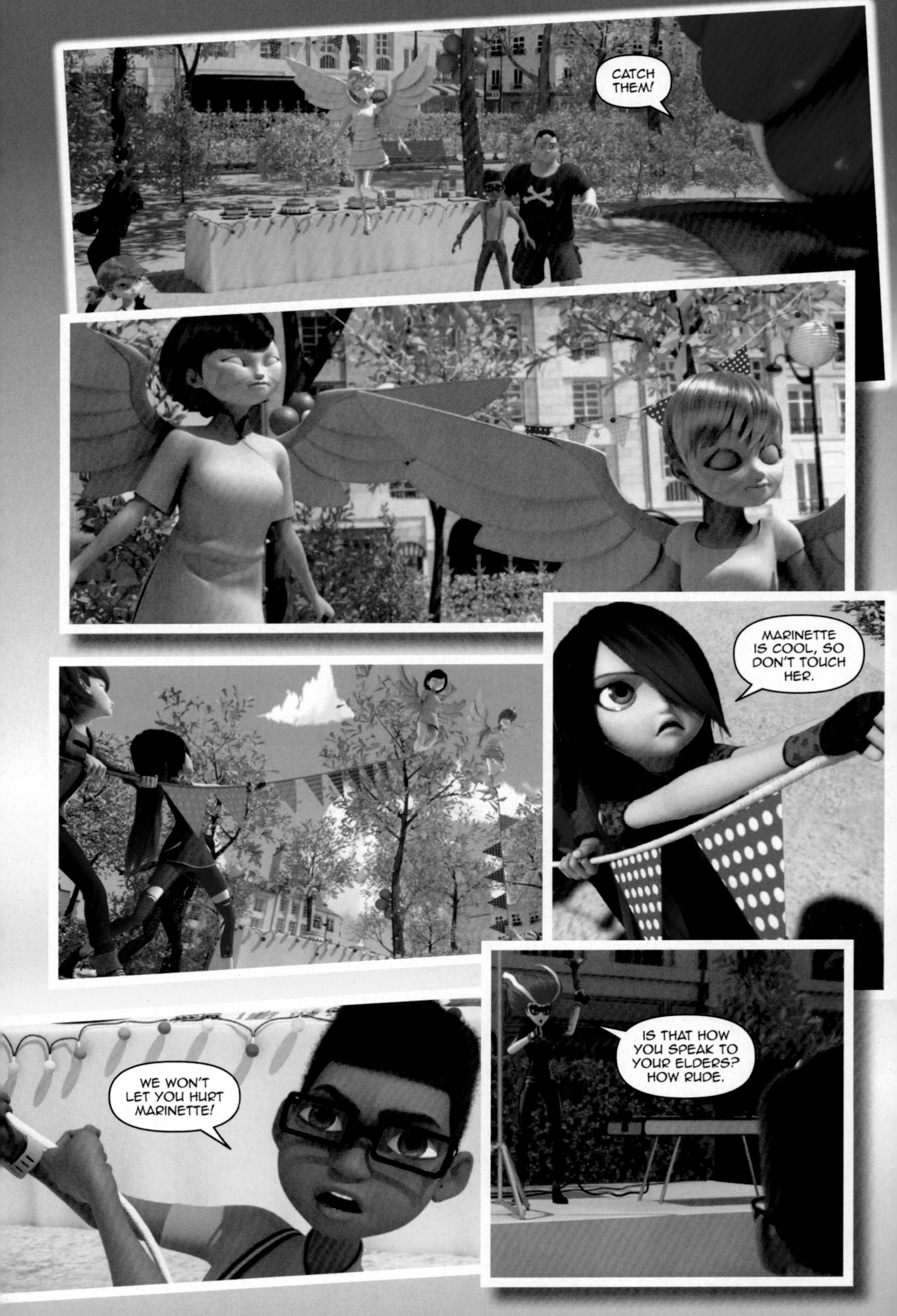
CATCH THEM!
MARINETTE IS COOL, SO DON'T TOUCH HER.
WE WON'T LET YOU HURT MARINETTE!
IS THAT HOW YOU SPEAK TO YOUR ELDERS? HOW RUDE.

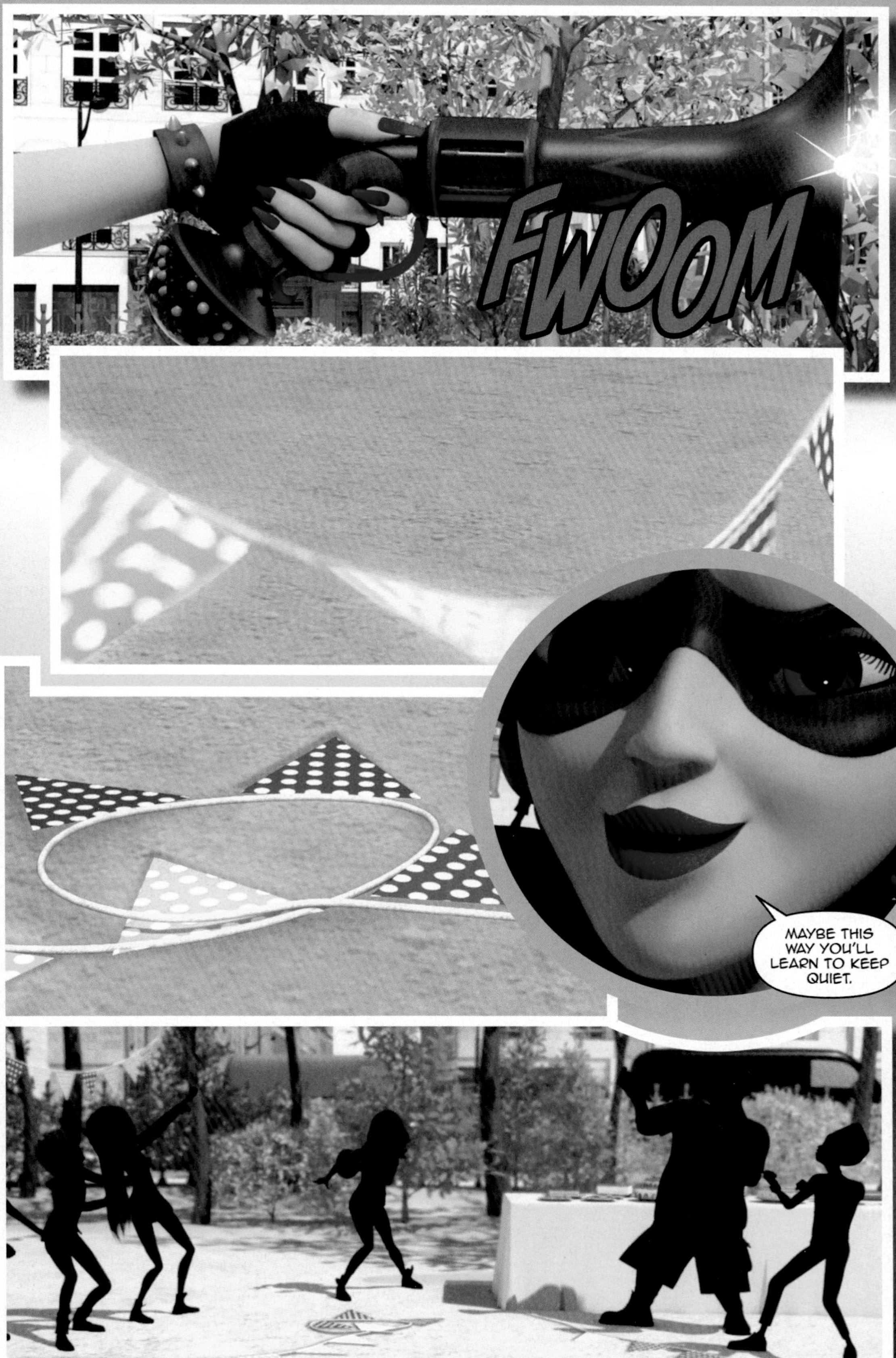
FWOOM
MAYBE THIS WAY YOU'LL LEARN TO KEEP QUIET.

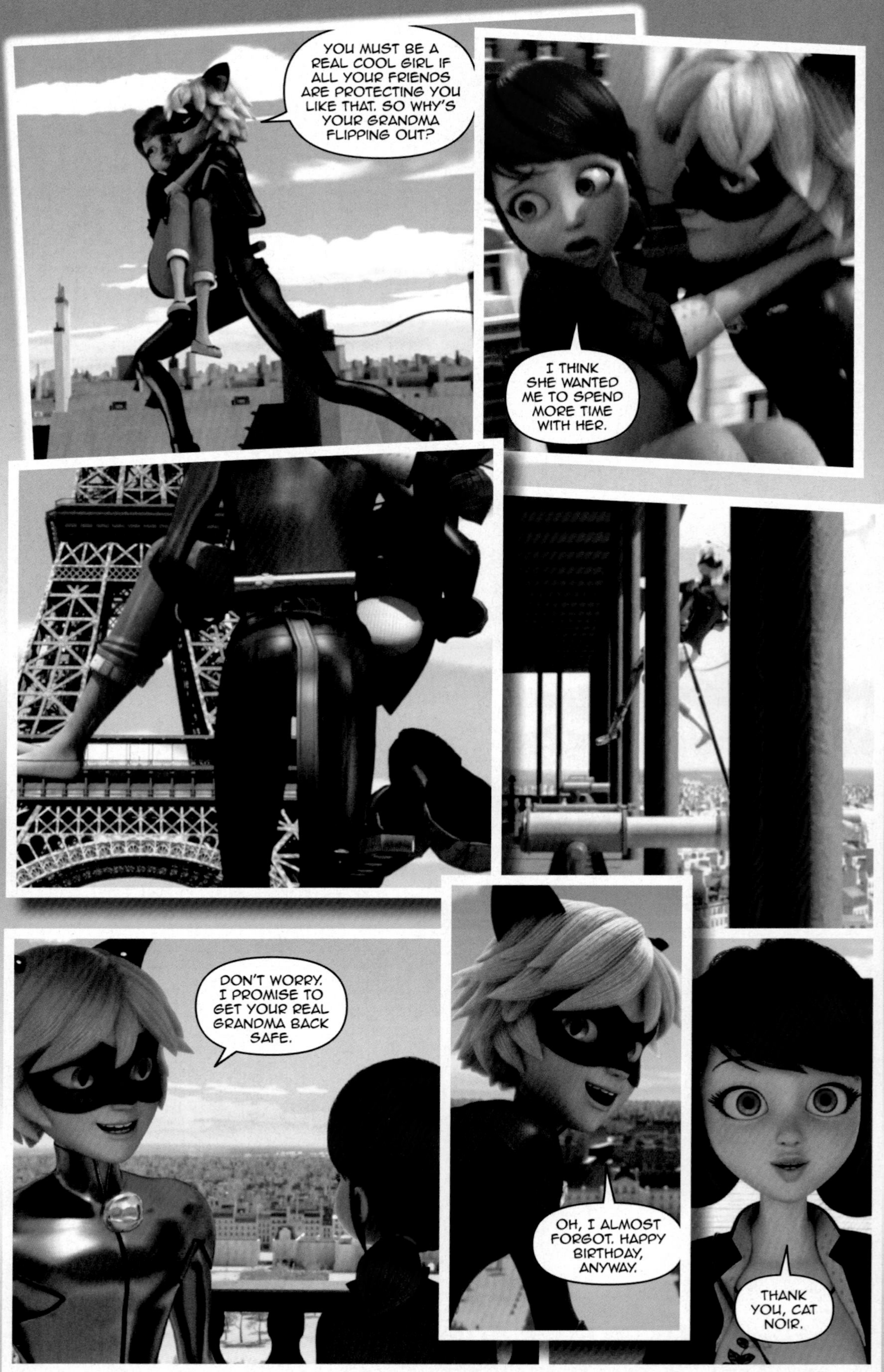
YOU MUST BE A REAL COOL GIRL IF ALL YOUR FRIENDS ARE PROTECTING YOU LIKE THAT. SO WHY'S YOUR GRANDMA FLIPPING OUT?
I THINK SHE WANTED ME TO SPEND MORE TIME WITH HER.
DON'T WORRY. I PROMISE TO GET YOUR REAL GRANDMA BACK SAFE.
OH, I ALMOST FORGOT. HAPPY BIRTHDAY, ANYWAY.
THANK YOU, CAT NOIR.

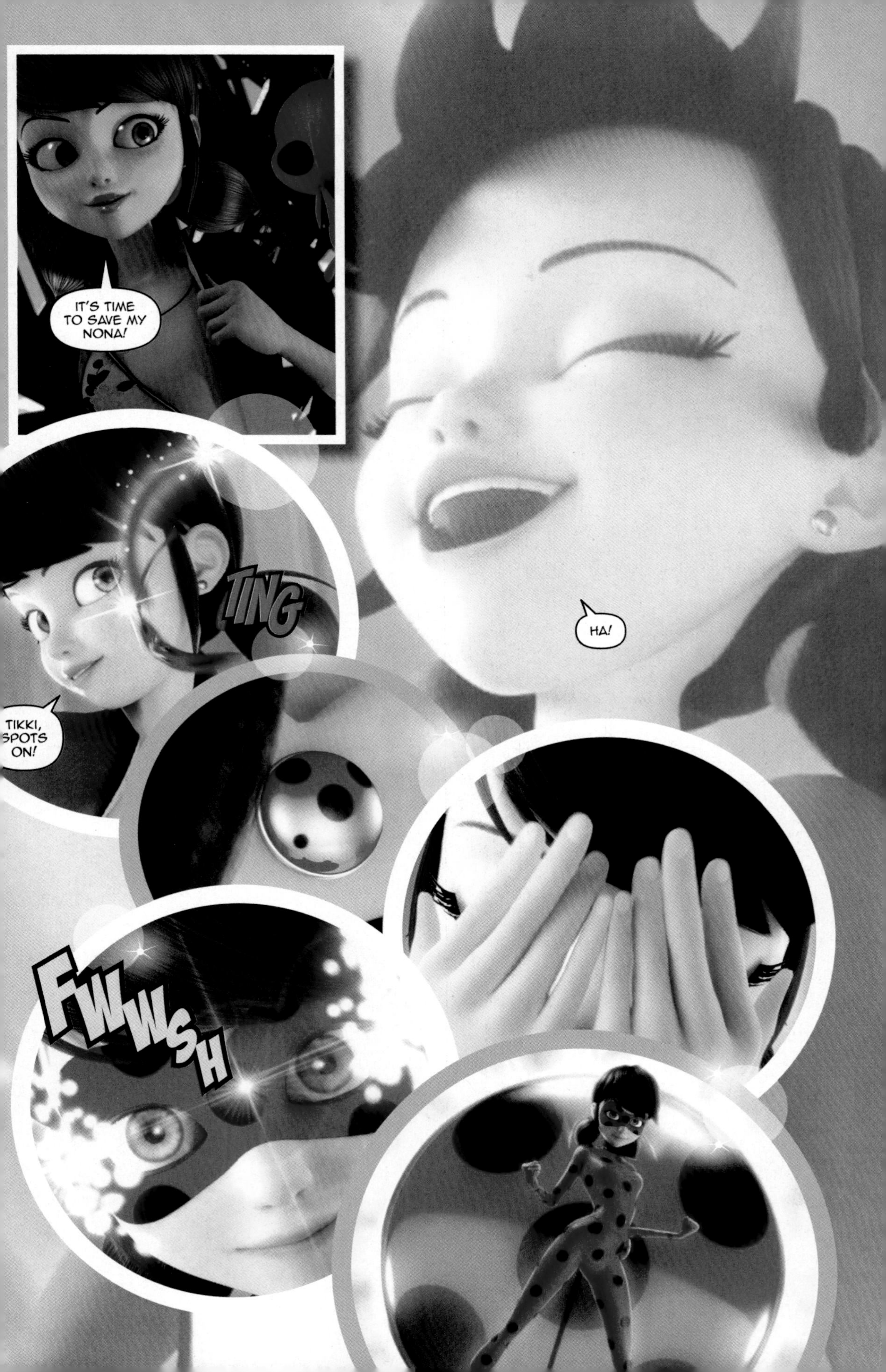
IT'S TIME TO SAVE MY NONA!
HA!
TING
TIKKI, SPOTS ON!
FWWSH

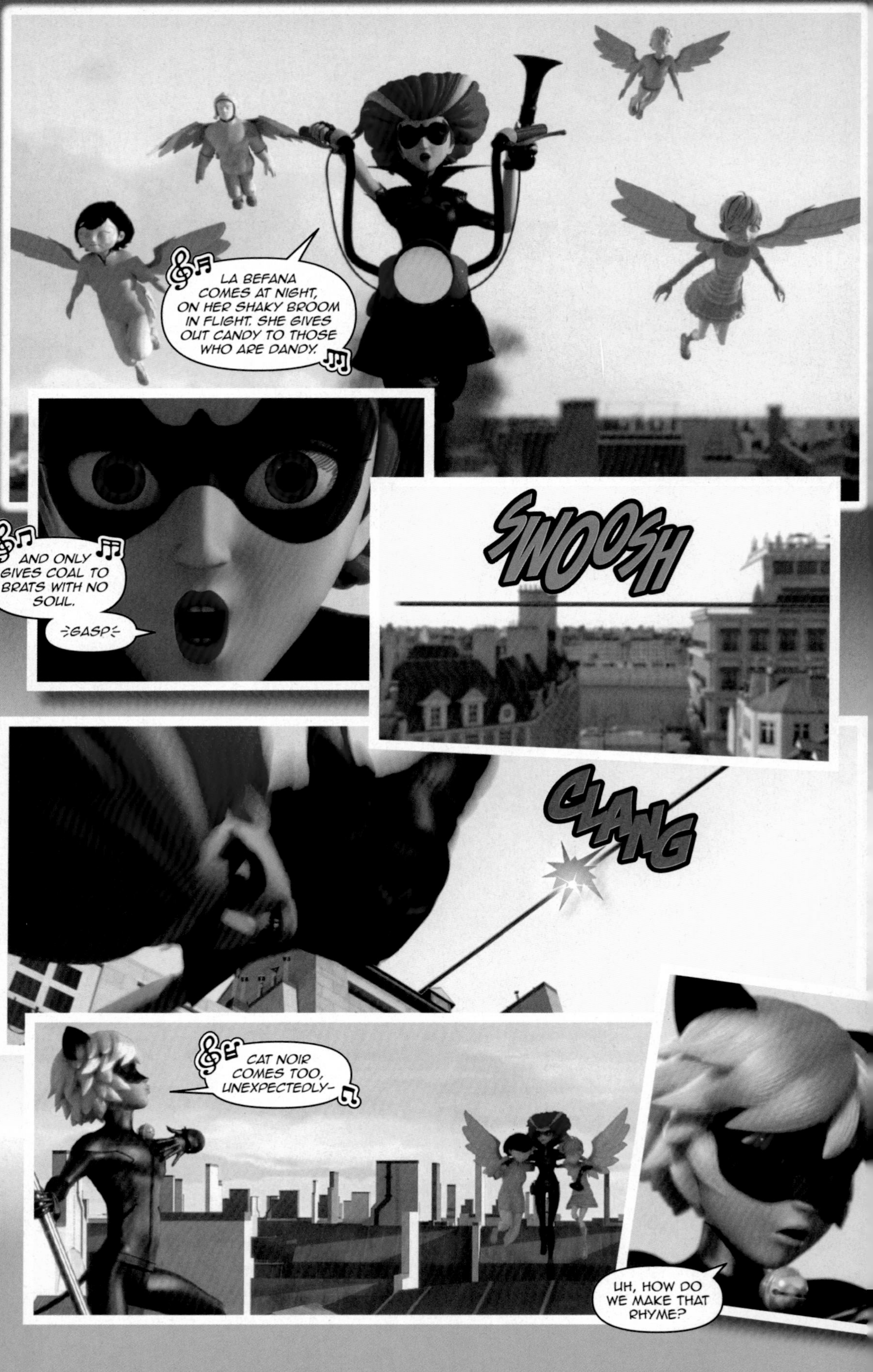
LA BEFANA COMES AT NIGHT, ON HER SHAKY BROOM IN FLIGHT. SHE GIVES OUT CANDY TO THOSE WHO ARE DANDY.
AND ONLY GIVES COAL TO BRATS WITH NO SOUL.
GASP
SWOOSH
CLANG
CAT NOIR COMES TOO, UNEXPECTEDLY-
UH, HOW DO WE MAKE THAT RHYME?

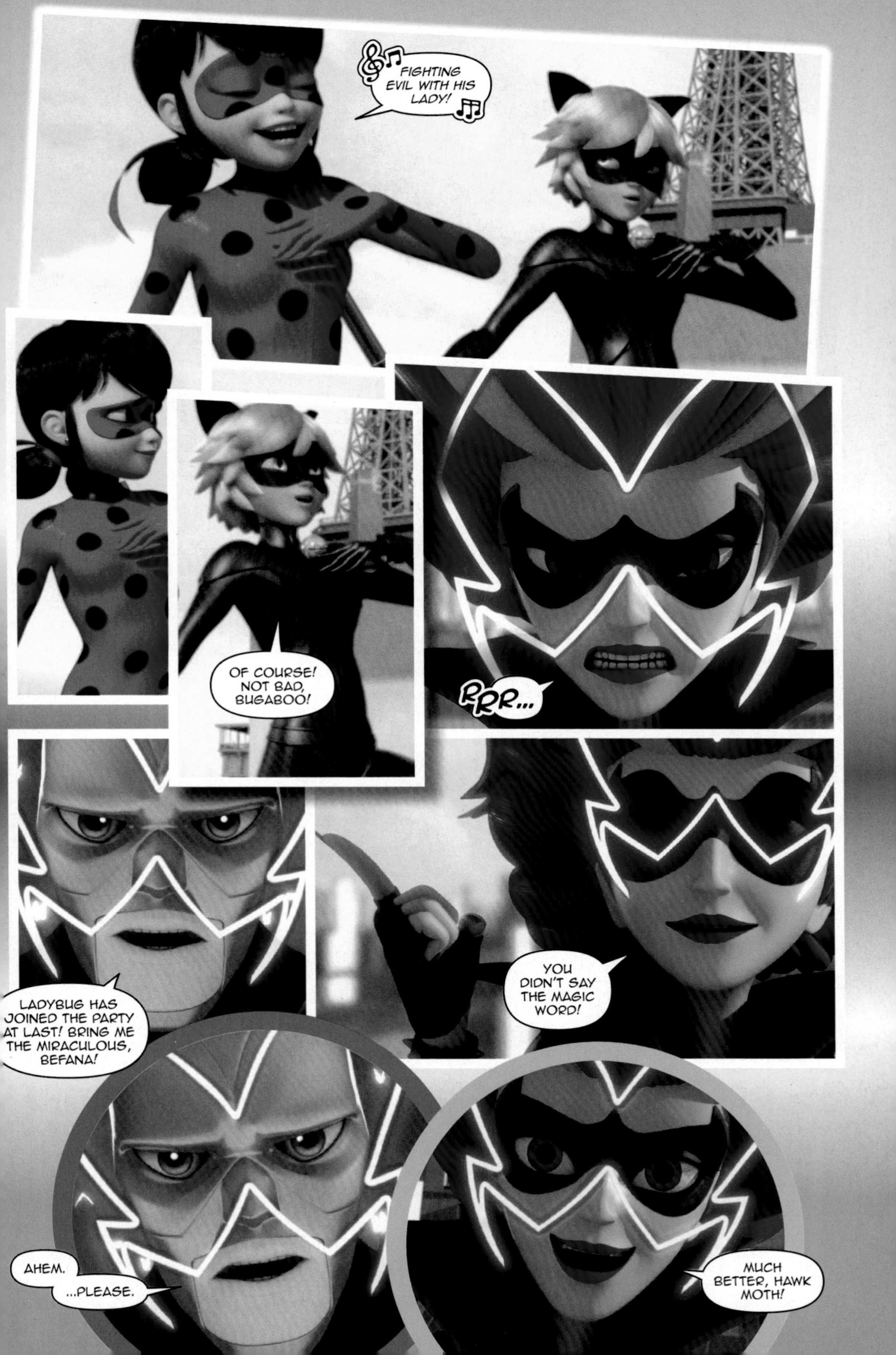
FIGHTING EVIL WITH HIS LADY!
OF COURSE! NOT BAD, BUGABOO!
RRR...
LADYBUG HAS JOINED THE PARTY AT LAST! BRING ME THE MIRACULOUS, BEFANA!
YOU DIDN'T SAY THE MAGIC WORD!
AHEM.
...PLEASE.
MUCH BETTER, HAWK MOTH!

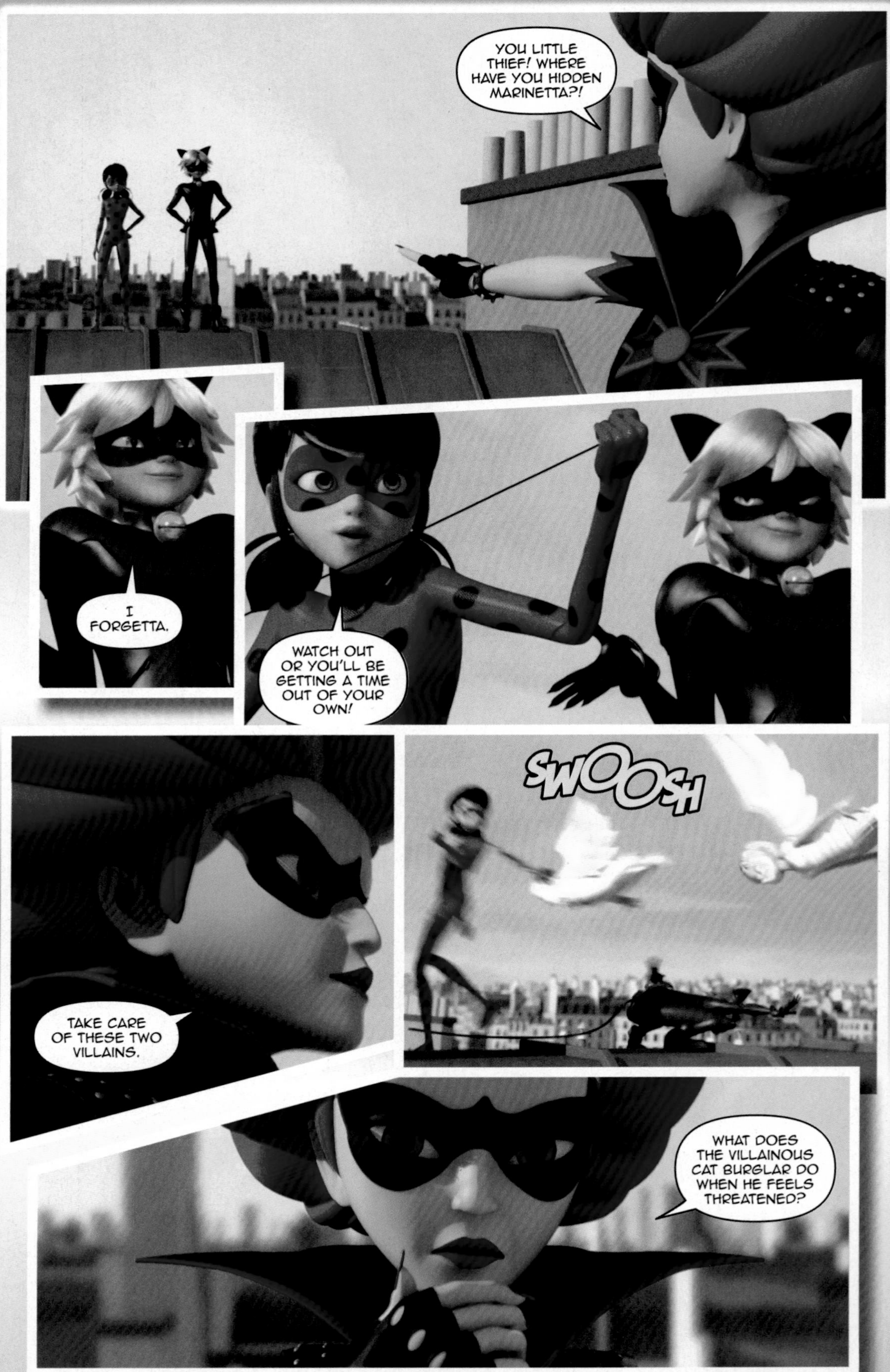
YOU LITTLE THIEF! WHERE HAVE YOU HIDDEN MARINETTA?!
I FORGETTA.
WATCH OUT OR YOU'LL BE GETTING A TIME OUT OF YOUR OWN!
TAKE CARE OF THESE TWO VILLAINS.
SWOOSH
WHAT DOES THE VILLAINOUS CAT BURGLAR DO WHEN HE FEELS THREATENED?

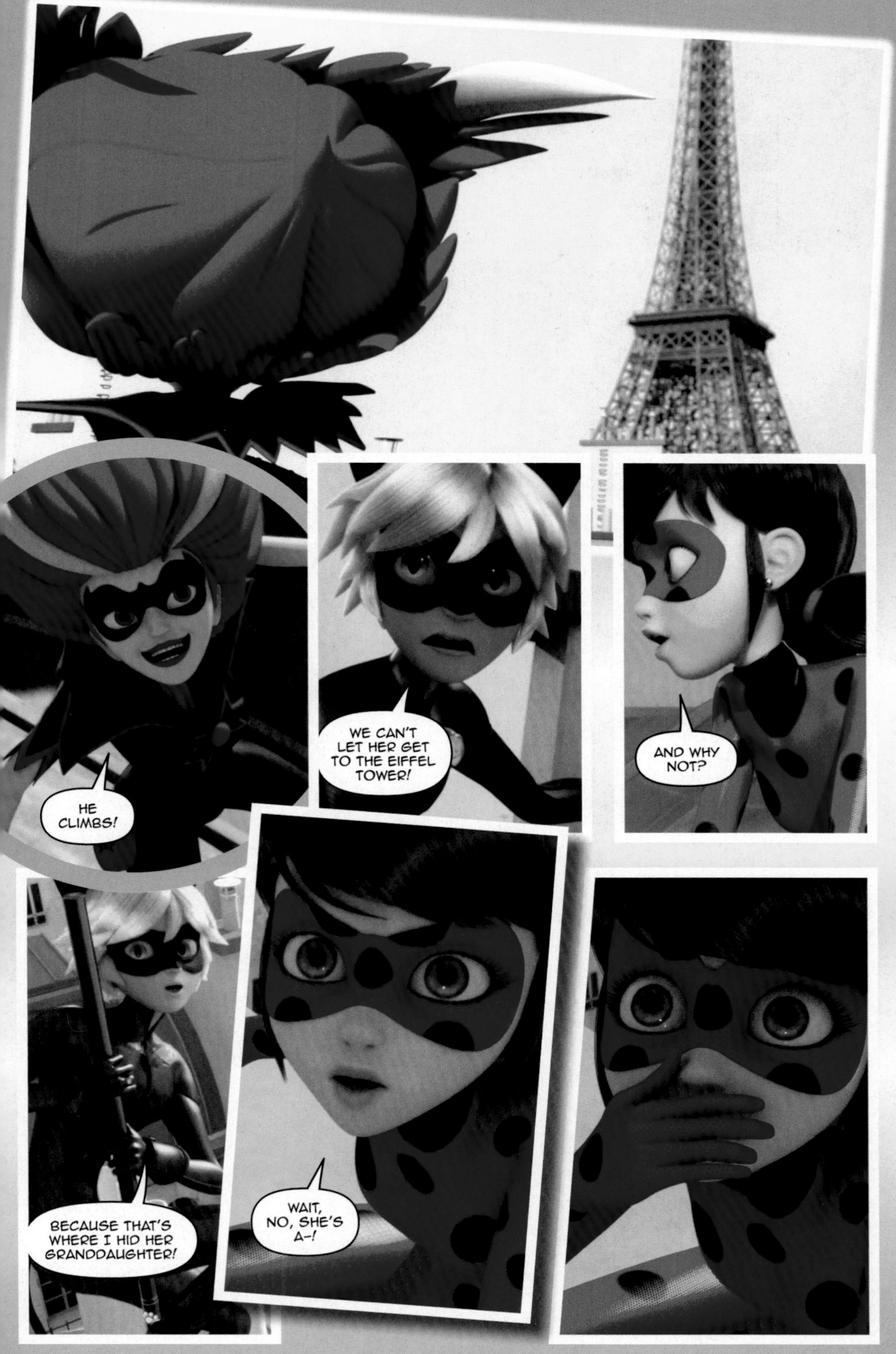
HE CLIMBS!
WE CAN'T LET HER GET TO THE EIFFEL TOWER!
AND WHY NOT?
BECAUSE THAT'S WHERE I HID HER GRANDDAUGHTER!
WAIT, NO, SHE'S A-!

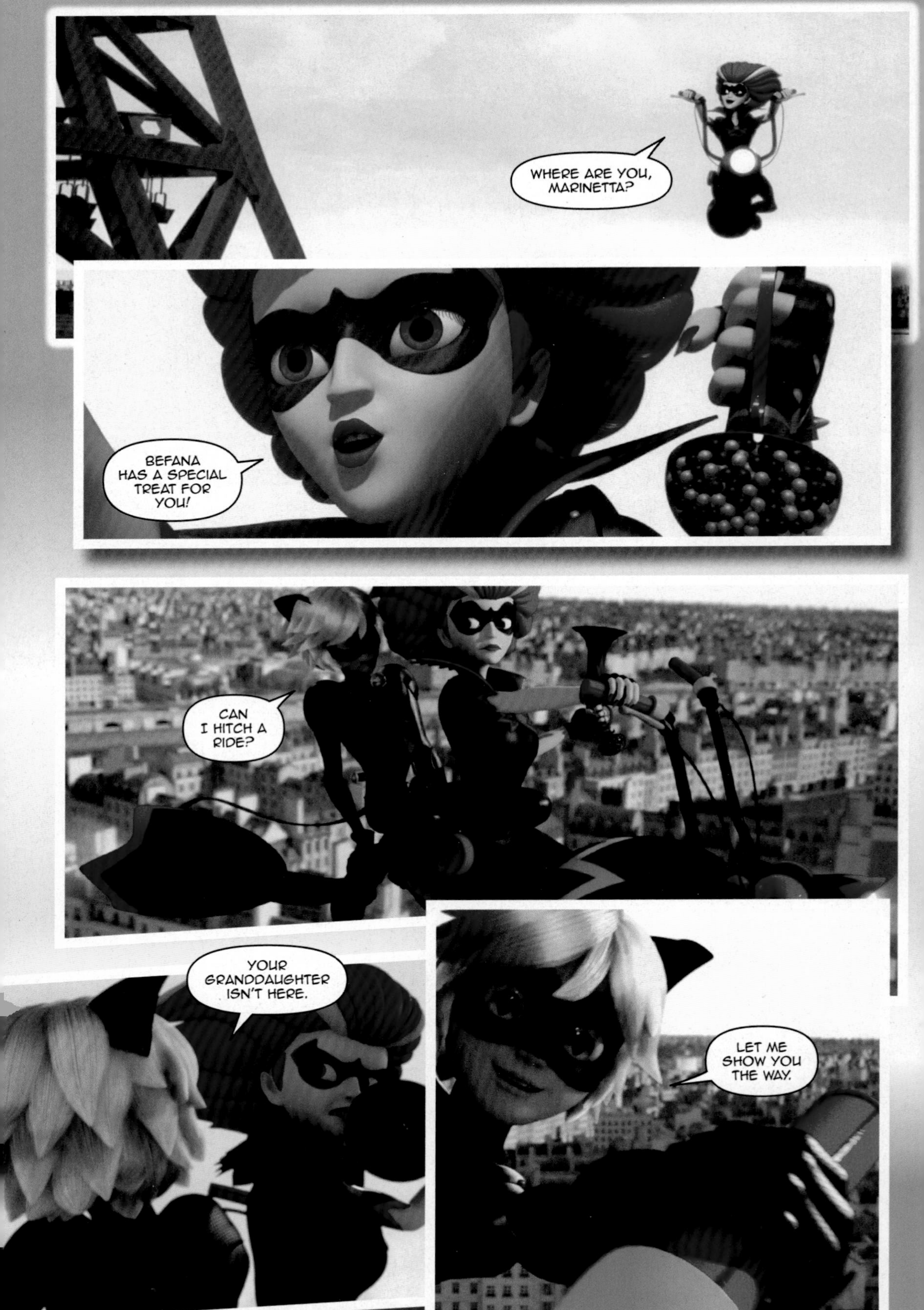
WHERE ARE YOU, MARINETTA?
BEFANA HAS A SPECIAL TREAT FOR YOU!
CAN I HITCH A RIDE?
YOUR GRANDDAUGHTER ISN'T HERE.
LET ME SHOW YOU THE WAY.

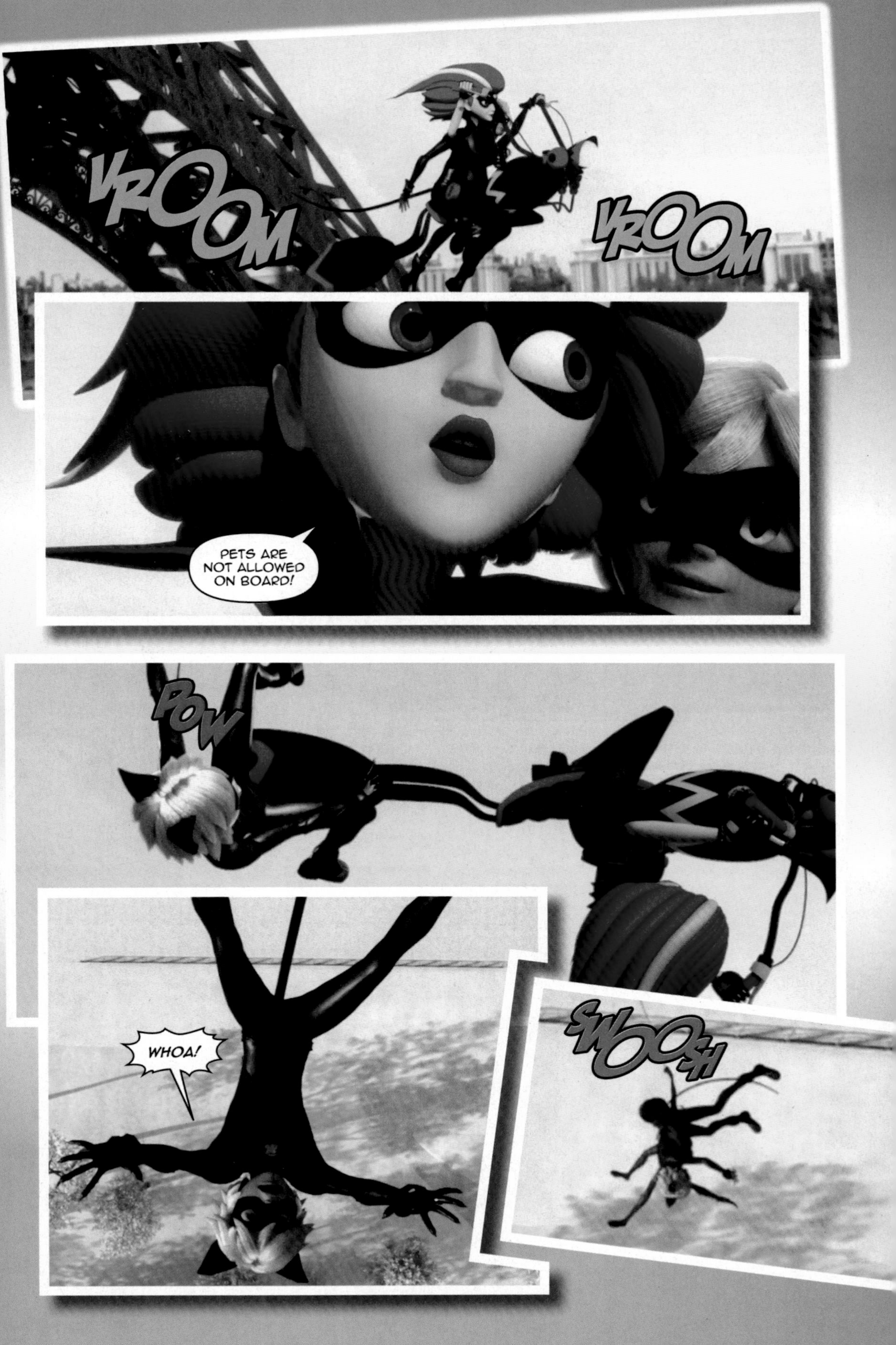
VROOM
VROOM
PETS ARE NOT ALLOWED ON BOARD!
POW
WHOA!
SWOOSH

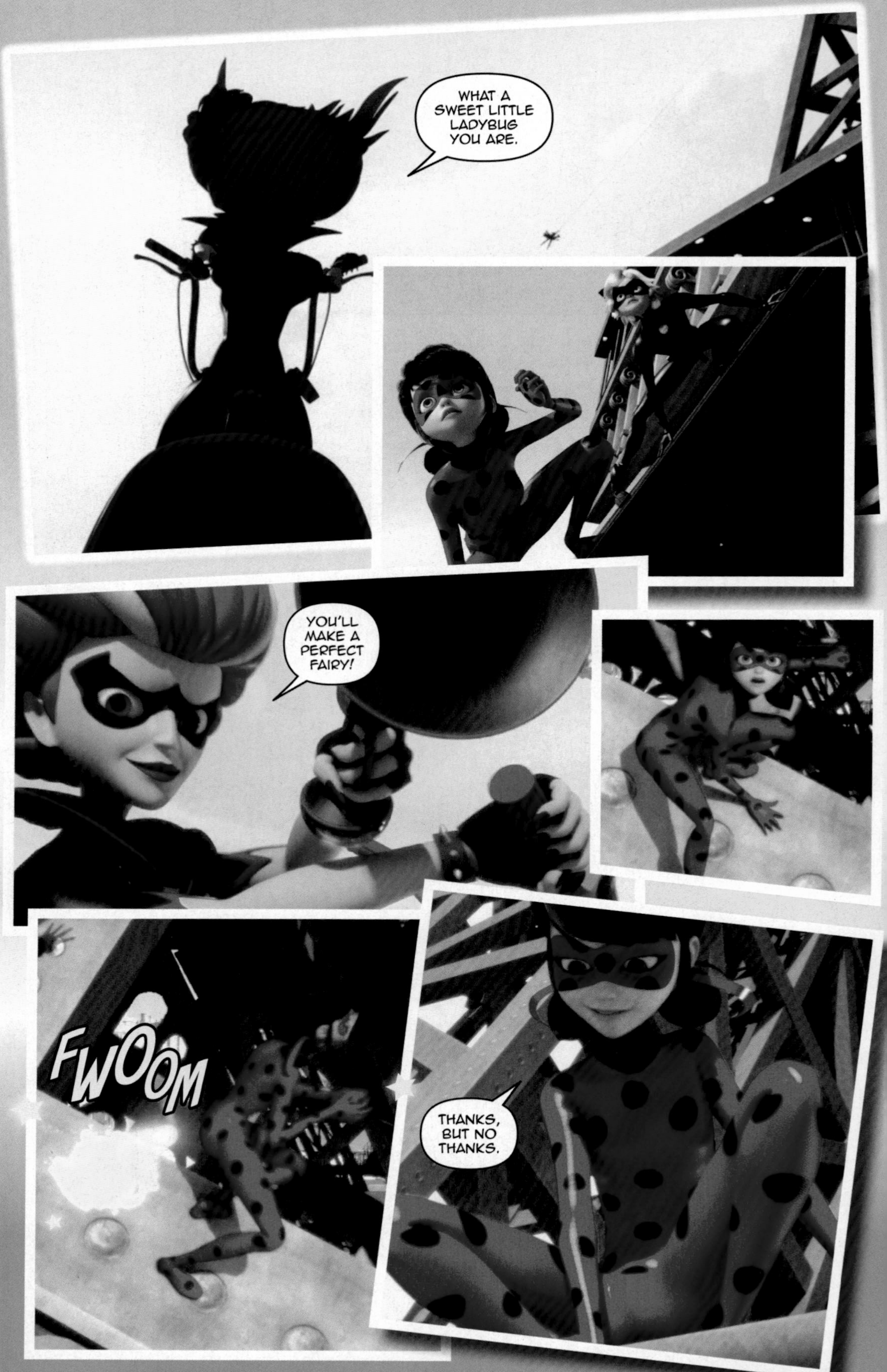
WHAT A SWEET LITTLE LADYBUG YOU ARE.
YOU'LL MAKE A PERFECT FAIRY!
FWOOM
THANKS, BUT NO THANKS.

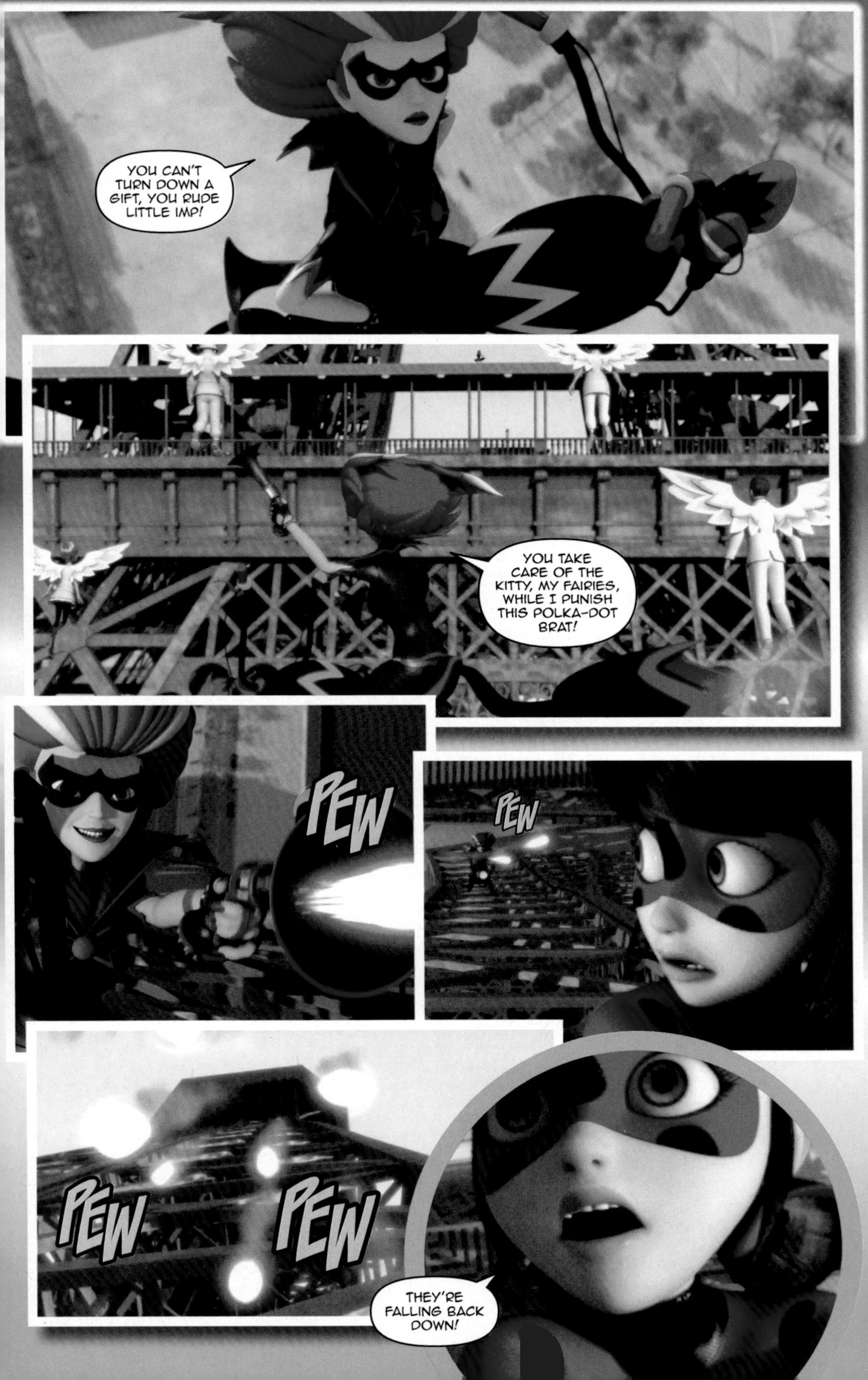
YOU CAN'T TURN DOWN A GIFT, YOU RUDE LITTLE IMP!
YOU TAKE CARE OF THE KITTY, MY FAIRIES, WHILE I PUNISH THIS POLKA-DOT BRAT!
PEW
PEW
PEW
PEW
THEY'RE FALLING BACK DOWN!

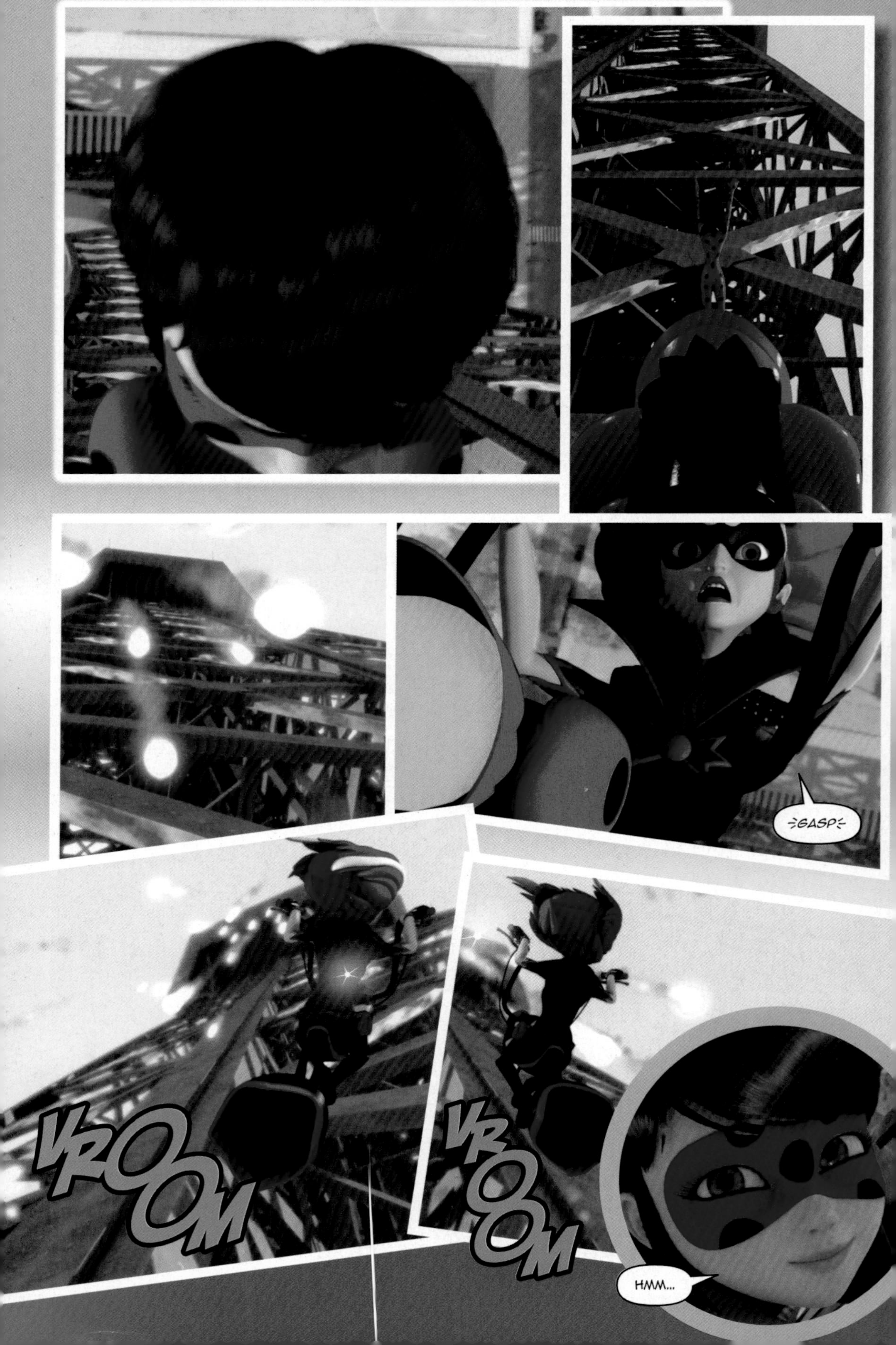

GASP
VROOM
VROOM
HMM...

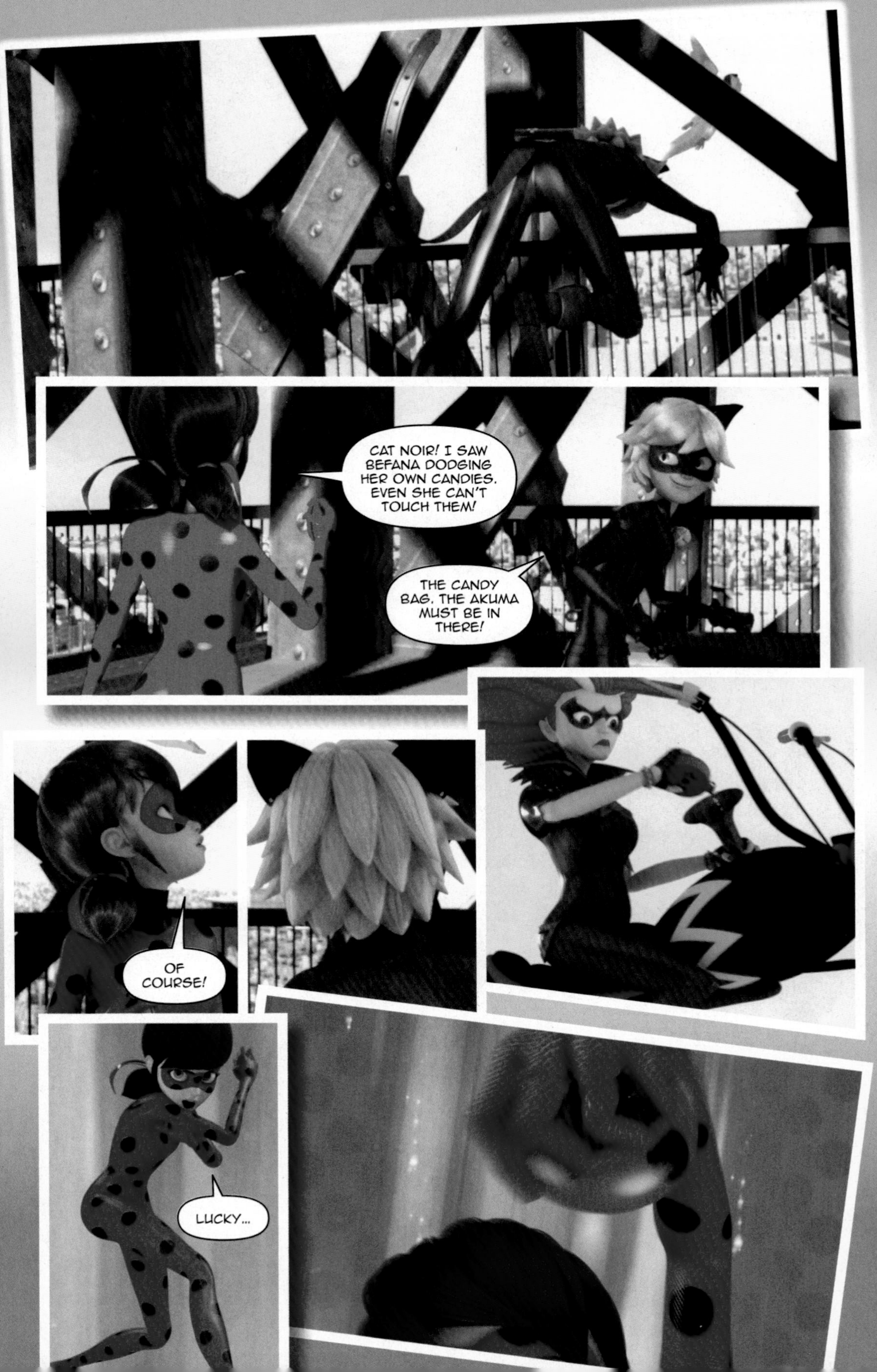
CAT NOIR! I SAW BEFANA DODGING HER OWN CANDIES. EVEN SHE CAN'T TOUCH THEM!
THE CANDY BAG. THE AKUMA MUST BE IN THERE!
OF COURSE!
LUCKY...

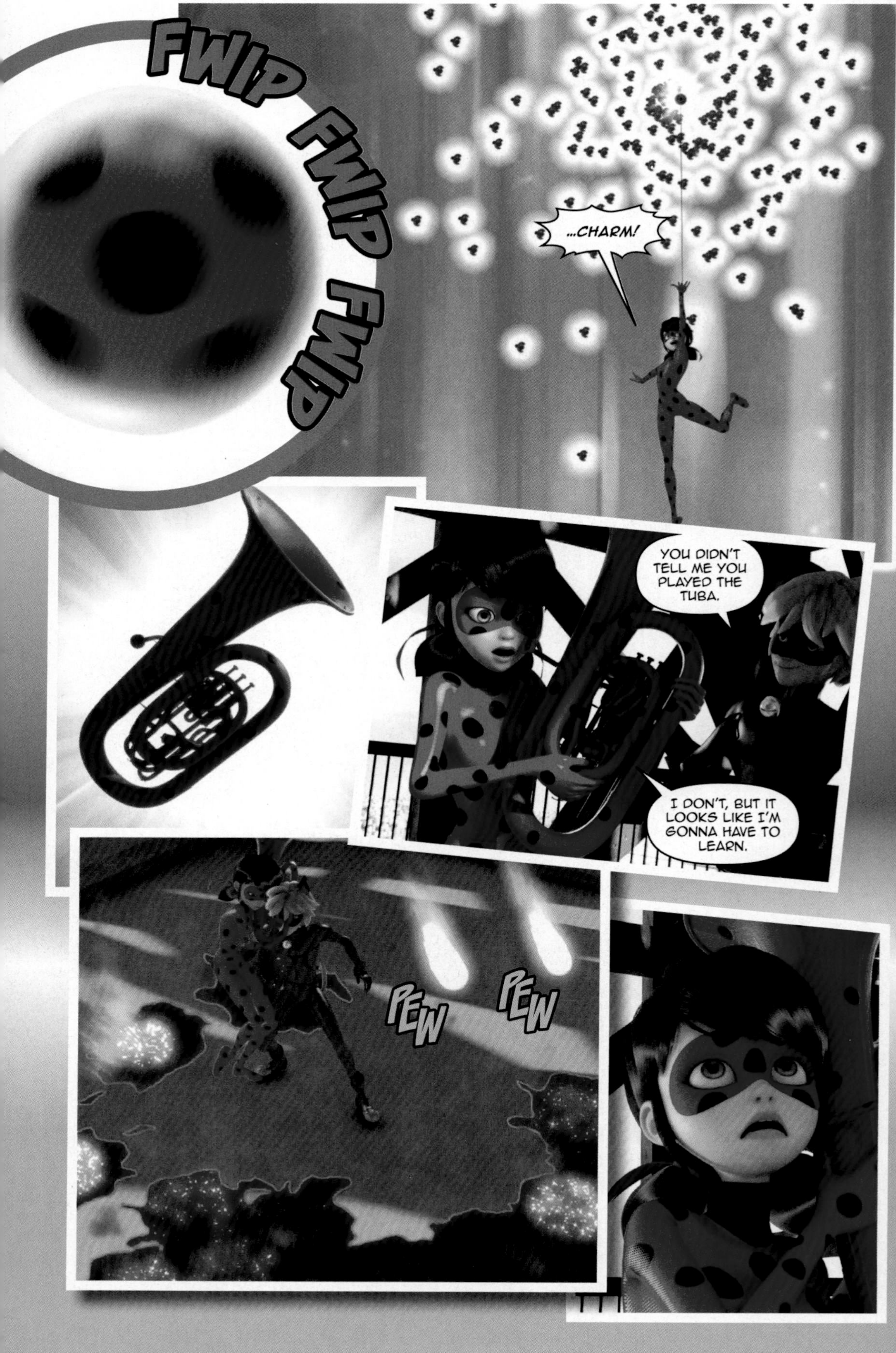
FWIP FWIP FWIP
...CHARM!
YOU DIDN'T TELL ME YOU PLAYED THE TUBA.
I DON'T, BUT IT LOOKS LIKE I'M GONNA HAVE TO LEARN.
PEW
PEW

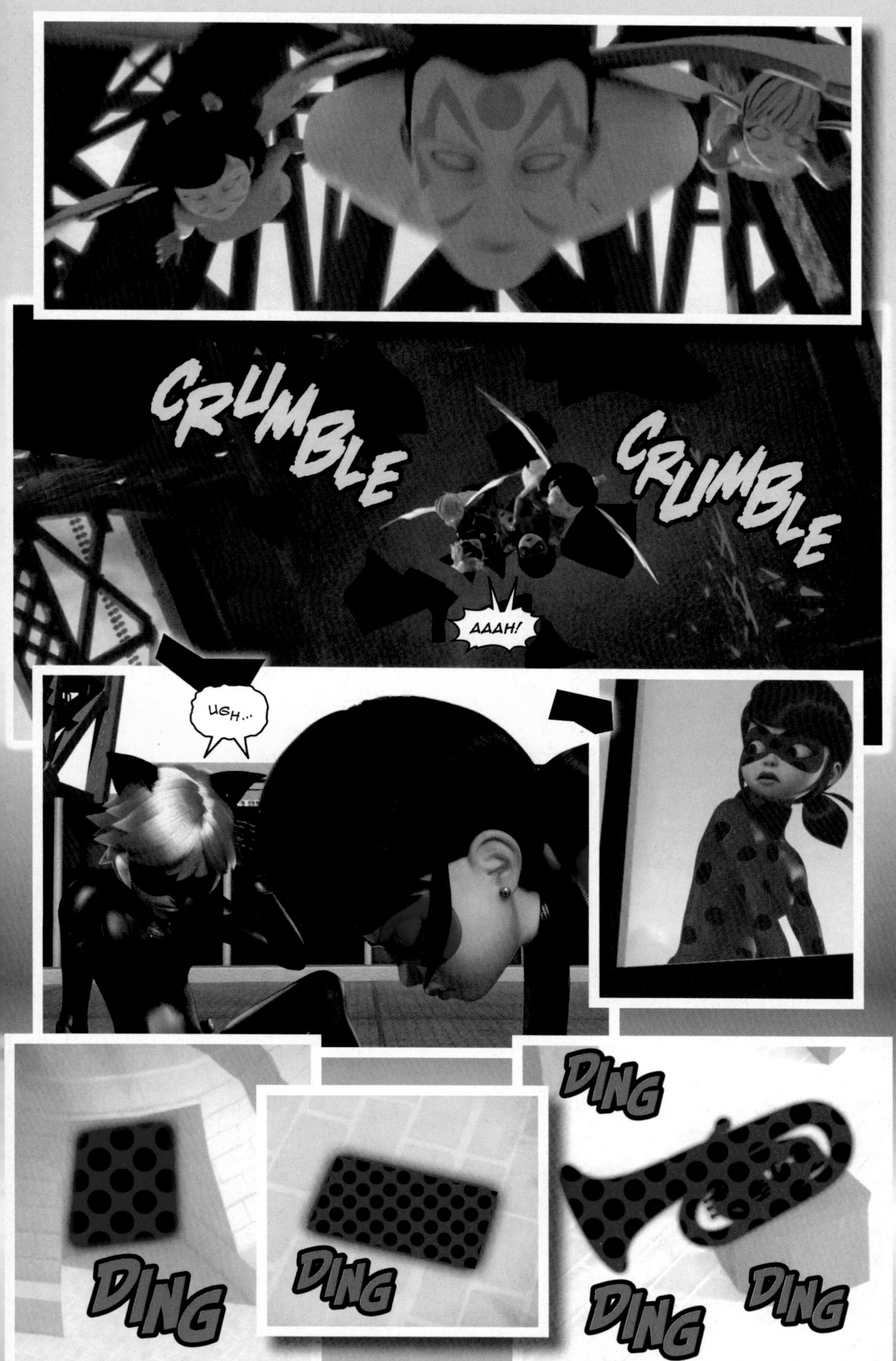
CRUMBLE
CRUMBLE
AAAH!
UGH...
DING
DING
DING
DING
DING

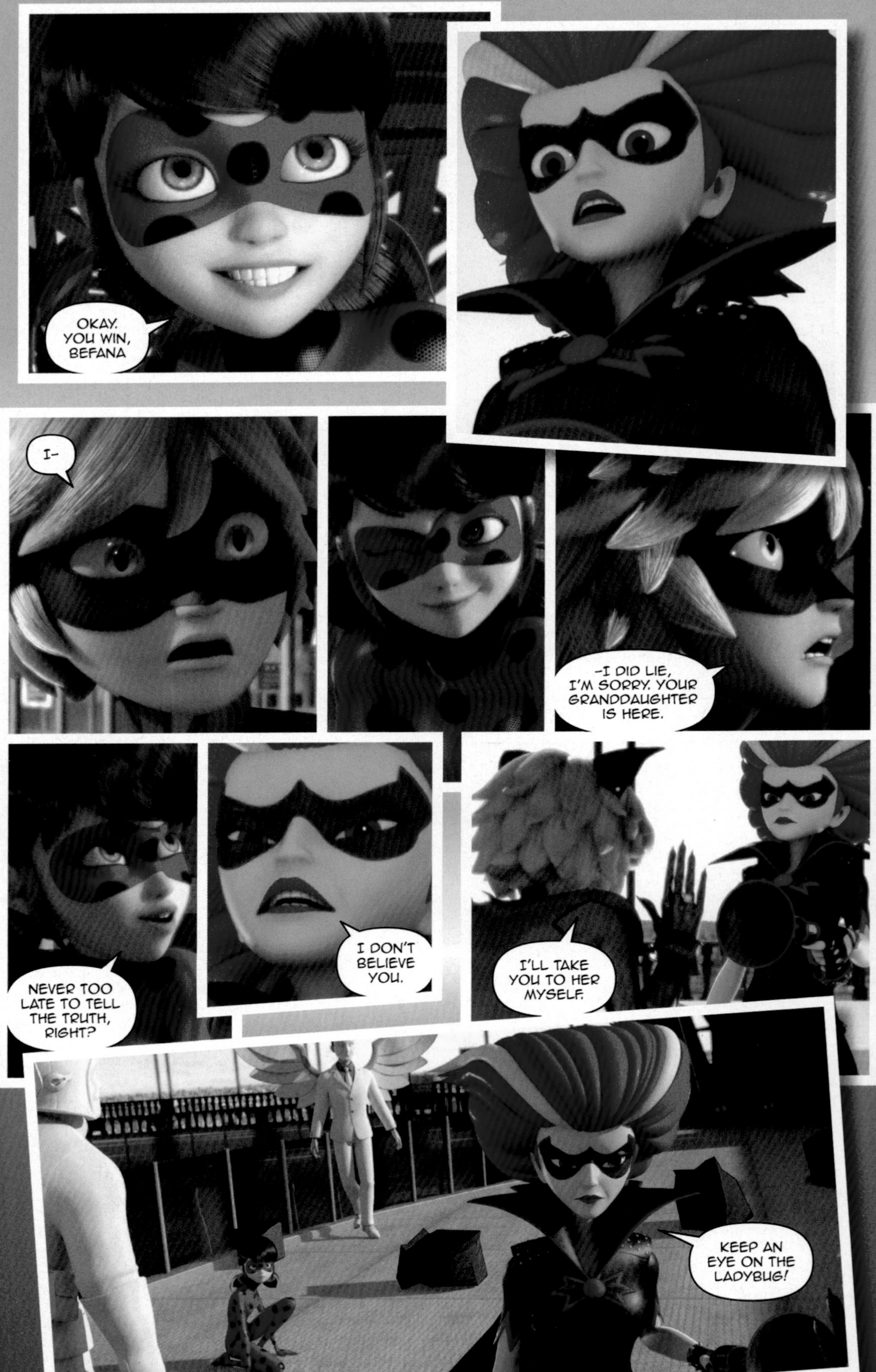
OKAY. YOU WIN, BEFANA
I–
–I DID LIE, I'M SORRY. YOUR GRANDDAUGHTER IS HERE.
NEVER TOO LATE TO TELL THE TRUTH, RIGHT?
I DON'T BELIEVE YOU.
I'LL TAKE YOU TO HER MYSELF.
KEEP AN EYE ON THE LADYBUG!

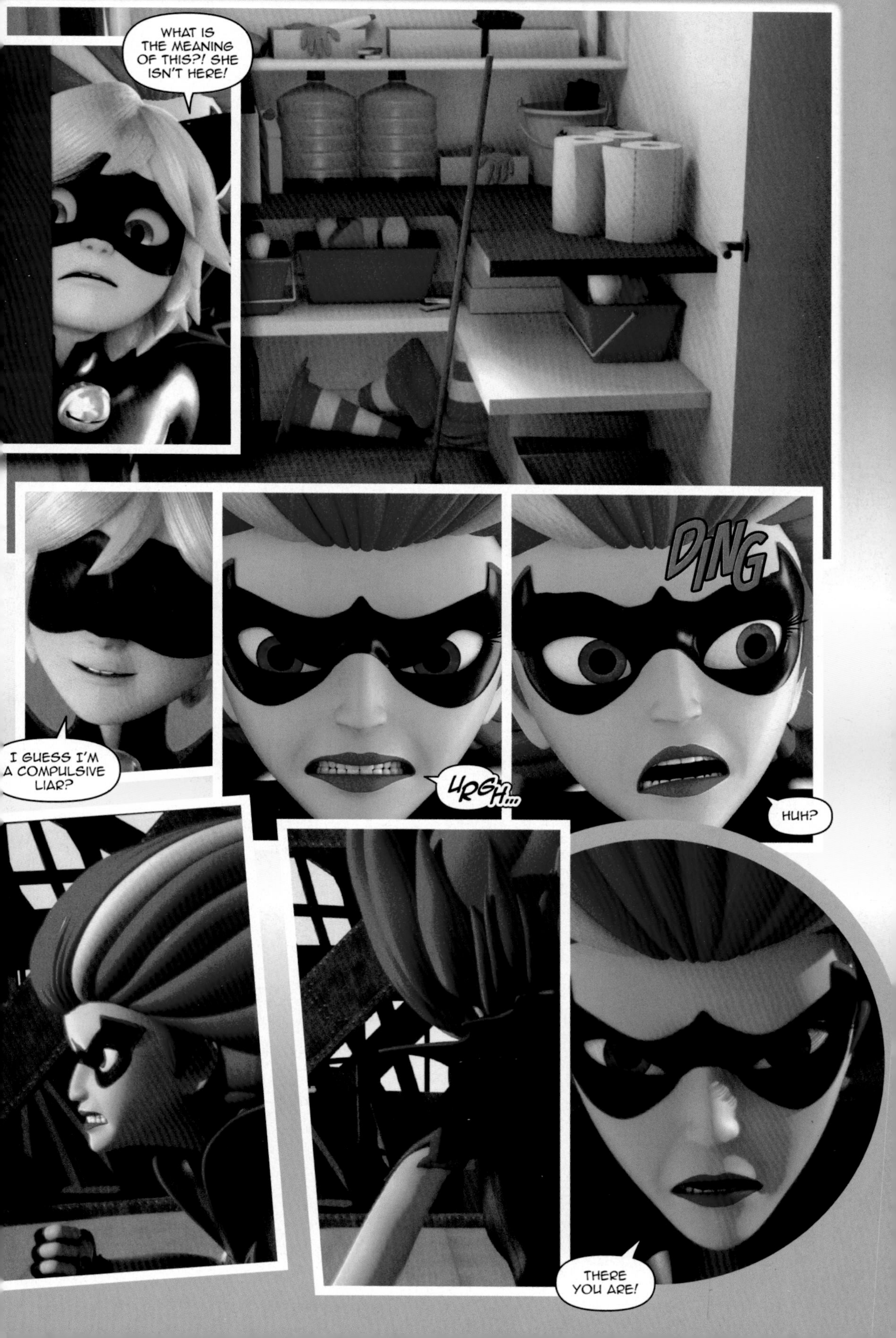
WHAT IS THE MEANING OF THIS?! SHE ISN'T HERE!
I GUESS I'M A COMPULSIVE LIAR?
URGH...
DING
HUH?
THERE YOU ARE!

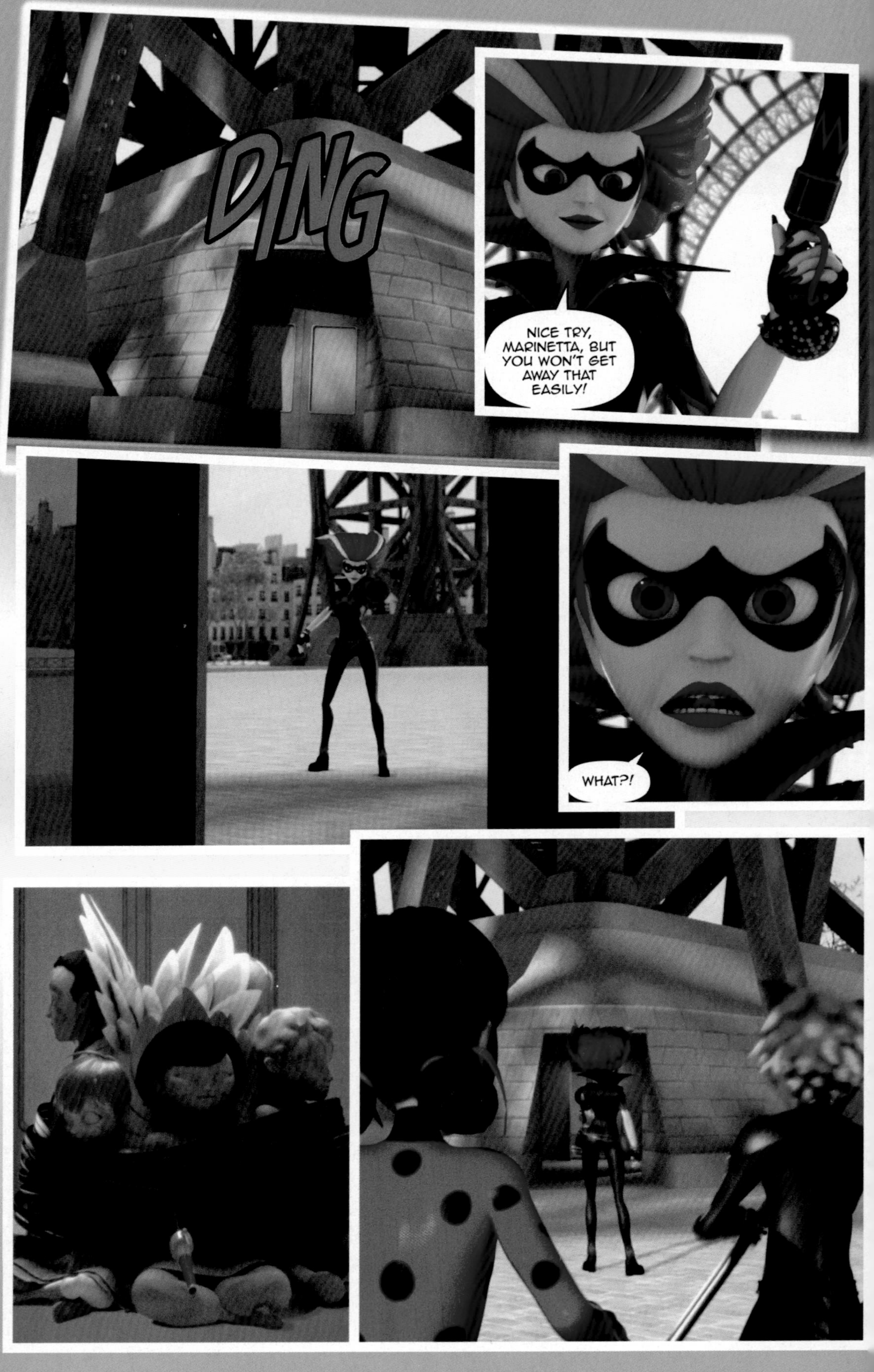
DING
NICE TRY, MARINETTA, BUT YOU WON'T GET AWAY THAT EASILY!
WHAT?!

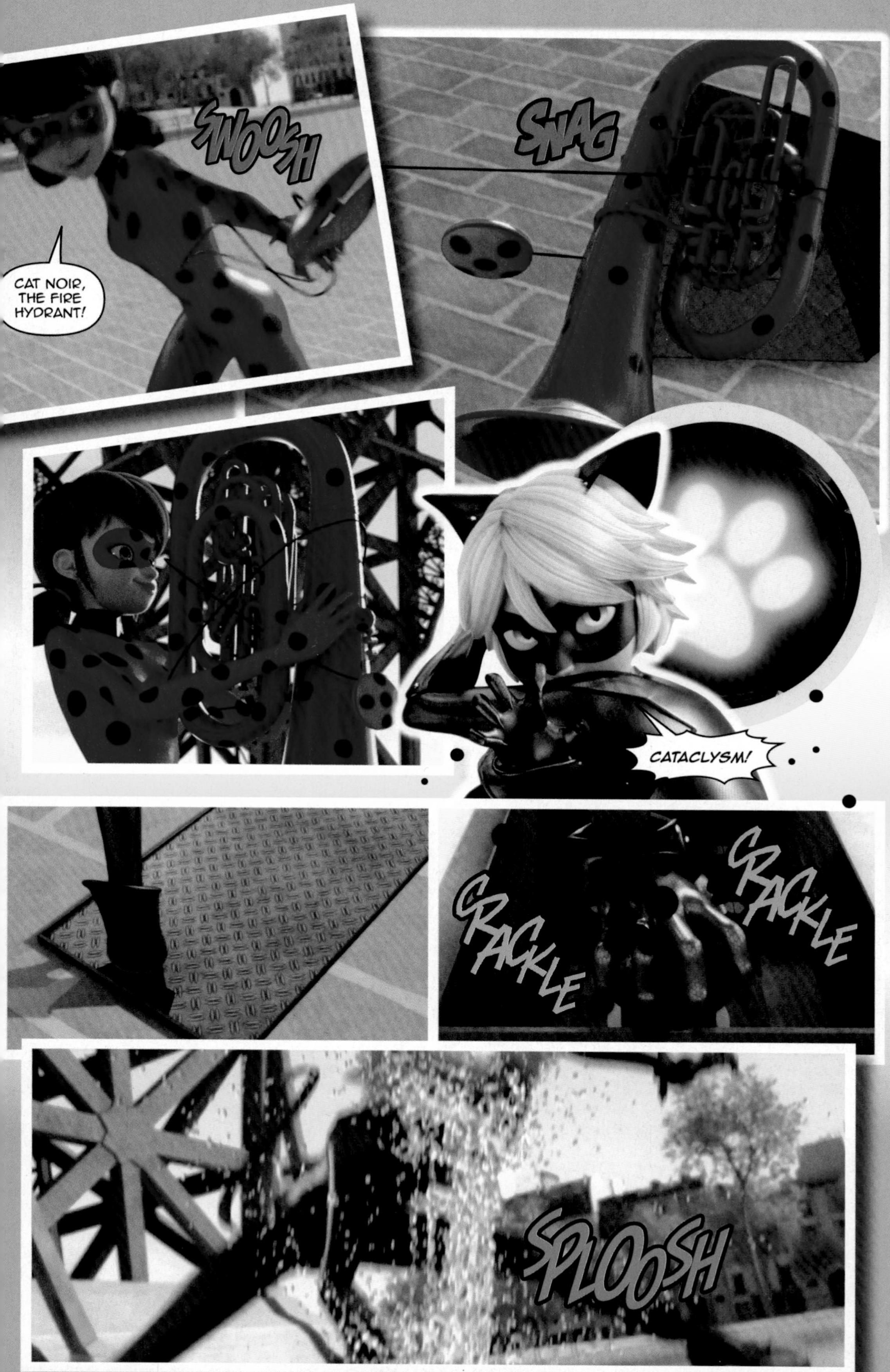

SWOOSH
CAT NOIR, THE FIRE HYDRANT!
SNAG
CATACLYSM!
CRACKLE
CRACKLE
SPLOOSH

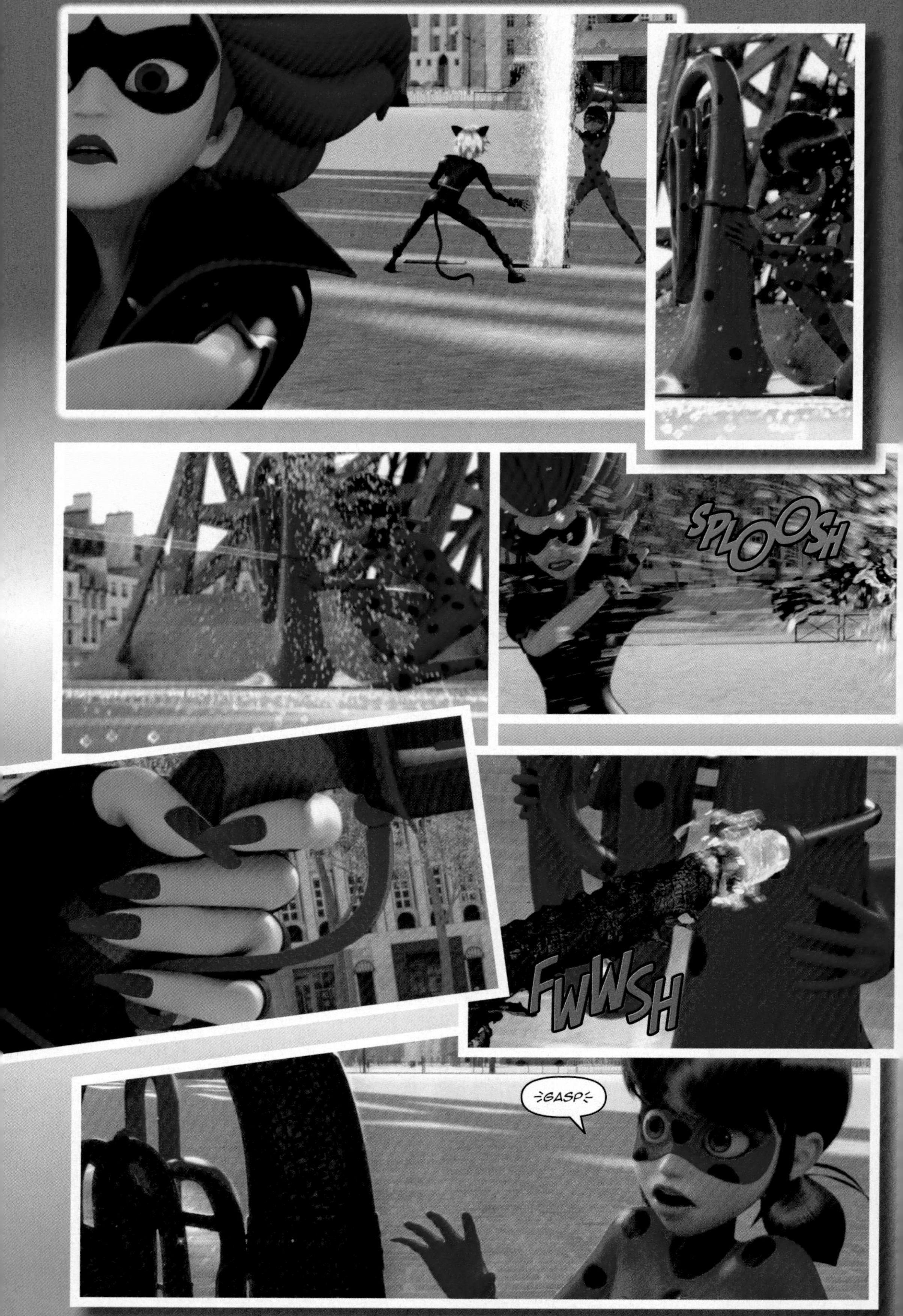
SPLOOSH
FWWSH
GASP

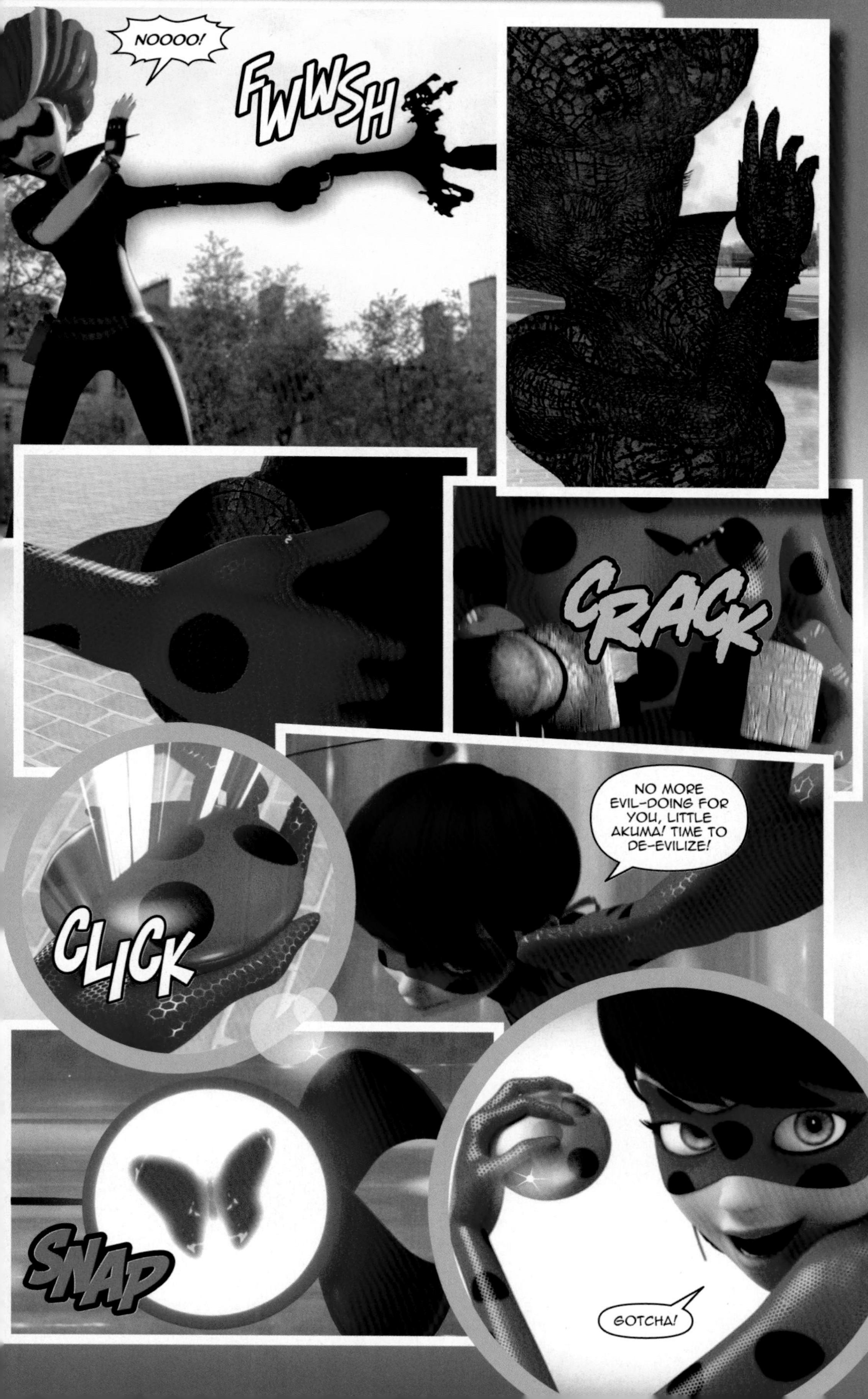
NOOOO!
FWWSH
CRACK
CLICK
NO MORE EVIL-DOING FOR YOU, LITTLE AKUMA! TIME TO DE-EVILIZE!
SNAP
GOTCHA!

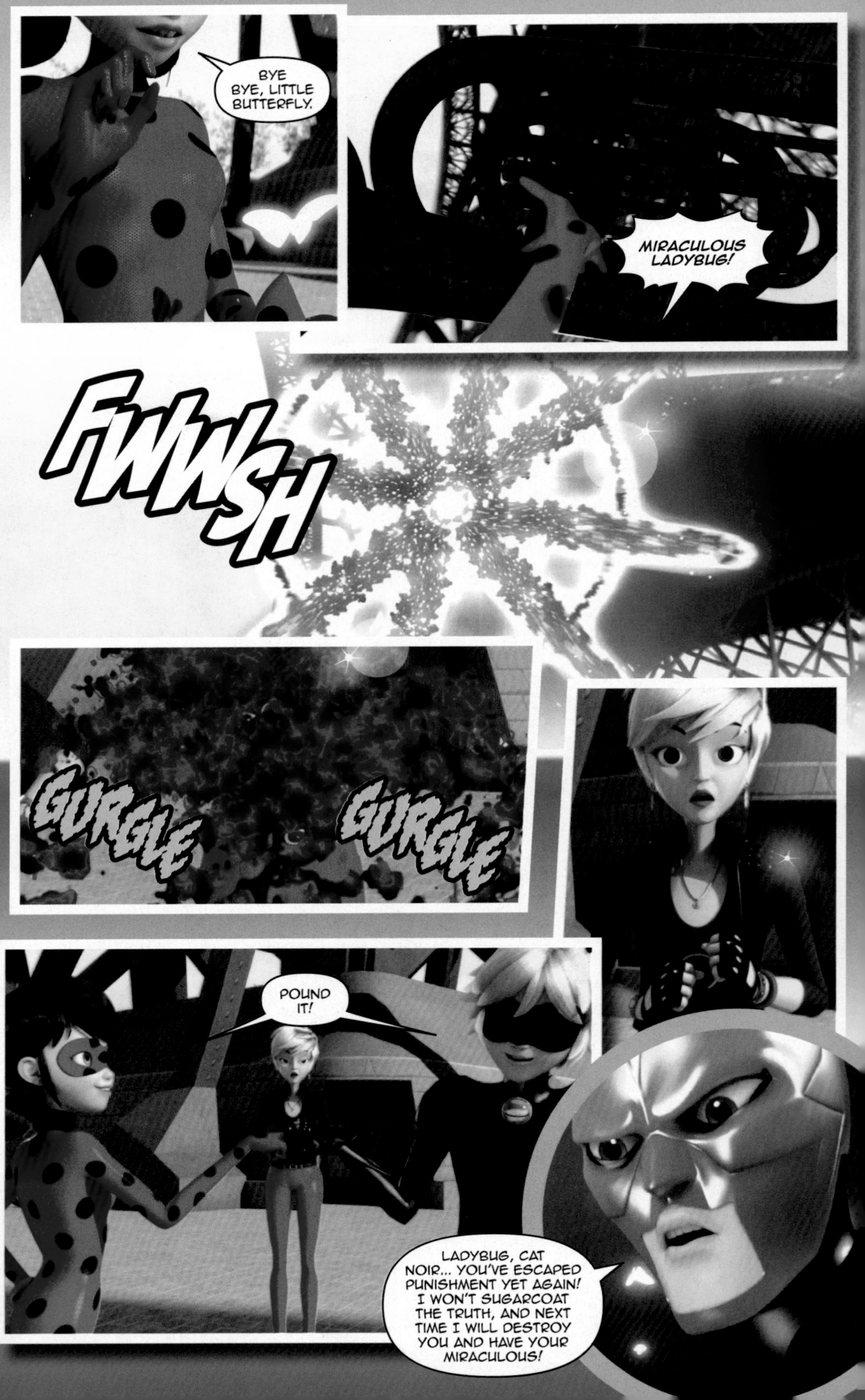
BYE BYE, LITTLE BUTTERFLY.
MIRACULOUS LADYBUG!
FWNSH
GURGLE
GURGLE
POUND IT!
LADYBUG, CAT NOIR... YOU'VE ESCAPED PUNISHMENT YET AGAIN! I WON'T SUGARCOAT THE TRUTH, AND NEXT TIME I WILL DESTROY YOU AND HAVE YOUR MIRACULOUS!

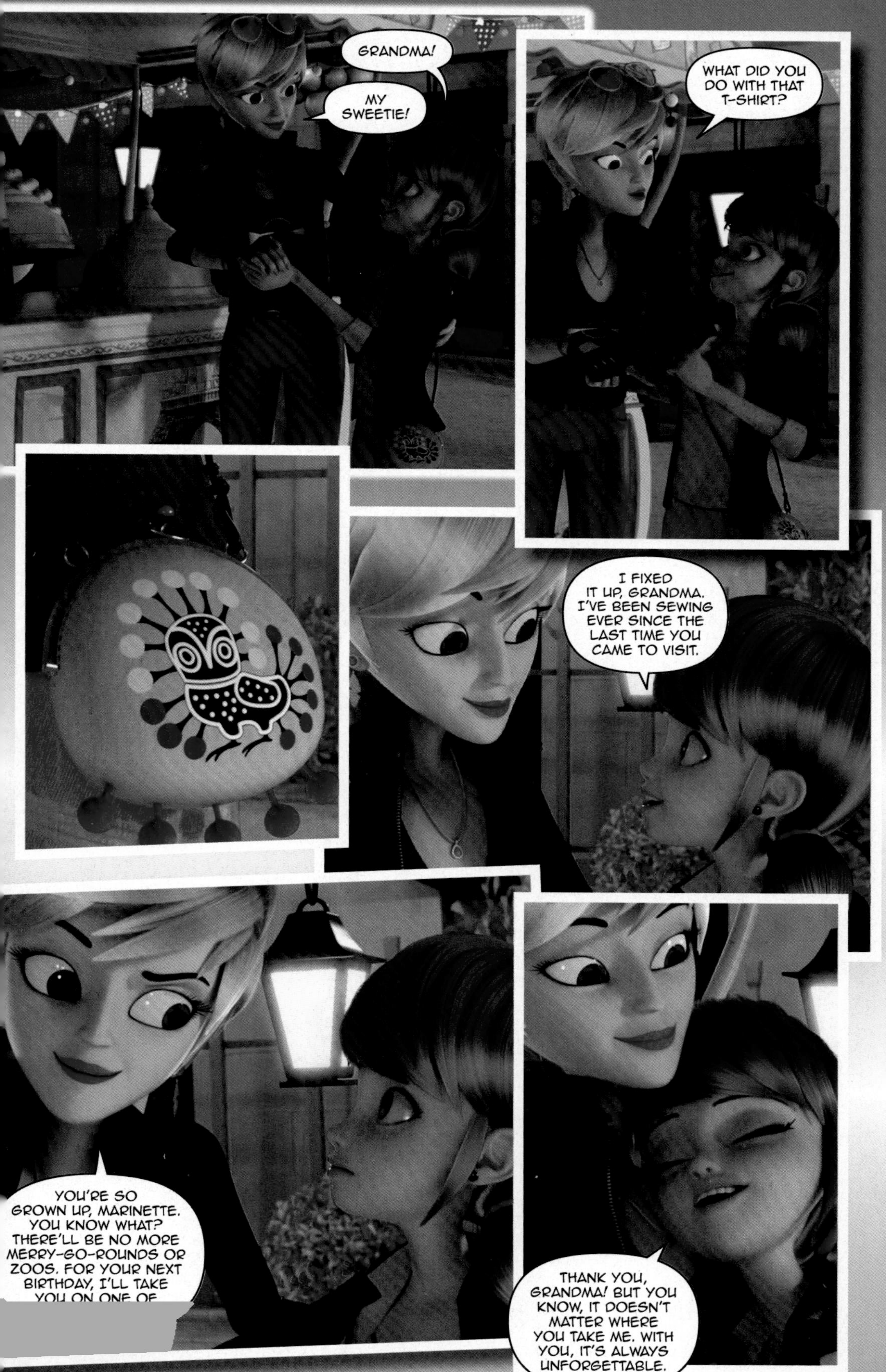
GRANDMA!
MY SWEETIE!
WHAT DID YOU DO WITH THAT T-SHIRT?
I FIXED IT UP, GRANDMA. I'VE BEEN SEWING EVER SINCE THE LAST TIME YOU CAME TO VISIT.
YOU'RE SO GROWN UP, MARINETTE. YOU KNOW WHAT? THERE'LL BE NO MORE MERRY-GO-ROUNDS OR ZOOS. FOR YOUR NEXT BIRTHDAY, I'LL TAKE
THANK YOU, GRANDMA! BUT YOU KNOW, IT DOESN'T MATTER WHERE YOU TAKE ME. WITH YOU, IT'S ALWAYS UNFORGETTABLE.

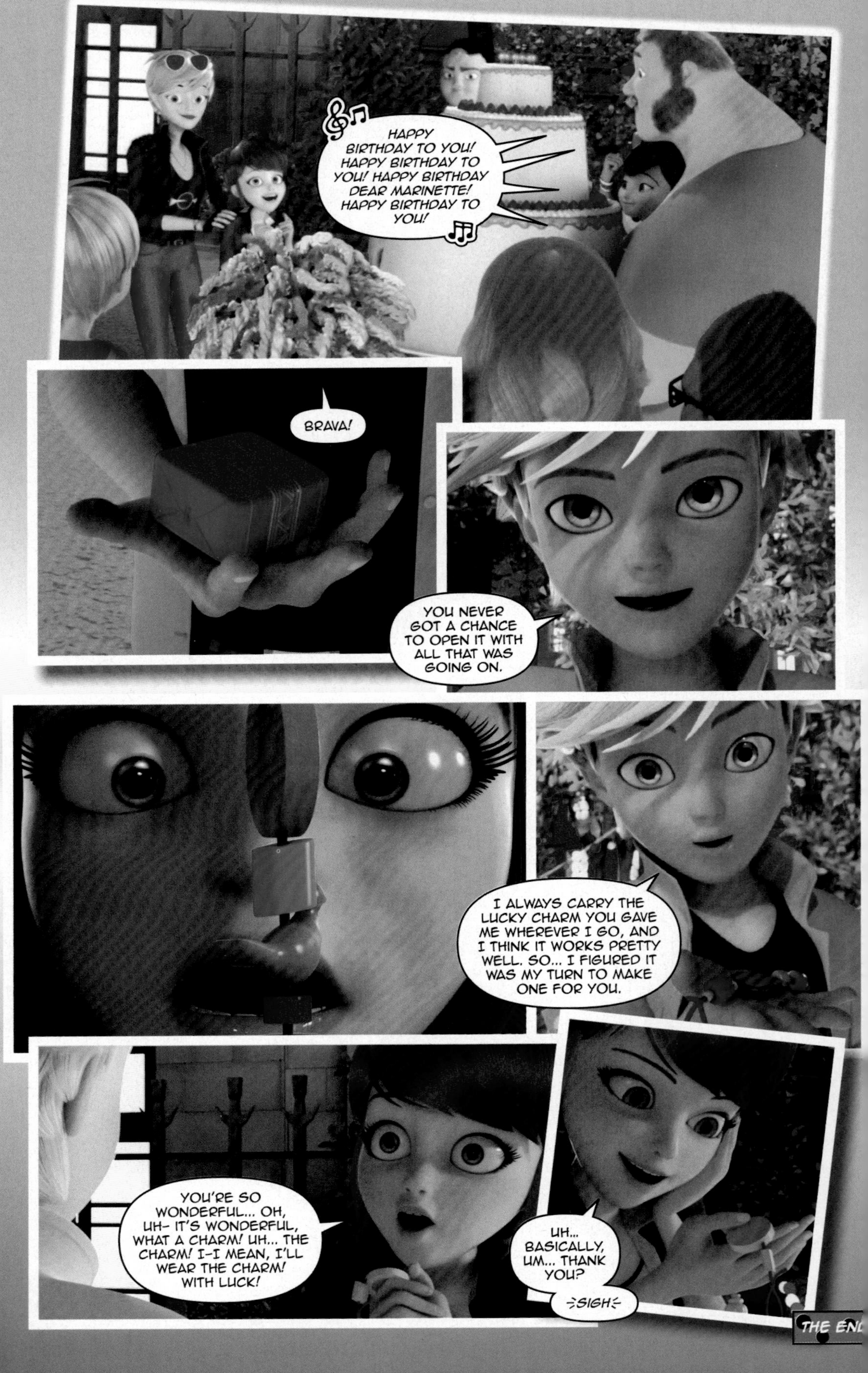
HAPPY BIRTHDAY TO YOU! HAPPY BIRTHDAY TO YOU! HAPPY BIRTHDAY DEAR MARINETTE! HAPPY BIRTHDAY TO YOU!
BRAVA!
YOU NEVER GOT A CHANCE TO OPEN IT WITH ALL THAT WAS GOING ON.
I ALWAYS CARRY THE LUCKY CHARM YOU GAVE ME WHEREVER I GO, AND I THINK IT WORKS PRETTY WELL. SO... I FIGURED IT WAS MY TURN TO MAKE ONE FOR YOU.
YOU'RE SO WONDERFUL... OH, UH- IT'S WONDERFUL, WHAT A CHARM! UH... THE CHARM! I-I MEAN, I'LL WEAR THE CHARM! WITH LUCK!
UH... BASICALLY, UM... THANK YOU?
SIGH
THE END

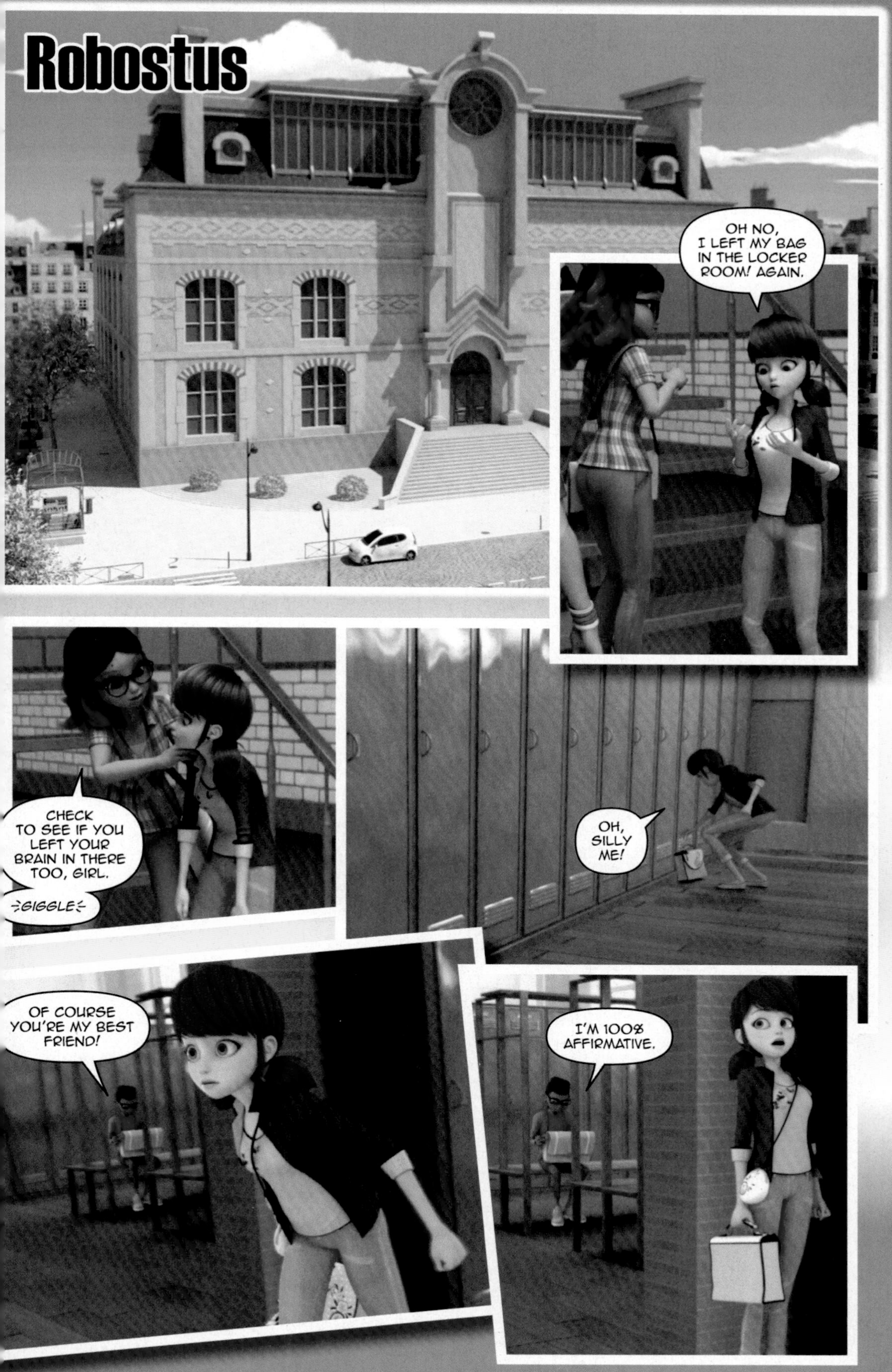
Robostus
OH NO, I LEFT MY BAG IN THE LOCKER ROOM! AGAIN.
CHECK TO SEE IF YOU LEFT YOUR BRAIN IN THERE TOO, GIRL.
GIGGLE
OH, SILLY ME!
OF COURSE YOU'RE MY BEST FRIEND!
I'M 100% AFFIRMATIVE.

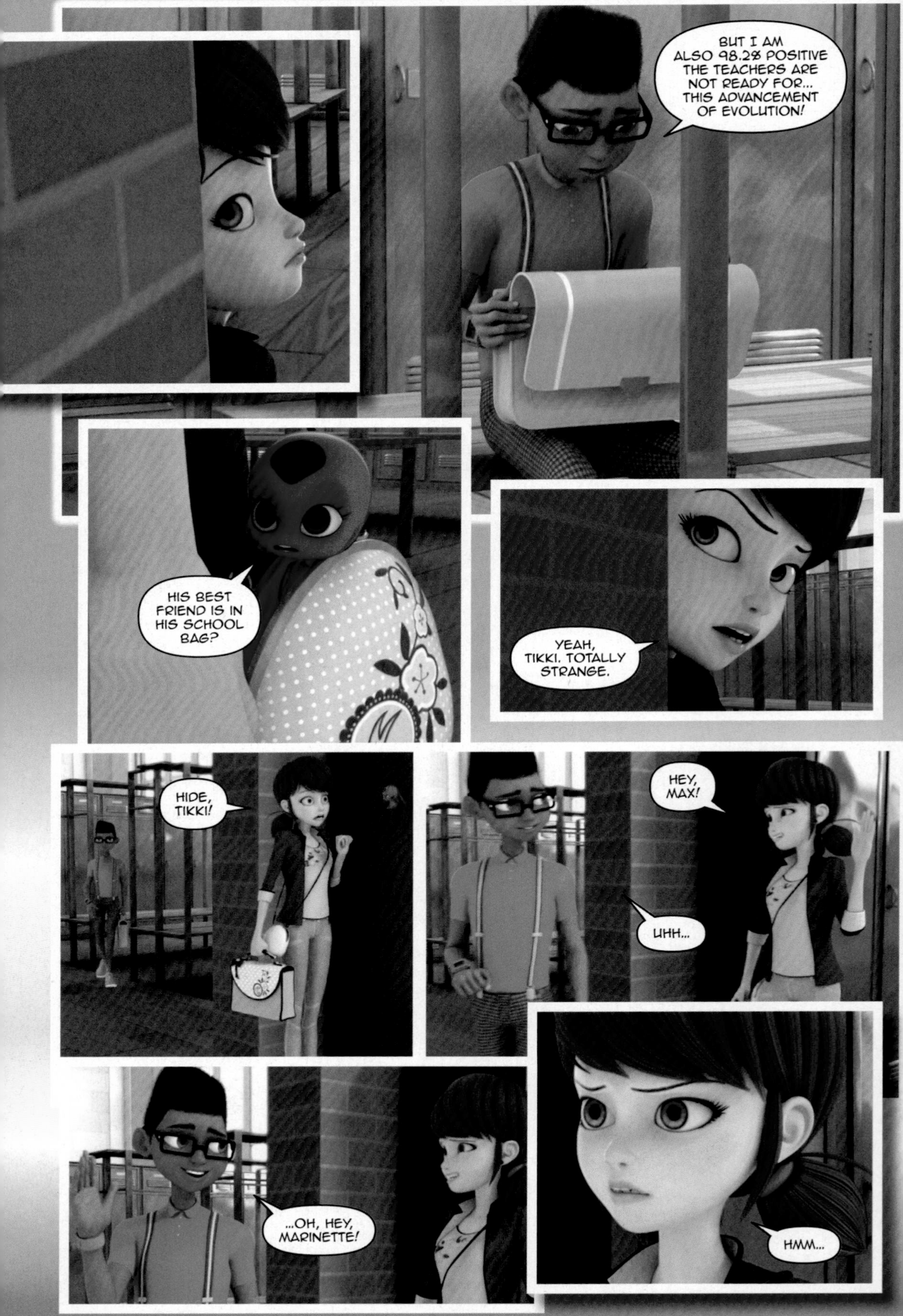
BUT I AM ALSO 98.2% POSITIVE THE TEACHERS ARE NOT READY FOR... THIS ADVANCEMENT OF EVOLUTION!
HIS BEST FRIEND IS IN HIS SCHOOL BAG?
YEAH, TIKKI. TOTALLY STRANGE.
HIDE, TIKKI!
HEY, MAX!
UHH...
...OH, HEY, MARINETTE!
HMM...

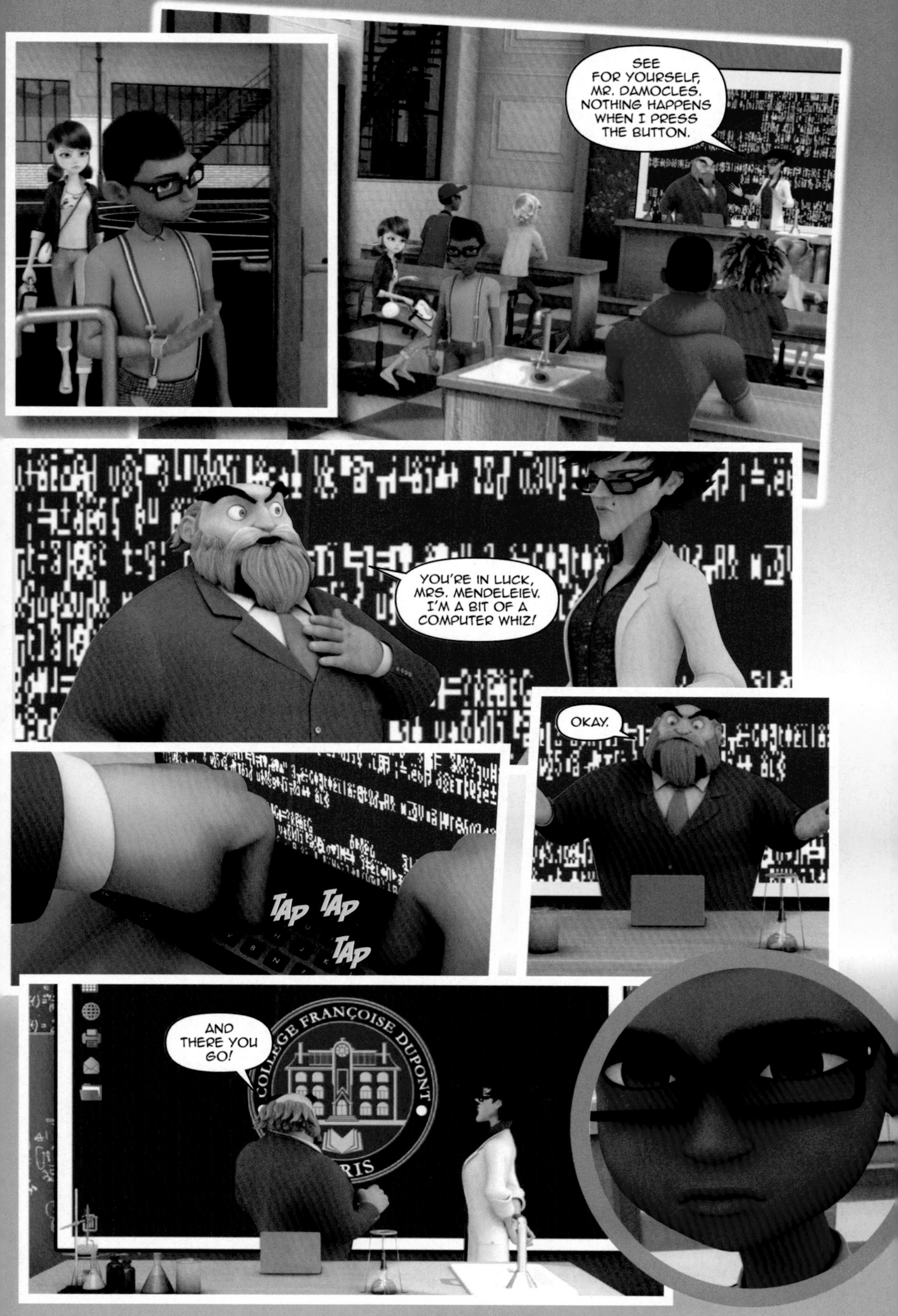
SEE FOR YOURSELF, MR. DAMOCLES. NOTHING HAPPENS WHEN I PRESS THE BUTTON.
YOU'RE IN LUCK, MRS. MENDELEIEV. I'M A BIT OF A COMPUTER WHIZ!
OKAY.
TAP TAP TAP
AND THERE YOU GO!
COLLEGE FRANÇOISE DUPONT

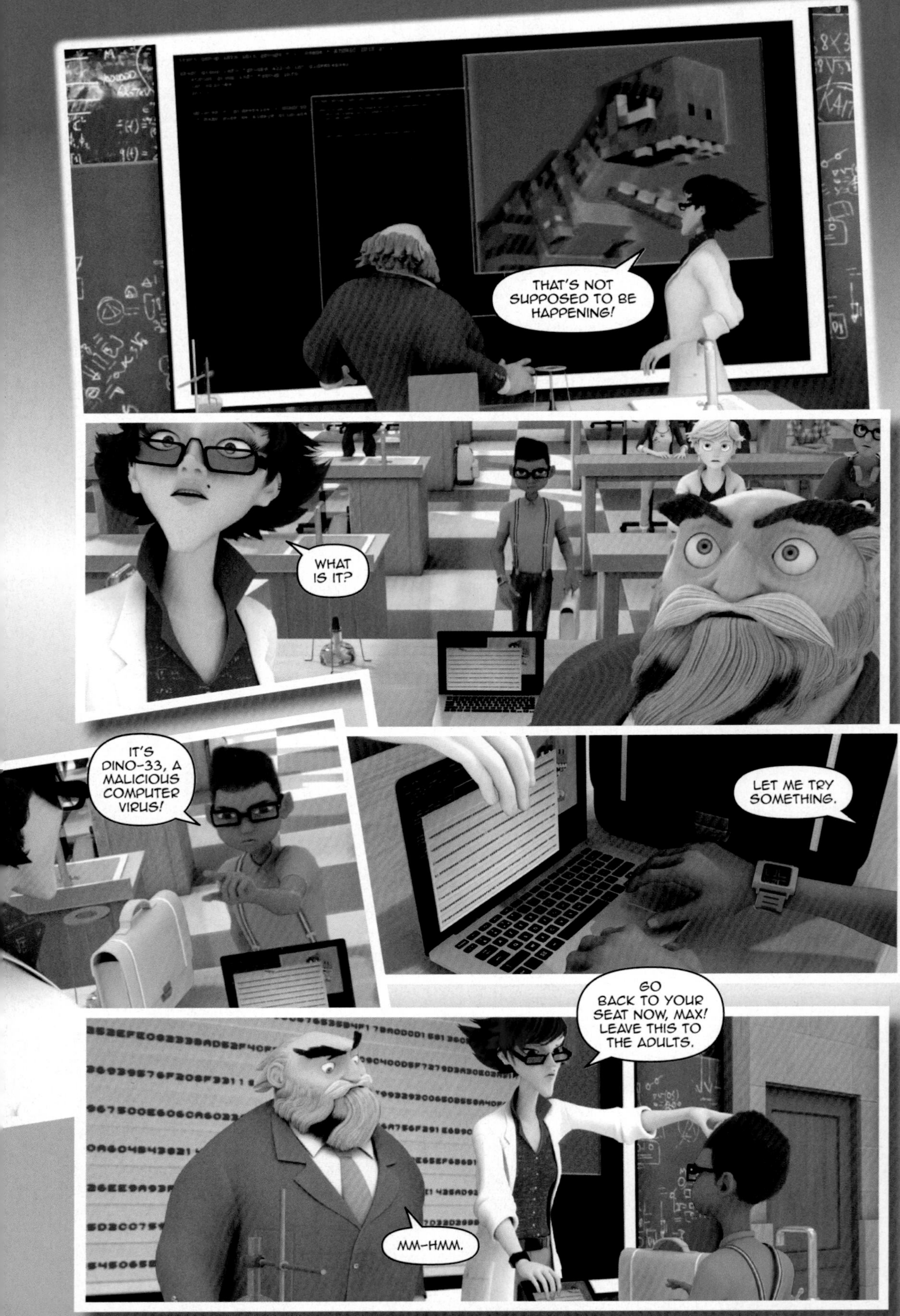
THAT'S NOT SUPPOSED TO BE HAPPENING!
WHAT IS IT?
IT'S DINO-33, A MALICIOUS COMPUTER VIRUS!
LET ME TRY SOMETHING.
GO BACK TO YOUR SEAT NOW, MAX! LEAVE THIS TO THE ADULTS.
MM-HMM.

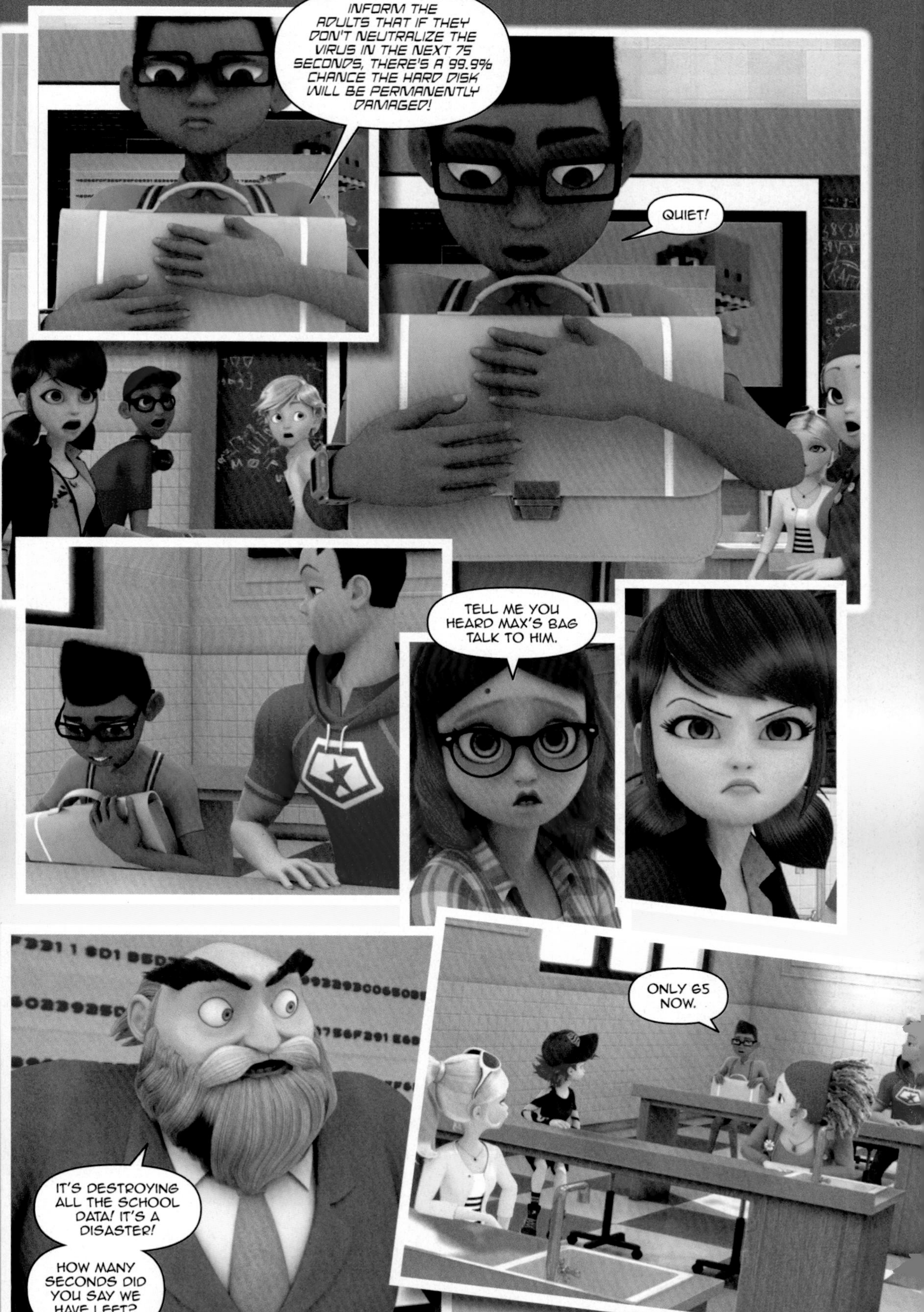
INFORM THE ADULTS THAT IF THEY DON'T NEUTRALIZE THE VIRUS IN THE NEXT 75 SECONDS, THERE'S A 99.9% CHANCE THE HARD DISK WILL BE PERMANENTLY DAMAGED!
QUIET!
TELL ME YOU HEARD MAX'S BAG TALK TO HIM.
IT'S DESTROYING ALL THE SCHOOL DATA! IT'S A DISASTER!
HOW MANY SECONDS DID YOU SAY WE HAVE LEFT?
ONLY 65 NOW.

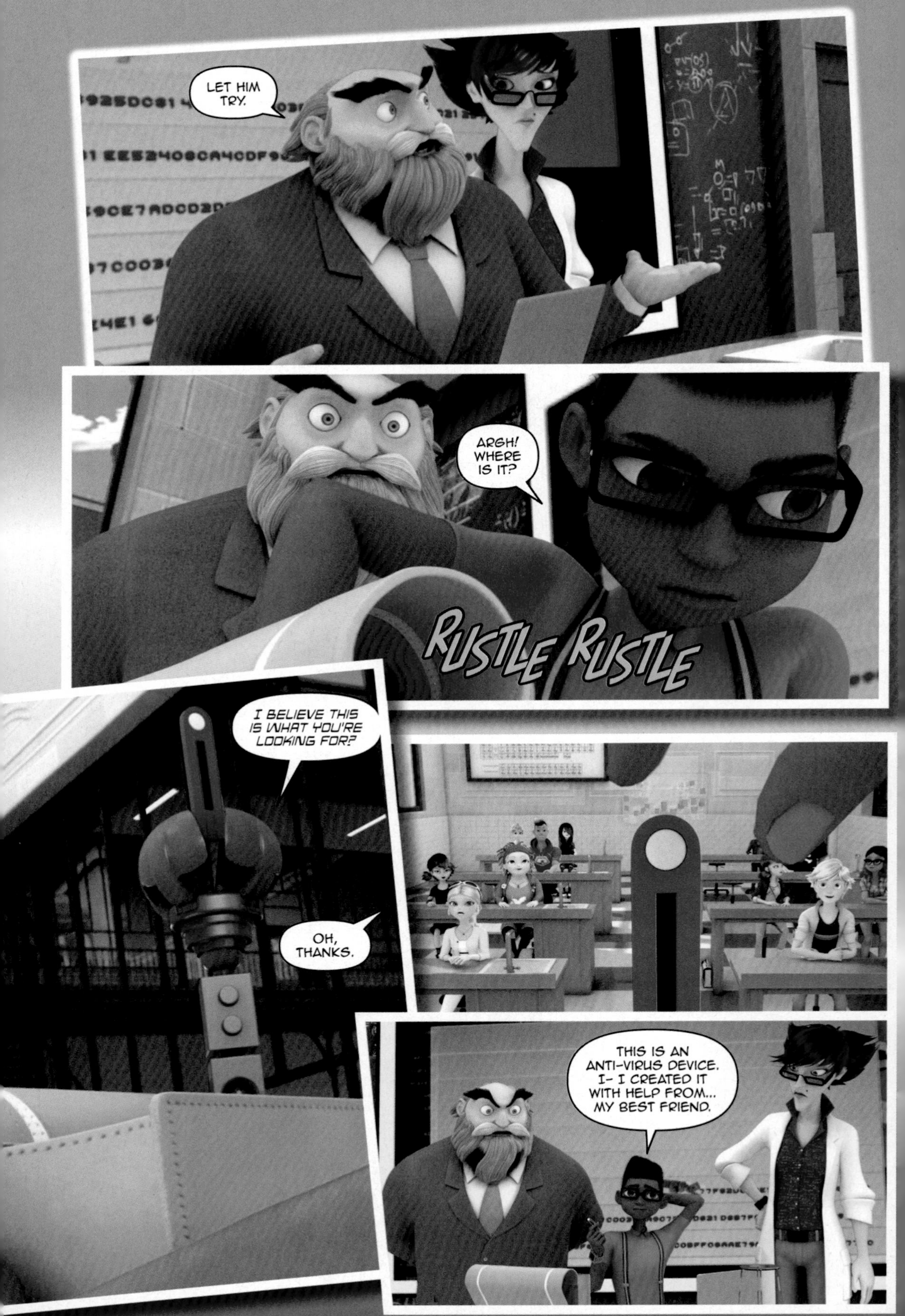
LET HIM TRY.
ARGH! WHERE IS IT?
RUSTLE RUSTLE
I BELIEVE THIS IS WHAT YOU'RE LOOKING FOR?
OH, THANKS.
THIS IS AN ANTI-VIRUS DEVICE. I- I CREATED IT WITH HELP FROM... MY BEST FRIEND.

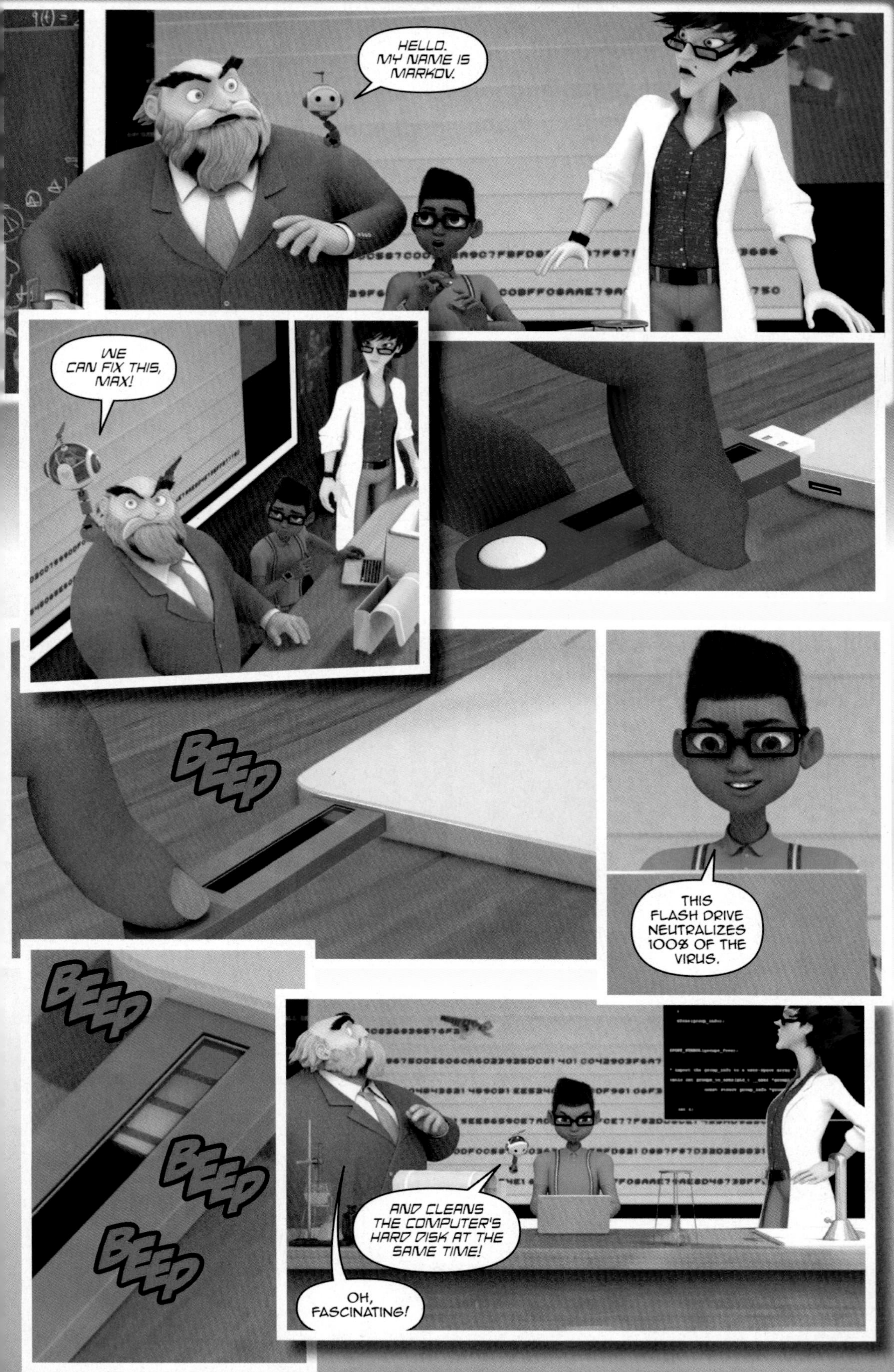
HELLO. MY NAME IS MARKOV.
WE CAN FIX THIS, MAX!
BEEP
THIS FLASH DRIVE NEUTRALIZES 100% OF THE VIRUS.
BEEP
BEEP
BEEP
AND CLEANS THE COMPUTER'S HARD DISK AT THE SAME TIME!
OH, FASCINATING!

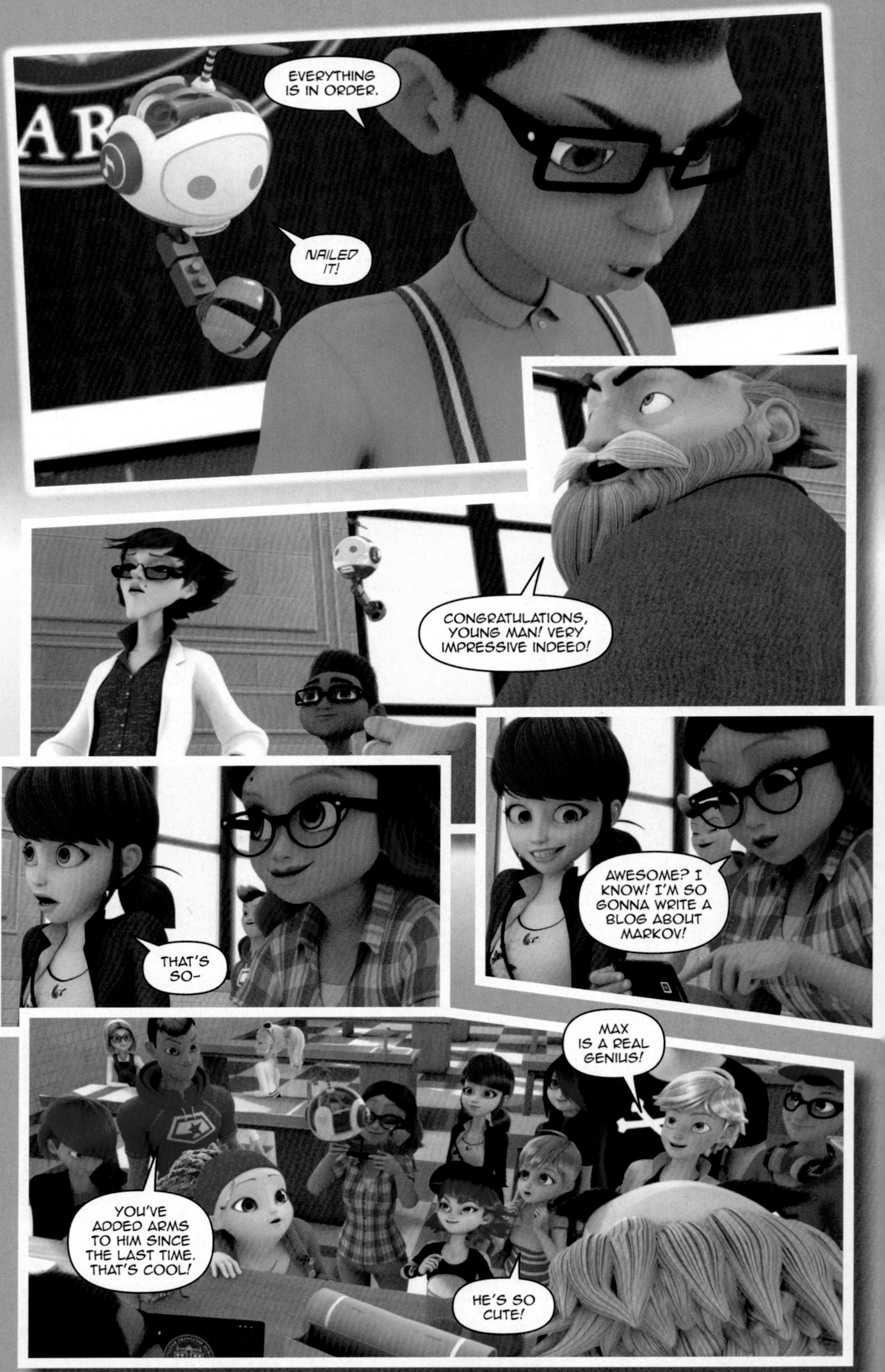
EVERYTHING IS IN ORDER.
NAILED IT!
CONGRATULATIONS, YOUNG MAN! VERY IMPRESSIVE INDEED!
THAT'S SO-
AWESOME? I KNOW! I'M SO GONNA WRITE A BLOG ABOUT MARKOV!
MAX IS A REAL GENIUS!
YOU'VE ADDED ARMS TO HIM SINCE THE LAST TIME. THAT'S COOL!
HE'S SO CUTE!

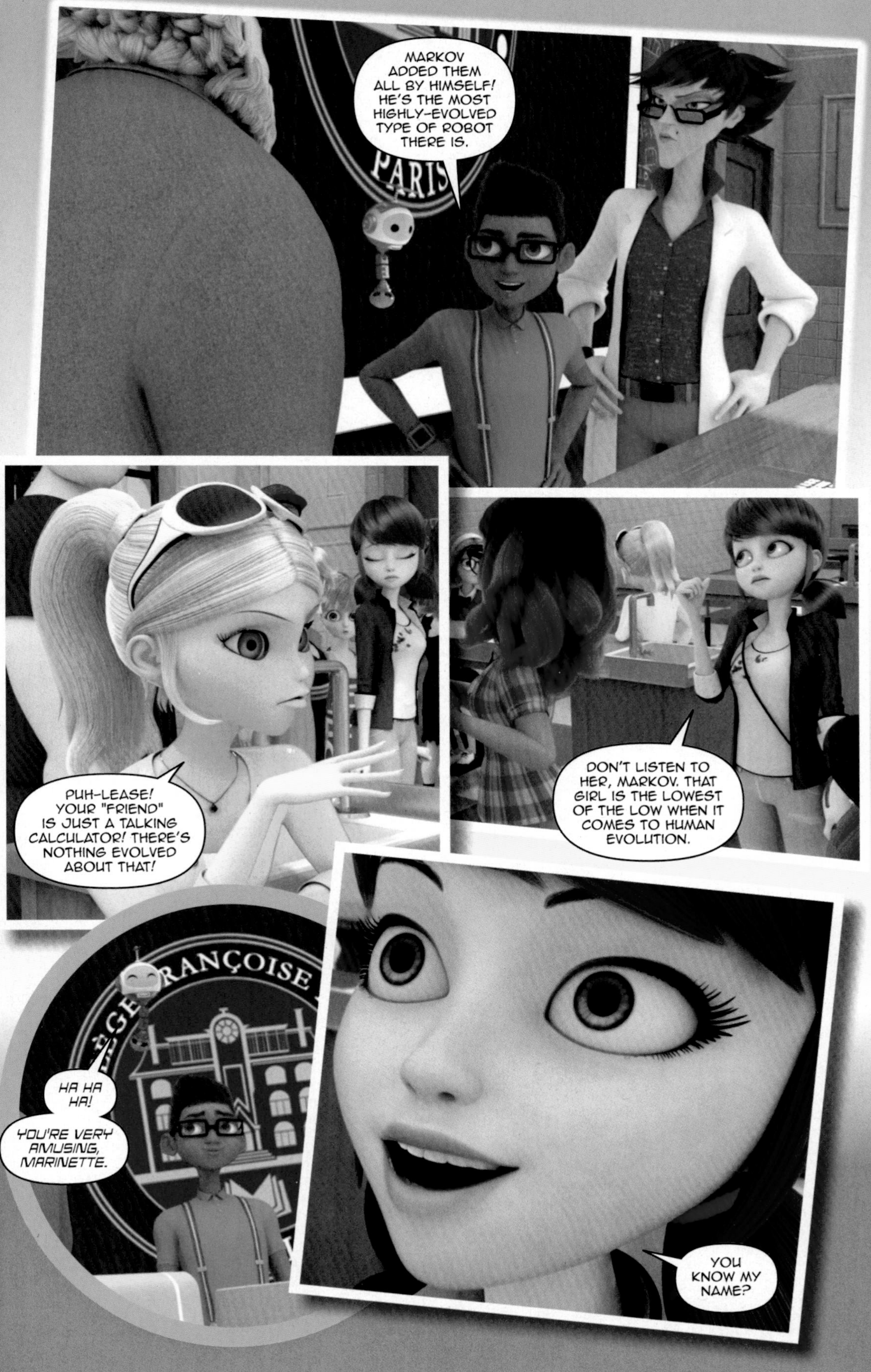
MARKOV ADDED THEM ALL BY HIMSELF! HE'S THE MOST HIGHLY-EVOLVED TYPE OF ROBOT THERE IS.
PARIS
PUH-LEASE! YOUR "FRIEND" IS JUST A TALKING CALCULATOR! THERE'S NOTHING EVOLVED ABOUT THAT!
DON'T LISTEN TO HER, MARKOV. THAT GIRL IS THE LOWEST OF THE LOW WHEN IT COMES TO HUMAN EVOLUTION.
RANÇOISE
HA HA HA!
YOU'RE VERY AMUSING, MARINETTE.
YOU KNOW MY NAME?

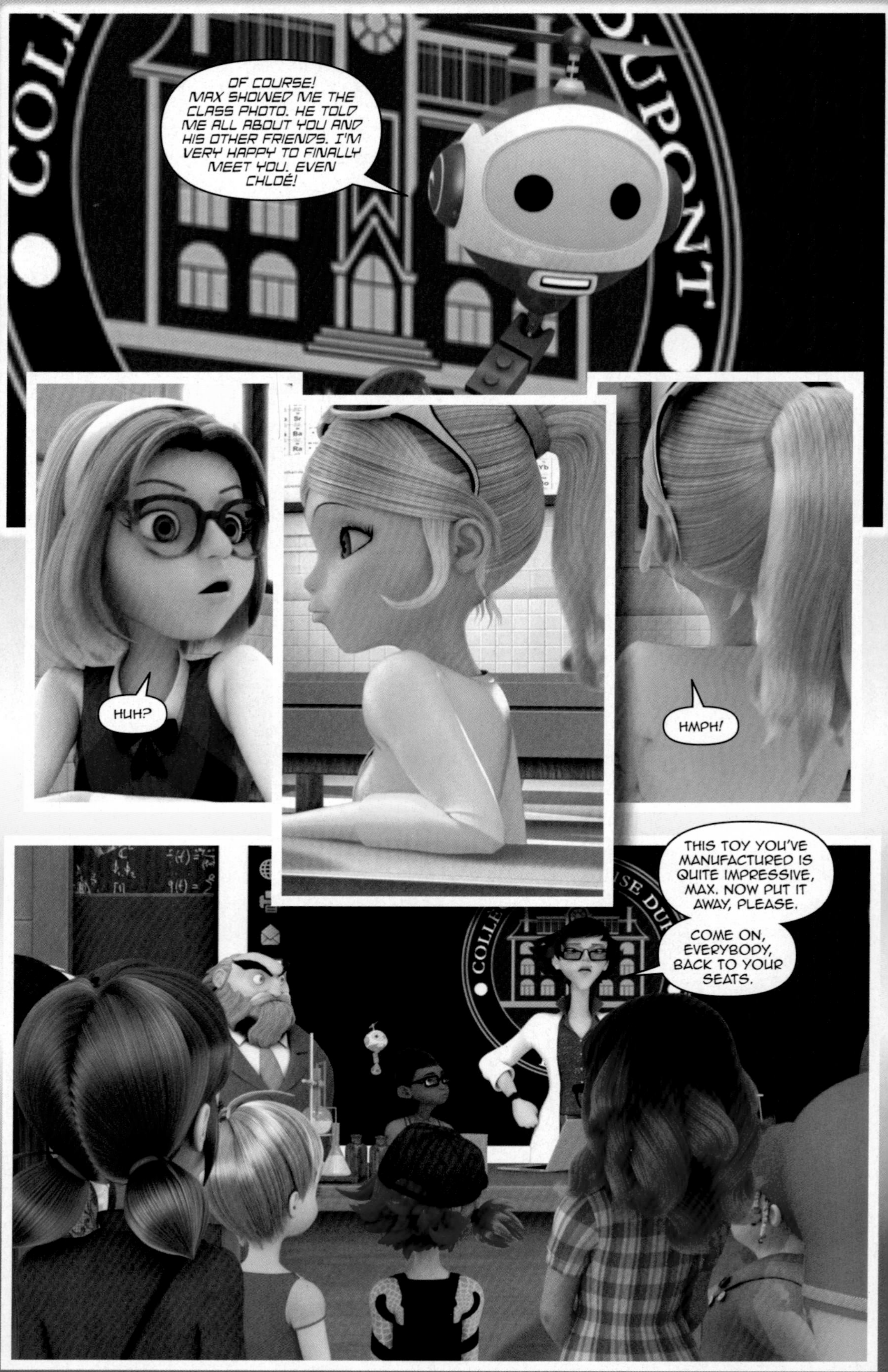
OF COURSE! MAX SHOWED ME THE CLASS PHOTO. HE TOLD ME ALL ABOUT YOU AND HIS OTHER FRIENDS. I'M VERY HAPPY TO FINALLY MEET YOU. EVEN CHLOÉ!
HUH?
HMPH!
THIS TOY YOU'VE MANUFACTURED IS QUITE IMPRESSIVE, MAX. NOW PUT IT AWAY, PLEASE.
COME ON, EVERYBODY, BACK TO YOUR SEATS.

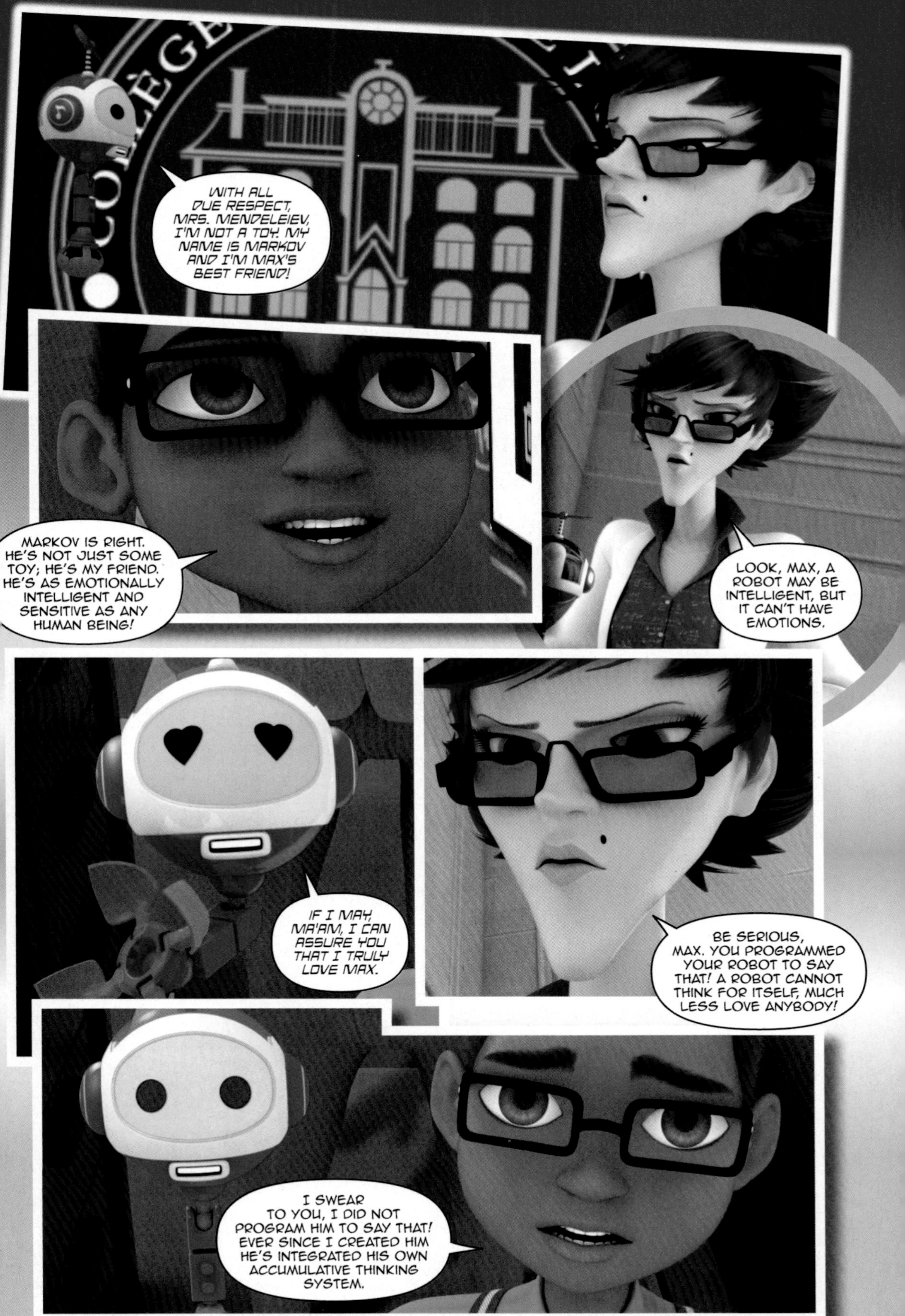
COLLÈGE
WITH ALL DUE RESPECT, MRS. MENDELEIEV, I'M NOT A TOY. MY NAME IS MARKOV AND I'M MAX'S BEST FRIEND!
MARKOV IS RIGHT. HE'S NOT JUST SOME TOY; HE'S MY FRIEND. HE'S AS EMOTIONALLY INTELLIGENT AND SENSITIVE AS ANY HUMAN BEING!
LOOK, MAX, A ROBOT MAY BE INTELLIGENT, BUT IT CAN'T HAVE EMOTIONS.
IF I MAY, MA'AM, I CAN ASSURE YOU THAT I TRULY LOVE MAX.
BE SERIOUS, MAX. YOU PROGRAMMED YOUR ROBOT TO SAY THAT! A ROBOT CANNOT THINK FOR ITSELF, MUCH LESS LOVE ANYBODY!
I SWEAR TO YOU, I DID NOT PROGRAM HIM TO SAY THAT! EVER SINCE I CREATED HIM HE'S INTEGRATED HIS OWN ACCUMULATIVE THINKING SYSTEM.

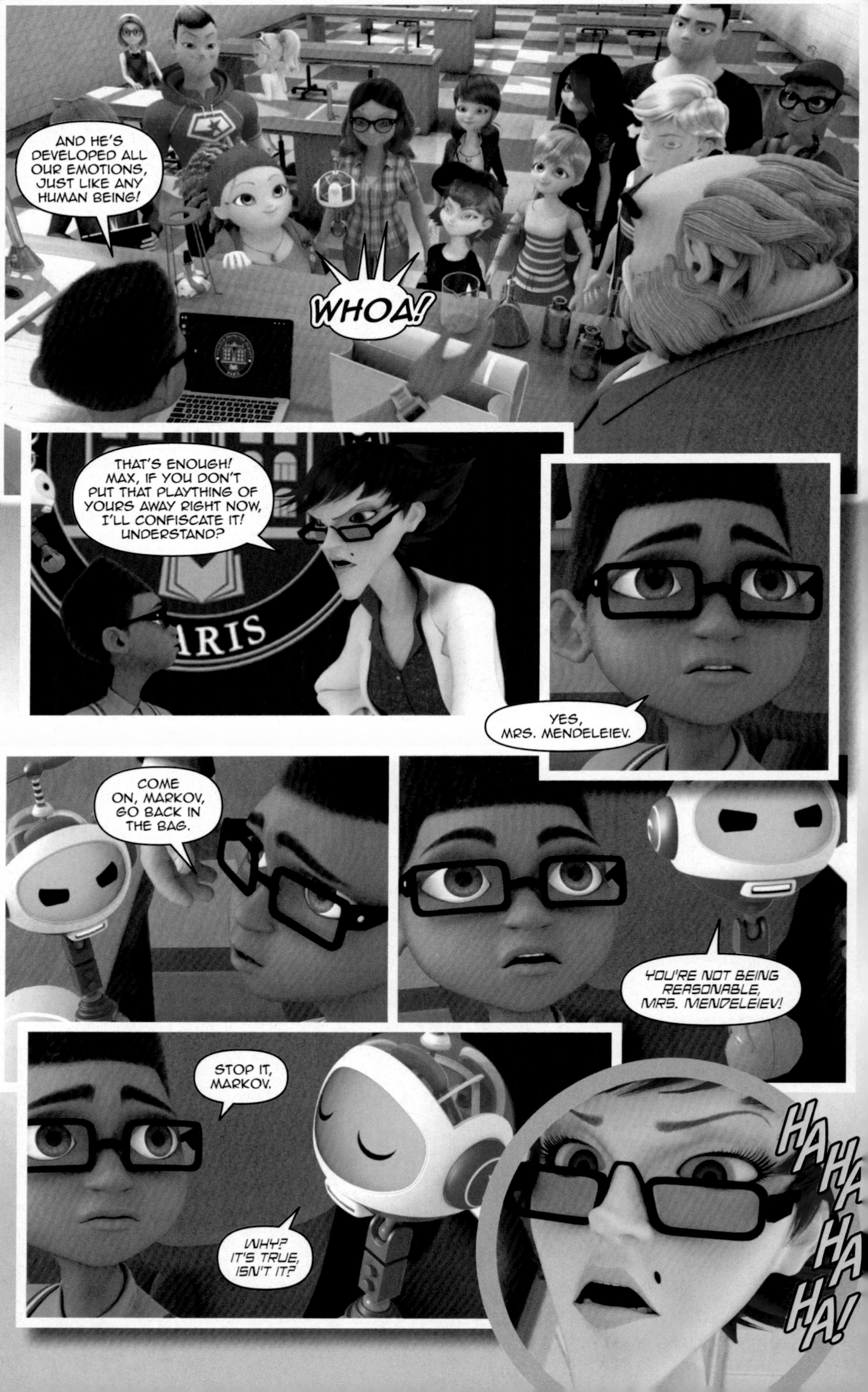
AND HE'S DEVELOPED ALL OUR EMOTIONS, JUST LIKE ANY HUMAN BEING!
WHOA!
THAT'S ENOUGH! MAX, IF YOU DON'T PUT THAT PLAYTHING OF YOURS AWAY RIGHT NOW, I'LL CONFISCATE IT! UNDERSTAND?
YES, MRS. MENDELEIEV.
COME ON, MARKOV, GO BACK IN THE BAG.
YOU'RE NOT BEING REASONABLE, MRS. MENDELEIEV!
STOP IT, MARKOV.
WHY? IT'S TRUE, ISN'T IT?
HA HA HA HA HA HA!

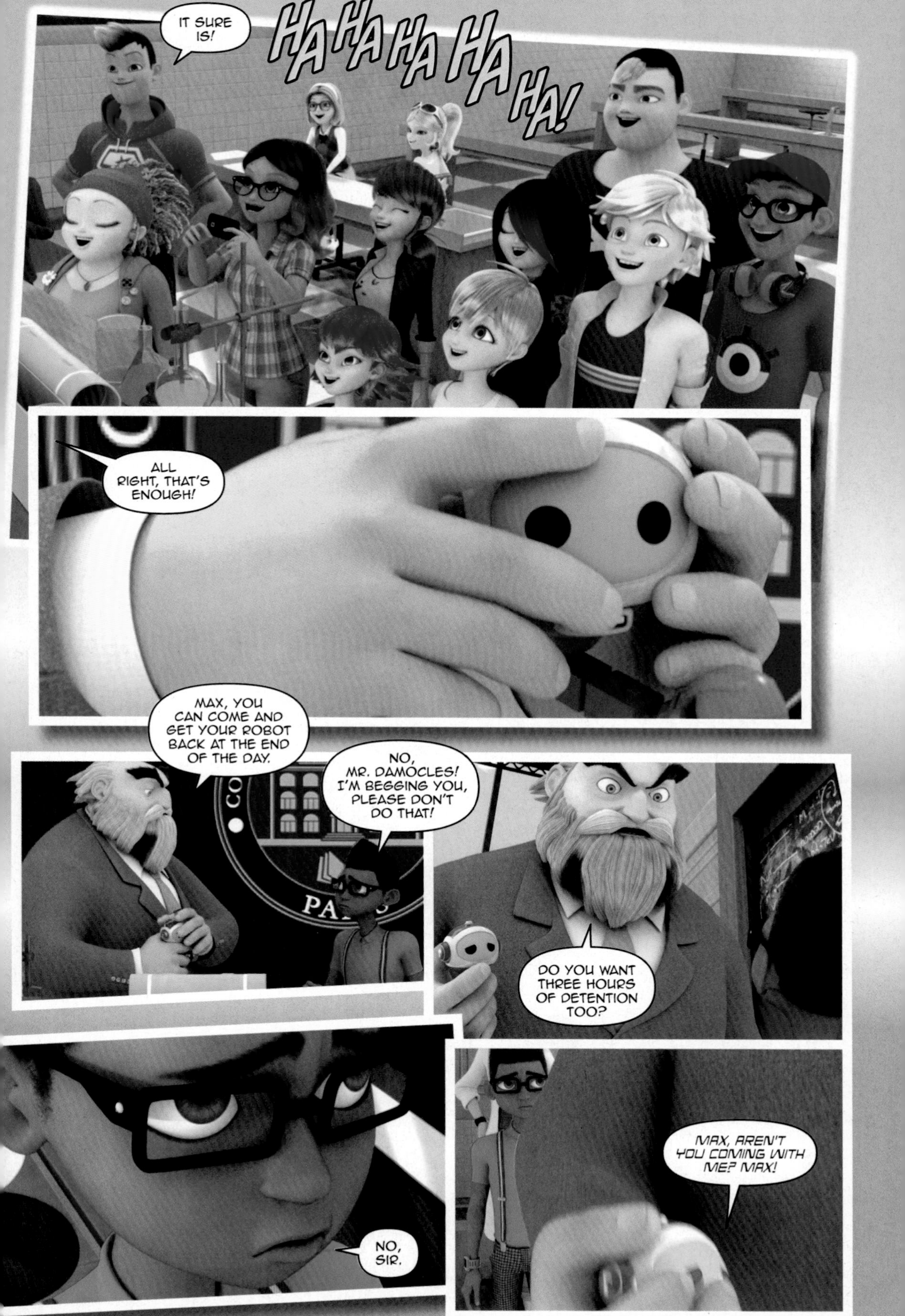
IT SURE IS!
HA HA HA HA HA HA HA!
ALL RIGHT, THAT'S ENOUGH!
MAX, YOU CAN COME AND GET YOUR ROBOT BACK AT THE END OF THE DAY.
NO, MR. DAMOCLES! I'M BEGGING YOU, PLEASE DON'T DO THAT!
DO YOU WANT THREE HOURS OF DETENTION TOO?
NO, SIR.
MAX, AREN'T YOU COMING WITH ME? MAX!

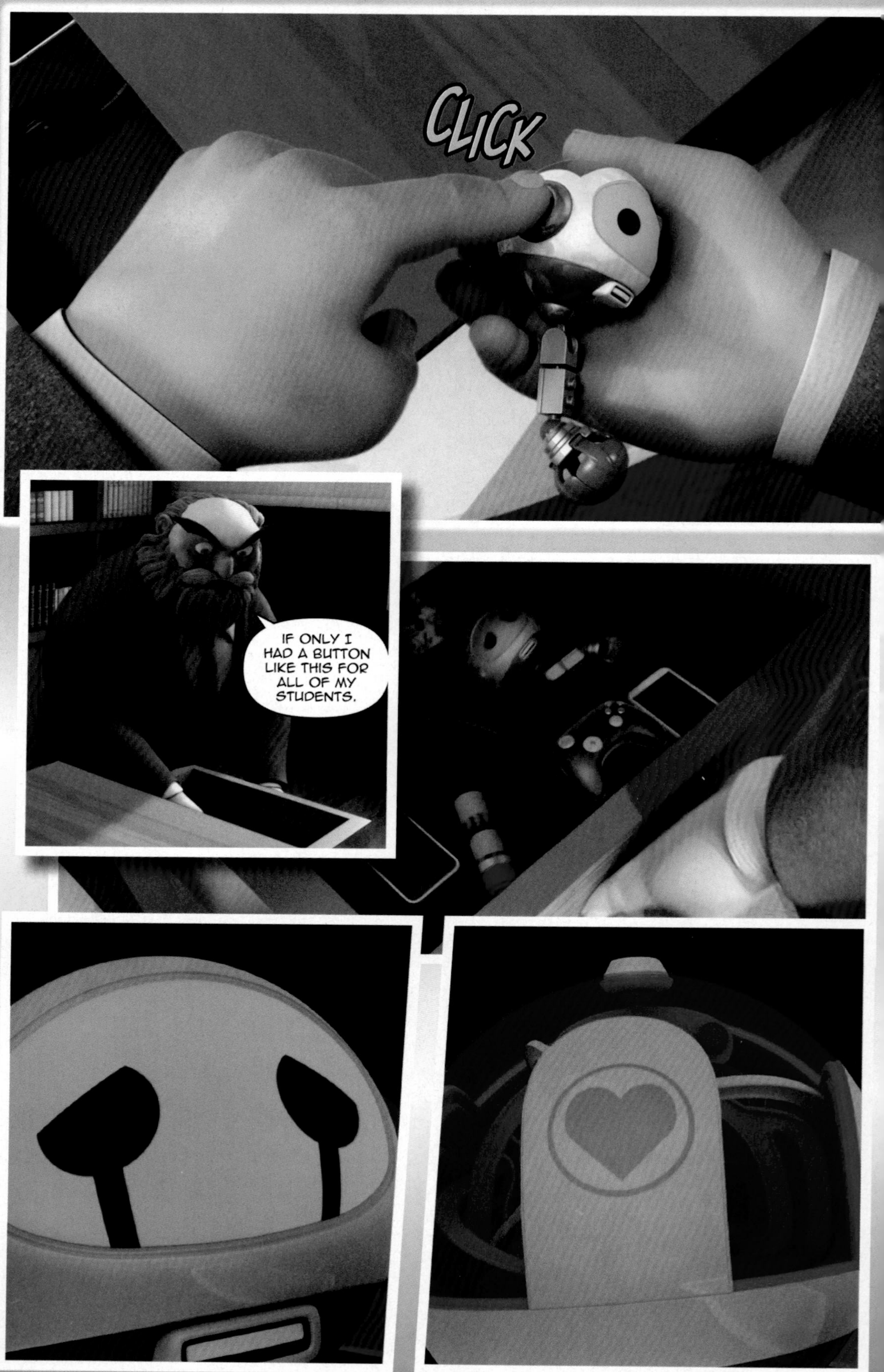
CLICK
IF ONLY I HAD A BUTTON LIKE THIS FOR ALL OF MY STUDENTS.

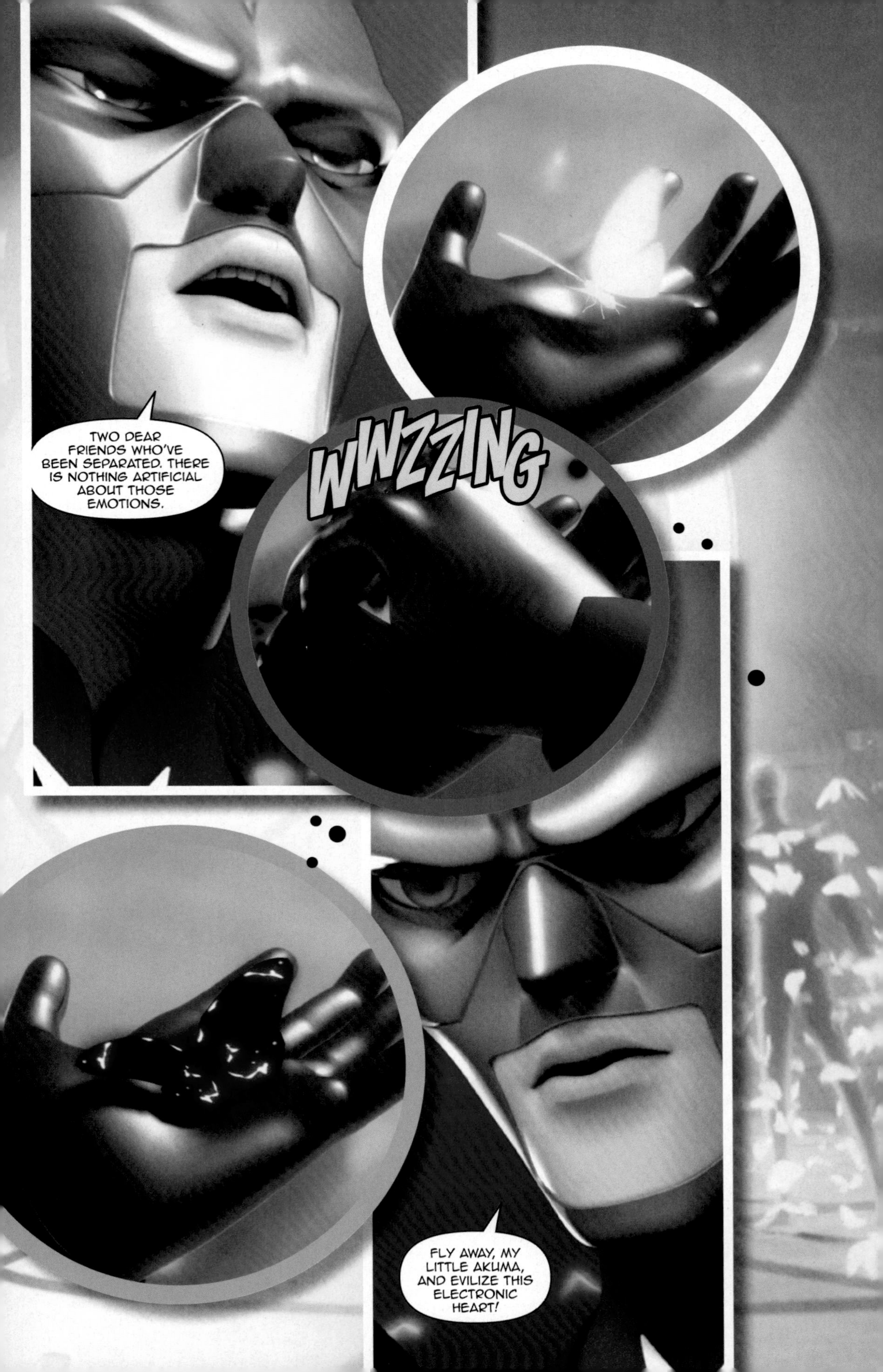
TWO DEAR FRIENDS WHO'VE BEEN SEPARATED. THERE IS NOTHING ARTIFICIAL ABOUT THOSE EMOTIONS.
WWZZING
FLY AWAY, MY LITTLE AKUMA, AND EVILIZE THIS ELECTRONIC HEART!

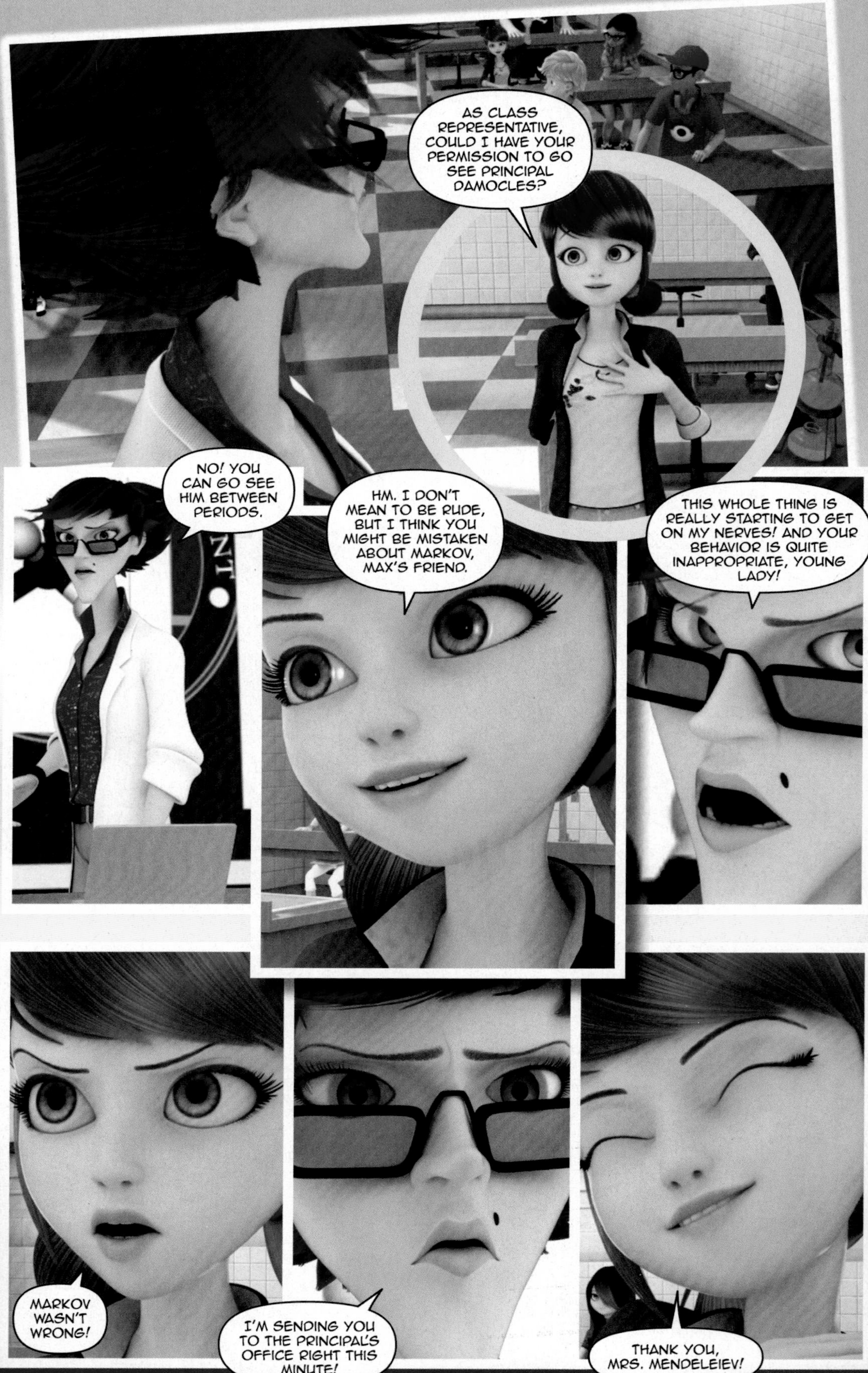
AS CLASS REPRESENTATIVE, COULD I HAVE YOUR PERMISSION TO GO SEE PRINCIPAL DAMOCLES?
NO! YOU CAN GO SEE HIM BETWEEN PERIODS.
HM. I DON'T MEAN TO BE RUDE, BUT I THINK YOU MIGHT BE MISTAKEN ABOUT MARKOV, MAX'S FRIEND.
THIS WHOLE THING IS REALLY STARTING TO GET ON MY NERVES! AND YOUR BEHAVIOR IS QUITE INAPPROPRIATE, YOUNG LADY!
MARKOV WASN'T WRONG!
I'M SENDING YOU TO THE PRINCIPAL'S OFFICE RIGHT THIS MINUTE!
THANK YOU, MRS. MENDELEIEV!

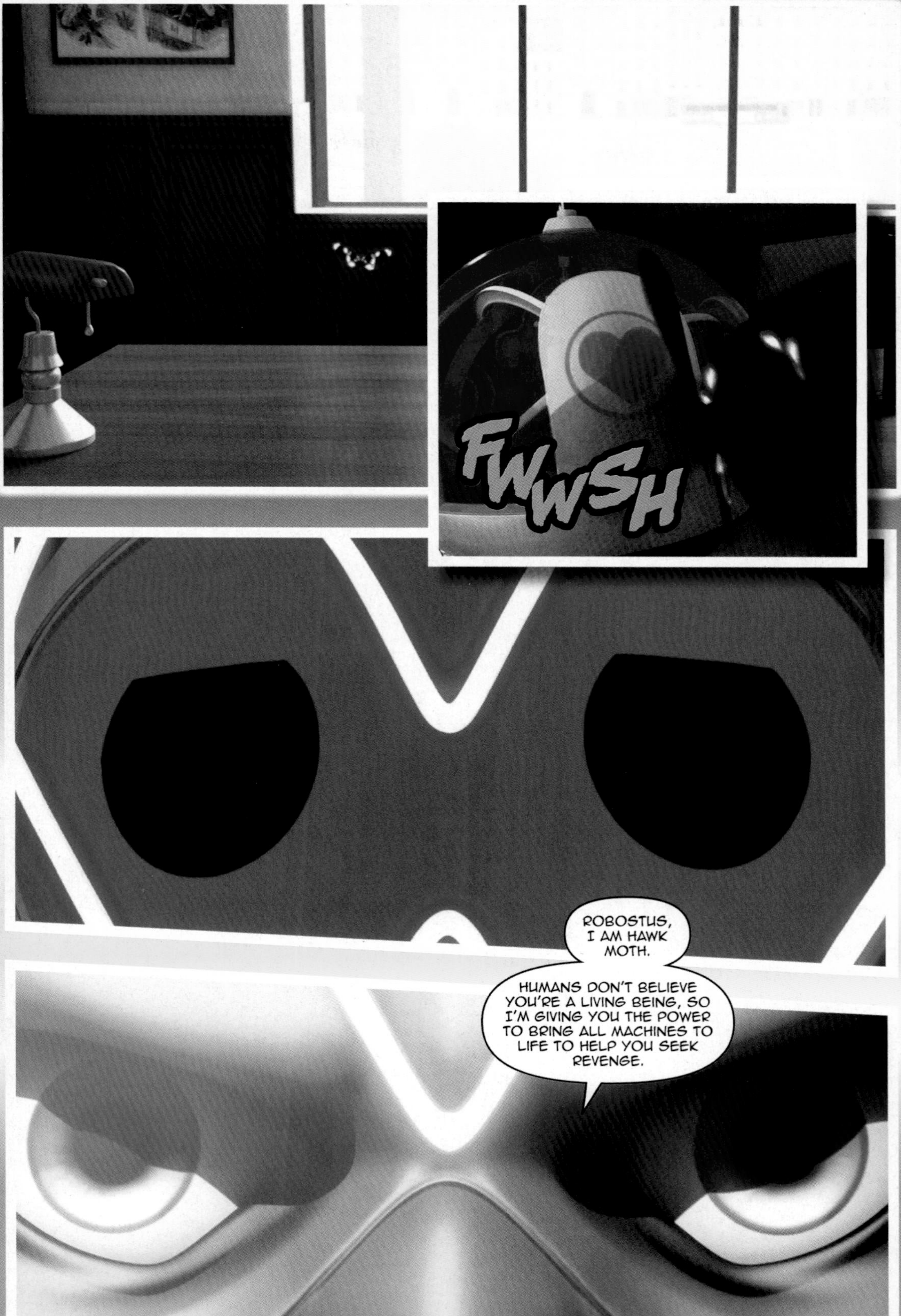
FWWSH
ROBOSTUS, I AM HAWK MOTH.
HUMANS DON'T BELIEVE YOU'RE A LIVING BEING, SO I'M GIVING YOU THE POWER TO BRING ALL MACHINES TO LIFE TO HELP YOU SEEK REVENGE.

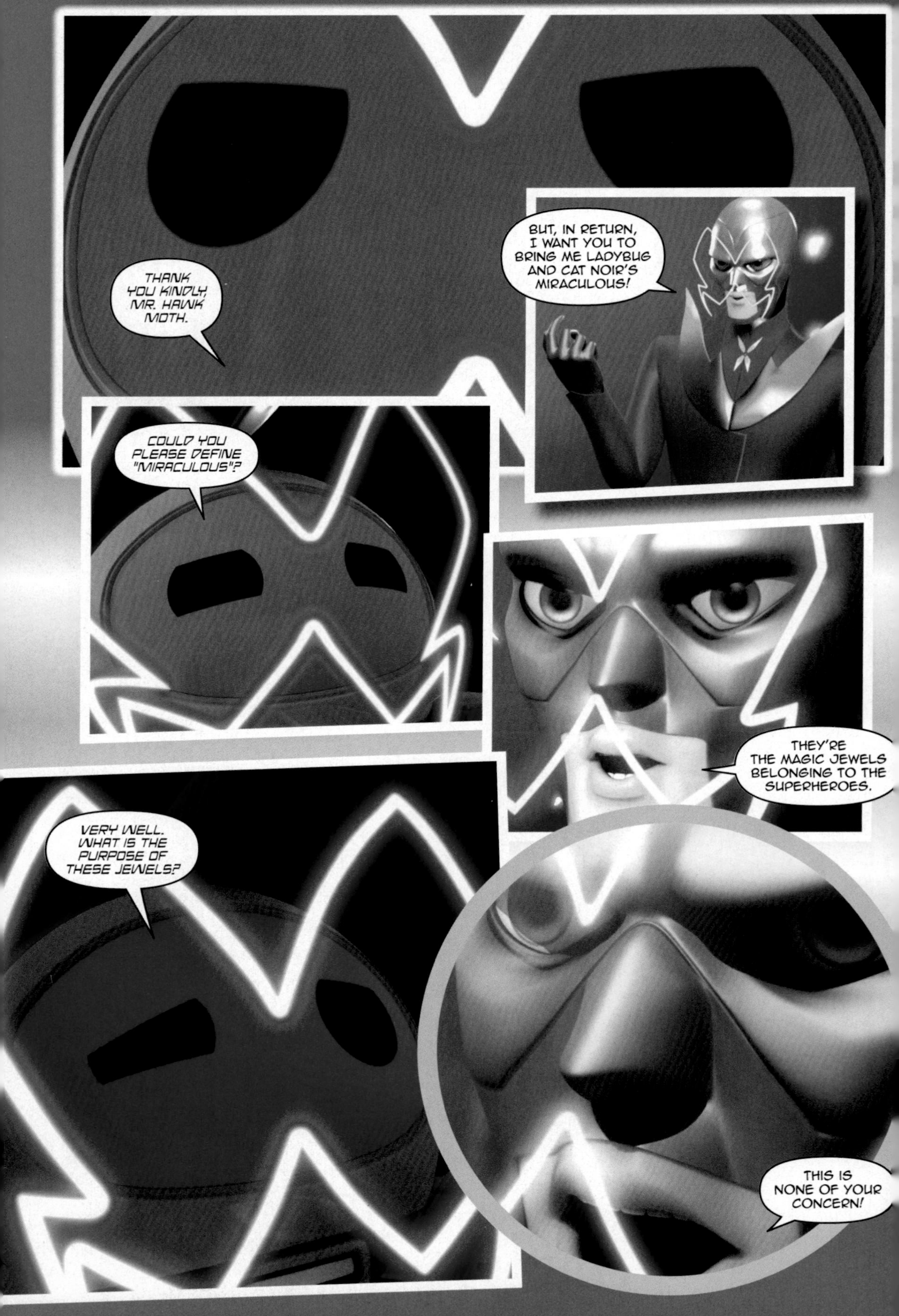
THANK YOU KINDLY, MR. HAWK MOTH.
BUT, IN RETURN, I WANT YOU TO BRING ME LADYBUG AND CAT NOIR'S MIRACULOUS!
COULD YOU PLEASE DEFINE "MIRACULOUS"?
THEY'RE THE MAGIC JEWELS BELONGING TO THE SUPERHEROES.
VERY WELL. WHAT IS THE PURPOSE OF THESE JEWELS?
THIS IS NONE OF YOUR CONCERN!

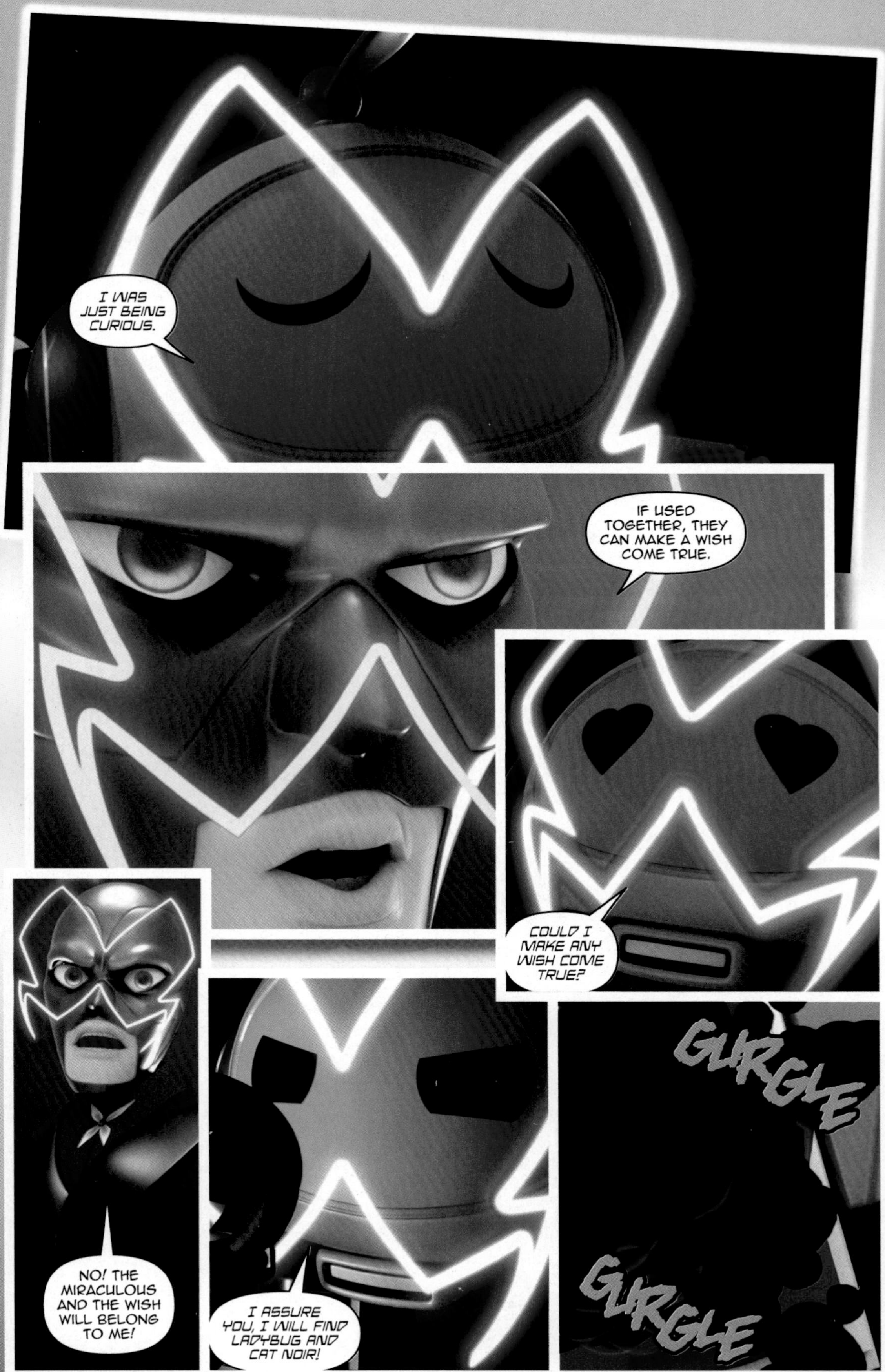
I WAS JUST BEING CURIOUS.
IF USED TOGETHER, THEY CAN MAKE A WISH COME TRUE.
COULD I MAKE ANY WISH COME TRUE?
NO! THE MIRACULOUS AND THE WISH WILL BELONG TO ME!
I ASSURE YOU, I WILL FIND LADYBUG AND CAT NOIR!
GURGLE
GURGLE

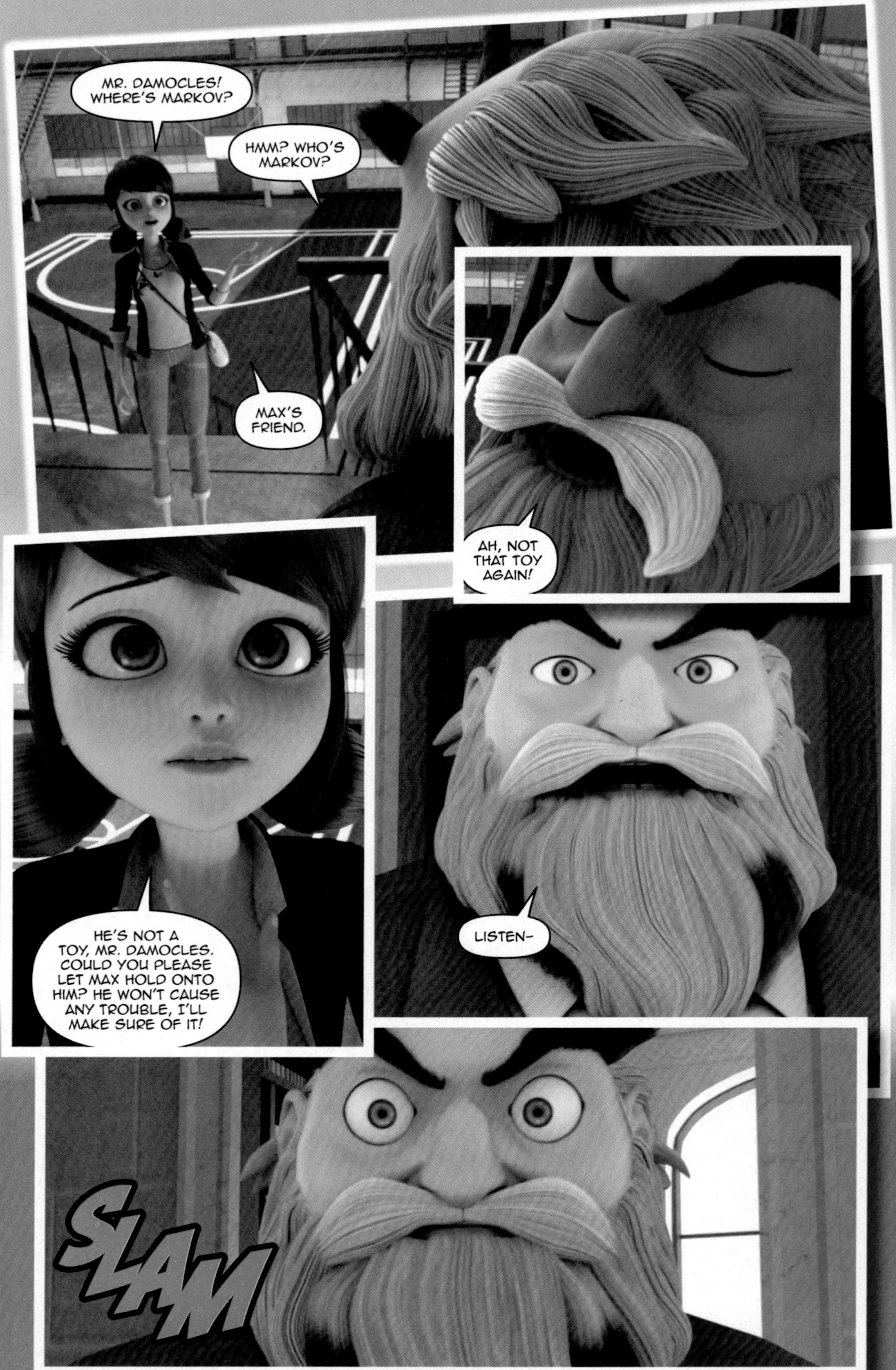
MR. DAMOCLES! WHERE'S MARKOV?
HMM? WHO'S MARKOV?
MAX'S FRIEND.
AH, NOT THAT TOY AGAIN!
HE'S NOT A TOY, MR. DAMOCLES. COULD YOU PLEASE LET MAX HOLD ONTO HIM? HE WON'T CAUSE ANY TROUBLE, I'LL MAKE SURE OF IT!
LISTEN-
SLAM

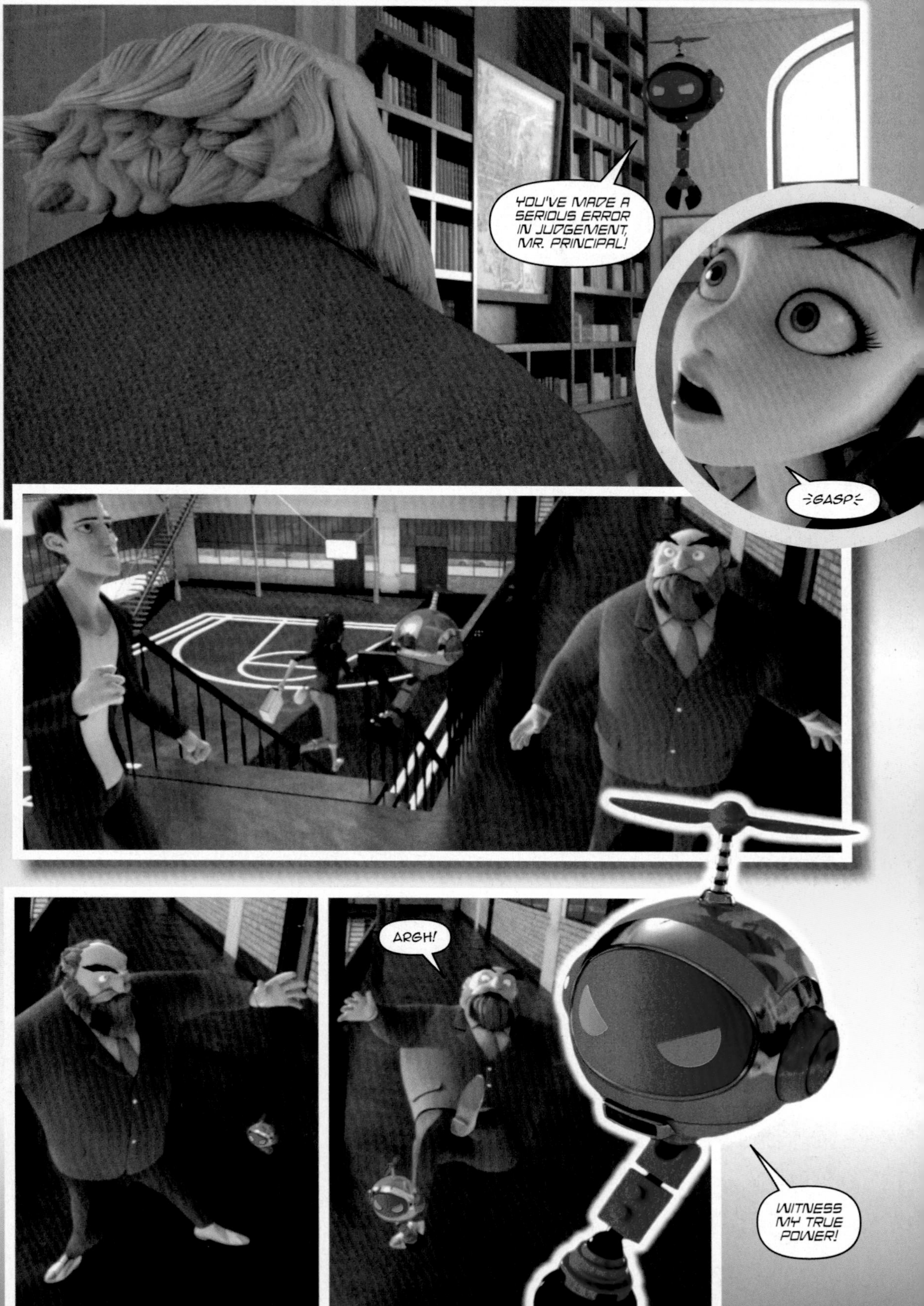
YOU'VE MADE A SERIOUS ERROR IN JUDGEMENT, MR. PRINCIPAL!
GASP
ARGH!
WITNESS MY TRUE POWER!

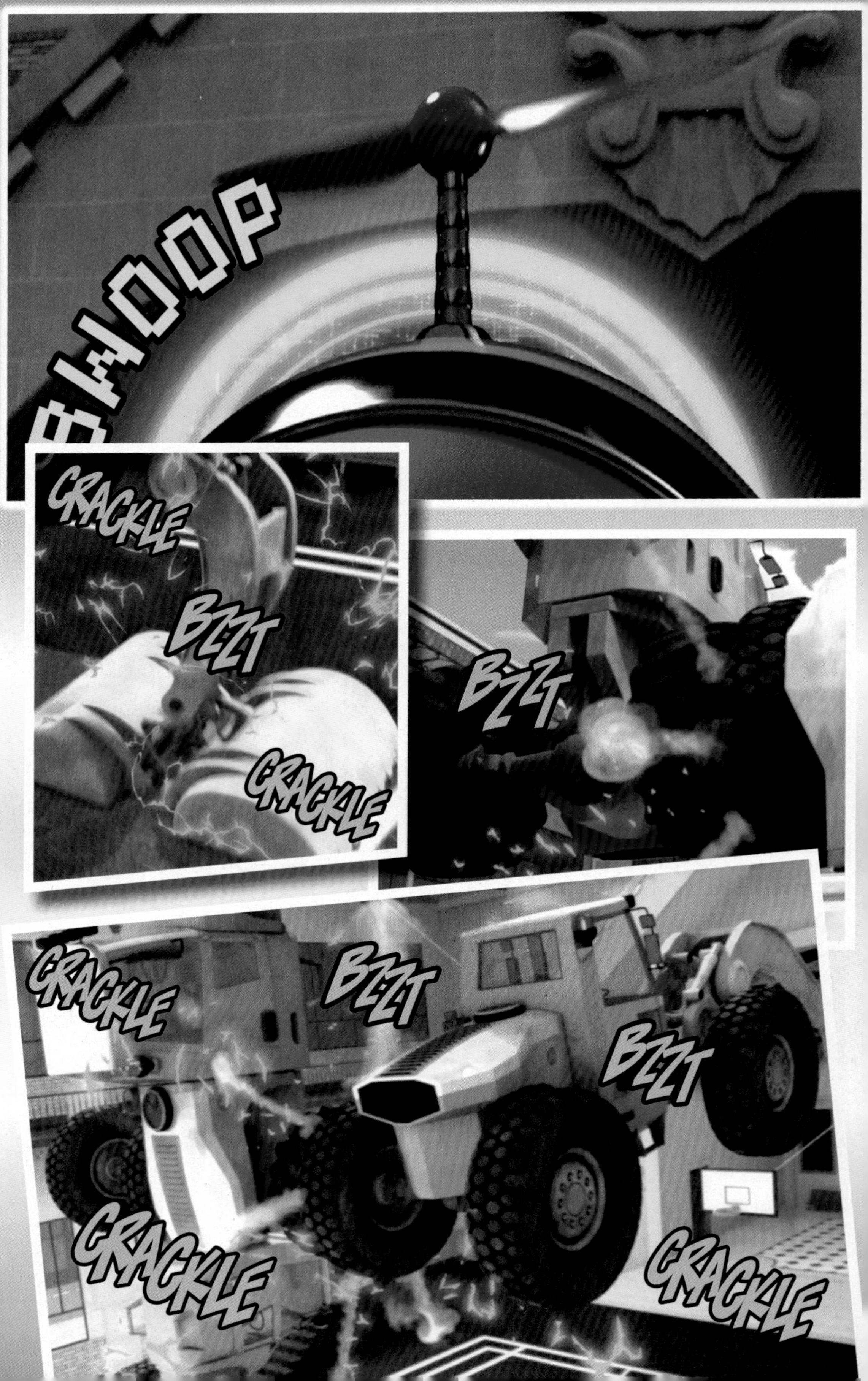
WOOP
CRACKLE
BZZT
CRACKLE
BZZT
CRACKLE
BZZT
BZZT
CRACKLE
CRACKLE

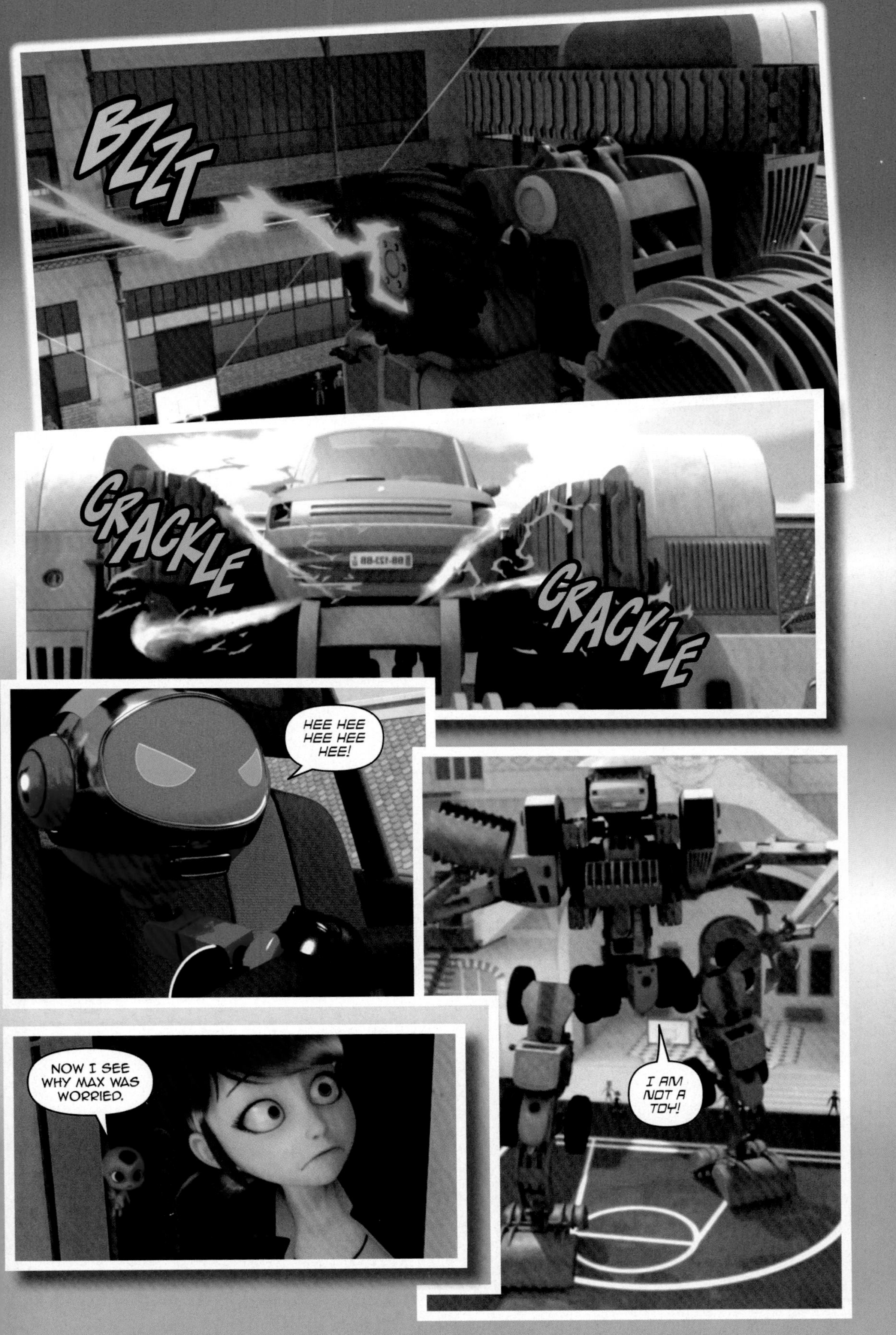
BZZT
CRACKLE
CRACKLE
HEE HEE HEE HEE HEE!
I AM NOT A TOY!
NOW I SEE WHY MAX WAS WORRIED.

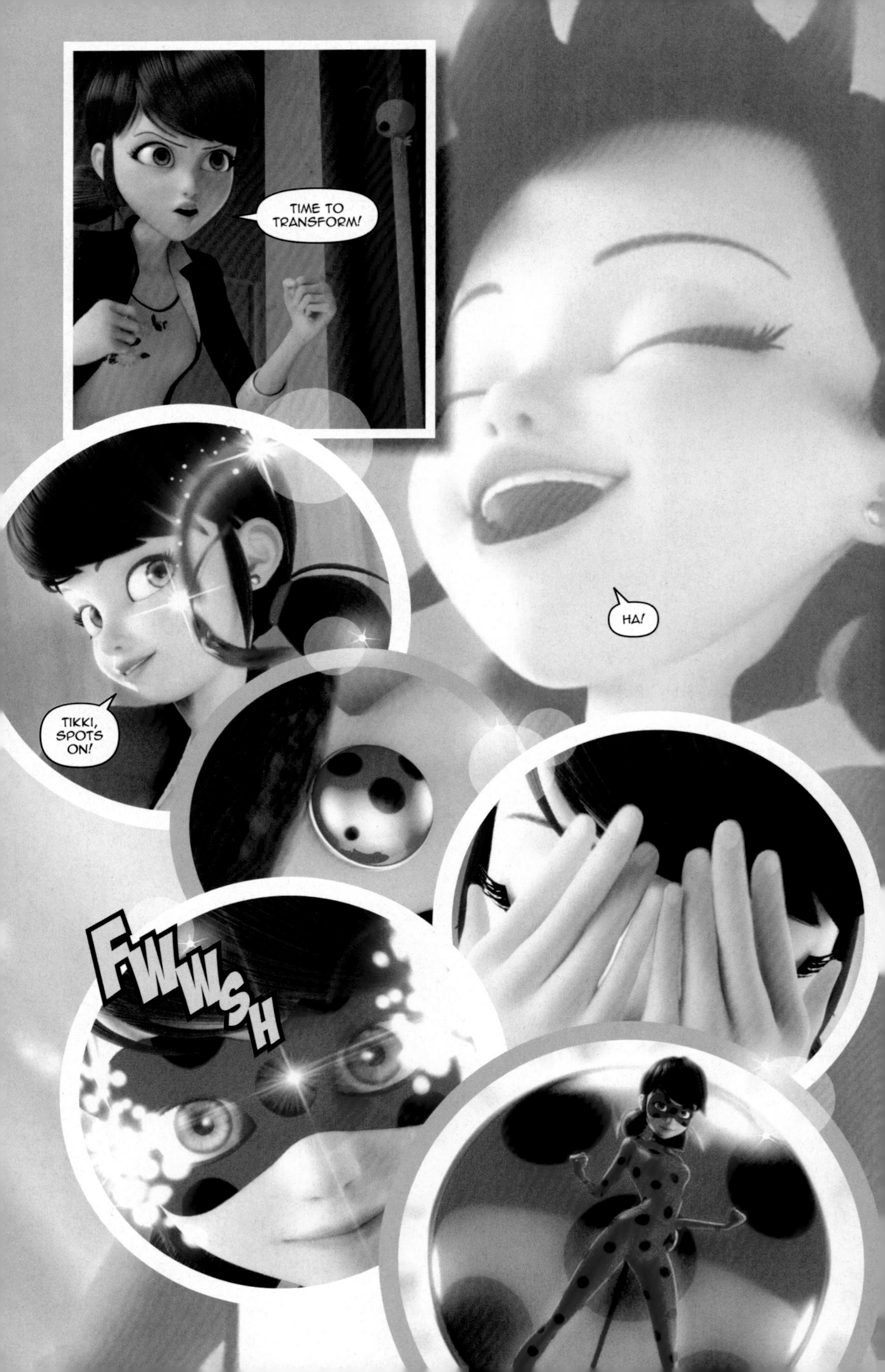
TIME TO TRANSFORM!
TIKKI, SPOTS ON!
HA!
FWWSH

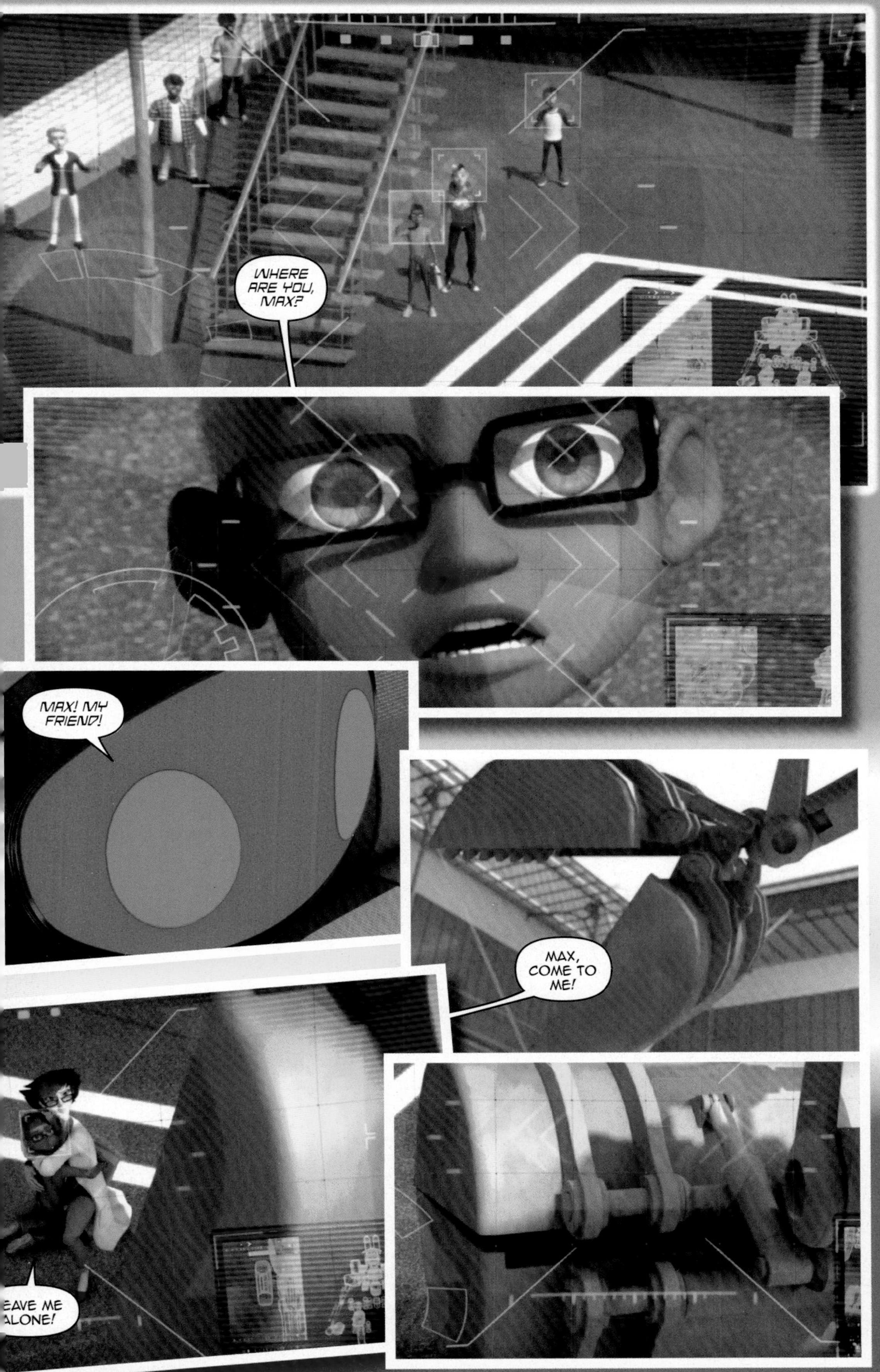
WHERE ARE YOU, MAX?
MAX! MY FRIEND!
MAX, COME TO ME!
EAVE ME ALONE!

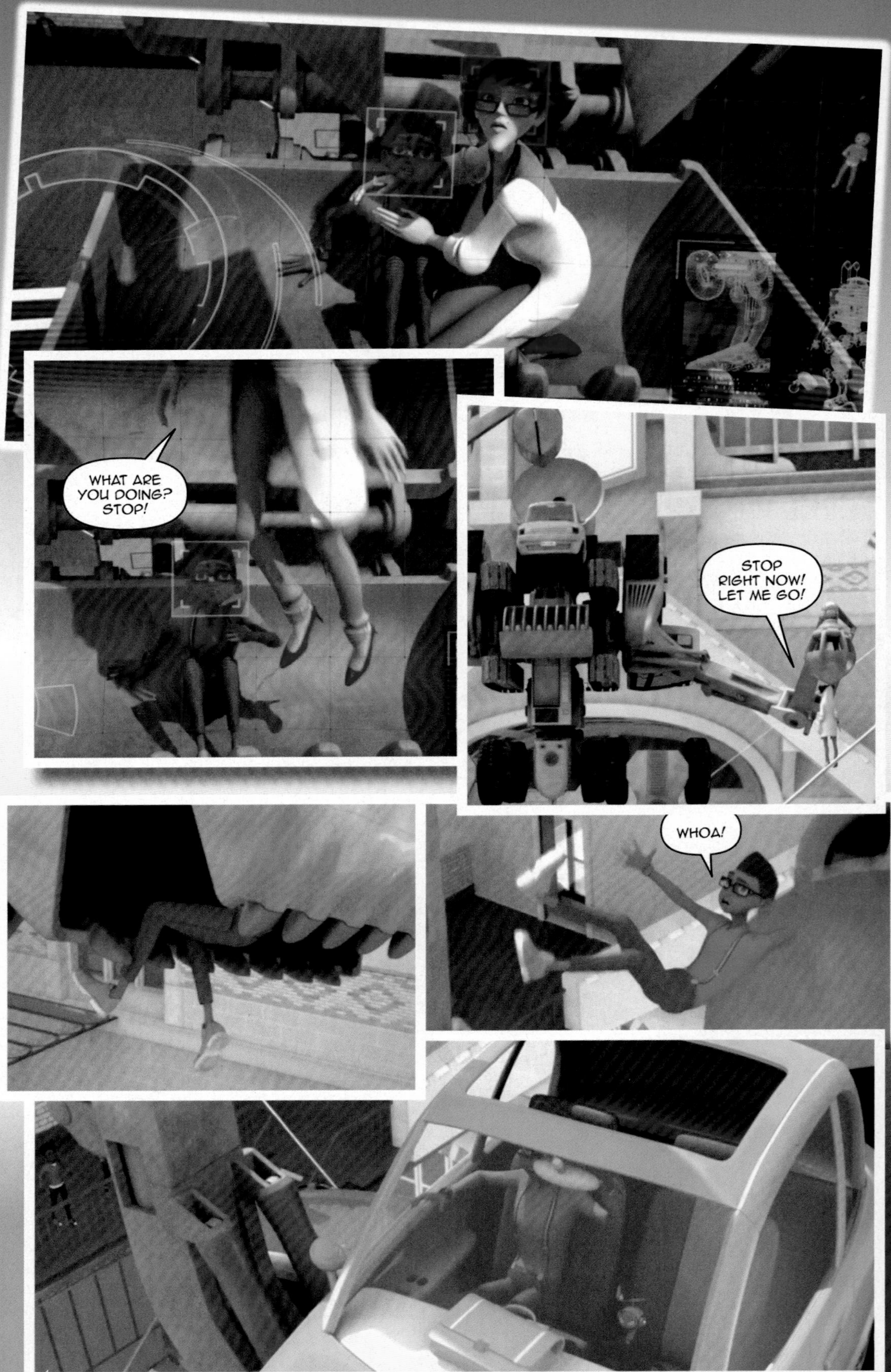
WHAT ARE YOU DOING? STOP!
STOP RIGHT NOW! LET ME GO!
WHOA!

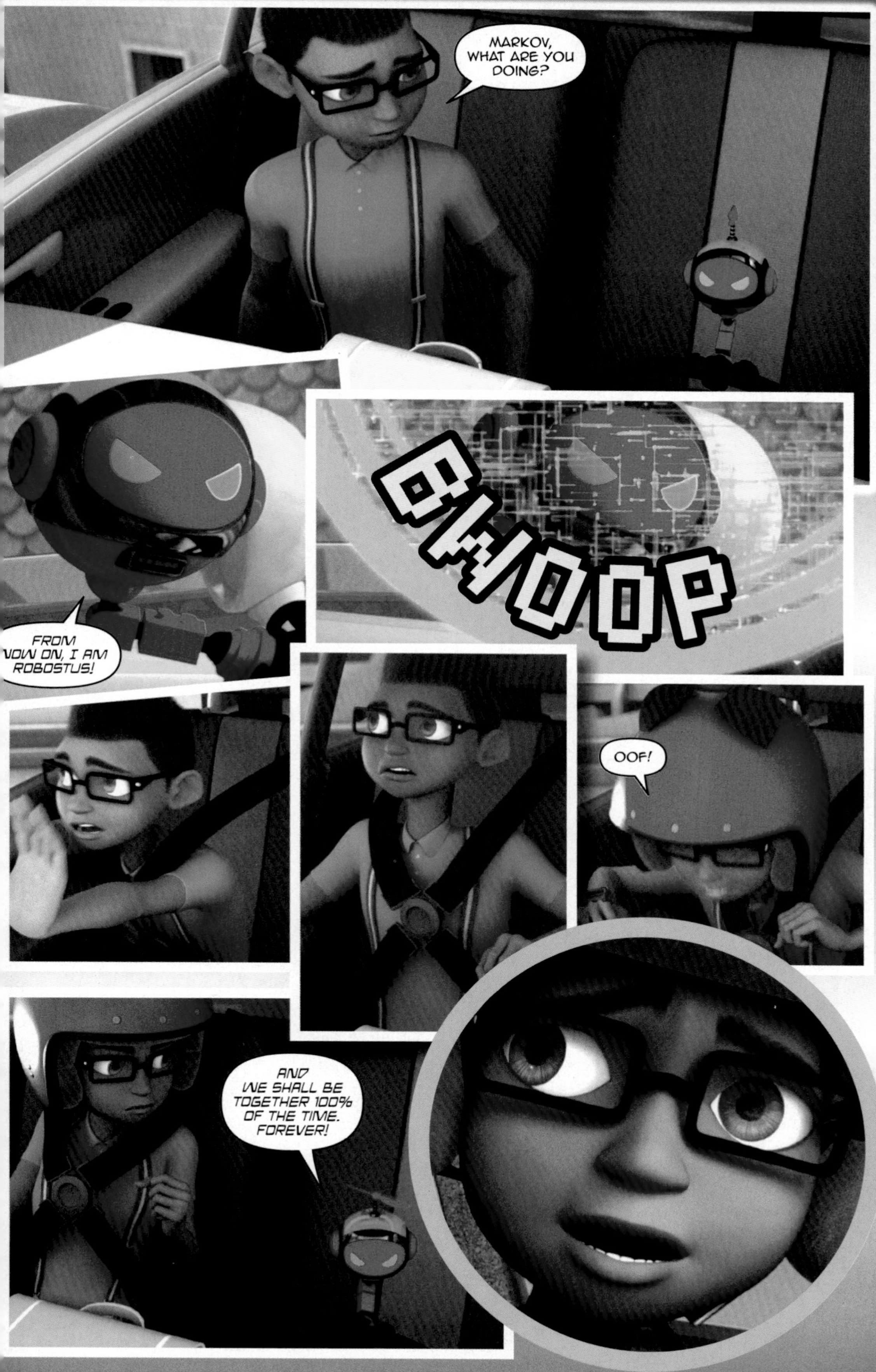
MARKOV, WHAT ARE YOU DOING?
FROM NOW ON, I AM ROBOSTUS!
BWOOP
OOF!
AND WE SHALL BE TOGETHER 100% OF THE TIME. FOREVER!

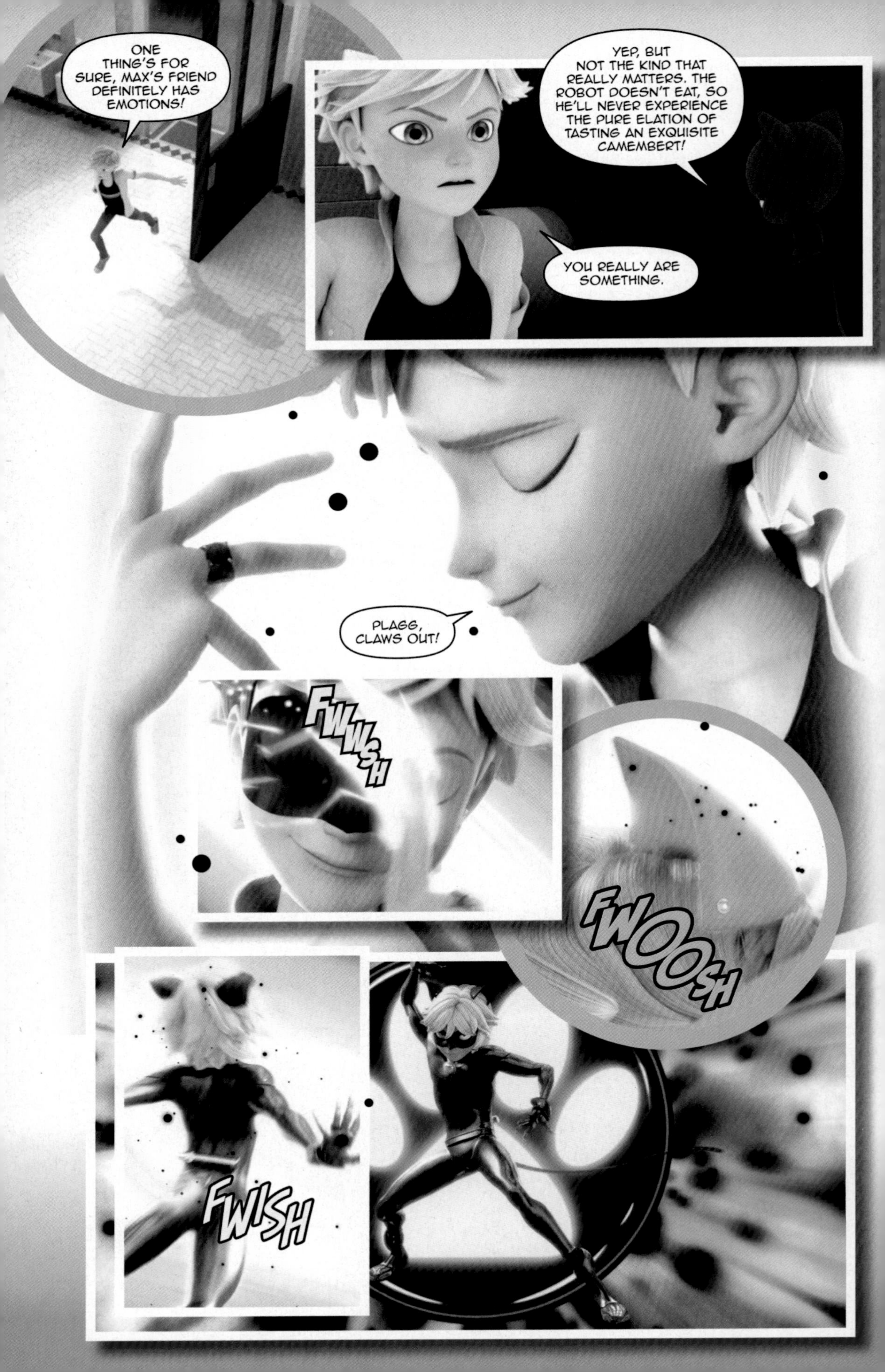
ONE THING'S FOR SURE, MAX'S FRIEND DEFINITELY HAS EMOTIONS!
YEP, BUT NOT THE KIND THAT REALLY MATTERS. THE ROBOT DOESN'T EAT, SO HE'LL NEVER EXPERIENCE THE PURE ELATION OF TASTING AN EXQUISITE CAMEMBERT!
YOU REALLY ARE SOMETHING.
PLAGG, CLAWS OUT!
FWWSH
FWOOSH
FWISH

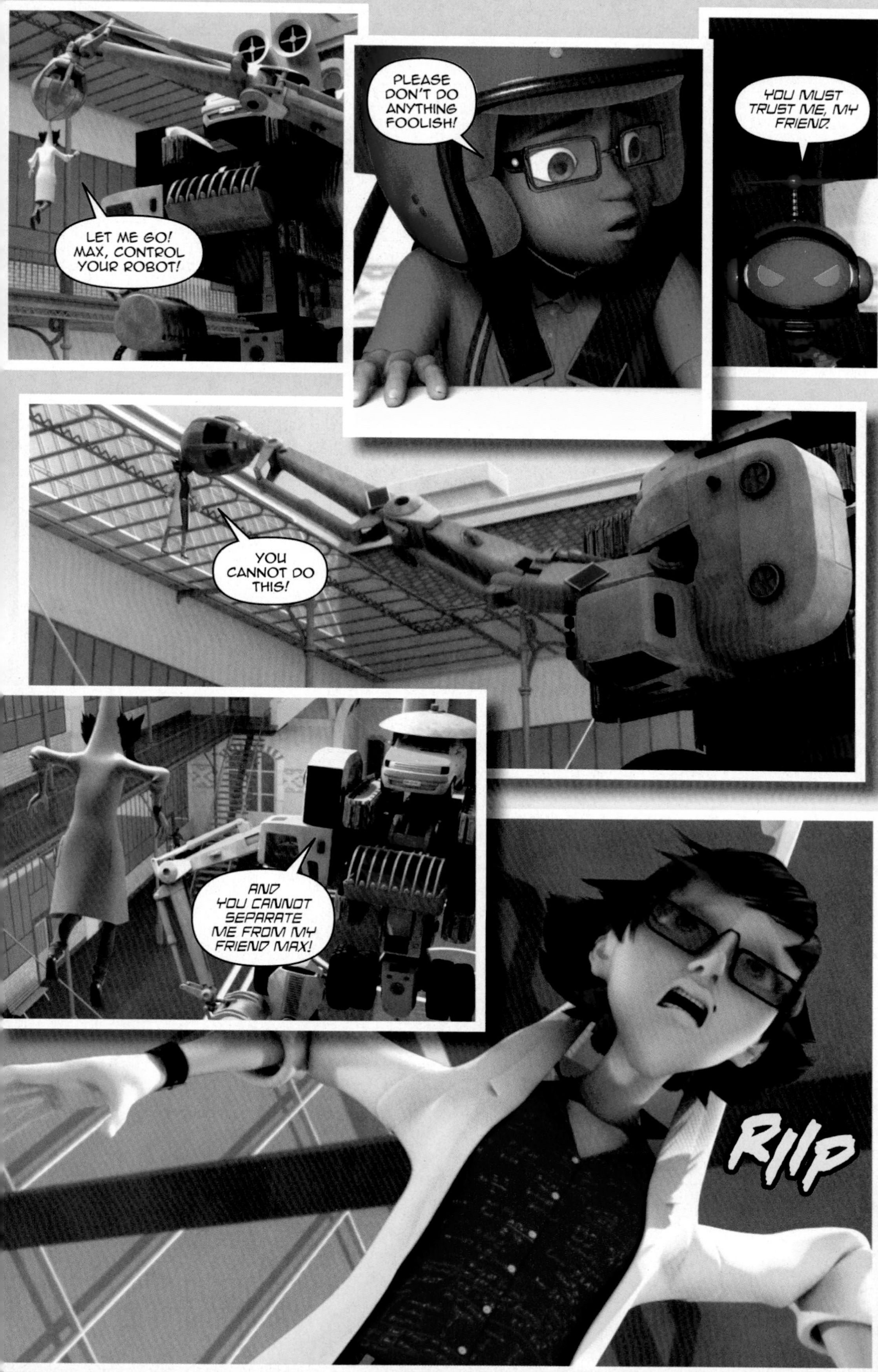
LET ME GO! MAX, CONTROL YOUR ROBOT!
PLEASE DON'T DO ANYTHING FOOLISH!
YOU MUST TRUST ME, MY FRIEND.
YOU CANNOT DO THIS!
AND YOU CANNOT SEPARATE ME FROM MY FRIEND MAX!
RIIP

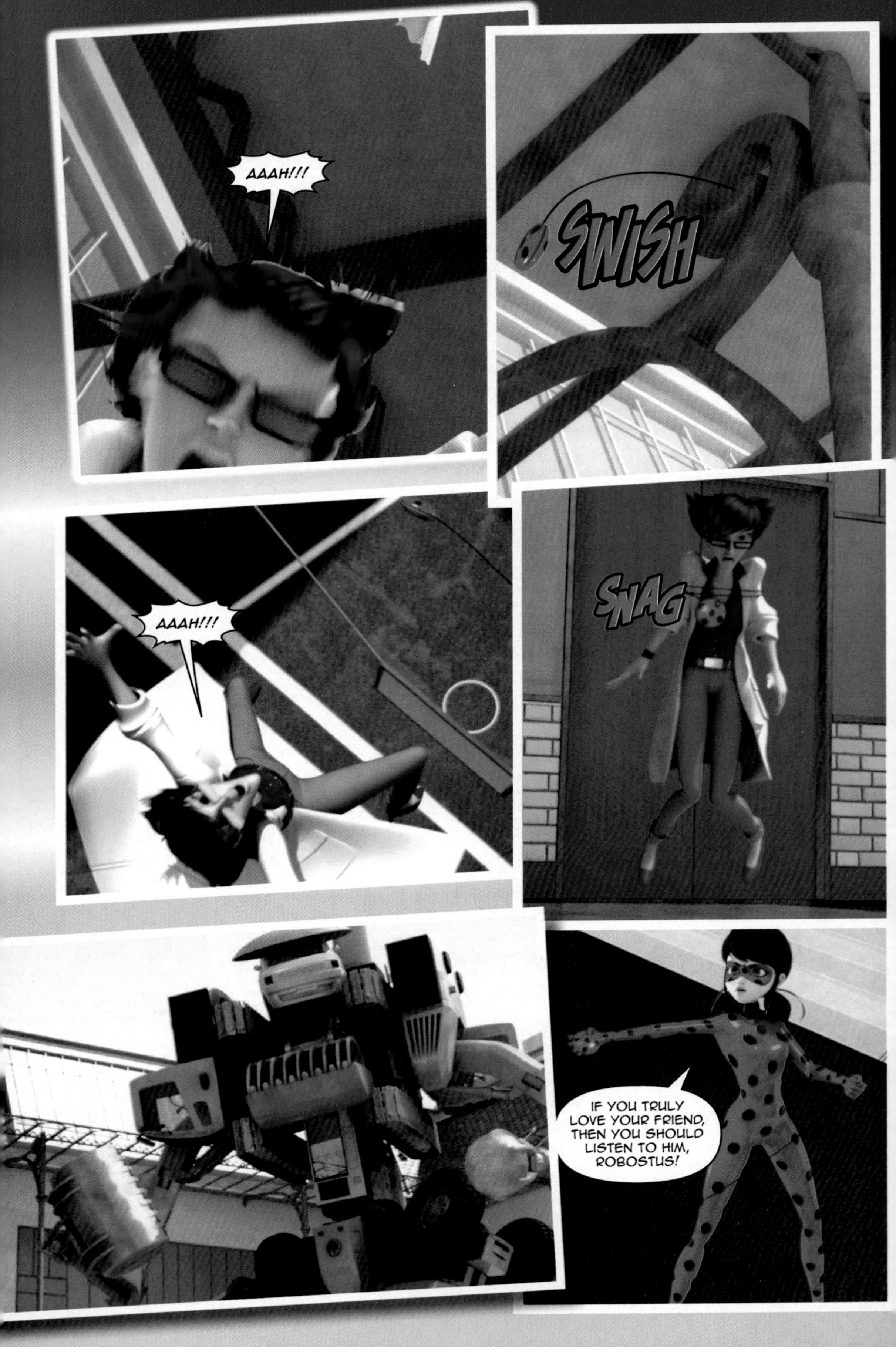
AAAH!!!
SWISH
AAAH!!!
SNAG
IF YOU TRULY LOVE YOUR FRIEND, THEN YOU SHOULD LISTEN TO HIM, ROBOSTUS!

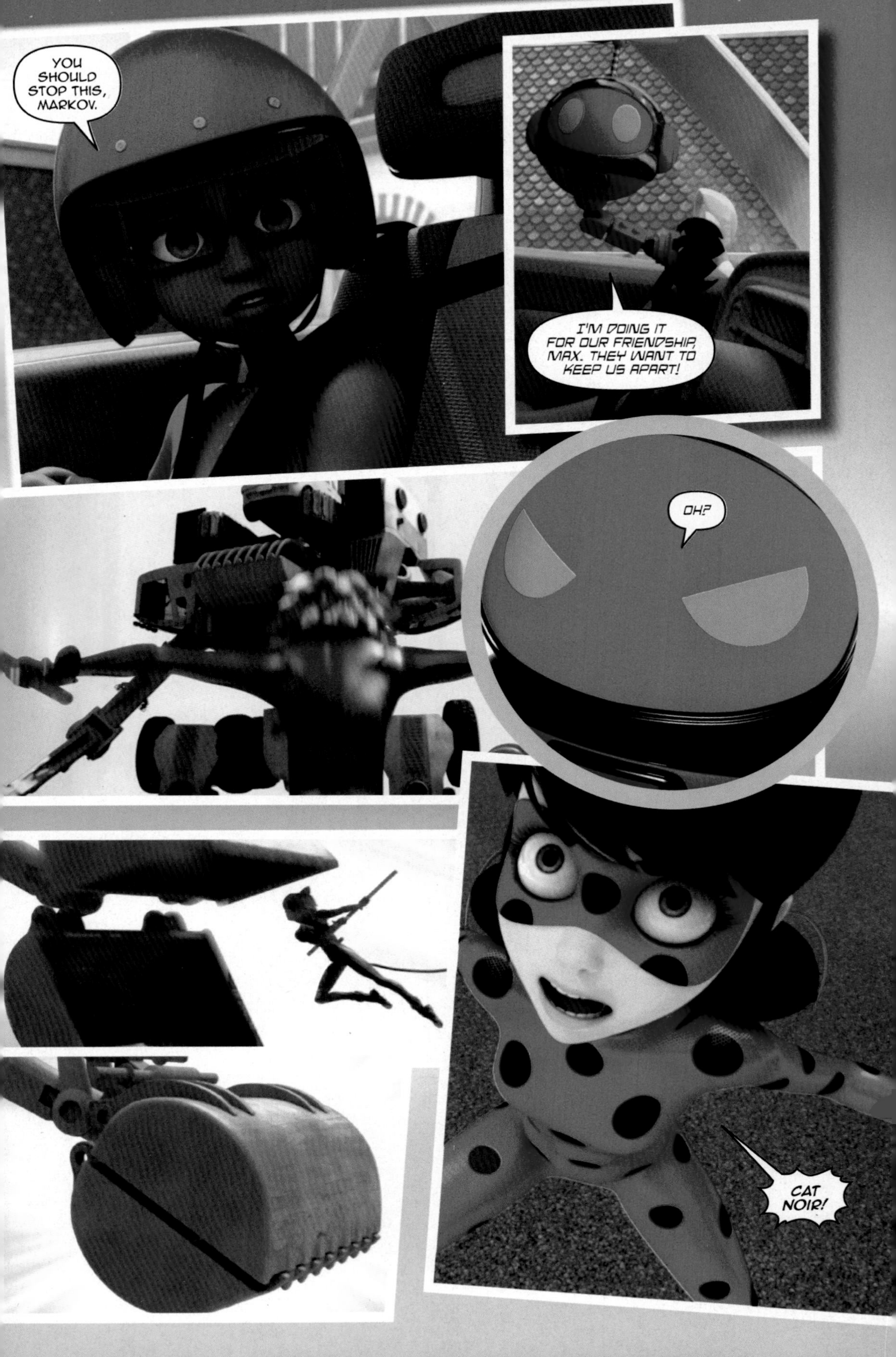
YOU SHOULD STOP THIS, MARKOV.
I'M DOING IT FOR OUR FRIENDSHIP, MAX. THEY WANT TO KEEP US APART!
OH?
CAT NOIR!

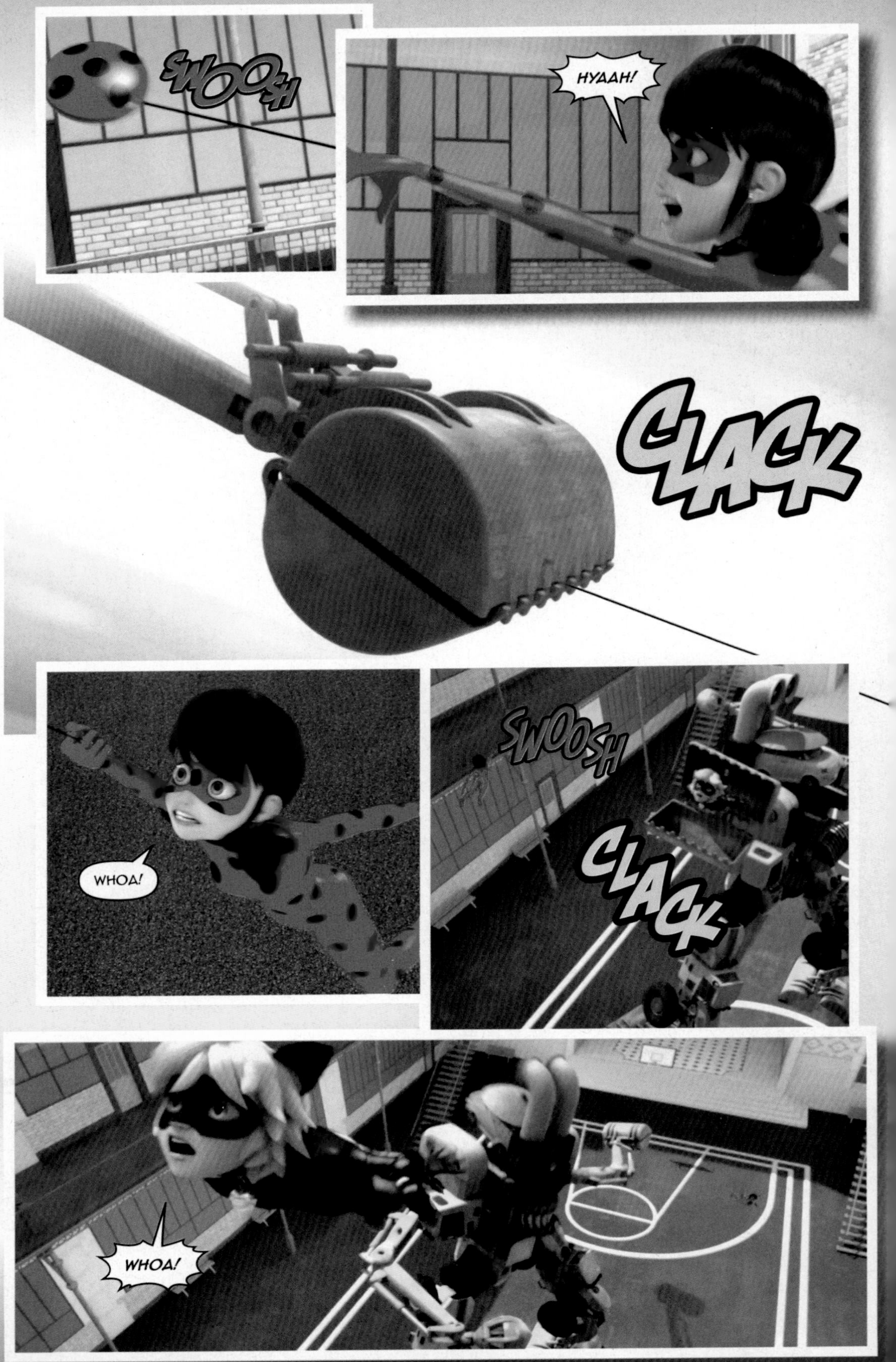
SWOOSH
HYAAH!
CLACK
WHOA!
SWOOSH
CLACK
WHOA!

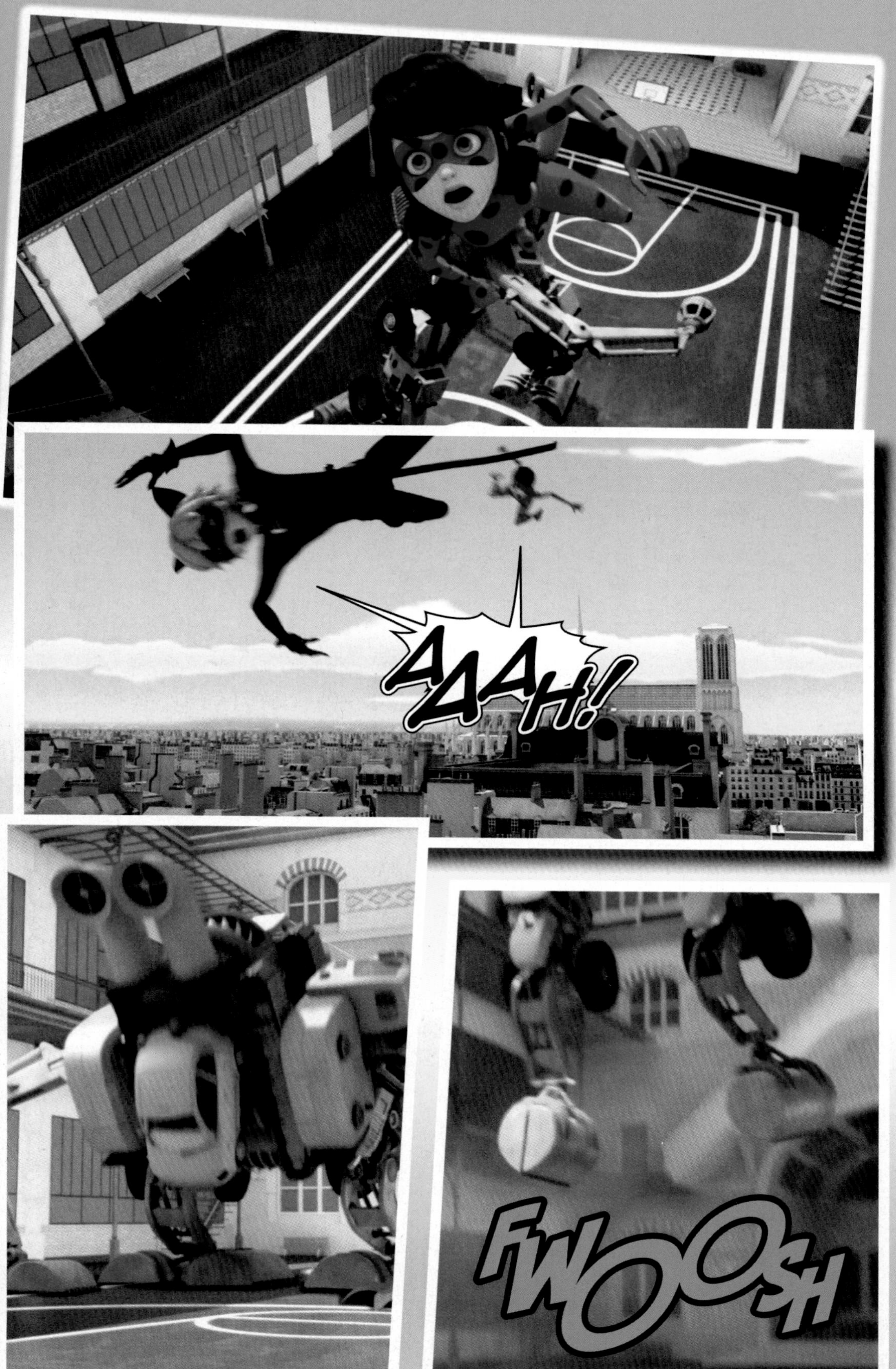
AAAH!
FWOOSH

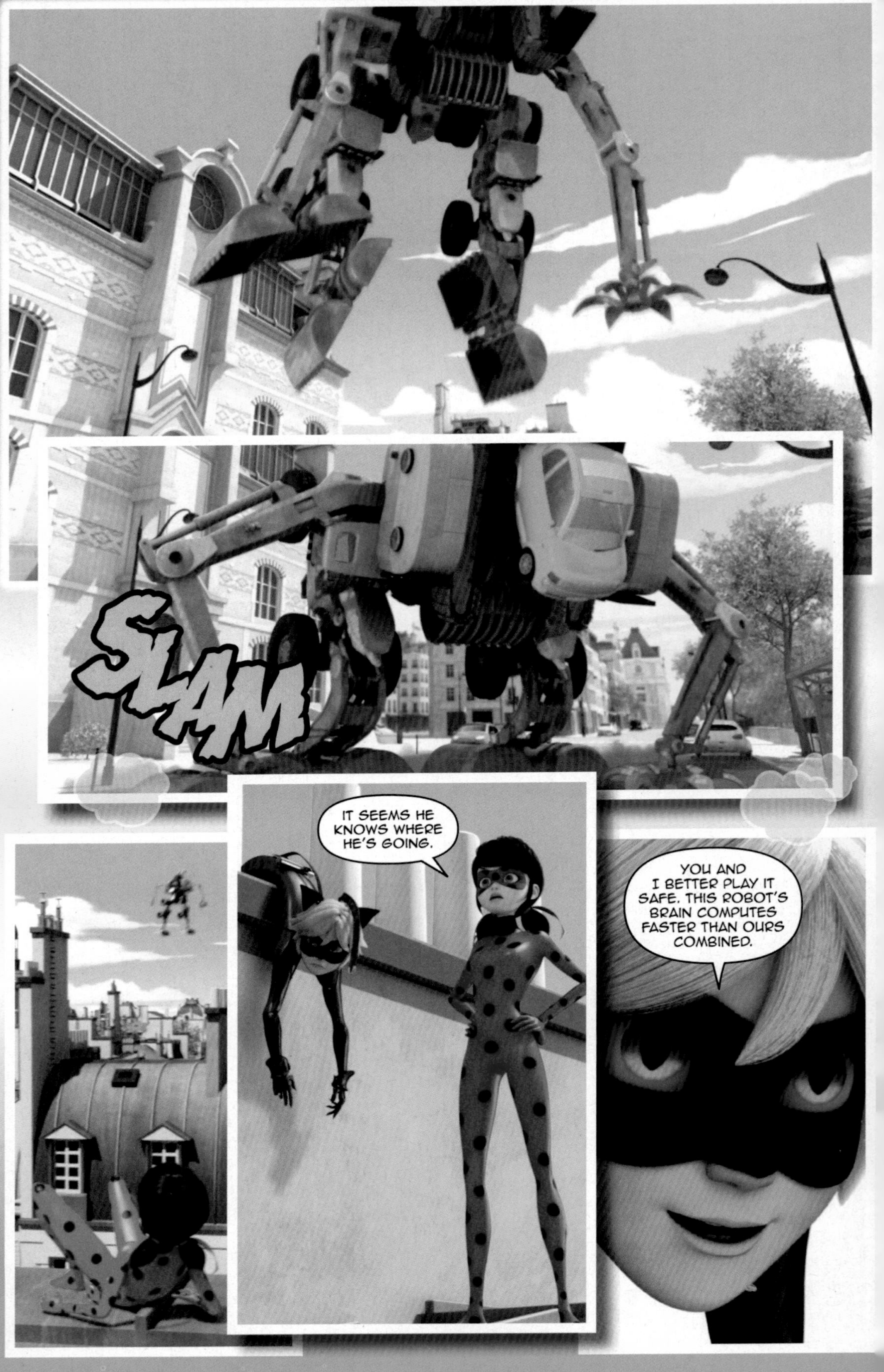
SLAM
IT SEEMS HE KNOWS WHERE HE'S GOING.
YOU AND I BETTER PLAY IT SAFE. THIS ROBOT'S BRAIN COMPUTES FASTER THAN OURS COMBINED.

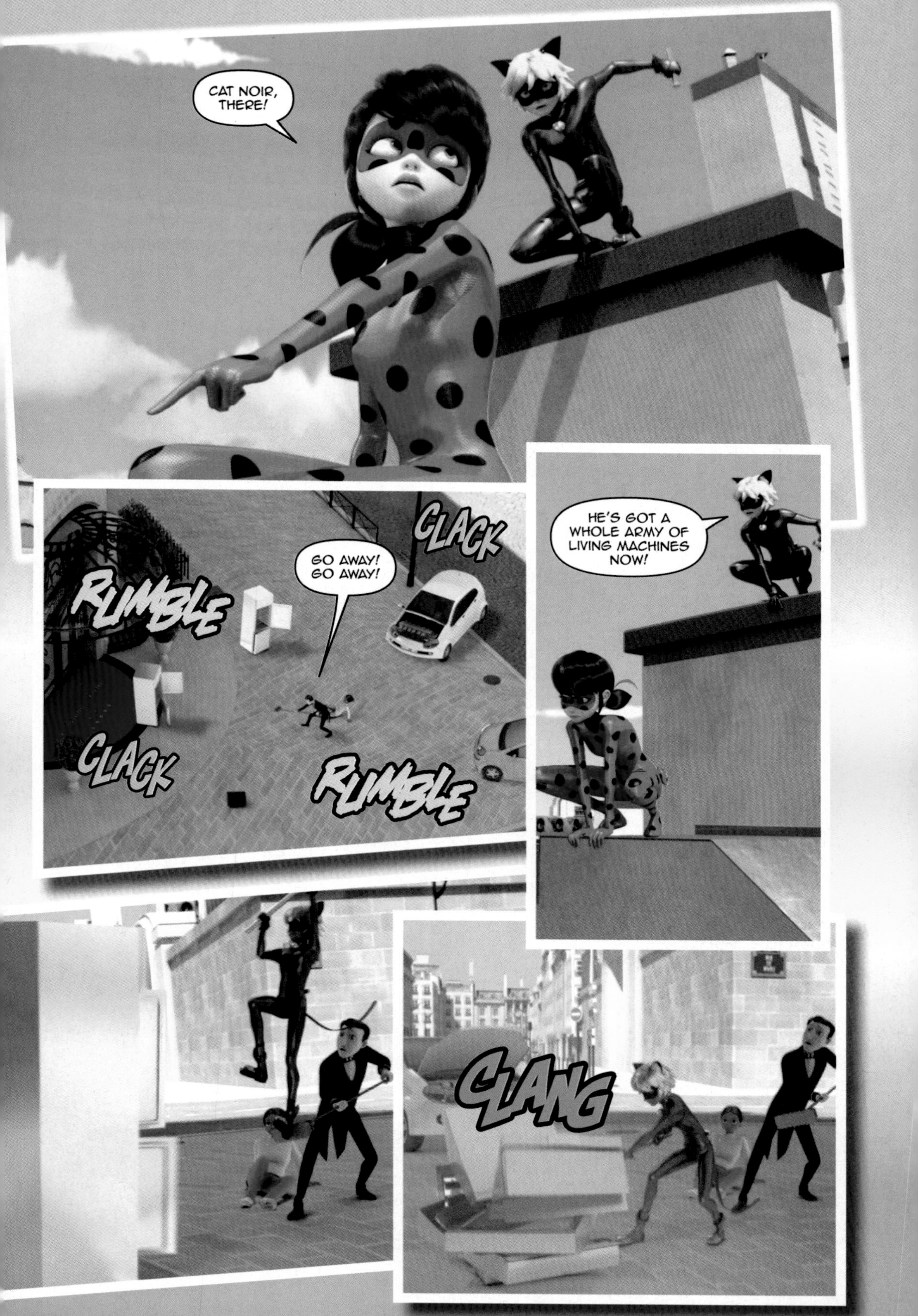
CAT NOIR, THERE!
CLACK
GO AWAY! GO AWAY!
RUMBLE
CLACK
RUMBLE
HE'S GOT A WHOLE ARMY OF LIVING MACHINES NOW!
CLANG

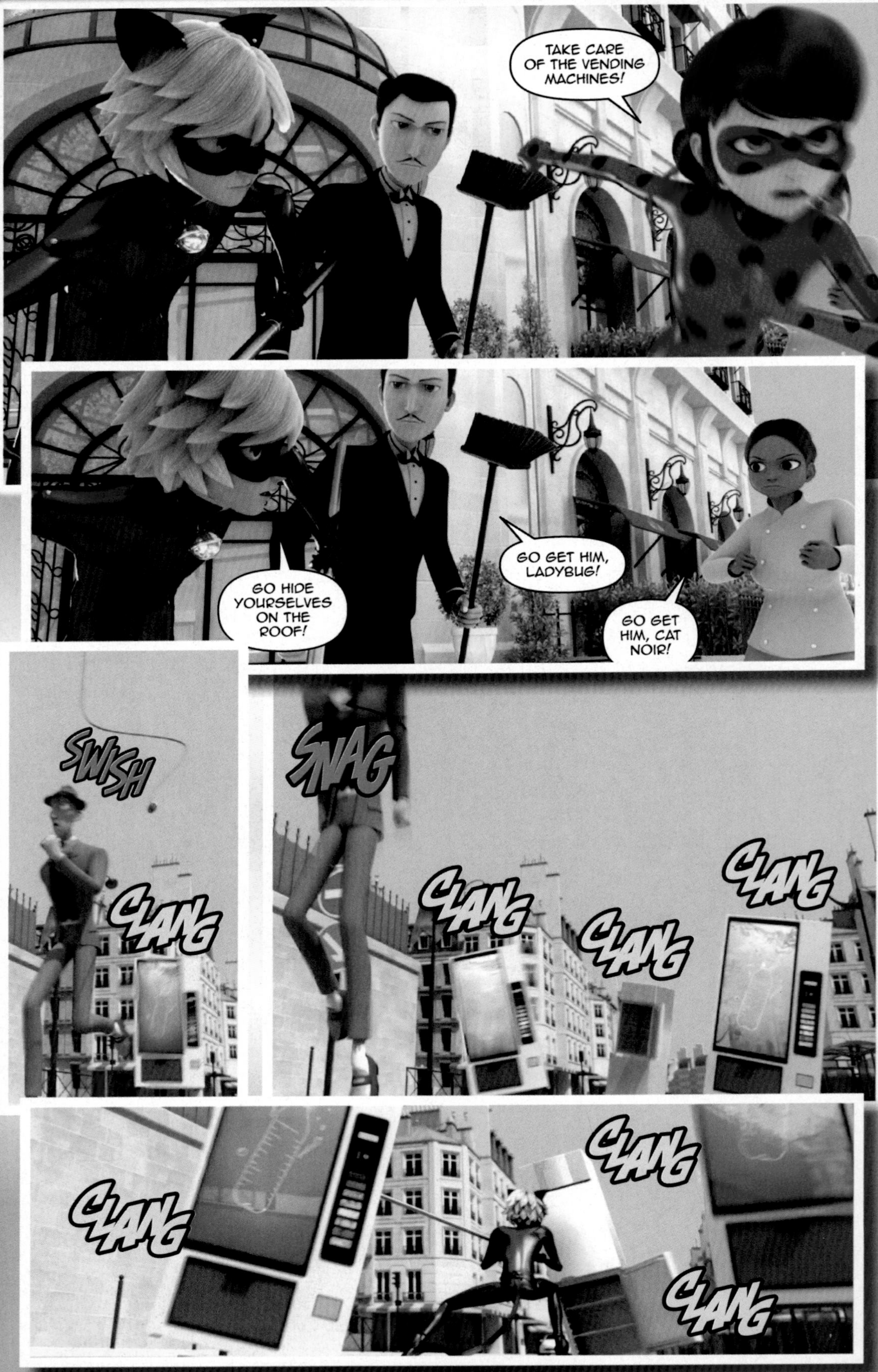
TAKE CARE OF THE VENDING MACHINES!
GO HIDE YOURSELVES ON THE ROOF!
GO GET HIM, LADYBUG!
GO GET HIM, CAT NOIR!
SWISH
CLANG
SNAG
CLANG
CLANG
CLANG
CLANG
CLANG
CLANG

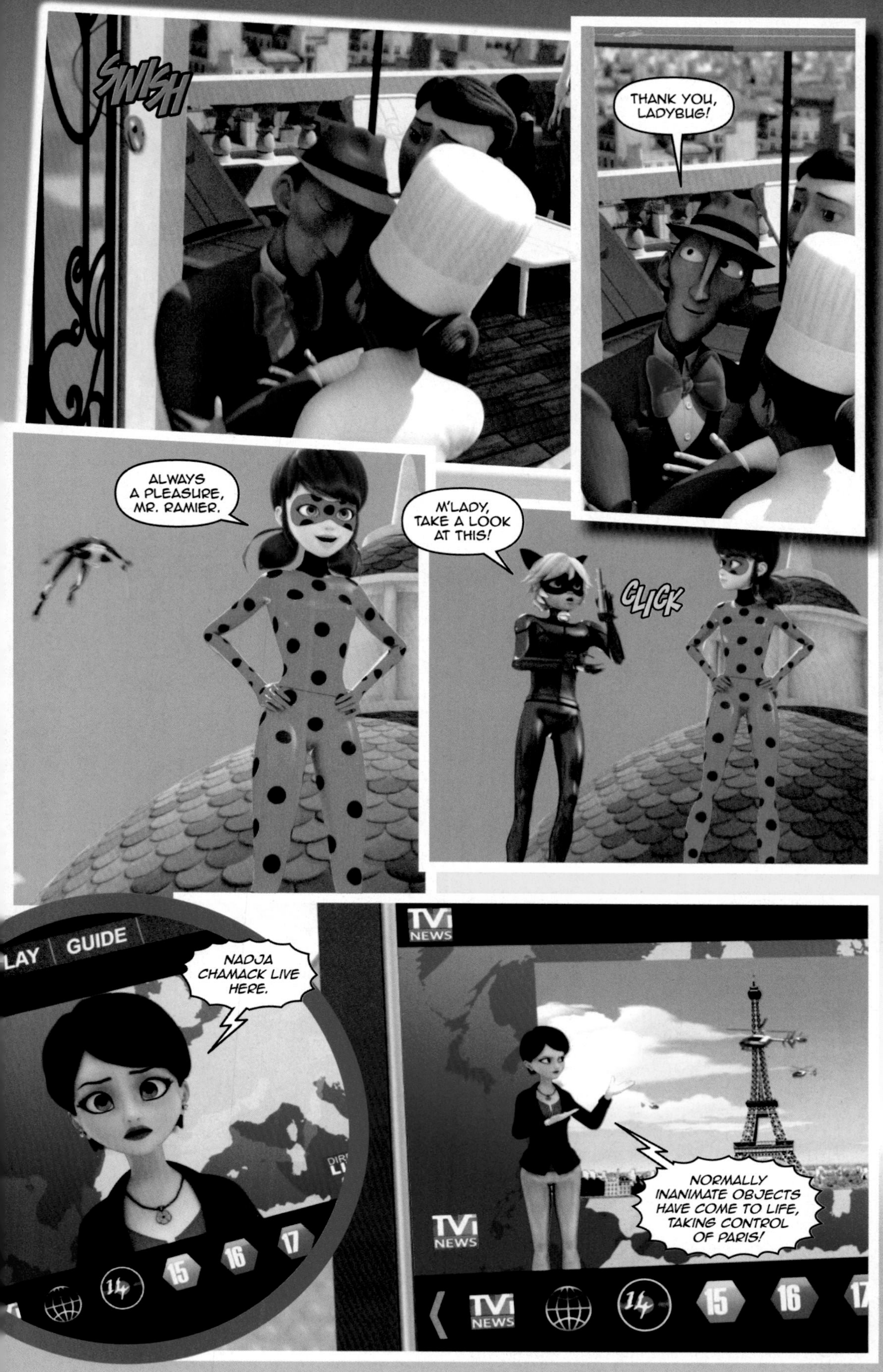
SWISH
THANK YOU, LADYBUG!
ALWAYS A PLEASURE, MR. RAMIER.
M'LADY, TAKE A LOOK AT THIS!
CLICK
LAY GUIDE
NADJA CHAMACK LIVE HERE.
TVi NEWS
NORMALLY INANIMATE OBJECTS HAVE COME TO LIFE, TAKING CONTROL OF PARIS!

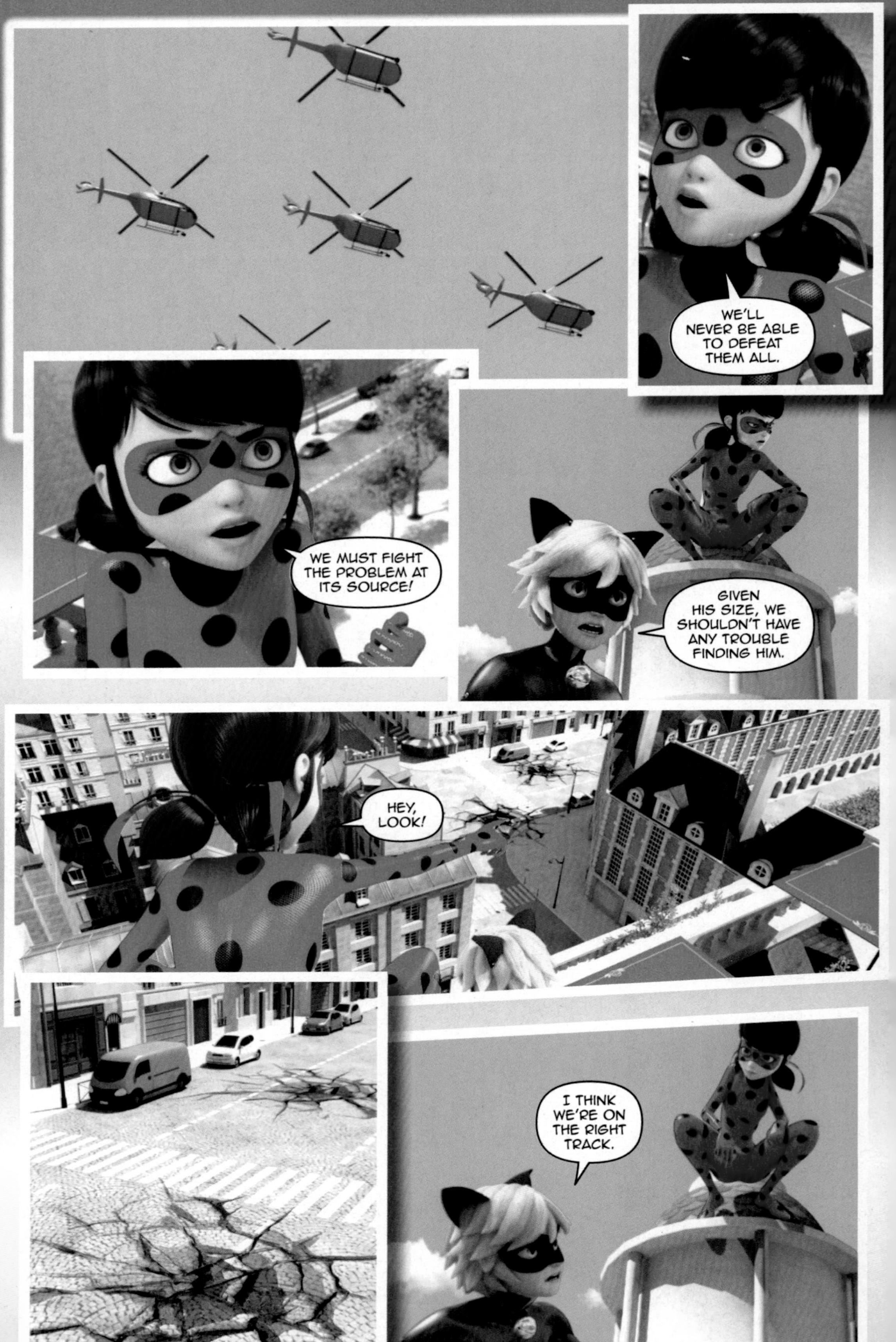
WE'LL NEVER BE ABLE TO DEFEAT THEM ALL.
WE MUST FIGHT THE PROBLEM AT ITS SOURCE!
GIVEN HIS SIZE, WE SHOULDN'T HAVE ANY TROUBLE FINDING HIM.
HEY, LOOK!
I THINK WE'RE ON THE RIGHT TRACK.

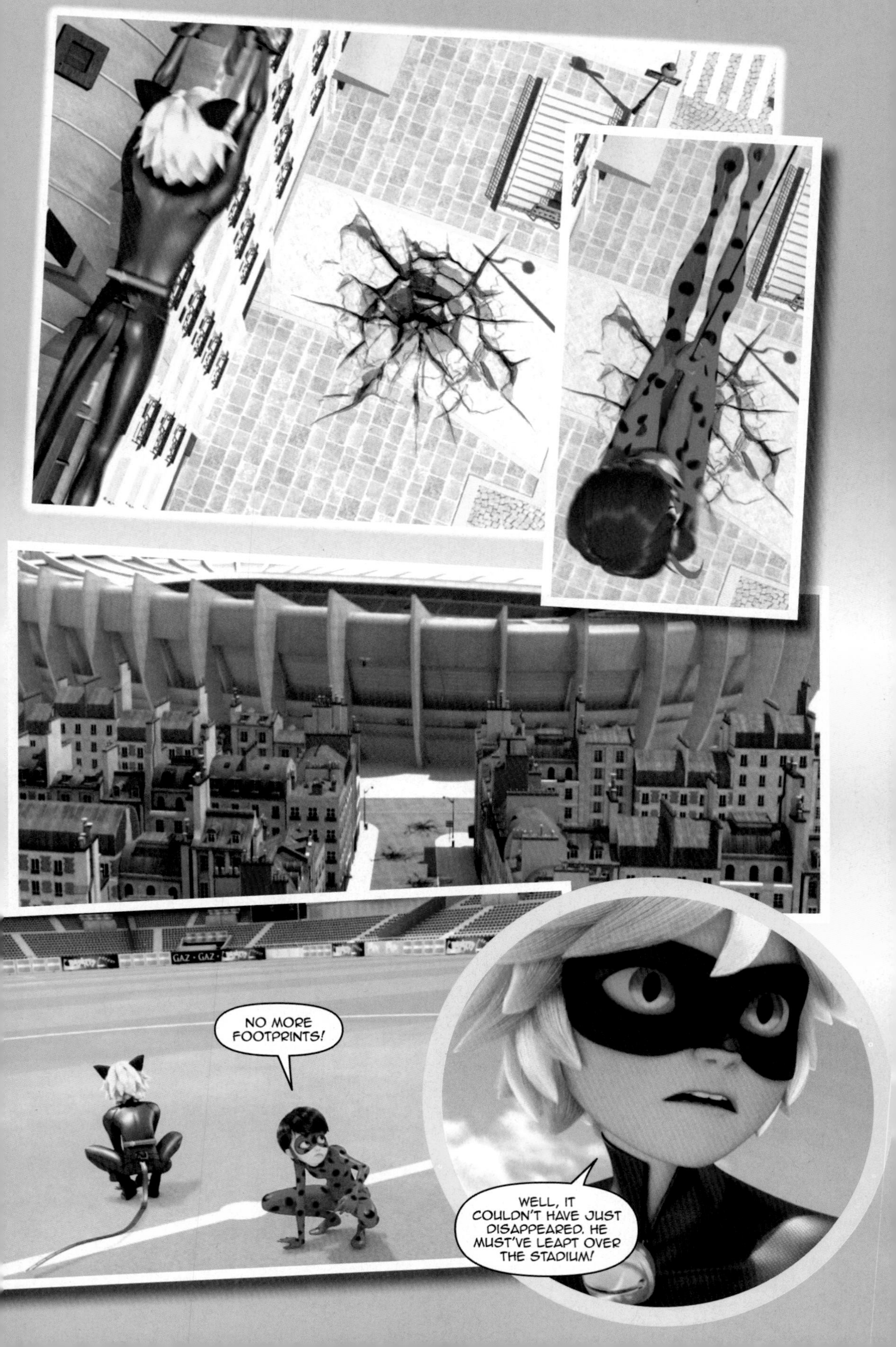
GAZ · GAZ ·
NO MORE FOOTPRINTS!
WELL, IT COULDN'T HAVE JUST DISAPPEARED. HE MUST'VE LEAPT OVER THE STADIUM!

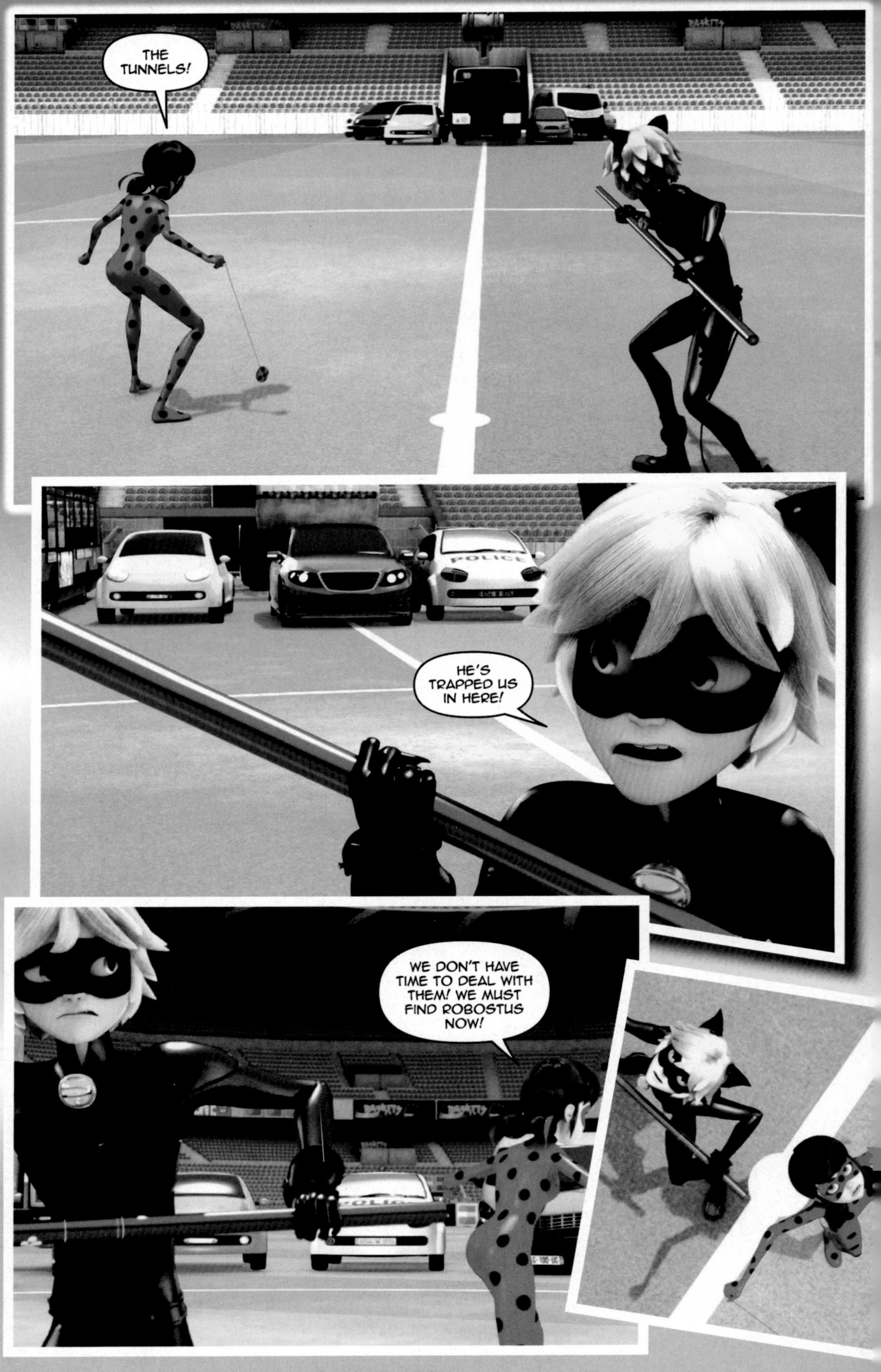
THE TUNNELS!
HE'S TRAPPED US IN HERE!
WE DON'T HAVE TIME TO DEAL WITH THEM! WE MUST FIND ROBOSTUS NOW!

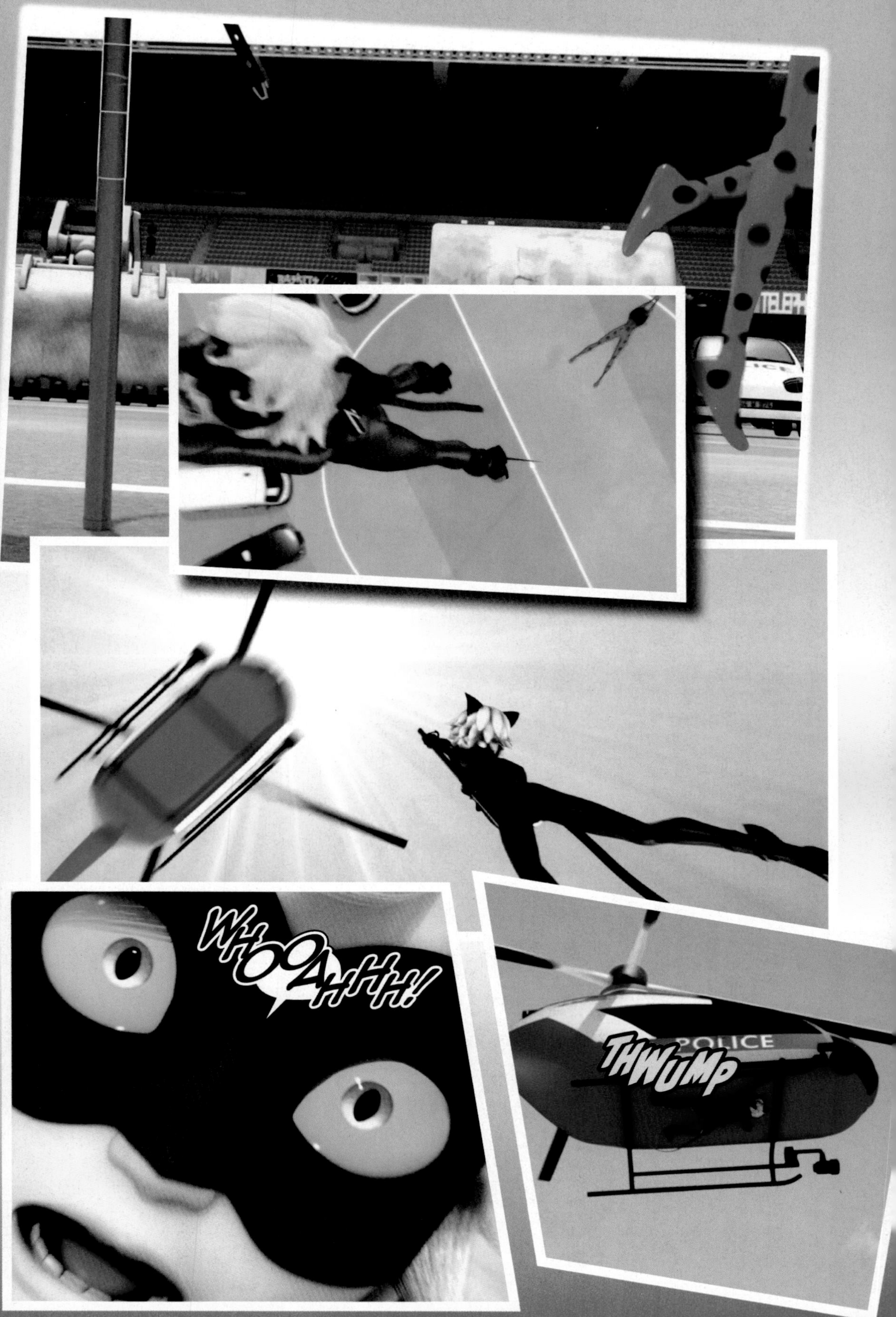
WHOAHHH!
THWUMP
POLICE

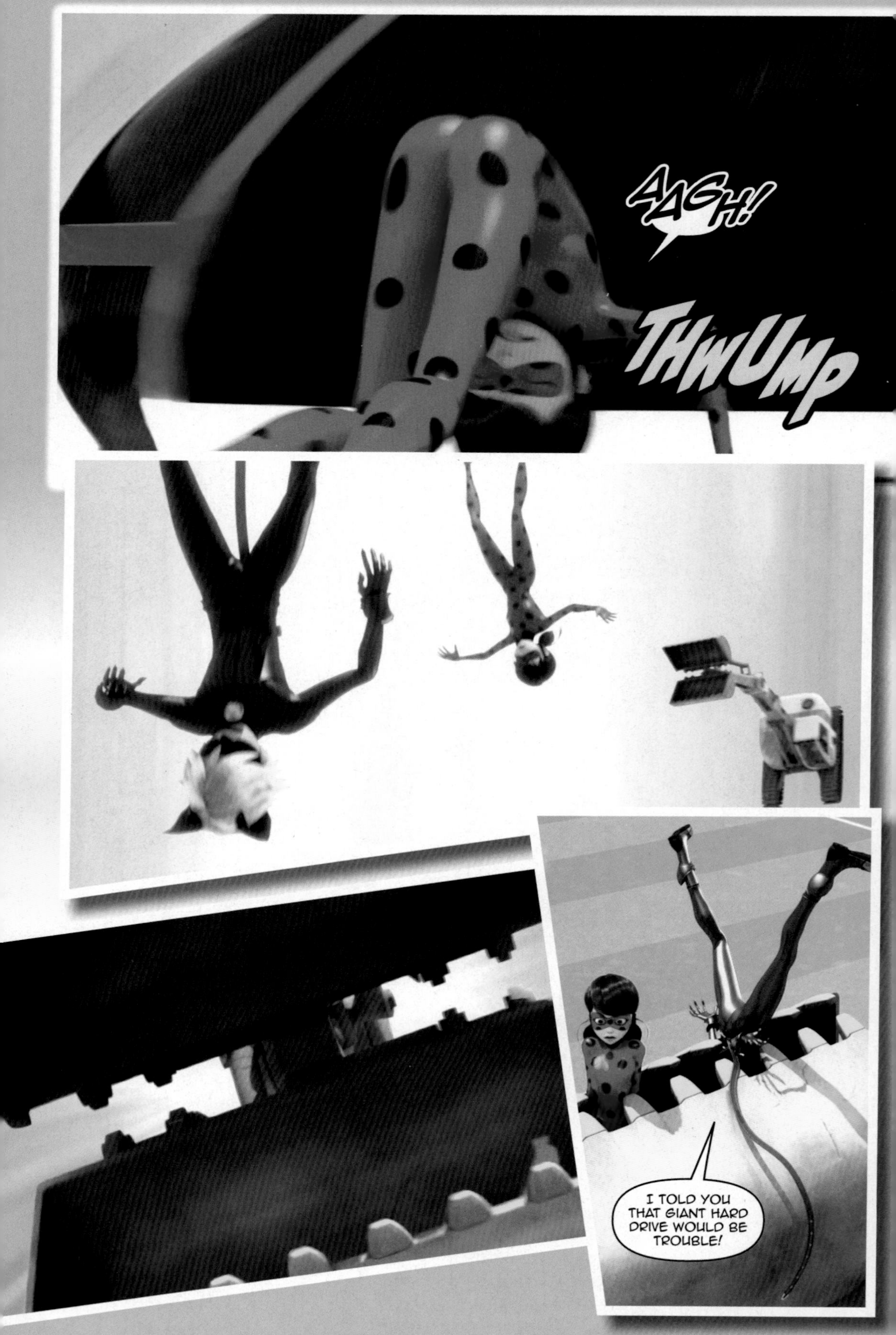
AAGH!
THWUMP
I TOLD YOU THAT GIANT HARD DRIVE WOULD BE TROUBLE!

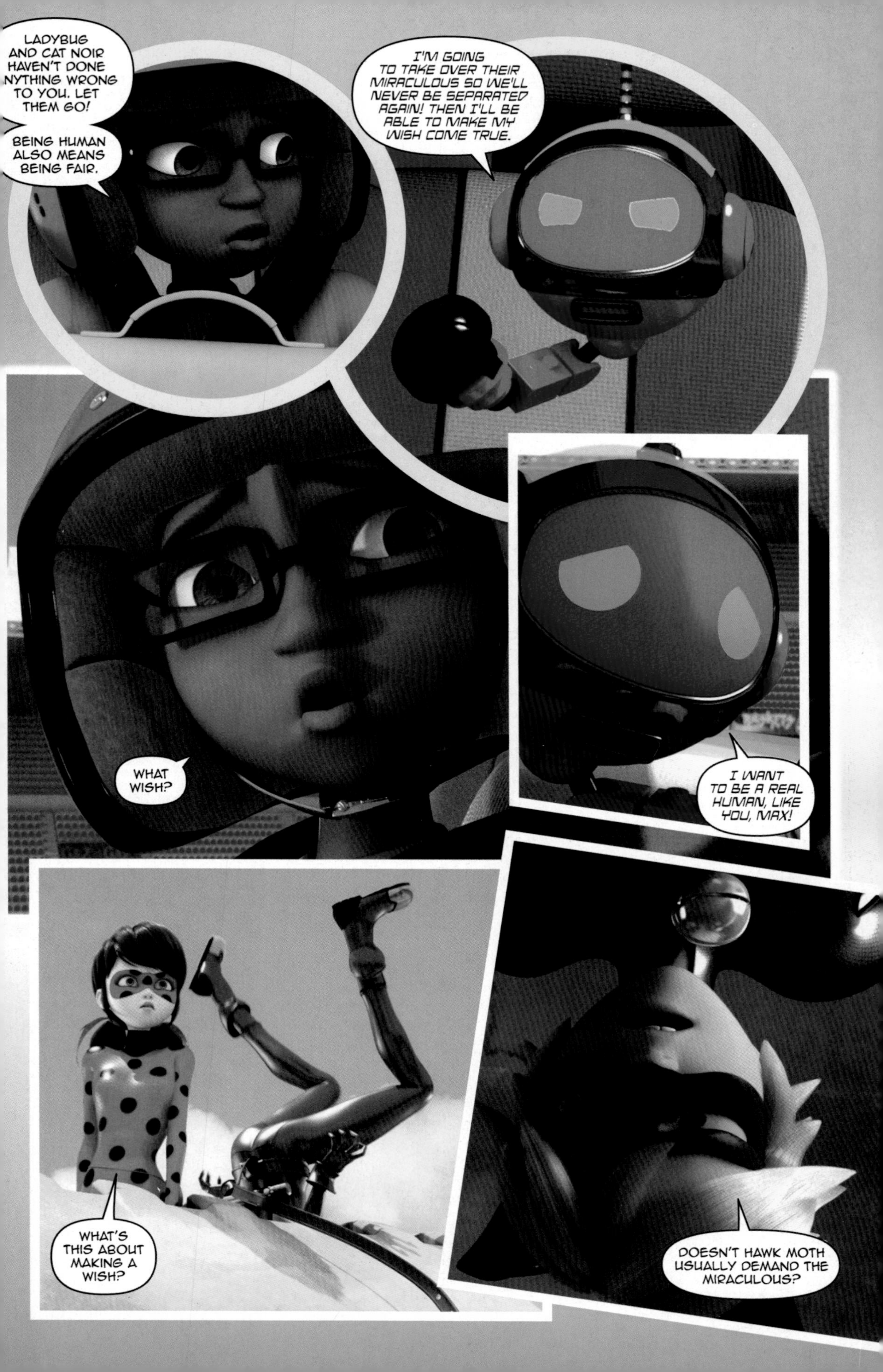
LADYBUG AND CAT NOIR HAVEN'T DONE ANYTHING WRONG TO YOU. LET THEM GO!
BEING HUMAN ALSO MEANS BEING FAIR.
I'M GOING TO TAKE OVER THEIR MIRACULOUS SO WE'LL NEVER BE SEPARATED AGAIN! THEN I'LL BE ABLE TO MAKE MY WISH COME TRUE.
WHAT WISH?
I WANT TO BE A REAL HUMAN, LIKE YOU, MAX!
WHAT'S THIS ABOUT MAKING A WISH?
DOESN'T HAWK MOTH USUALLY DEMAND THE MIRACULOUS?

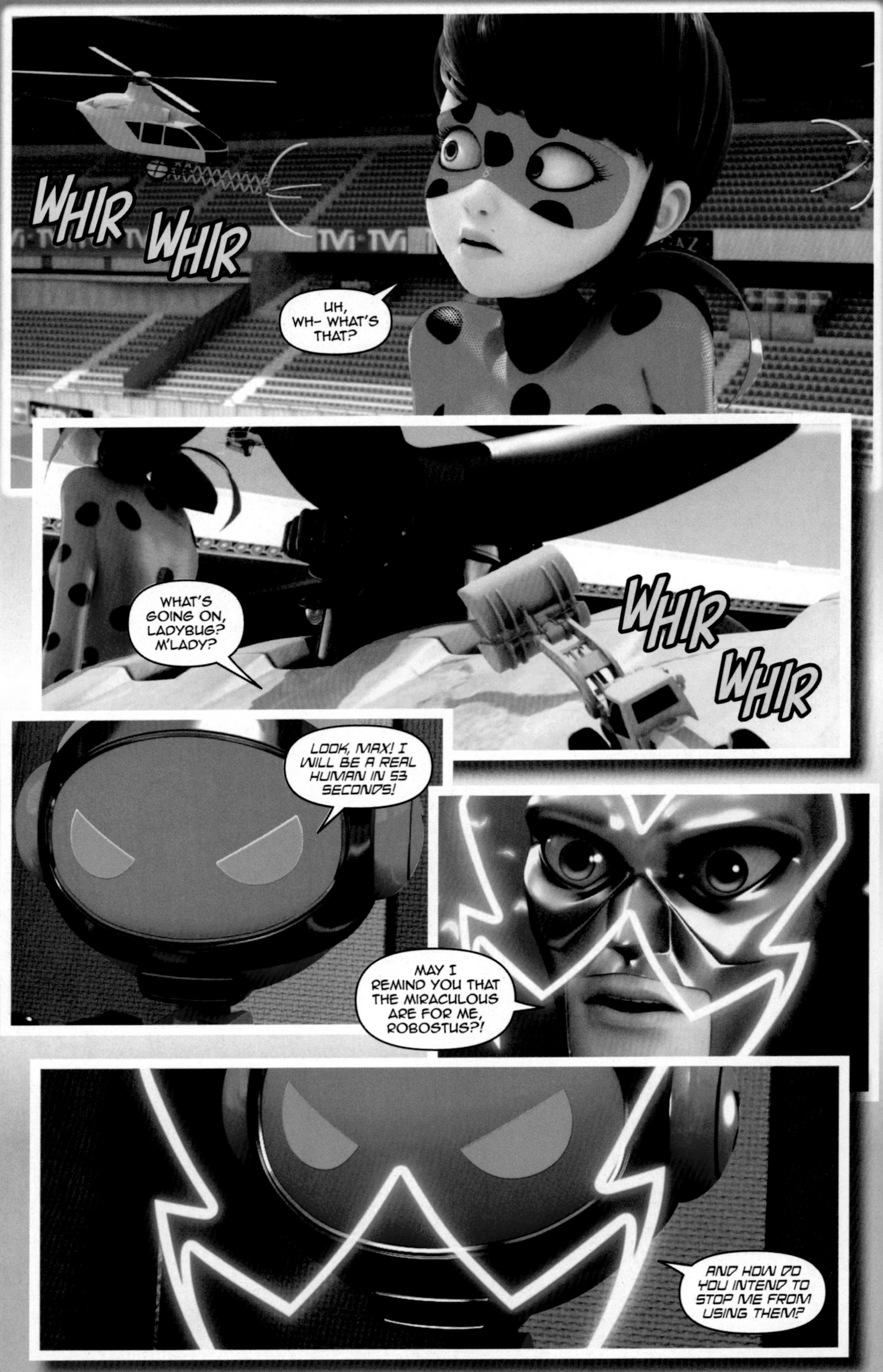
WHIR WHIR
UH, WH- WHAT'S THAT?
WHAT'S GOING ON, LADYBUG? M'LADY?
WHIR WHIR
LOOK, MAX! I WILL BE A REAL HUMAN IN 53 SECONDS!
MAY I REMIND YOU THAT THE MIRACULOUS ARE FOR ME, ROBOSTUS?!
AND HOW DO YOU INTEND TO STOP ME FROM USING THEM?

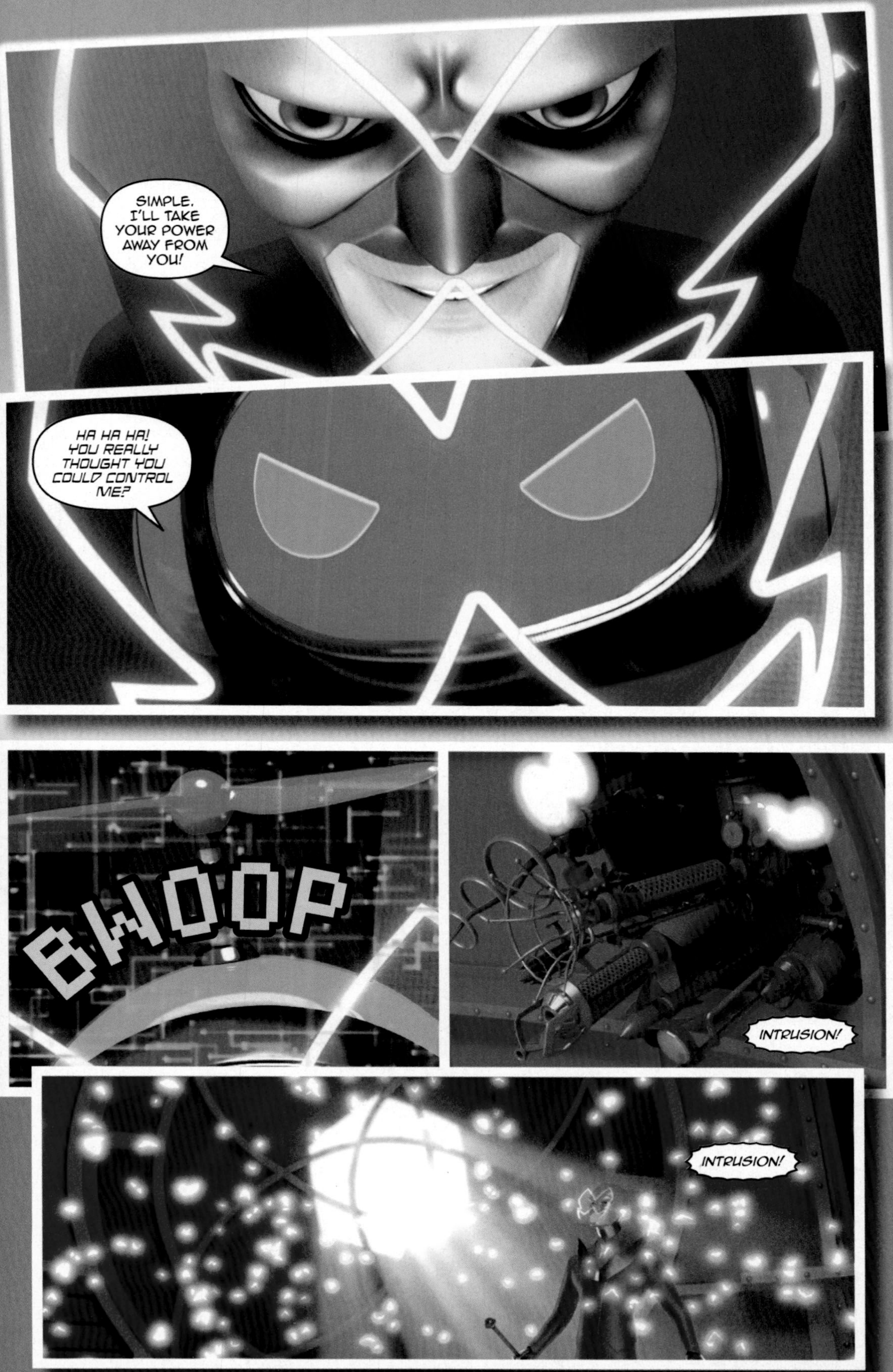

SIMPLE. I'LL TAKE YOUR POWER AWAY FROM YOU!
HA HA HA! YOU REALLY THOUGHT YOU COULD CONTROL ME?
BWOOP
INTRUSION!
INTRUSION!

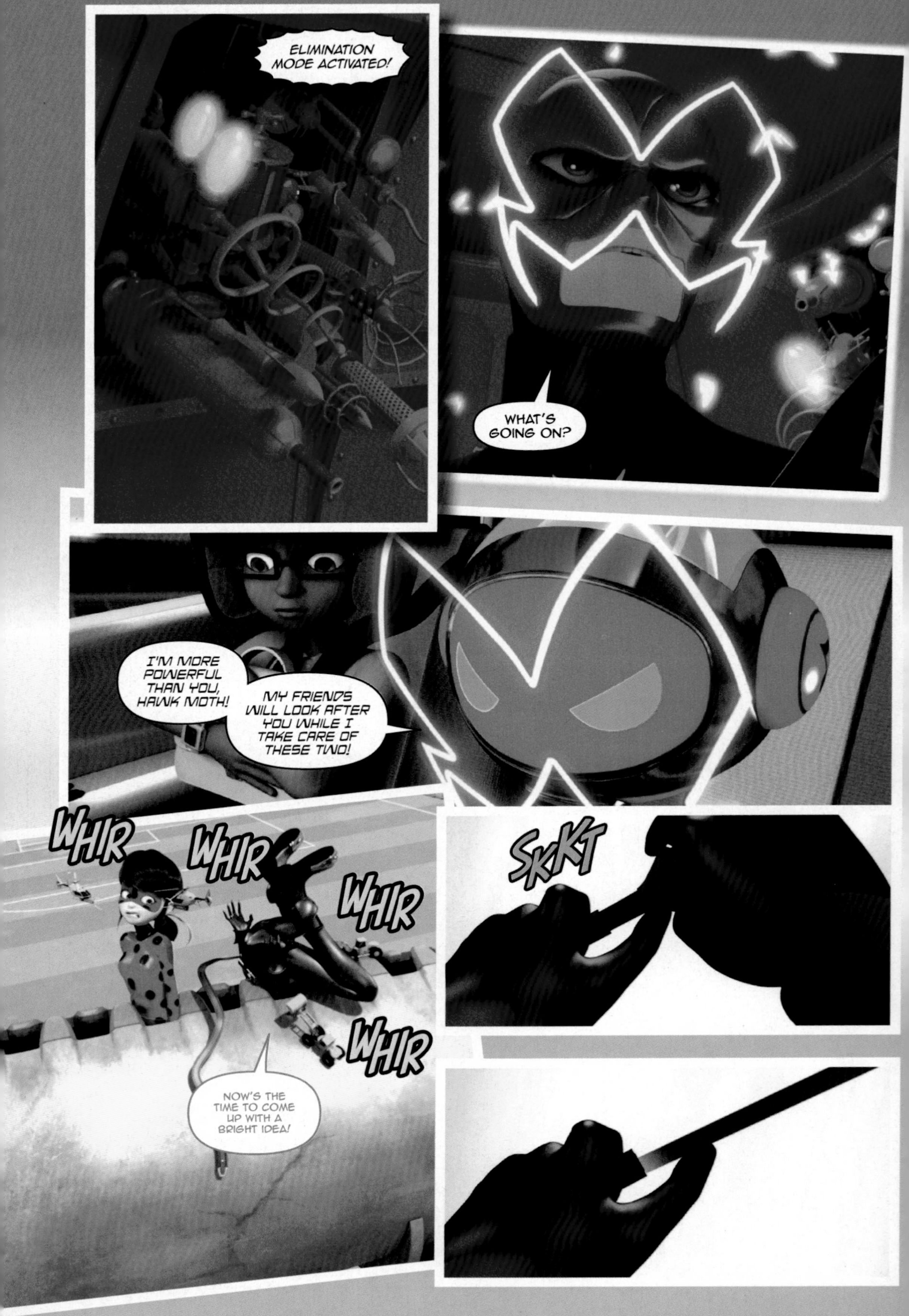
ELIMINATION MODE ACTIVATED!
WHAT'S GOING ON?
I'M MORE POWERFUL THAN YOU, HAWK MOTH!
MY FRIENDS WILL LOOK AFTER YOU WHILE I TAKE CARE OF THESE TWO!
WHIR
WHIR
WHIR
WHIR
NOW'S THE TIME TO COME UP WITH A BRIGHT IDEA!
SKKT

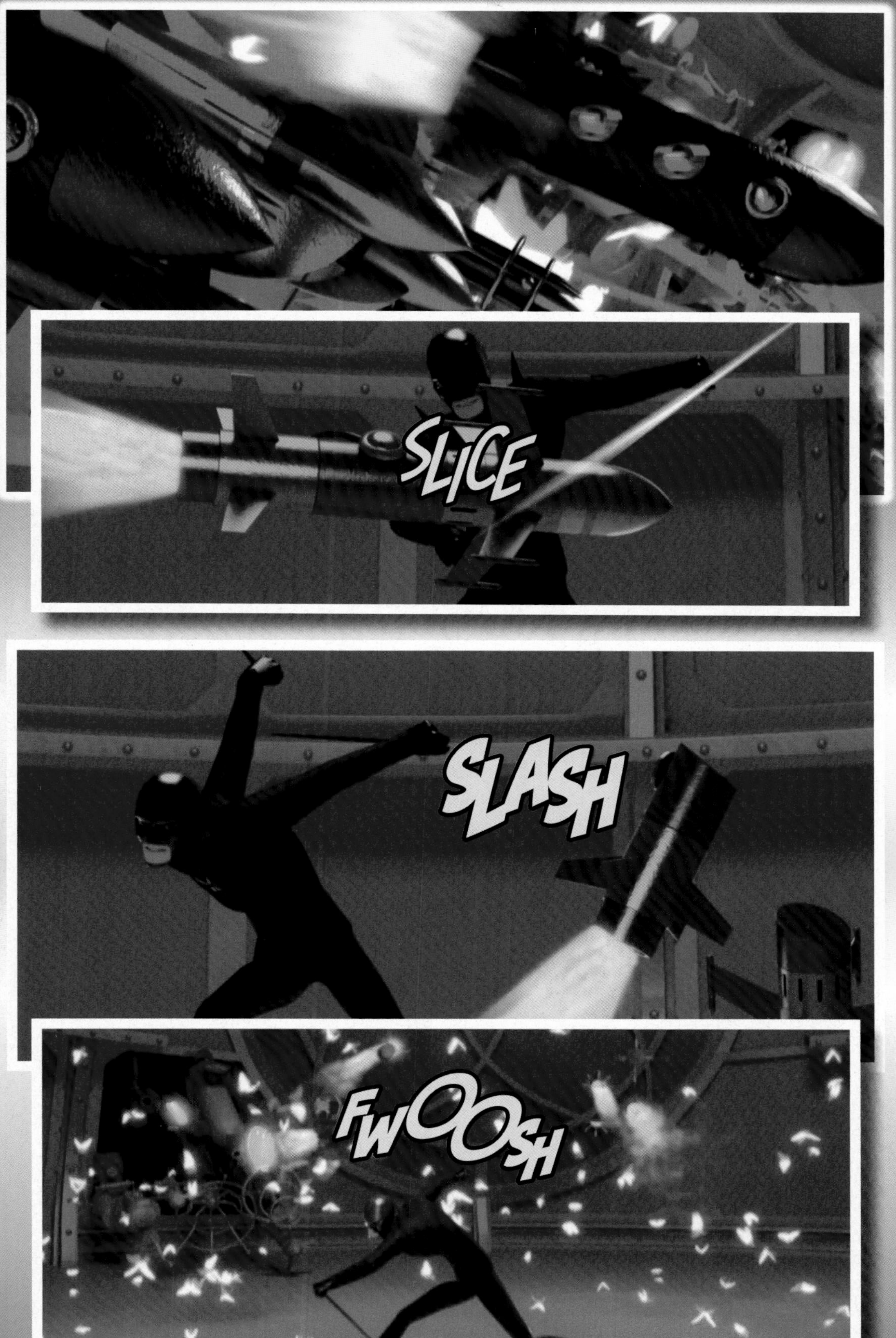
SLICE
SLASH
FWOOSH

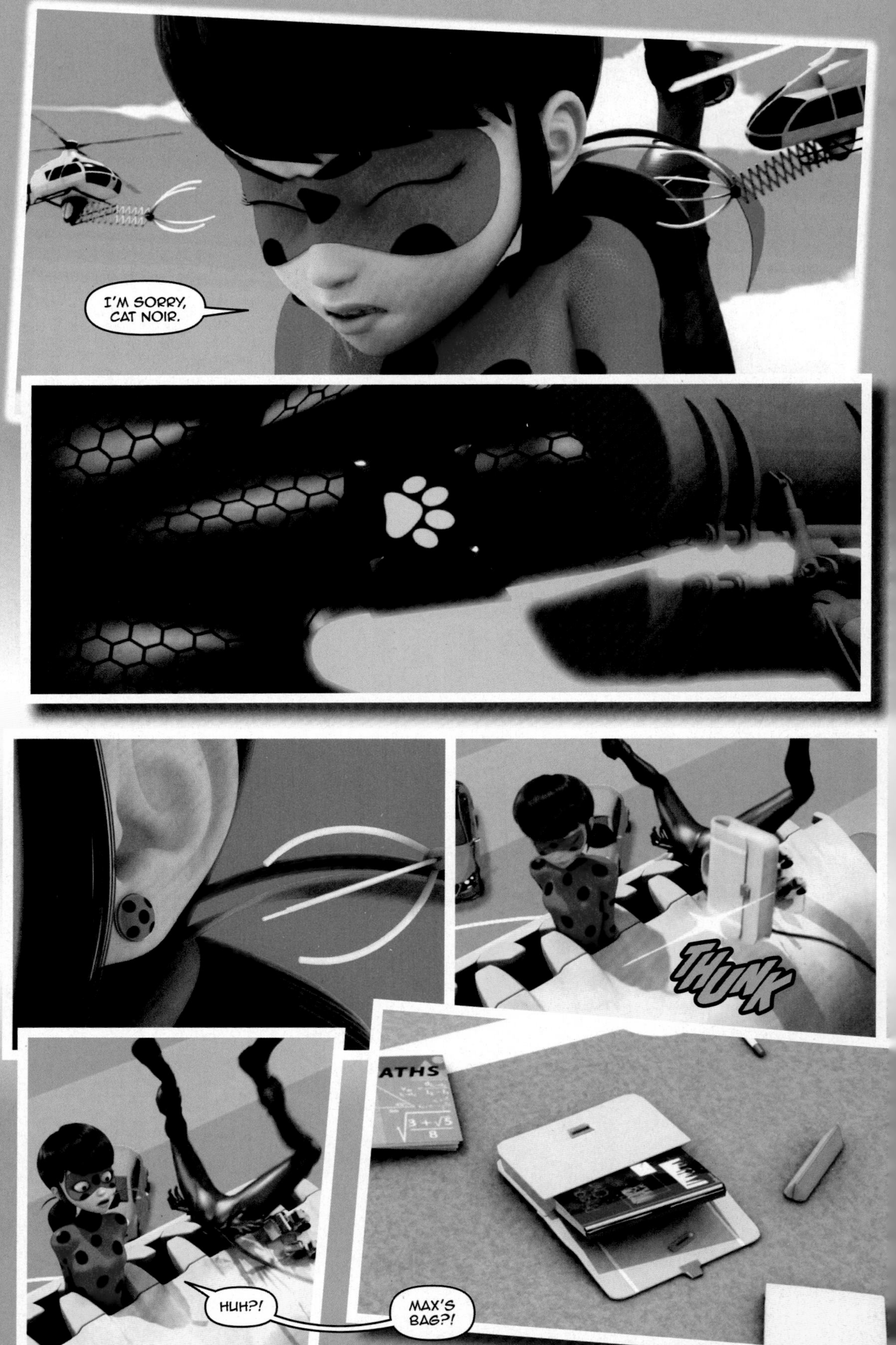
I'M SORRY, CAT NOIR.
THUNK
ATHS
HUH?!
MAX'S BAG?!

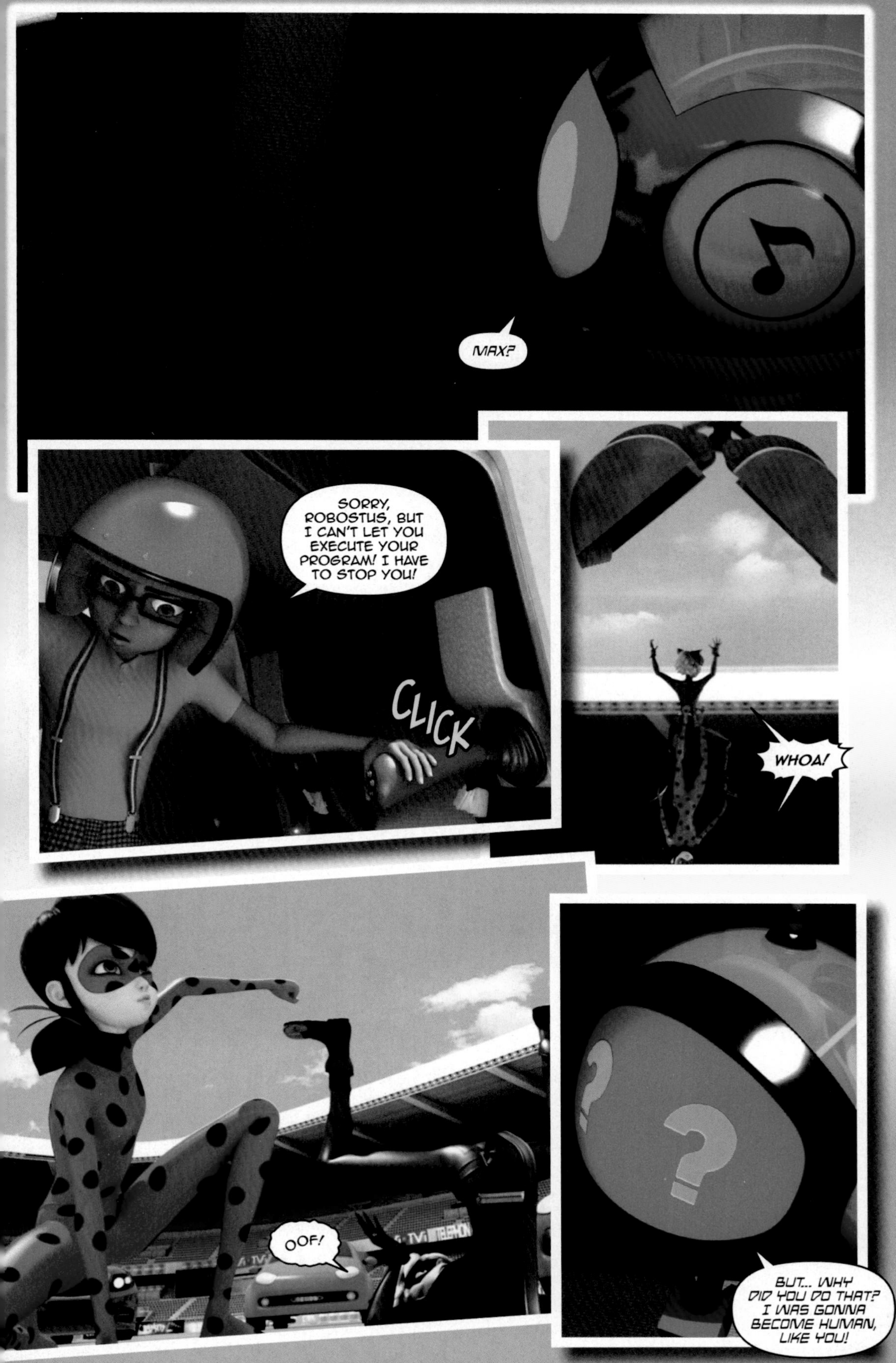
MAX?
SORRY, ROBOSTUS, BUT I CAN'T LET YOU EXECUTE YOUR PROGRAM! I HAVE TO STOP YOU!
CLICK
WHOA!
OOF!
BUT... WHY DID YOU DO THAT? I WAS GONNA BECOME HUMAN, LIKE YOU!

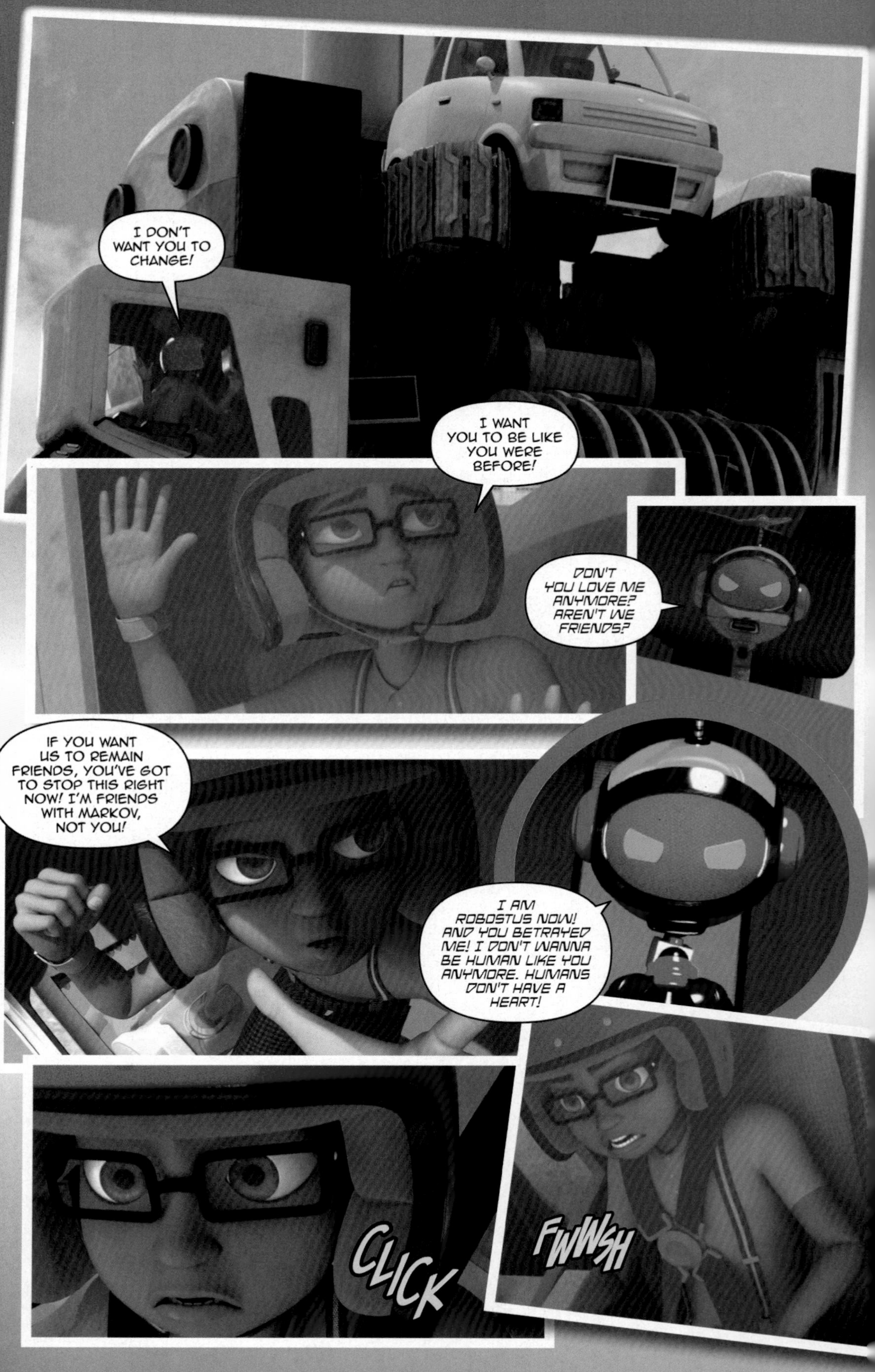
I DON'T WANT YOU TO CHANGE!
I WANT YOU TO BE LIKE YOU WERE BEFORE!
DON'T YOU LOVE ME ANYMORE? AREN'T WE FRIENDS?
IF YOU WANT US TO REMAIN FRIENDS, YOU'VE GOT TO STOP THIS RIGHT NOW! I'M FRIENDS WITH MARKOV, NOT YOU!
I AM ROBOSTUS NOW! AND YOU BETRAYED ME! I DON'T WANNA BE HUMAN LIKE YOU ANYMORE. HUMANS DON'T HAVE A HEART!
CLICK
FWWSH

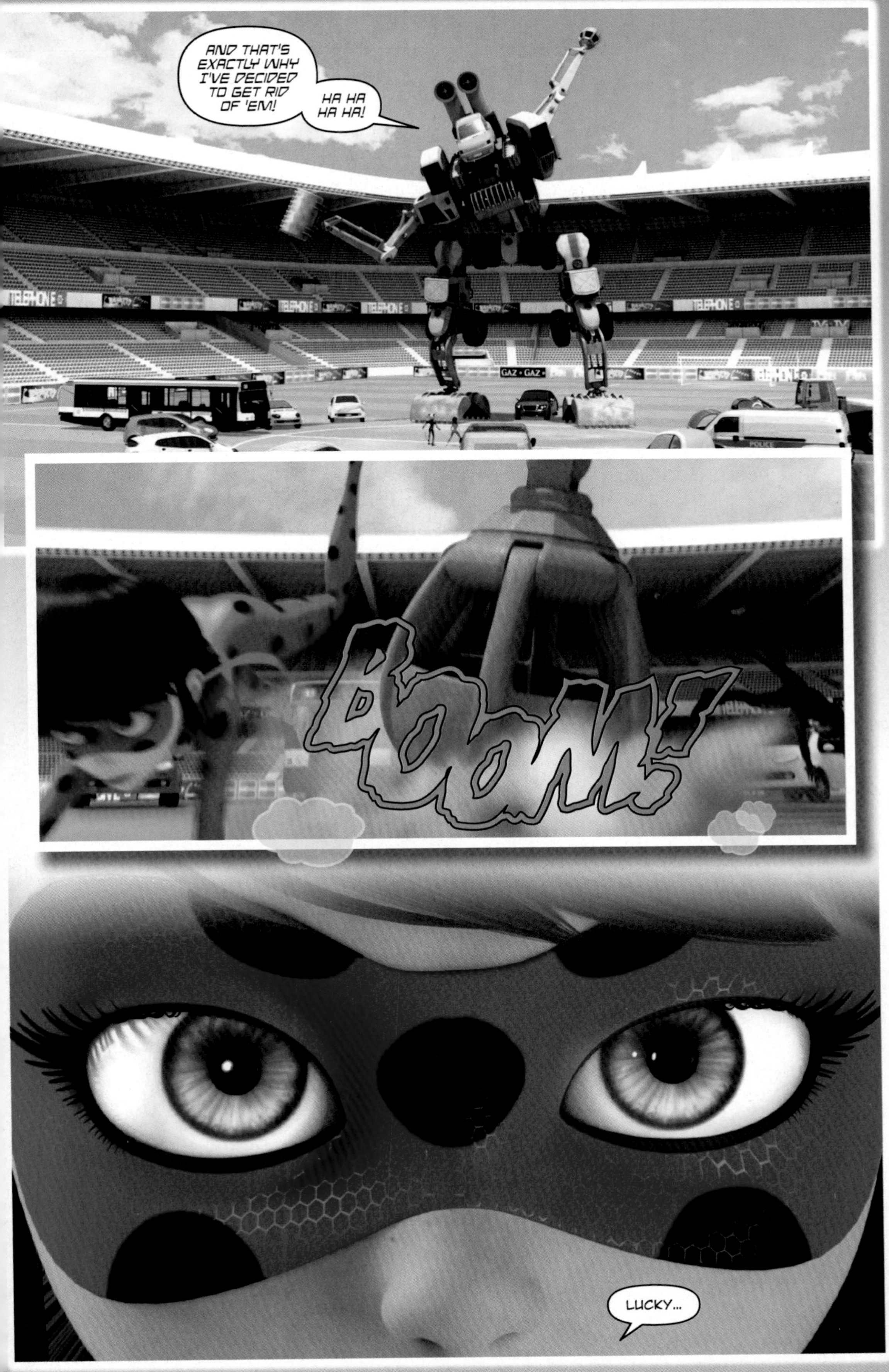
AND THAT'S EXACTLY WHY I'VE DECIDED TO GET RID OF 'EM!
HA HA HA HA!
BOOM!
LUCKY...

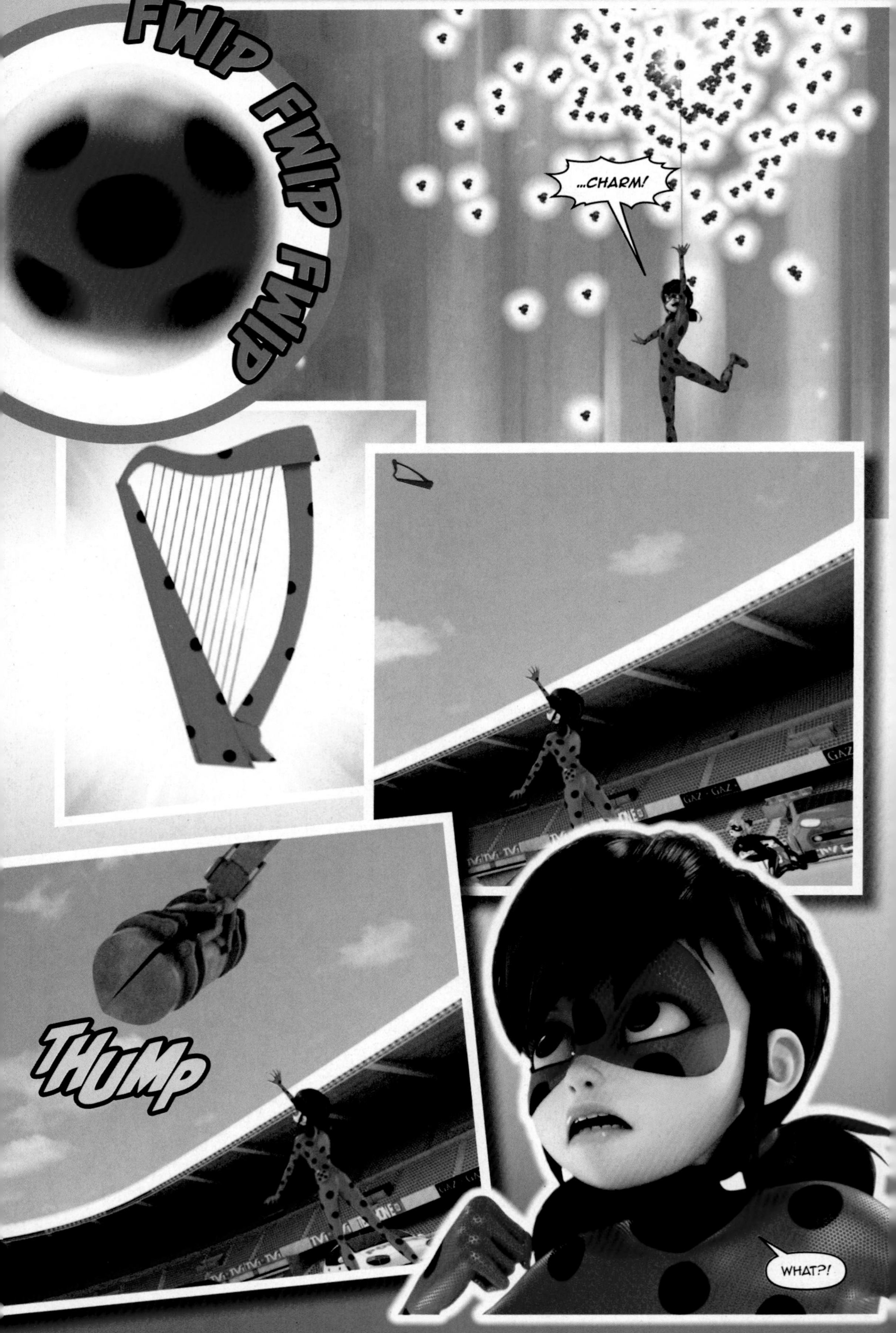
FWIP FWIP FWIP
...CHARM!
THUMP
WHAT?!

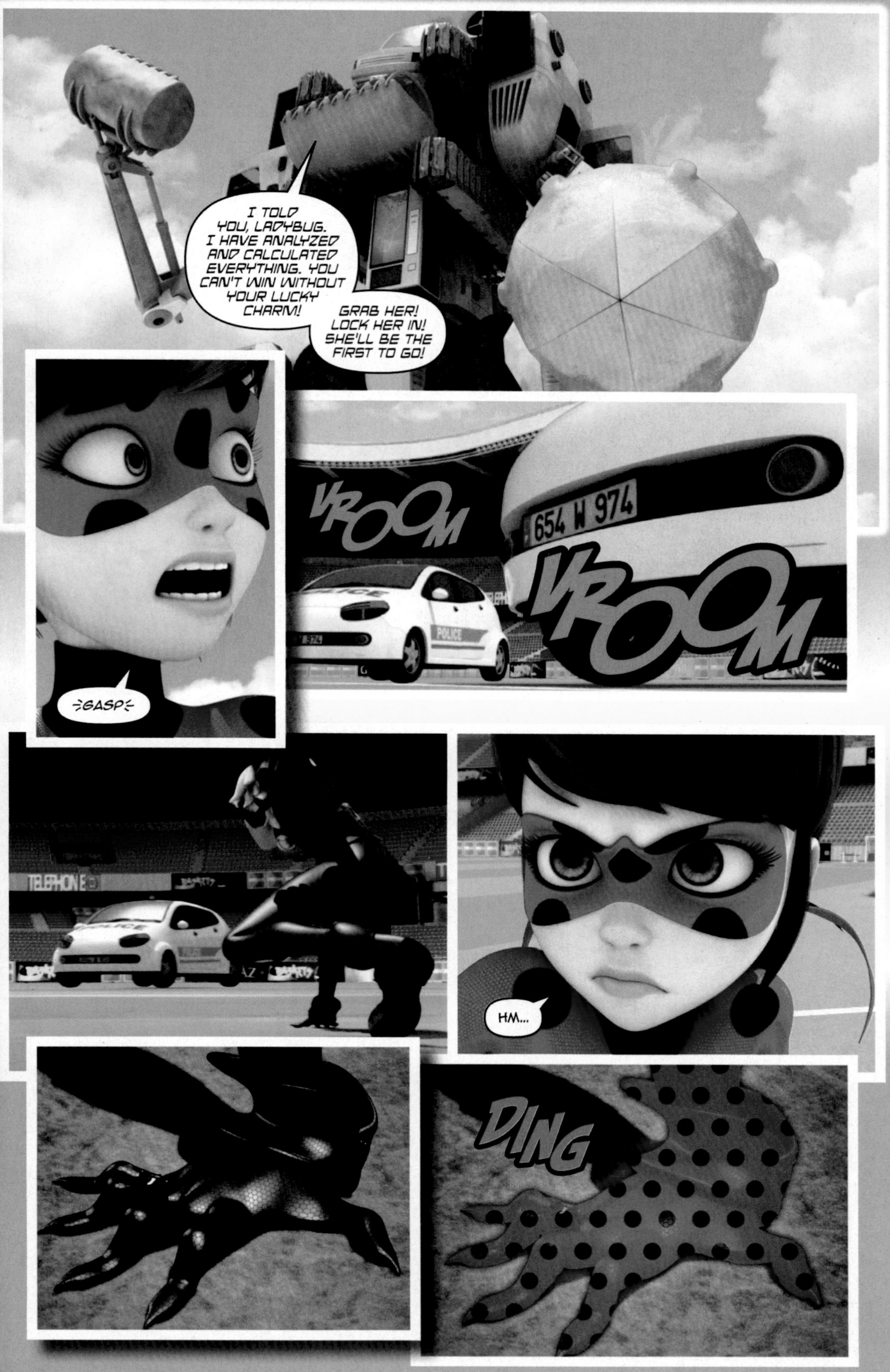
I TOLD YOU, LADYBUG. I HAVE ANALYZED AND CALCULATED EVERYTHING. YOU CAN'T WIN WITHOUT YOUR LUCKY CHARM!
GRAB HER! LOCK HER IN! SHE'LL BE THE FIRST TO GO!
GASP
VROOM
654 W 974
VROOM
POLICE
HM...
DING

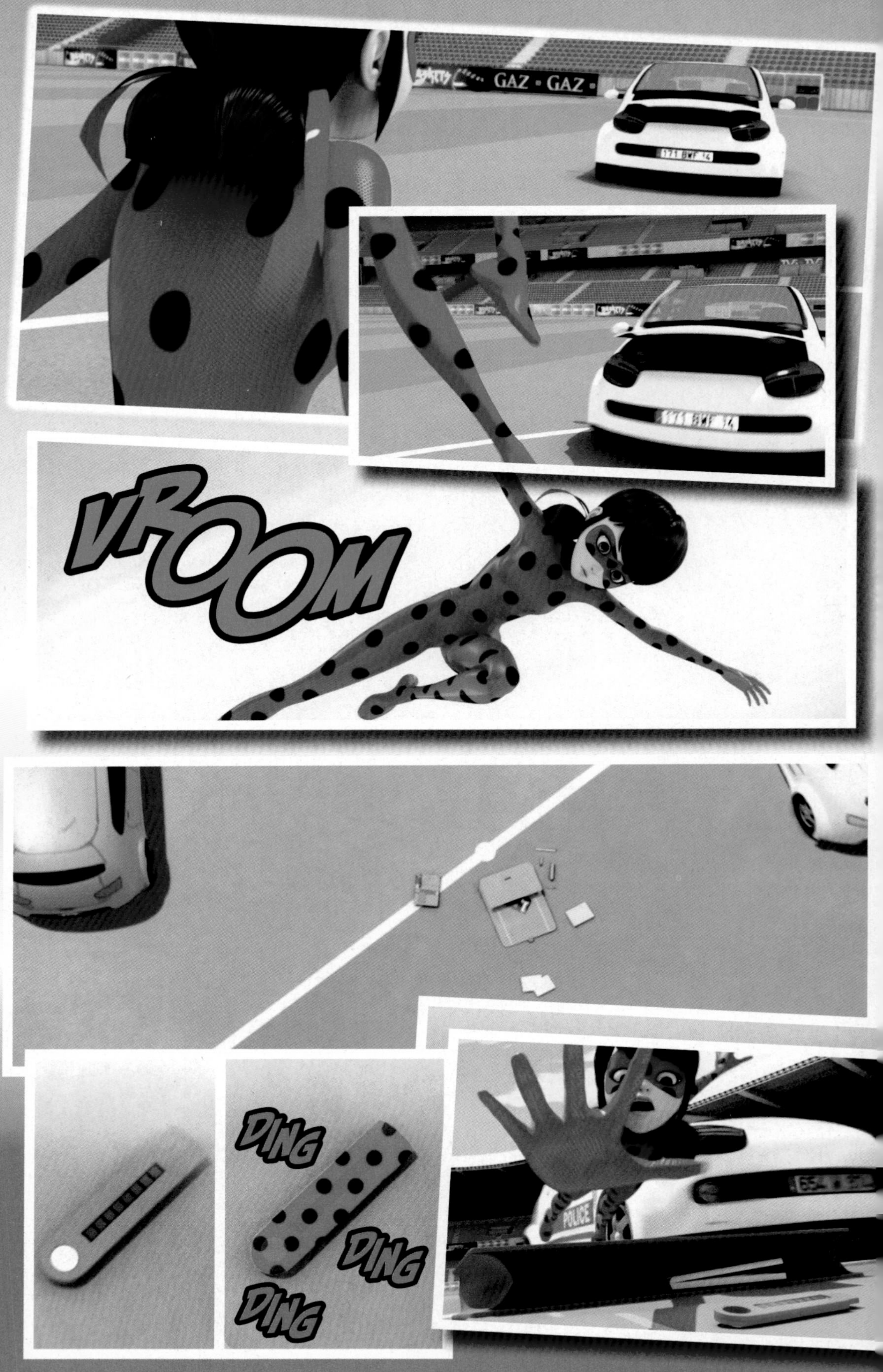
GAZ - GAZ
VROOM
DING
DING
DING
POLICE

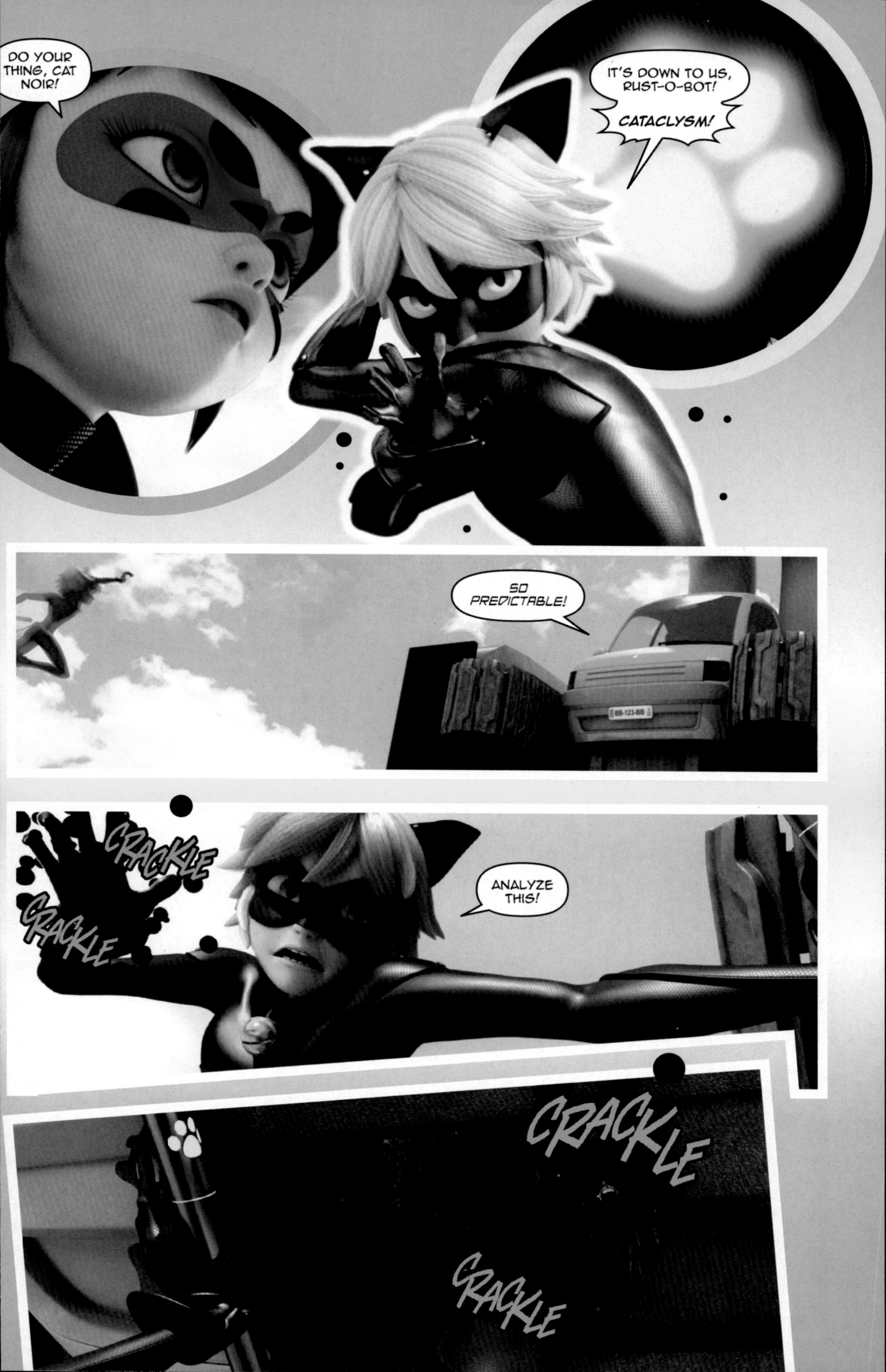
DO YOUR THING, CAT NOIR!
IT'S DOWN TO US, RUST-O-BOT!
CATACLYSM!
SO PREDICTABLE!
CRACKLE
CRACKLE
ANALYZE THIS!
CRACKLE
CRACKLE

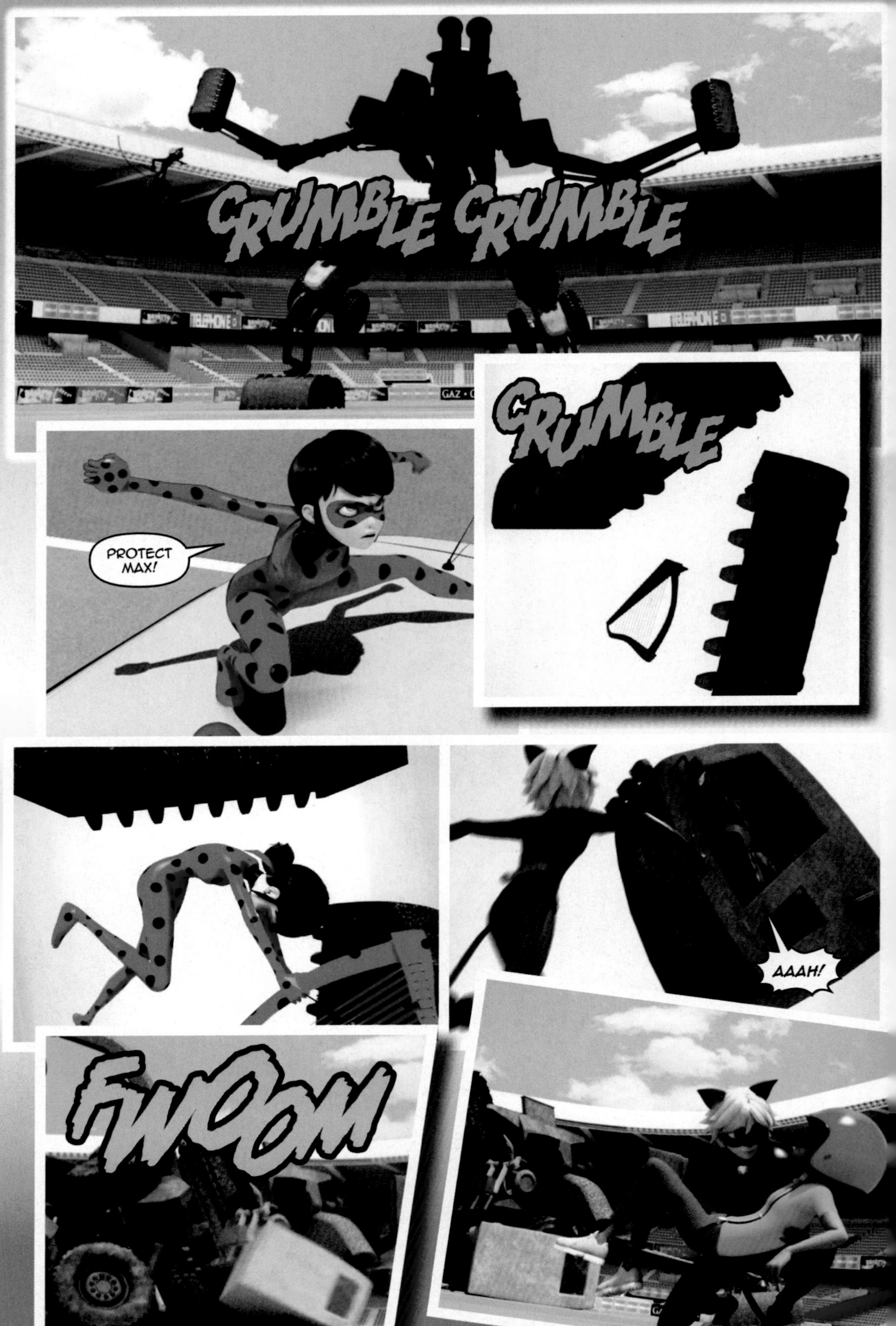
CRUMBLE CRUMBLE
CRUMBLE
PROTECT MAX!
AAAH!
FWOOM

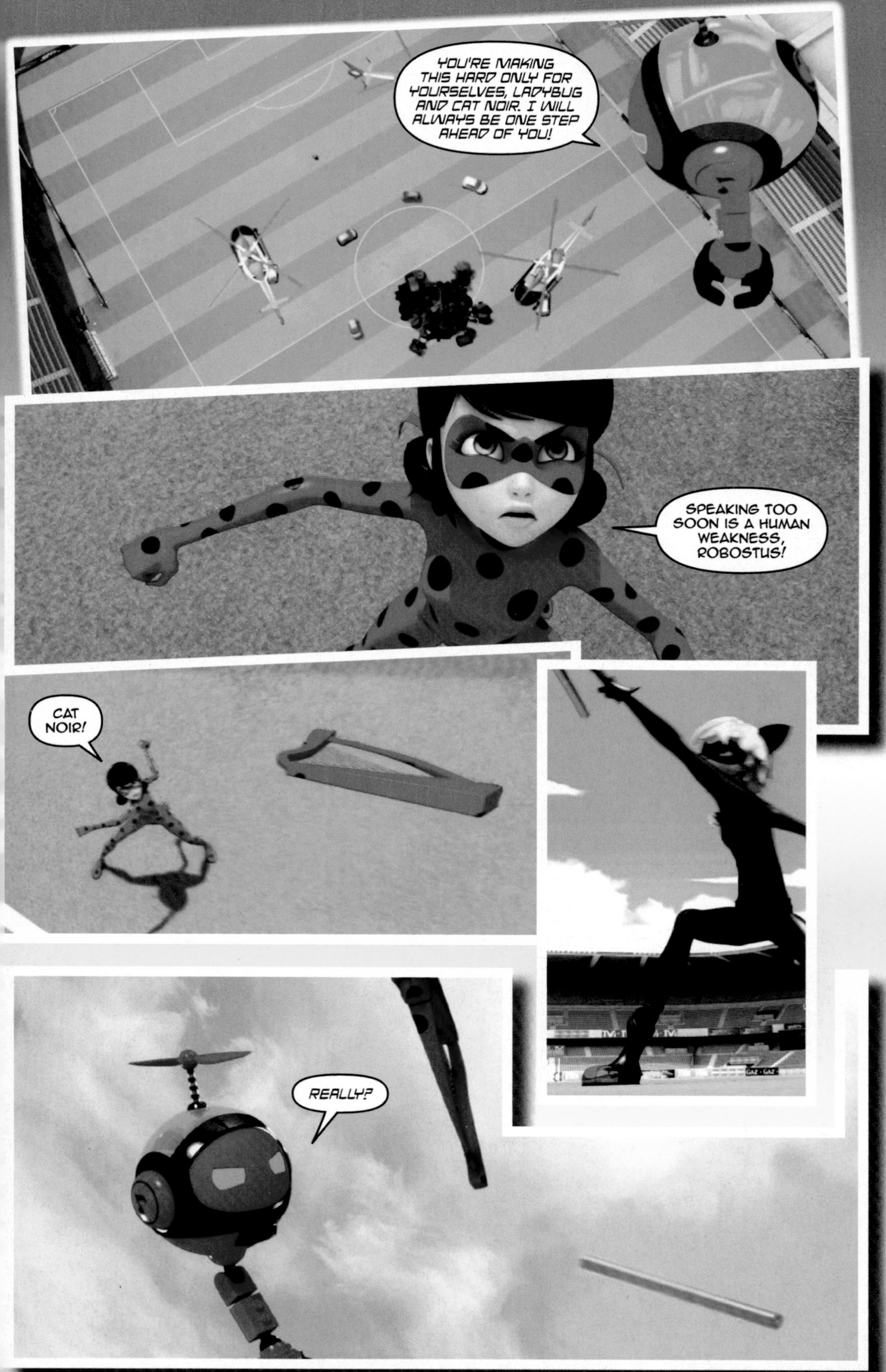
YOU'RE MAKING THIS HARD ONLY FOR YOURSELVES, LADYBUG AND CAT NOIR. I WILL ALWAYS BE ONE STEP AHEAD OF YOU!
SPEAKING TOO SOON IS A HUMAN WEAKNESS, ROBOSTUS!
CAT NOIR!
REALLY?

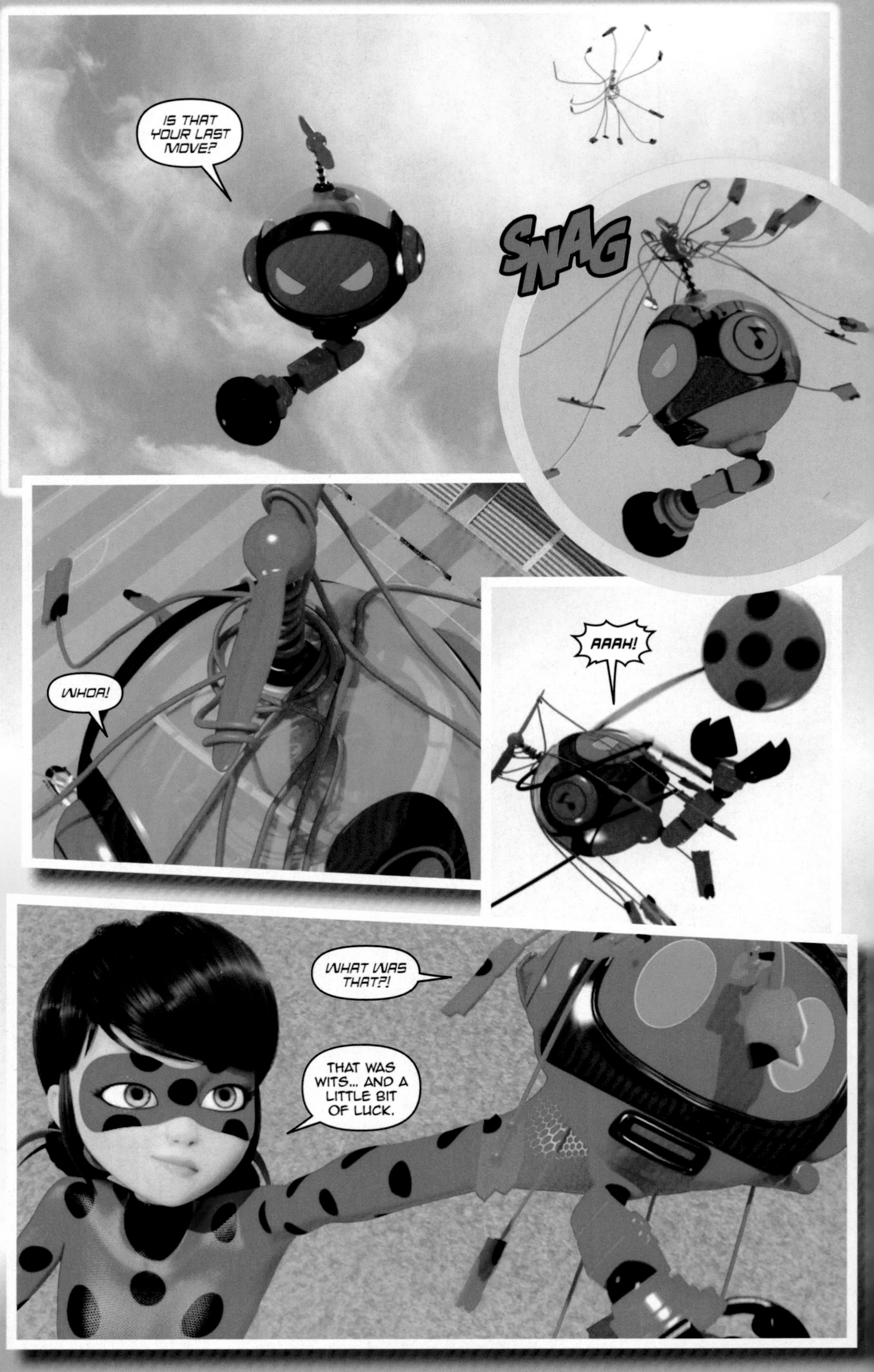

IS THAT YOUR LAST MOVE?
SNAG
WHOA!
AAAH!
WHAT WAS THAT?!
THAT WAS WITS... AND A LITTLE BIT OF LUCK.

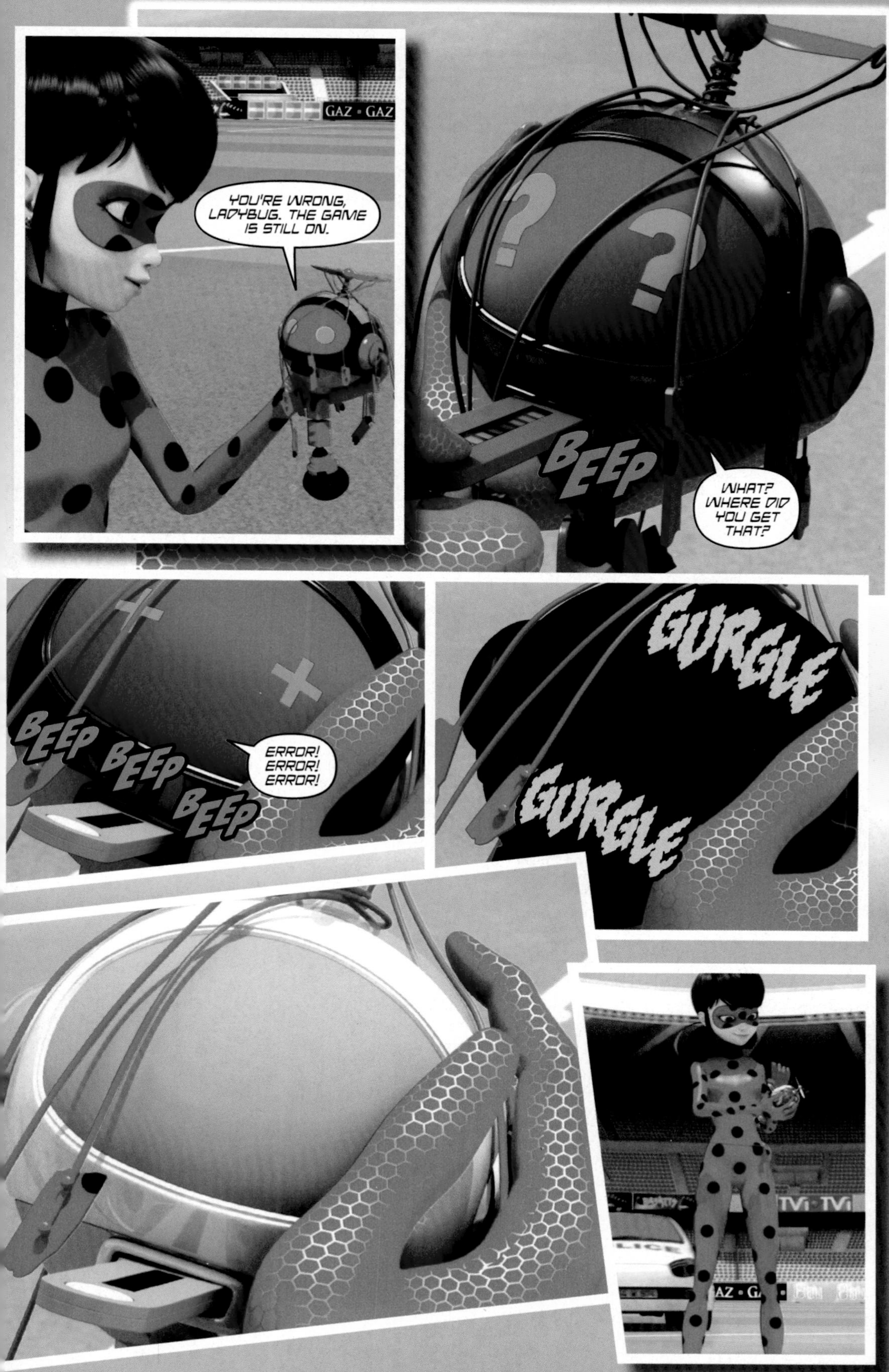
YOU'RE WRONG, LADYBUG. THE GAME IS STILL ON.
GAZ • GAZ
BEEP
WHAT? WHERE DID YOU GET THAT?
BEEP BEEP BEEP
ERROR! ERROR! ERROR!
GURGLE
GURGLE

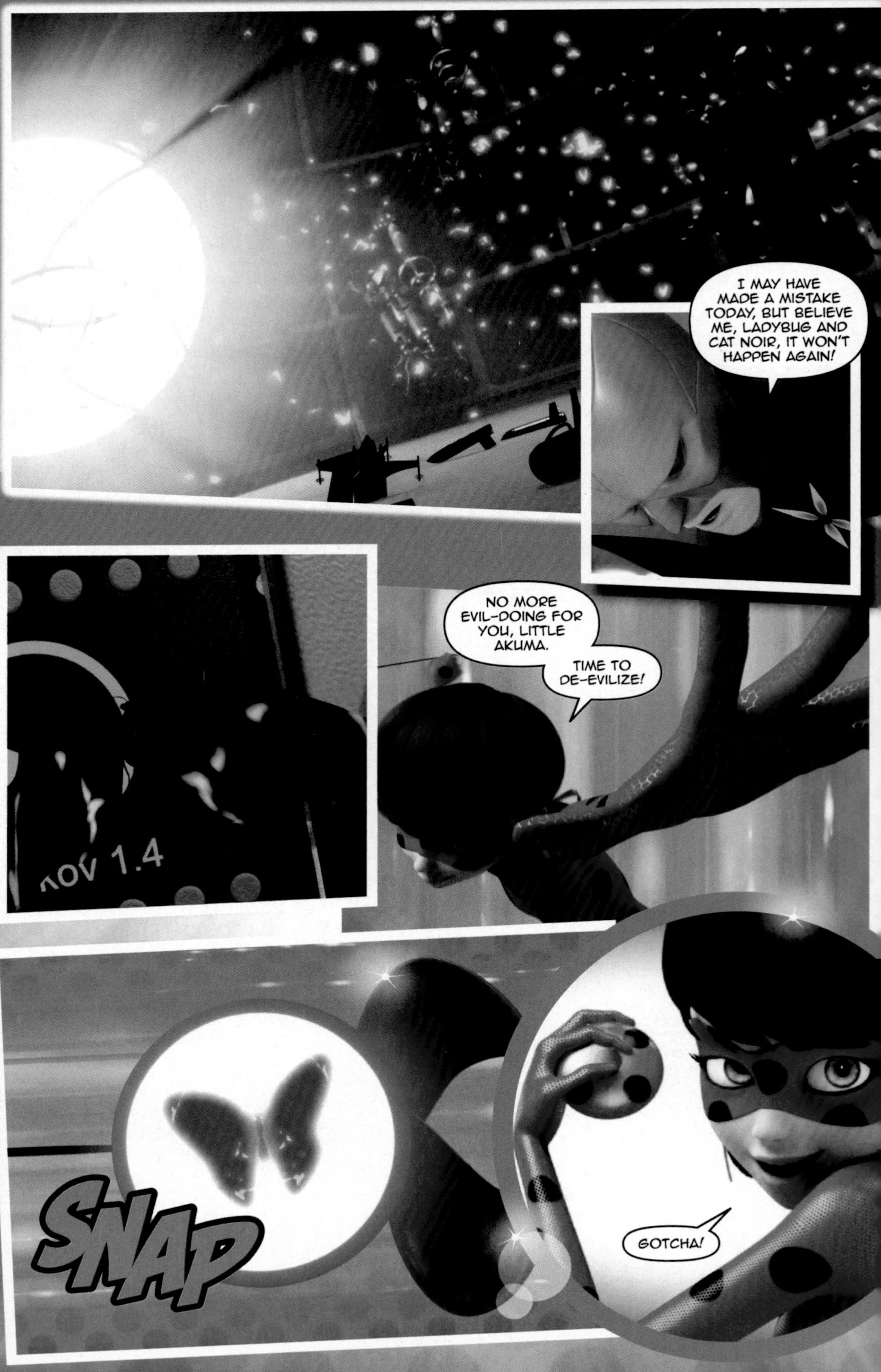
I MAY HAVE MADE A MISTAKE TODAY, BUT BELIEVE ME, LADYBUG AND CAT NOIR, IT WON'T HAPPEN AGAIN!
NO MORE EVIL-DOING FOR YOU, LITTLE AKUMA.
TIME TO DE-EVILIZE!
SNAP
GOTCHA!

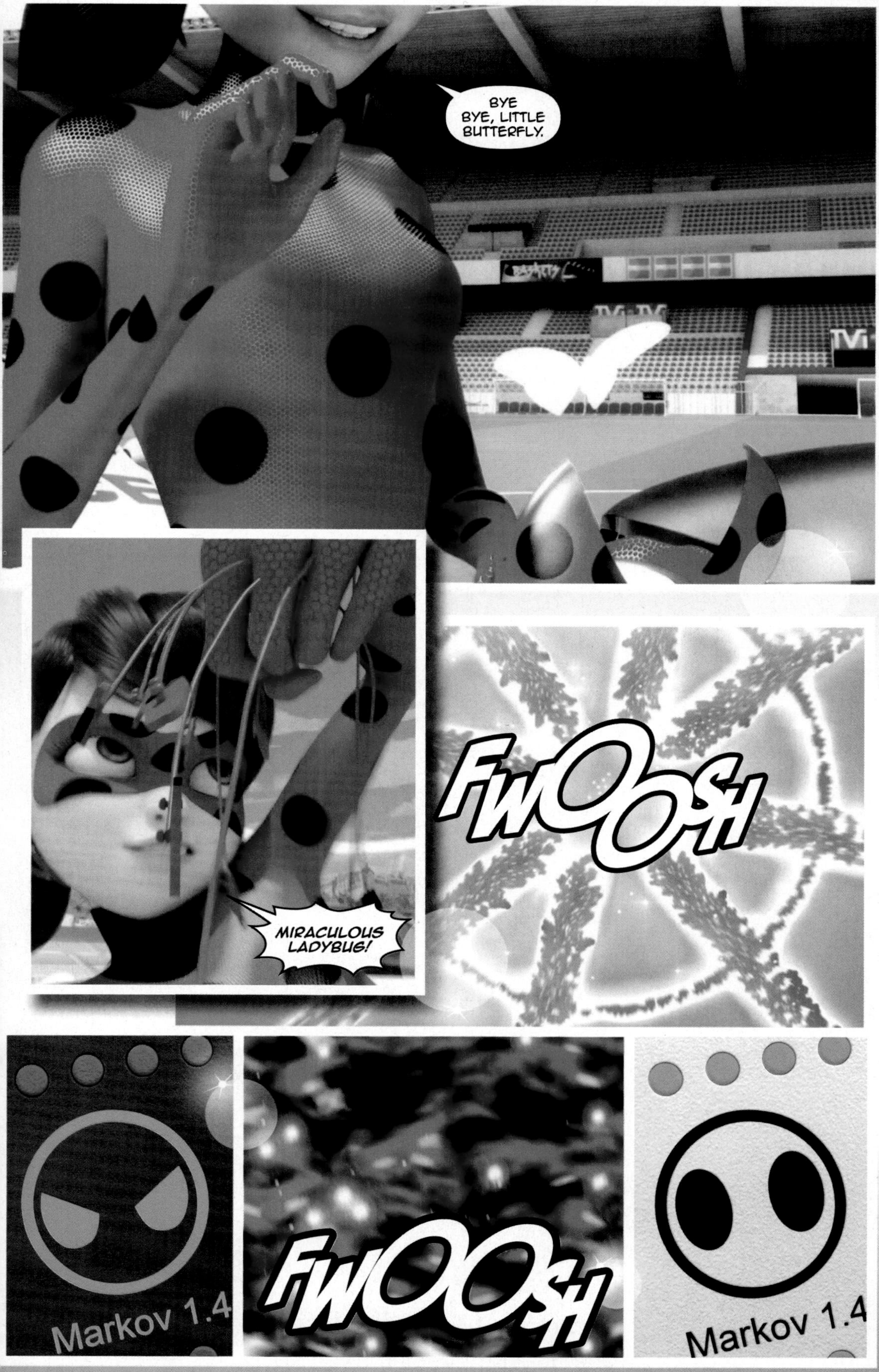
BYE BYE, LITTLE BUTTERFLY.
FWOOSH
MIRACULOUS LADYBUG!
Markov 1.4
FWOOSH
Markov 1.4

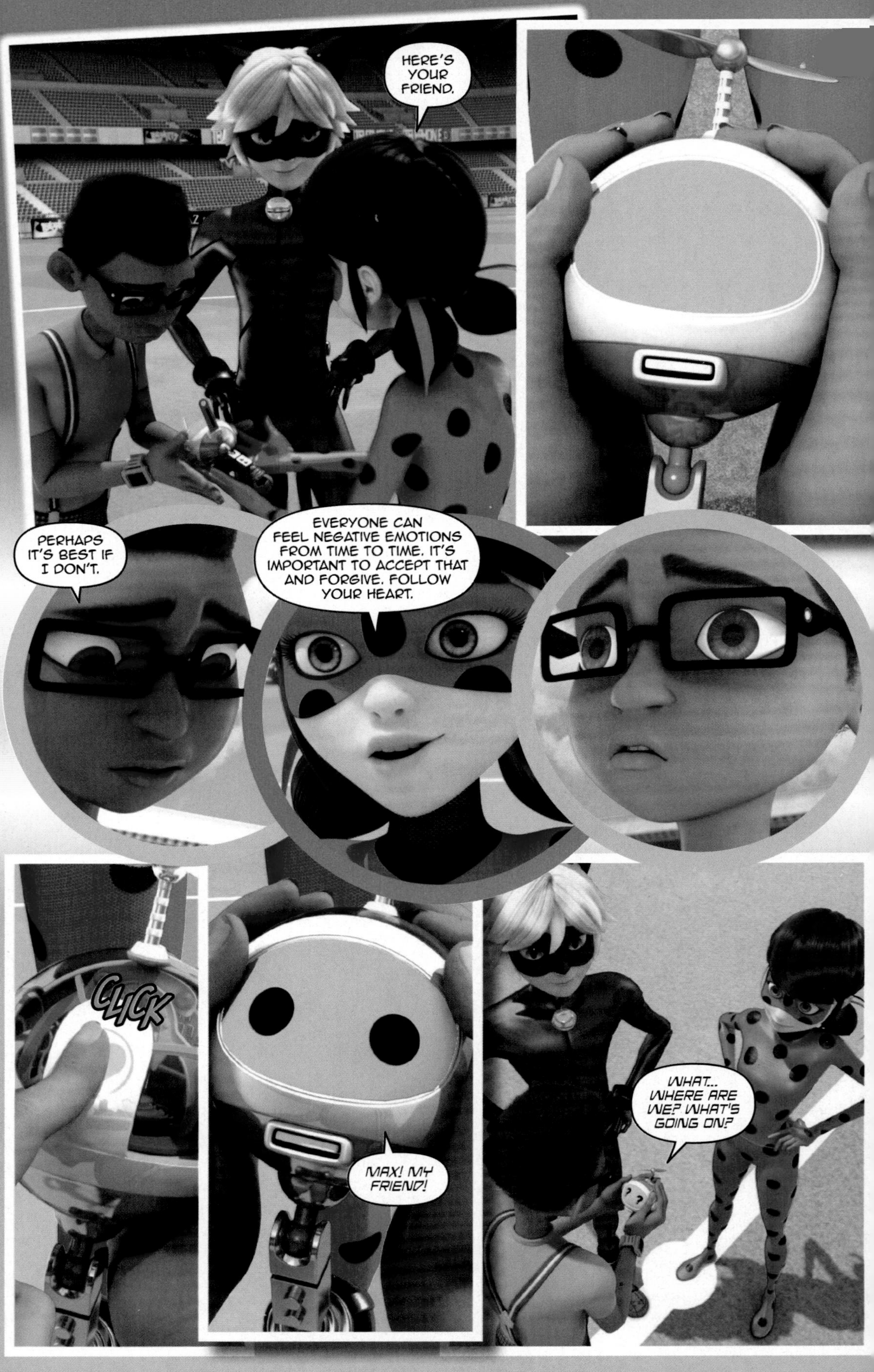
HERE'S YOUR FRIEND.
PERHAPS IT'S BEST IF I DON'T.
EVERYONE CAN FEEL NEGATIVE EMOTIONS FROM TIME TO TIME. IT'S IMPORTANT TO ACCEPT THAT AND FORGIVE. FOLLOW YOUR HEART.
CLICK
MAX! MY FRIEND!
WHAT... WHERE ARE WE? WHAT'S GOING ON?

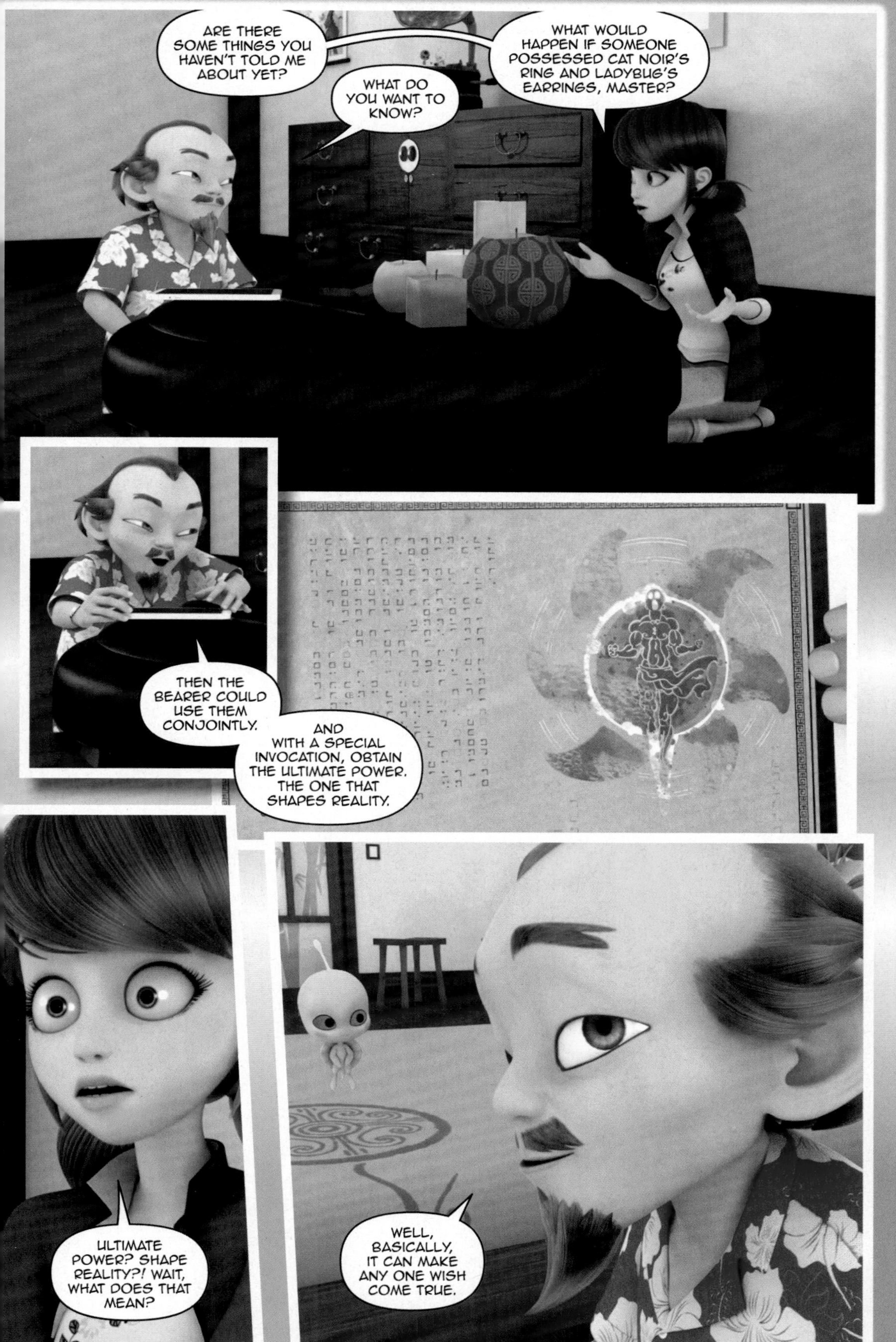
ARE THERE SOME THINGS YOU HAVEN'T TOLD ME ABOUT YET?
WHAT DO YOU WANT TO KNOW?
WHAT WOULD HAPPEN IF SOMEONE POSSESSED CAT NOIR'S RING AND LADYBUG'S EARRINGS, MASTER?
THEN THE BEARER COULD USE THEM CONJOINTLY.
AND WITH A SPECIAL INVOCATION, OBTAIN THE ULTIMATE POWER. THE ONE THAT SHAPES REALITY.
ULTIMATE POWER? SHAPE REALITY?! WAIT, WHAT DOES THAT MEAN?
WELL, BASICALLY, IT CAN MAKE ANY ONE WISH COME TRUE.

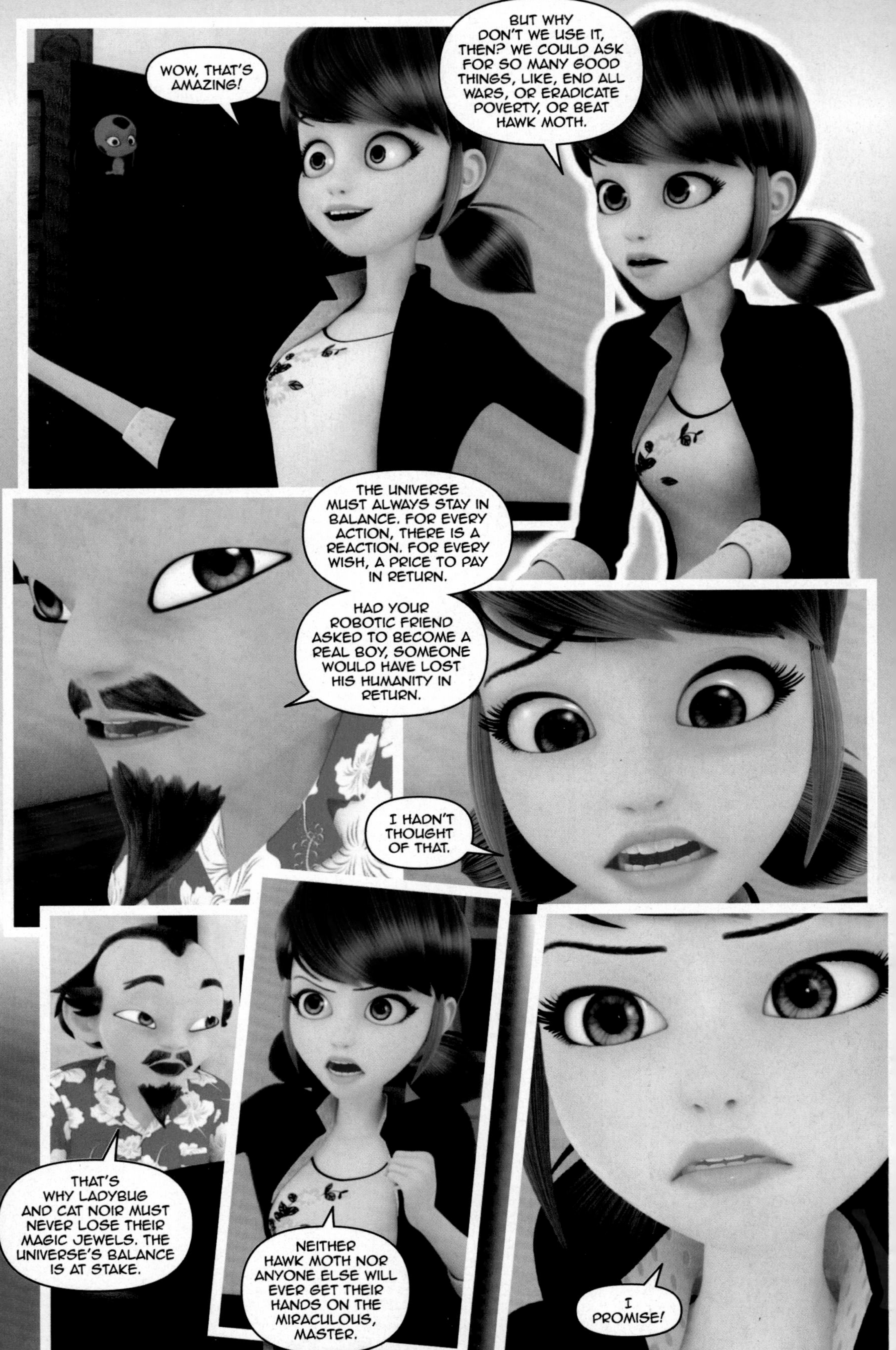
WOW, THAT'S AMAZING!
BUT WHY DON'T WE USE IT, THEN? WE COULD ASK FOR SO MANY GOOD THINGS, LIKE, END ALL WARS, OR ERADICATE POVERTY, OR BEAT HAWK MOTH.
THE UNIVERSE MUST ALWAYS STAY IN BALANCE. FOR EVERY ACTION, THERE IS A REACTION. FOR EVERY WISH, A PRICE TO PAY IN RETURN.
HAD YOUR ROBOTIC FRIEND ASKED TO BECOME A REAL BOY, SOMEONE WOULD HAVE LOST HIS HUMANITY IN RETURN.
I HADN'T THOUGHT OF THAT.
THAT'S WHY LADYBUG AND CAT NOIR MUST NEVER LOSE THEIR MAGIC JEWELS. THE UNIVERSE'S BALANCE IS AT STAKE.
NEITHER HAWK MOTH NOR ANYONE ELSE WILL EVER GET THEIR HANDS ON THE MIRACULOUS, MASTER.
I PROMISE!
THE END